2nd Amendment Remedies

A Novel by

S.L. Shelton

The 2nd novel in the Scott Wolfe Series

This book is a work of fiction. Names, characters, places and incidents are products of the author's imagination or are used fictitiously. Any resemblance to actual events, locales or persons, living or dead, is entirely coincidental.

Copyright © 2013 by S.L. Shelton

All rights reserved, including the right to reproduce this book or portions thereof in any form whatsoever.

Front cover, maps and artwork contained in this book are Copyright © S.L. Shelton

The cover image is a modified and stylized rendering based on a photo obtained courtesy of the Department of Defense photo library. Photo credit, Cpl. Melissa Tugwell

---

Other books by S.L. Shelton:

The Scott Wolfe Series:
A Lamb in Wolfe's Clothing
2nd Amendment Remedies

Back story: Lt. Marsh

For Don Cooper

Thank you for being my friend and an endless source of information on all things from law enforcement to chemical compounds. Your value to me is immeasurable.

Prologue

Friday, July 9th, 2010—Arlington, Virginia

QUINN BLACK, Vice President of the Tactical Division at Baynebridge Security, felt a little ridiculous. He'd been driving around in random circles for almost an hour, but he had to be sure he wasn't being followed. If caught, the information he was carrying would not only endanger his position at the firm, it could potentially cost him his life.

As he pulled into the garage structure at Ballston Common Mall in Arlington, he checked his rearview again.

I'm just being paranoid, he thought. *If anyone suspected, I'd be in the basement at Baynebridge Headquarters, getting waterboarded.*

He drove up to the third level parking area as instructed and parked as far away from the mall entrance as was possible. Before he had even put his car in park, someone tapped on his window.

The surprise made his chest contract. He half expected a gunshot until he saw it was the person he was there to meet—Mark. That was the only name he had for the man who had stood quietly in the corner when the DOJ investigator had given him the ultimatum two weeks ago in Fayetteville, North Carolina—cooperate or be indicted.

"You scared the shit out of me," Black hissed after taking a deep breath to release the tension in his chest.

Mark stepped back and let him get out of the car.

"Sorry," Mark quipped with a grin. "I saw you coming up and figured I'd save you some time finding me." He cocked his head to the side. "Are you sure you're with tactical division?" A jab at his skittishness.

"I've been looking over my shoulder since I pulled the data," Black complained as he closed his door. "This is a really bad idea. If I get caught, they'll kill me after they torture me for your name."

"Then it would probably be in *my* best interest to just whack you now," Mark replied with sarcasm.

Black tensed. He had only been VP of Tactical at Baynebridge for nine months. His predecessor had died under mysterious circumstances—made even more mysterious by the sudden appearance of fake shell companies that had been generated from his division's accounting system.

"Relax," Mark ordered impatiently. "Just give me the information and go home to your wife. No one's going to come after you unless you were sloppy getting to me."

Black reached into his folio, extracted a large manila envelope, and then handed it to Mark, who grasped it—but Black didn't let go immediately.

Black had been approached by a company board member only a month ago, and the man had introduced him to Heinrich Braun of Spryte Industries. That was when he'd discovered how deep in the shit he already was just by accepting the job in the first place. Unfortunately for him, he had already sent inquiries about the accounts and the high volume and large amounts in the transactions before he'd met Braun…and those inquiries had ended up in the hands of a forensic accountant with the Department of Justice.

Stupid, stupid, stupid!

And now he was standing in front of *Mark*, about to hand over a package that could end his life if discovered. It contained a listing of corporate dividend payouts—except the people on the list didn't hold stock in the companies paying them, and the companies that were making the payments didn't exist.

"This buys me immunity when the arrests start?" Black asked.

"Don't ask me," Mark replied, yanking the envelope from Black's hand. "I'm just helping a friend. That's between you and the Department of Justice."

"That's not what I was told when I was directed to meet you here," Black snapped.

"Look, man. I'm not a lawyer or an Agent. I'm just supposed to pick up an envelope, hand you a thumb drive, then get the hell outta here," Mark replied. "Your deal is whatever your deal is with them. If you aren't down with that, then I need to call Justice and start this over again."

Panic seized Black.

"No, no. It's all there," he sputtered, caving to the veiled threat. He couldn't back out—he knew they already had evidence on him. This was his only chance to extract himself from the mess. "Wait! You aren't with Justice?"

Mark shook his head. "Just doing a favor for a friend," he replied.

"Then why should I trust you?" he asked with a slight squeak to his voice. "I'm risking my life here."

"Did you look at the printouts?" Mark asked knowingly.

Black stared at him blankly for several long seconds, and then nodded. "Yeah," he mumbled finally in almost a whisper.

"Then you know that trust is running pretty thin at the moment."

"I get it," Black replied as he got back into his car. "I'm sorry. I'm just—"

"Yeah, yeah," Mark interrupted sarcastically. "Just on edge." He handed him a thumb drive. "Here. This is yours."

Black looked at it hesitantly, as if it would bite him if he didn't keep an eye on it, but then he took it from Mark anyway.

"Put it on the routing system the next time a payment comes through, and you'll never have to see me or do a drop like this again," Mark said. "Don't screw it up, or the deal is off."

"Thank God," Black sighed. "Getting these printouts was a nightmare. They track every output device."

"Like I said," Mark reiterated. "Get this on the system and your job is done."

Black nodded and then closed his door. He watched Mark out of the corner of his eye as he pulled out of his parking space. As soon as he turned a corner and couldn't see him any longer, he breathed a sigh of relief.

When he was clear of the garage and had turned right onto Glebe Road, he pulled out his phone and dialed. The person at the other end answered on the first ring.

"The package has been delivered," Black reported nervously.

"Good," came a thick German accent at the other end. "We've got tracking. It would be best if you caught the first flight back to Charlotte. You don't want to be around when this goes down."

"Understood," Black replied, ending the call.

He had just betrayed his company and the Justice Department. But more dangerous for him, he had also just betrayed Heinrich Braun, head of security for Spryte Enterprises.

The data he had handed over was real account information—he had replaced the data Braun had given him in an effort to hedge his bets.

If Justice made their connections, he would get immunity—and if Braun succeeded in shutting down the investigation, then he'd have the trust of Braun and Combine for planting the tracker—unless Braun or his bosses found out he'd accessed the real payout data.

A cold weight filled his gut as sudden realization hit him.

What if Braun gets the folder and audits the data sheets? he thought. *He'll know I swapped out real data.*

"Shit!" he muttered as he drove toward Reagan National Airport. "How the hell did they get me over a barrel like this?"

**

MARK GAINES climbed into his SUV after watching Quinn Black's vehicle exit the garage below.

"How did it go?" the woman in the passenger seat asked as he closed the door.

Deidre "Dee" Faulks looked at him with anticipation. Mark knew she was out on a limb investigating this on her own. She had gotten only mild support from her bosses at the Justice Department but a promise of full support *if* she could tie the phantom payments through the Cayman shell accounts Baynebridge had created to any agencies or the list of media outlets Mark had discovered for her. He was being as supportive of her as he could without revealing his involvement.

"He's skittish," Gaines replied. "And I think he's holding something back."

"Do you think Baynebridge got to him?" she asked as they drove down the ramp of the garage.

Gaines shook his head. "Look for yourself," he replied, handing her the envelope. "The data is real. There's no way Baynebridge would let him walk out the door with that if they suspected him."

Dee flipped through the pages and then whistled.

"I know, right?" Gaines said as they merged into traffic on Glebe Road. "And that's just one set of payments."

"Do they match the media list you have?" she asked.

"I just glanced at it, but I saw about a half-dozen names from my list on there," he replied. "I saw Buck Grimwall on there for sure."

She laughed. "Well, we should have known that bloated blowhard was on someone's payroll. Look at all the political weight he carries."

"That's not political weight," Mark joked. "It's pasta."

Dee laughed again.

"Who's financing it?" she mused, though it was clearly a rhetorical question.

Gaines shook his head. "Someone with a lot of money," he replied. "That's just about two weeks' worth of payments in that package."

"Maybe we should shake the tree," she suggested as an SUV pulled up beside them in traffic and then dropped back again.

Gaines smiled.

"What?" she asked.

"I was just thinking how easy it would be to spot the rest of them if we made a few of the payees disappear," he retorted with an ironic tone.

"Hey!" she exclaimed with a knowing grin. "This is a Justice Department investigation. We don't '*disappear*' people."

Gaines just smiled.

"You spent too much time with the CIA," she said—it wasn't a compliment.

Gaines laughed. "Don't I know it," he sniped, then leaned over and stole a kiss. "It's a good thing I have you to keep me on the straight and narrow."

Their tender moment was interrupted by a tremendous crash as a dump truck rammed them from behind. It began pushing them down the street like snow in front of a plow.

The SUV that had pulled up beside them before was suddenly speeding back to Dee's side as the dump truck began shoving them toward the intersection of Columbia Pike.

Gaines knew what was coming next.

"DOWN!" he yelled at his female passenger as he pulled his weapon from under his jacket and stepped down harder on the accelerator.

The windows on the passenger side erupted in splinters of glass as the automatic weapons in the SUV began spitting bullets at them.

Sound suppressors, Gaines thought as he fired back through the broken window. *That means professionals.*

He pulled away from the dump truck just as they reached the intersection and turned hard onto the other road, wheels squealing through the maneuver. The assault team in the SUV tried to make the turn to follow, but the dump truck got in their way, forcing them to wait to go around. Gaines sped south on Columbia Pike, his SUV dragging its bumper on the street.

"Dee, are you hit?" he asked intensely, his voice all business.

She shook her head.

"Fucking Black!" he exclaimed. "He rolled on us."

"This is elaborate," Dee gasped as they sped down the road, barely masking her terror as she pulled out her phone. "I'm calling for backup."

She began to dial and then suddenly held her phone out in front of her.

"Shit!" she exclaimed. "No signal."

Gaines dropped his Glock in his lap and then reached for his own phone.

"Me too," he added, looking at the signal. "They've got us jammed. We have to get clear or we're toast. I've only got this and two spare mags."

"How'd they find us so fast?" she asked, turning to look for the other SUV.

Gaines thought for a second and then a realization struck him. He grabbed the envelope Black had given him and dropped it in Dee's lap.

"Look in there," he ordered as he returned his attention to the road.

She ripped it open, revealing an adhesive-backed metallic strip on the inside of the envelope.

"Shit," she exclaimed again.

"Toss it," he commanded, but it was already on its way out the window.

"I wish I had taken your advice on the gun," she said as she looked in the side mirror and saw the other SUV closing on them again from her side.

"Me too," he muttered, cutting hard to turn off of Columbia Pike, the tires on their SUV squealing all the way through the intersection.

"Damn it, Mark. I'm a forensic accountant," she quipped as her panic began to rise. "There's not much call for tactical training when bankers go rogue."

As they straightened from the turn, a fresh round of automatic fire began peppering the back of the vehicle. The back window exploded inward, and Mark heard two thuds beside him.

"Ungh," Dee grunted.

Gaines looked and saw her arching her back in pain.

"DEE!" he yelled as she began to fall forward against her seatbelt.

As he reached over to her, he lost focus on the road for a split second and hit a car that was pulling through the intersection. His SUV spun sideways and skidded to a halt, half on the sidewalk on the other side of the street.

The attacker's SUV skidded to a stop next to his. Through the trickle of blood in his eyes he saw Dee slouched forward in her seat, her eyes open. He struggled against the darkness that was closing in on him as the assault team approached them on foot.

Gaines heard men talking next to Dee's side of the vehicle.

"That's her," he heard a man say with a thick German accent. "Search her, make sure she's dead, and then let's get out of here."

Gaines opened one eye to a slit, searching for his Glock without moving his head or giving any indication of consciousness. He saw it, but it was on the floor in front of Dee. He looked to the side and in his peripheral vision saw a shock of white hair disappear toward the rear of the crashed vehicle.

"What about him," another asked from Gaines's side.

"Make sure he's dead, and get his ID," the German ordered from somewhere behind him.

As the door on his side of the vehicle opened, Gaines lashed out with his left fist while simultaneously unlatching his seatbelt. In a flash, the punch to his assailant's throat had loosened his grip on his weapon. Gaines grabbed for it as he unwound himself from the seat belt and fell to the street.

He had the attacker's weapon hand in his grasp as he hit the pavement with a thud. He bent the man's wrist, pointing the 9mm Beretta up at its owner's head. Fear flashed through the man's eyes as Gaines hooked his finger over the trigger, firing a silenced round up through the man's chin and out the top of his head. He quickly stripped the weapon free of the dead man's hand.

On the passenger side of the SUV, another attacker was firing his weapon at the seat on Gaines' side. From the ground, Gaines had a clear shot at the man's ankles from under the vehicle. Two shots spat from the barrel of the stolen weapon, sending the man falling to the asphalt. The attacker didn't even have time to react before Mark had fired, punching nine millimeters of hot lead through the man's skull.

Behind him, he heard suppressed shots being fired again, thwacking against the metal of Gaines' wrecked vehicle. He quickly jumped back into the SUV and began firing through the blown out rear window.

He struck one man in the chest, sending him sprawling to the pavement and then reached out urgently with his fingers to touch Dee's neck, checking for a pulse.

There was none.

"I'm sorry, Dee," he muttered through gritted teeth, and then he grabbed the documents that were tucked between her seat and the center console.

He fired three more rounds before the slide locked back on his borrowed weapon, and then reached over to the floorboard in front of Dee to retrieve his own Glock. Once in hand, he emptied the magazine through the back window. Unlike the sound-suppressed Beretta, his weapon was loud and certain to draw more attention.

He quickly dropped the empty magazine and slapped in one of two spares before dropping back down onto the asphalt of the street.

He wasted no time seeing if the others had recovered. He got up and ran, keeping the SUV between him and the assault team's vehicle. As he ran, he stuffed the documents Black had given him into his waistband. He was three blocks from the crash site before he slowed down to look behind him. He didn't see anyone following, so he changed direction again, running through the backyards of a row of townhouses.

He repeated that course of action for more than twenty minutes, running, changing direction, running again. When he was certain there was no way anyone had followed him, he turned once more into a backyard with a high hedge and pushed his way into a tool shed.

Once there, he sank to the floor in front of the rakes and shovels and tried to breathe some calm into himself.

"Shit, shit, shit," he muttered, holding his head in his hands.

When he pulled them down, there was blood. He touched the throbbing spot on his forehead and felt the sting of a deep laceration. He reached over to a small workbench and grabbed a mostly clean rag, pressing it to his forehead.

After a few moments of deep breathing, he pulled his phone out and began dialing the office of Dee's boss at the Department of Justice. Just before pressing send, he had a sudden thought.

He reached into his waistband and extracted the transaction documents Black had delivered to him. Running his finger down the lists, he was through ten pages before it came to rest on a name he recognized at the Justice Department—Rubin Paul.

Paul. He thought to himself. *Isn't that the communications director at Justice?*

Instead of dialing, he pulled up the web browser on his phone and searched for the name. His suspicion had been correct.

"Fuck," he muttered again as panic threatened to seize him.

They don't know who I am, he thought, trying to calm himself. *They didn't know I was helping Dee.*

But he also knew that anonymity wouldn't last long under scrutiny.

All they had to do was cross reference her phone records and they'd find his cell phone. From there, it would only be a hop, skip, and a jump to his cover ID. He shook his head as he dropped his phone to the ground.

"Don't worry, Dee," he said to the phone. "I'll find them."

He stomped on his phone, shattering it under the heel of his boot.

All they'll find is a cover ID, he thought. *That gives me a few days to get a plan together—unless they have access to CIA data.*

That thought drove him out of the shed and then down the street.

As soon as he found a suitable vehicle, he broke the radio antenna off and used it to gain entry, bending the end and slipping it into the driver's side window.

If I were still with the Agency, I could call in a hot extraction, he thought as he climbed in and began to hotwire the old Chevy sedan.

"What did you get me mixed up in, Dee?" he muttered.

He paused momentarily at the thought of Dee slouched over against her seatbelt. A wave of guilt washed over him for thinking of himself while she was laying dead several blocks back. It suddenly occurred to him that this was not the first time he had survived an attack and a love interest had not. A brief feeling of déjà vu swept over him, and he noted the lack of deep regret. That upset him.

"I'm sorry, Dee," he muttered again sadly.

With that, he started the vehicle, sat up, and drove away.

Years ago, he had worried that his time with the CIA had turned him into a robot. One of the Agency shrinks had encouraged him to find something that *did* upset him and then use it as a gauge of his emotional detachment. As long as his "reality check" thought was still upsetting, he was still "human." The reality check he had come up with was his sister. Picturing her in trouble was the only thing that caused him emotional distress.

He took a moment to visit his "reality check" thought. Tension instantly filled his gut and a pinch formed in his chest.

Still human after all, he thought.

On the way down the street, his earlier conversation with Dee came back to him and he looked over at the empty seat next to him. "Maybe it *is* time to 'disappear' some people," he sneered, and then began plotting his next actions.

"Huntsville," he muttered, thinking of his stash of IDs and cash. "But first I need a better vehicle."

one
Tuesday, July 13th

4:15 a.m.—Fairfax Virginia

I woke just before sunrise—sweating again. I had been doing that a lot.

I slipped out of bed, quietly, so as not to disturb Barb, and then padded as quietly as I could to the closet. I heard her stir as I gathered my clothes and started to leave the bedroom.

She had taken to sleeping at my condo after we'd arrived back in the US. At first she would sleep on the couch next to the window in my bedroom, but as my night terrors got worse, she began coming to bed with me because she feared I'd reopen my wounds. The injuries had healed over enough not to be a threat any longer, but my dreams had gotten worse—and Barb was now a regular bed partner.

"Trouble sleeping?" she asked sleepily.

"Yeah. I'm sorry I woke you," I replied.

"Scott, it's okay," she insisted, rising from bed. "I'll get up and make some coffee,"

"Don't do that," I complained, already feeling the guilt swell up in me. "You can't get up every time I have a bad dream or get a cramp. One of us needs to have our wits about us."

She paused, looking at me, a worried crease on her brow. I walked over, kissed her, and pulled the covers back over her shoulders.

"Go back to sleep," I whispered gently.

That was enough to undermine her resolve and she lay back down. I knew she was tired. I had woken her nearly every night for the past two months with shouts and thrashing in bed.

The past few weeks had been hard—on both of us. I felt guilty for being such a burden, especially when she tried so desperately to baby me. But I was constantly reminding her that she had been kidnapped and nearly blown up as well.

I tried to open the front door quietly so as not to disturb Barb any more than I already had. But the annoying squeak that had developed was impossible to silence no matter how the door was opened and despite the copious amount of lubricant I'd doused it with. It would take a resetting of the hinges, and I wasn't in the mood for a woodworking project when all I had on my mind was getting the hell out of the house.

I got into my car and drove away from Fairfax in the dark. I could just see the beginnings of pink in the horizon in my rearview mirror as I drove west on Route 50 toward the Loudoun County/Clark County line.

I needed a climb—my first climb since Europe. Actually my first climb since the day before I left for Europe.

During my appointment the day before, my doctor had given me the green light to work out, which had made my decision easy. I, of course, had not disclosed that by "work out" I meant "rock climbing."

My brain quickly gave me the various displays of the time since my last climb:

2.13 months

65 days

1,560 hours

93,600 minutes

5,616,000 seconds

I remembered that I had started climbing at around 1:30 p.m. on that day in May, so my brain graciously adjusted the hours, minutes, and seconds in the virtual readout that was constantly assaulting my vision.

1,568.5 hours

94,110 minutes

5,646,600 seconds

Roughly.

God, I need a climb, I thought as I raced down Route 50.

I chose Crescent Rock because of its remoteness—it was on the Appalachian Trail. There, the hike alone would keep most weekday climbers away. Add in the extra heat this summer, and I figured I'd have the rock to myself. That, at least, was as I had planned.

Crescent Rock was a cliff that popped up in the middle of a stretch of the Appalachian Trail. It was surrounded by dark green foliage, bugs, and the occasional outcropping of rock…until you reached the cliff. It sort of snuck up on you. You'd be hiking along, swatting flies and sweating pints of water under the canopy of green, and then you would suddenly be standing in front of a magnificent wall of rock.

If a hiker wished to continue north on the trail, they'd either have to climb the impressive face *or* snoop around until they found the trail that led up the side.

I preferred the climb. In fact, the only reason I could think of to strap several dozen pounds of equipment to my back and walk through rough terrain *was* to climb. I didn't understand the appeal of hiking for the sake of the stroll. It seemed like wasted effort with no reward—but, to each their own.

It only took me ten minutes to tie in my protection point after the forty-five minute hike, and then I warmed up on a low free climb to get my fingers warmed up for the main event—a craggy overhang nearly fifty feet above the base.

My performance was less satisfying than I had imagined it would be.

The climb route I had chosen would have given me little trouble just a few months earlier. But the recovery from my burn, stabbing, and gunshot wounds had been slow and painful—as was the climb. But I wasn't going to be happy until I could climb without feeling the internal tension and bruising caused by my last adventure.

At that moment, however, I would have been happy just to be able to finish the damned climb.

Each time I reached for a handhold above my head, my shoulder and the skin on my arm would tighten, pull, and then flash with pain. When I switched arms and reached with my right, my gut would tighten and flash with pain.

I had been told by my doctors that I could attempt outside exercise within reason, but to take it easy and not to over stress my wounds. But the emotional wounds were pushing me further than my physical wounds would allow. Between the near-death experience, my apparent schizophrenia, and my lack of emotional enthusiasm for the new depth of my relationship with Barb, I felt like my head was going to explode. It almost felt as if I were trying to put on a pair of shoes I had worn when I was ten: *I remember them fitting before; why won't they fit now?*

I had also been dreaming about my dad. I thought of my dad often when I climbed… I'm not exactly sure why, but I rarely if ever dreamed about him. So the new 'visits' I was receiving from him in my dreams weren't welcome.

I was still ten feet below the overhang when I reached for a decent-sized hand hold above my head. It was slightly out of reach, so I stepped forward, off balance for a fraction of a second to grab for it.

Pain flashed like a lightning strike across my belly. I hesitated and lost my footing.

CRASH.

Down on my harness I fell, sending yet another jolt of pain through my bruised body.

As I dangled there, trying to shift my weight onto muscles that weren't sore—a losing proposition in itself—I wondered if I would ever feel whole again…physically or mentally.

Why am I doing this to myself? I wondered. *It's too soon to be climbing again.*

Bone and meat heal on their own, came the whisper from my schizophrenic hitchhiker. **Healing your mind requires effort.**

"Aren't you afraid if I heal my mind, you'll be cast into the void?" I muttered to the ghostly *other* voice in my ear.

I heard snickering in my head. Apparently it *wasn't* worried.

"How about some help then?" I asked sarcastically.

Nothing.

"As expected," I muttered and then leaned forward to grasp the rock and try again.

I had become eerily accustomed to the intrusions from the voice in my head—a recent addition to my personality that had occurred for the first time in Amsterdam when the Bosnian Serb mercenary, Majmun, had tortured me. The voice didn't intrude often, but I became less concerned, though more irritated, each time I heard it.

I still hadn't told the CIA psychiatrist about it. Each time I got close, my extra voice would warn me not to.

The sessions were doing some good though—and some

damage. They were dredging up questions about myself that I had never addressed.

I had resisted going at first, but between the weekly calls from John Temple and the urging from Barb and her father, I finally gave in and made the appointment.

The catalyst for the call had been an unpleasant midnight awakening; I'd found myself on the bedroom floor trying to drag Barb under the bed.

That thought pushed my attention away from my climb again, and I popped off the rock. My harness caught my weight with a sharp jerk, making my side hurt again.

I was usually very comfortable solo climbing. My ascender, attached to my climbing rope, was tied to my harness with a short piece of tubular webbing. It was long enough, though, to give me a jolt when I reached the end of it after a fall.

The image of my dad's face flitted across my mind. He was looking up at me.

When did he ever look up at me? I asked myself.

No answer from my other voice.

"Fat lot of help you are," I said aloud.

The memory had probably just been part of my dream. My dad never climbed with me—not that I could remember anyway.

I rested, suspended thirty-five feet off the ground, before getting my feet back on the rock wall and attempting to climb again. I reached out for the rock, straining beyond the tightness in my shoulder.

I settled my feet down into a thin bump of granite and arched my back to lean into it, reaching higher this time and finding a solid handhold with my fingertips. My fingers walked across a thin lip of the stone, looking for a solid grip. When they found a crevasse, I sank them in as far as they would go, and then, pulling with agonizing difficulty, I rose back to where I had been before.

A memory assaulted me. "Hang on. Please hang on," I remembered myself saying… I knew the scene was from my childhood, but I couldn't place the context. The memory was vivid enough to startle me. I looked down at my right hand, turning my palm over to see the thin white scar that cut across the center. The memory of my dad looking up at me filled my head again.

A panic attack set in.

POP. I came off the rock again.

CRASH. Down into my harness.

I swore to myself, dangling from my safety line, looking up toward my protection point still some twenty-five feet above me and fifteen feet above the overhang I was attempting.

I took several deep breaths, shaking out my arms and hands, and then launched back onto the rock.

Willpower, Scott. Willpower.

My fingers reached, stretched, then closed on a hold. My leg moved up and my toe found a ripple in the rock about the thickness of a pen, rounded on the top but thick enough for the edge of my climbing shoe to grab. I reached up with my left hand, feeling for the crack I could knuckle jam, leaning, stretching past the pain in my abdomen.

I was approaching my limit on the effort when my finger found the crack and I slipped my pinky and ring finger into the opening.

As I closed my hand, expanding my finger joints to lock them into the crevasse, a violin began playing. It echoed off the rock and ridge, filling the air with a ghostly whine.

I wondered if I was hearing things again.

I looked around but saw no sign of anyone.

My foot began to fail, so my I brought my other leg up to find a better perch. I pulled up hard with my left arm, feeling the pain seep outward from my wounds as my back arched, and I pulled myself nearly parallel to the ground beneath the massive rock jutting out from the rock wall.

Agony!

I threw my foot up and let my toe slide down until it came to rest on a crag deep enough for me to hook my heel. Once I latched it in place, I let it take most of my weight.

I hugged the stone face with my right arm, cupping the tips of my fingers over a small point of rock, suspended now with my head slightly lower than the rest of my body, like a spider walking across the ceiling.

I looked backwards toward the ground as I shook out the pain and tension from my left hand and then dipped it into my chalk bag.

As soon as I caught my breath, I resumed my upward movement. Left hand over my head, I grasped the outside edge of the overhang, then, taking a deep breath, I let go of my right hand and the heel hook.

My legs swung down like a pendulum, the entire weight of my body suspended by my left hand. The pain that maneuver created in my abdomen was enormous, and I suddenly had the panicked notion that the sensation in my gut was muscle ripping—but I held on.

Almost done, I thought.

I reached up with my right hand, placing it on top of my left, and then pulled myself up in a pull-up motion. My shoulder was screaming in agony. I almost decided to let go out of fear of doing damage to myself.

Bone and meat heal on their own, came the whisper of my other voice.

I pressed up until I could swing my leg over the edge and hook my heel again.

"Finally!" I exclaimed as I reached up for a more secure hold with my hands.

I breathed heavily, resting my overexerted body and listening to the music. I could tell now it was coming from above me.

Once rested, I continued. It became a technical climb from that point up, so there was less stress on my damaged body. It was only another minute before I reached my protection pivot at the top. My hand closed on a thick bucket hold just above the twin carabineers.

As I pulled myself over the top of my rope, I saw her—a dark-haired woman in black spandex, a climbing harness, and a blue sports bra, facing the valley and playing a violin.

I grunted up and over the edge of the cliff and then laid on my back, catching my breath and listening to her play. I didn't recognize the music. It was classical, beautifully played, and haunting, with slow, sad rises and falls. The echo from the valley seemed to make the piece a duet of sorts.

When she finished, I turned my head and greeted her.

"That was beautiful," I said, still on my back, catching my breath.

"Thanks!" she exclaimed, smiling. "I've always wondered what that would sound like here."

She set her violin into its open case. "It looked like you were struggling down there," she stated plainly, still smiling.

"Yeah. Trying to get back into form," I responded mildly, feeling an imaginary twinge and putting my hand to my side.

"Ah. An accident?" she asked.

"Something like that," I muttered jokingly. That was usually sufficient to derail questions about my injuries.

She smiled as she reached for my hand to help me up. I winced as I rose, and she shot me a worried look. I looked at her and shook my head.

"It's alright. So much better now than it was a couple months ago," I said reassuringly.

I lifted my shirt to inspect my abdomen, looking for any

telltale bruising under the skin. But it was fine—with the exception of the throbbing. I looked up in time to see the expression of horror on her face.

"Seriously. It's not as bad as it looks," I lied.

It had, in fact, been worse than it looked. My heart had stopped three times between being shot and arriving at the US Military hospital in Landstuhl, Germany. At one point, it had stopped for more than five minutes.

"What happened?" she asked.

I ignored her question. "I'm Scott," I offered, deflecting.

"Nice to meet you, Scott. I'm Arlia. What happened?" she repeated, not missing a beat.

"I made some questionable decisions that resulted in an unpleasant confrontation," I confessed. "I'll survive. None of the damage is permanent."

Her eyes narrowed accusingly, though playfully. "You still didn't answer my question—but I guess that's an answer of sorts. I guess you could tell me, but then you'd have to kill me, right?"

I laughed. "No. But I'd have to call the CIA in to debrief you." I spoke rigidly, making it sound like a joke.

She looked at me suspiciously and then smiled. "What do you do for a living, Scott?" she asked.

I hesitated for a second before answering. "I'm a programmer."

"Ah HA!" she exclaimed ironically, still grinning broadly. "Computer nerd. Well, it's nice to meet you anyway, Scott." She looked at the protection point for my top rope set up.

"That looks pretty bomb proof," she noted. "Mind if I rope in and give this route a whack?"

"Sure," I said. "Help yourself."

Before the words were completely out of my mouth, she was slipping my rope through a descender.

She began to slowly walk down the face of the rock. I linked up once she reached the bottom and yelled over my shoulder, "On rappel."

"On belay," she yelled from below, and then I began walking down the face as well.

Once at the bottom, I unhooked the figure eight descender and hooked up a belay device. She quickly and smoothly tied her harness into my rope with a bowline knot, chalked her fingers, and looked back at me, letting me know she was ready when I was. I nodded.

"Climbing," she informed, singingly.

"On belay," I replied.

She moved quickly.

Her movements were more evocative of a dancer than a climber. She stayed in nearly constant motion from place to place, flowing out of one position into the next. I kept a constant two-foot length of slack so that my tension did not interfere with her climb. In a matter of moments, she had sprung herself clear of the final crux move and was standing, waist level with the pivot point of my protection links.

She looked down on me from her perch and yelled, "Nice little workout. I can see why you had trouble. That fall back move is off center when you lose your heel hook…must have hurt like hell for you."

"Yeah," I replied. "Shoulder and stomach."

"Yep. Tweaked me a little bit too, and I'm not damaged." She flashed a toothy grin. "Not physically anyway."

Then she burst out in melodious laughter.

"Descending!" she yelled.

"Still on," I replied.

She walked her way backwards down the face until she reached the base and then leapt outward to land deftly like a cat on the ground.

"Nice climb," I said sincerely.

"Thanks," she replied. "—and thanks for letting me use your rig."

I nodded.

"Hey. You wouldn't be interested in grabbing some lunch, would you?" she asked as she began to coil my rope. "There's a great little place in Round Hill, just down the road."

I smiled. "Thanks. But I've been gone long enough. My girlfriend will probably be worrying about me, and I don't get cell signal out here," I replied—all truth.

"Gotcha," she replied knowingly.

She hefted my rope onto her shoulder and began the climb back to the top, this time taking the path that went around the side.

"My car's back on Route 7," I said. "You can leave the rope down here."

"Nah. That's the long way. I'm parked over at Raven's Rock. It's only four hundred yards from here. I'll take you back to your car."

Nice, I thought. I hadn't been looking forward to the hike back down the trail anyway.

We hiked back up to the top of the rock, untied my protection ropes and straps, and then loaded our gear on our shoulders before heading down the side trail to Raven's Rock. I hadn't known about the utility road up here to service the communications towers—I'd use it next time I was here.

We arrived at Arlia's car and then climbed in for the short drive to the Route 7 parking area. Once there, she helped me load my gear in the back of my car. I was really very sore, and it must have shown because she was being very helpful—much more than necessary.

"I try to get out here a couple times a month," she offered as she dropped my rope into the backseat. "It'd be nice to climb with you again—if you're up to it."

"Sure," I replied pensively. "If you want, I can let you know next time I'm coming out here." I reached for my phone to punch in her info.

She grabbed it out of my hand—no doubt noticing I was being truthful about my lack of signal—and began punching in her phone number and email address. She handed the phone back to me and smiled.

"Great. I'll look forward to hearing from you," she chirped with a grin and a wink. "You know…to climb."

Except for the straight black hair, she reminded me much of Kathrin.

"I'd like that," I offered honestly. "But my recovery has been slow. Don't think harshly of me if it takes a while."

"You got it," she said as she turned and walked back to her car. "Be well," she said as she got in.

That was the last thing Kathrin had said to me too.

As she drove away, I wondered how Kathrin was doing. I had sent her an email the week after I got back home, but had never received a reply. I had resisted the urge to send her a second email so as not to be a bother if she wasn't interested in communicating after all. I also got 'the look' from Barb when I told her the first message had remained unanswered.

I didn't want to upset the new stability Barb and I had found. But I had been close a couple of times. Barb had never come out and directly said she didn't want me to contact her, but her thoughts on the matter were pretty clear. I should have been angry about that—maybe I was angry about it. Or maybe I was dwelling on it because I was just looking for another excuse to be angry with her.

Damn! I thought. I've really gotten to be annoyingly passive aggressive.

I shook my head. Too many other unpleasant questions were

floating around in there. No time for that one.

I decided to send Kathrin another message. I missed her.

As I leaned against my car, typing out the short message, I began to feel guilty.

Why? I wondered silently. *Kathrin helped me rescue Barb and the other hostages. Barb should be thrilled and thankful if we could make contact with her again.*

My thumb hovered over the send button. I read the message again:

> *Out on another adventure? I hope all is well with you. Would like to hear from you if you are inclined. So much to talk about.*

Guilt.

"Why the hell am I feeling guilty?" I asked aloud.

My reply came in the form of a woodpecker tapping at a rotted branch.

It wasn't really the answer I'd hoped for, but tap, tap, tap, could be construed as a sign.

I tapped send, hopped into my car, and started the fifty-minute drive back to Fairfax.

**

BARB WHITNEY was doing the best she could not to think about how things "could be" with Scott as she readied herself for class. She had almost gotten used to the idea of being woken at night, and early on she'd learned to handle listening to him grunt and groan while trying to accomplish the simplest of physical tasks—such as trying to carry the laundry to the other end of the house. What she was having a problem with was his seeming inability to accept her help, her affection, or even her concern. Deep down, she was afraid he blamed her for his injuries—and she didn't know if she could live with that.

She looked at the time and saw it was just after 7:30 a.m. She wouldn't dare call him—he had been getting more irritated each time she called to check on him. Instead, she scrolled through her contacts until she reached Bonbon.

Scott had only been tying up loose ends at work, doing all of it from home—but he had been to see Storc and Bonbon a couple of times since coming home. Maybe he had said something to one of them.

She dialed Bonbon, knowing she would be up and getting ready for work.

"Hello, doll," Bonbon answered. "How's it goin' at AA?" she asked—her joke about Scott being in "Agents Anonymous" rehab.

"Hi, Bon," Barb replied. "Things are about the same."

"Oh," Bonbon replied with a sad tone. "I'm sorry to hear it."

"I was wondering if he might've mentioned anything to you or Storc the other day when he visited," Barb asked, knowing it was a long shot.

"No. I'm sorry, sweetie. He didn't talk much at all," she replied. "He seemed much more interested in how things were going with us and work. To be honest, I had a hard time not telling him about all the changes at TravTech, so it was mostly just dishing on work gossip."

"I'm having second thoughts about him doing the contract thing," Barb said. "Anything outside of his normal routine seems to be agitating the living shit out of him, excuse my French."

"I don't know. But I do know the management is excited about it. The new money from the Agency has got all the big muckity mucks dancing around like they struck oil or something," Bonny replied. "The only one who doesn't seem happy is Habib. I think he's a little upset he's losing Scott from his division."

"I honestly don't care how Habib feels about it," Barb said crossly. "I'm only worried about how Scott will handle the change. I'm almost sorry I gave Daddy my blessing when he suggested it."

"I don't know," Bonbon replied optimistically. "I think once he's back, he'll hop right into it. He's the hard charger, remember? It took him all of ten seconds to decide to come and save your little hiney."

Barb smiled at the memory of the cargo container door opening and seeing Scott standing there with a rifle strapped across his shoulder. He looked so amazing and heroic, even the thought of it made her weak in the knees again. The fact that she hadn't known at the time that he'd been burned, stabbed, and shot had turned her into a guilt-ridden wimp, second guessing everything about how she treated him. His tendency to get quiet and sullen when she insisted on something for his own good had made her uncomfortable taking the lead on his recovery...very unlike her usual "in-charge" self.

"I know how he *was*," Barb said, her eyes starting to water again. "I'm having trouble figuring out how he *is*."

"Awww, sweetheart," Bonny cooed, comforting her. "It'll be alright—look. I'm gonna be here. I'll keep an eye on him. If it looks like he's about to melt down or something, I'll send him home. I think between the two of us, we can steer him back to being the boy we know and love."

"I hope so, Bon. I'm just worried he won't be able to find his way back," she replied and then lowered her voice to a whisper. "I caught him looking up guns and tactical information on the web again."

"He went through a lot," Bonny offered supportively. "He'll come around. The new section will be good for him. It'll challenge him. You *know* how much he loves a challenge."

"Yeah," Barb muttered, clearly unconvinced. "You know where he is this morning?"

"Where?"

"He woke up at four a.m. and snuck out to go climbing," she

said incredulously.

"What?!" Bonny exclaimed. "Won't his doctors be pissed?"

"They cleared him for outside exercise yesterday," Barb replied with accusation in her tone. "But I don't think they had that in mind."

"Maybe he'll take it easy," Bonny replied supportively and then paused a second. "Maybe you should call to see how he is."

"I'm afraid to! That's what I'm talking about. The last time I questioned him about his recovery, he didn't say a word to me for twenty-four hours…exactly twenty-four hours…to the *minute*."

"God-damned, computer-brained geek," Bonny said in disgust. "Even his subconscious, passive-aggressive bullshit is digitally executed."

"He disappears up to the loft to do pushups and sit ups, thinking I can't hear him moaning in pain," Barb continued. "He was doing it in the bedroom in the morning until I got on him about it. He just grabbed his towel and left the room."

"Hey, at least he's trying to keep that hard body hot for you," Bonny offered.

Barb chuckled. "It wouldn't be so bad if he'd tell me what was going on in his head," she said, and then immediately realized that the last few times he had done that, she had overruled him anyway and insisted on her own course of action.

Maybe it's me who needs to adjust. She shook her head. *SHIT! There I go second-guessing myself again. Damn you, Scott Wolfe.*

"I'll set him straight the next time I see him," Bonny declared.

Barb panicked at the thought. "No," she said quickly and then softened her tone. "Let's see how he handles going back to work before we get nuts. You're right; it may be just what he needs."

"Maybe."

"What does Storc say?" she asked, knowing Scott was

actually closer to him.

"It's not important," Bonny muttered, diverting.

"Seriously. What?"

"He said he's surprised Scott's coming back at all," Bonny said cautiously. "That you can't just go back to the way things were after a life-altering event like that."

That statement made Barb's stomach churn.

"But I wouldn't worry about it," Bonny quickly added. "Storc's got some sort of a man-crush, hero-worship thing going on. I think he secretly hopes Scott is going to become an Agent or something and take him with on his next adventure."

The statement should have been funny, but it just left a cold feeling in Barb's gut.

"Well, that's not going to happen," Barb said. "I'll make sure of that."

"I'm right there with you, doll," Bonny replied. "Hey. I've got to go to work now, but let's get dinner one night this week and go over a plan for next week… If you still think he's coming to work next week."

"I'm pretty sure he will," Barb replied. "He's been chomping at the bit and begging his doctors and the psychiatrist to release him for work. I'm pretty sure Monday is the day."

"Okay," Bonny replied. "You, me, and a girl's night out. We'll figure it out. Okay?"

"Sounds good, Bon. Thanks," she said.

"That's why I'm here," Bonny said in a sing-song voice. "Gotta go. Chat later."

"Okay. Bye bye."

Barb grabbed her keys and headed for the door.

Damn it, Scott. One way or another, I'm going to drag you back to health…even if it kills us both.

two
Wednesday, July 14th

CIA Headquarters—Langley, Virginia

JOHN TEMPLE was in a heated discussion with a group of analysts.

"How could we just lose them?" John asked. "We had eyes on them in Turkey."

"No," replied Ruth, one of the analysts. "We had eyes on the Serbs. There was never any guarantee they had the devices with them."

John considered her point, jutting his jaw and holding it tight so he wasn't tempted to take his frustration out on her. They had recovered two of the warheads from the Serbs in the Czech Republic during the hostage incident—but two were still out there.

Without their leadership in place, the remaining Serb mercenaries appeared to be trying to unload them, but try as they might, the most well-funded intelligence organization on the planet couldn't seem to discover their location—and John was taking it as a personal reflection on his abilities.

"They wouldn't have pulled in that much security for no reason," John concluded, finally. "And shielding like that doesn't come standard on Range Rovers."

"It was pretty amateurish shielding…hospital radiology gowns and hand poured lead sheets over ceramic tile," Ruth pointed out. "It's not like they were using IAEA-approved transport."

"You can't just hide nukes in the backseat of your car," John said, exasperation rising in his voice. "They must've had the devices in mind when they installed the shielding."

"True," came the reply from another analyst. "Or it may have just been a decoy."

John shook his head in frustration. "We know the path of the two we captured, so we need to go back to the beginning—at some point they were all together."

"Sir," Ruth replied carefully. "There's been no chatter or a conspicuous absence of chatter from anyone who might be interested in a buy…and there was no back trail indication of a hand off. We should consider the possibility the Serbs are just sitting on them and testing our ability to track their movements."

"No," he grunted plainly.

"Why not?" Ruth asked.

Annoyance spread across his face. "Because if we assume that, then it means we are accepting we don't know anything. Accepting that is the same thing as saying, 'I give up.'"

"That's not what I meant," Ruth replied defensively. "Look—"

She pointed at her computer monitor indicating the flag

locations on a map.

"These are the twenty-two movement hits we've tracked and responded to," she continued, zooming out to show them all, spread out across Europe, the Middle East, and Africa. "Each one ended up being conventional weapons or a wild goose chase."

"What's your point?" John asked.

"If you were underground, being hunted, and had lost your leadership, would you be wasting resources on creating wild goose chases?" she asked.

He saw that she was hoping he'd put the pieces together.

"They are expending a lot of resources to give the impression they are moving the devices," he answered finally, satisfying her gaze.

"Right!" she replied enthusiastically. "That means one of two things: either they already have a buyer and have gotten fresh funds to make the move, or they think they have a buyer and are using their remaining resources to cover it."

"Show me just the pins that were a zero net gain on intel," John ordered, leaning toward her computer screen.

She clicked her mouse on a filter tab and removed the conventional weapons caches. John looked at it for a second when an idea struck him.

"Now toggle back to just the conventional weapons deliveries," he added.

She did as he instructed.

"What's unusual about this group of flags compared to the wild goose chases?" he asked, now testing her.

She toggled the screen back and forth a couple of times before it dawned on her.

"The delivery radius for the conventional arms transactions are fixed in a repeated, predictably defined limit and the phantom deliveries are all random," she acknowledged finally.

"And on how many of those arms deliveries do we have buyer info?" he asked.

She clicked a few more links and overlaid the data on the map. There were only four.

"That's odd."

"Yeah," John replied with a smile as the insight opened a new possibility for tracking.

Just then, his phone rang, and he walked a few feet away from the analysts before answering.

"Temple," he answered.

"Agent Temple," came the woman's voice from the other end. "This is Charlie Branch, up in the HUMINT Coordination Center."

"Hey, Charlie," John said, turning his back to the analysts. "What can I do for you?"

"We just got an all-agencies hit on one of your section's cover IDs," she relayed. "It's flagged to notify you."

"What ID?" he asked, suddenly very interested in the conversation.

"Dominic Tranum. It looks like it's an old travel ID," she said. "It was just an inquiry, but it still sets off a flag."

Mark Gaines. Now, why would you be using an Agency travel ID?

John paused to think about it for a moment. Gaines had left the Agency more than a year before. Technically, the ID should have been closed out with his departure—but as with any government agency, details often get missed. He decided to play it cool.

"Just an inquiry?" he asked.

"Yes," she replied. "Homeland Security."

John thought about giving the order to release the information, but at the last second, he decided to give Gaines the benefit of the doubt. The Tranum cover was just a travel ID, not a deep cover—any serious probing and it would fall apart anyway.

"As long as it's just an inquiry, I don't see a need to blow the cover," he replied. "Unless there's a warrant attached to the request, leave it buttoned up."

"Yes, sir," she replied. "Thank you."

"Yep," he said and then ended the call.

He stood there for a few seconds after he hung up, trying to figure out why Gaines would be using one of his old travel covers.

"What are you up to, Mark?" he muttered.

"Ehem." One of the male analysts cleared his throat.

John turned back to the group and headed back to the computer monitor in front of Ruth.

"Okay, dig deep and follow them all the way back to before their first movement," he ordered. "Stay on the conventional arm deals with no buyers. Maybe you're right. Maybe they are the real test and the empties were the decoys."

All of the analysts nodded and went back to work as John walked toward the elevator. As the doors closed, he got an overwhelming desire to call Mark and ask him what was going on. He toyed with the phone in his pocket before deciding against it.

It hadn't ended well when Gaines left the Agency. The fact that he trusted John enough to use one of his travel IDs was signal enough the blood wasn't as bad as it had seemed. John would let it play out.

I hope you're alright, Mark, John thought.

That thought made him think of someone else. He pulled his phone out of his pocket and dialed, but instead of calling Mark Gaines, he dialed Scott Wolfe's number.

**

My phone rang just as I was easing myself into my favorite green chair. I was still sore from my climb the day before, and I had spent most of the morning soaking in the tub after Barb left for school. I reached back and placed the ice pack on my shoulder before answering.

"Hello."

"Hey, Scott." I immediately recognized the voice as John Temple's.

"Hey, John. How's it going?"

"I'm doing well," he replied, but I heard tension in his voice. "How about you?"

"A little better every day," I said optimistically. "I actually climbed yesterday for the first time since Europe."

"That's great," he responded enthusiastically. "I know it felt good to be back on the rock."

"I wouldn't go that far," I muttered jokingly. "But it was good to get out of the house."

"Still a lot of pain?" he asked.

"Not until yesterday," I replied through a chuckle.

"I get it," he muttered. "Are you back to work yet?"

"Not really," I replied, feeling a tug of guilt for not being back in the office. "I've been working on projects from home, but I haven't been into the office yet."

"So, have you heard?" he asked.

"About the Agency contracts?" I confirmed. "Yeah. Bonny told me."

"Good. I hope you're okay with the contract set up," he probed cautiously.

"I haven't seen it yet," I replied. "Should I be worried?"

"Your boss seemed to be on board," John said with amusement in his voice.

"Who? Habib?"

"No. Bernard Evonitz," John replied.

"Bernie is the owner," I corrected. "I've met him all of twice and only seen him a dozen times since I've worked there."

"Well, don't be surprised if you see more of him," John said with a warning in his voice. "He seemed thrilled that you were responsible for the extra business."

"How much 'extra?'" I asked, suddenly concerned about a change in my role at the company.

"I wouldn't worry about it too much," John offered dismissively. "When are you going back?"

"Monday," I replied. "But I started wrapping up old projects last week."

"You're a better man than me," he said. "I'd be squeezing every minute out of my R&R, seeing how many hula girls I could get delivering my drinks at the same time."

"I'm climbing the walls here, John. If it hadn't been for Dr. Hebron, I would've started last week," I said, referring to the CIA psychiatrist John had set me up with. "She insisted I have at least a full week of physical health and a green light from the doctors before going back."

"If you were an Agent, she'd probably make you wait a month after you're cleared physically," he said, making me feel a little better.

"Okay," I replied in exhaustion. "I give up… Did you need something from me?"

"Nope," he replied. "We're golden. I was just calling to check in."

"Thanks, John. I appreciate it," I said sincerely.

"No problem. I'll check in again in a few days," he said before ending the call.

I relaxed back into the cushions of my chair and let the ice do its work on my shoulder. I couldn't help but wonder what was driving John to be so proactive in his contact with me. I didn't get the sense he was normally a social butterfly, but he'd called at least once a week since I got back from Germany.

I suddenly wondered if he was grooming me for recruitment.

"Good luck with that," I muttered with a chuckle.

Though, maybe working for the Agency wouldn't be that bad.

three
Thursday, July 15th

Afternoon—Dr. Rachel Hebron's Office in Langley, Virginia

In the weeks since I had returned home from Europe, I had slowly begun looking forward to my sessions with Dr. Hebron. Today was not one of those days.

She had given me homework to do in our last session and I had been unable—or unwilling—to focus on it enough to complete it. It had been a simple question: *What sort of adult is created when someone is bullied as a child?*

She had only managed to open up more emotional pain with that question, creating broader insecurities in my dreams. Instead of just reliving the trauma of killing and nearly being killed, I was now having dreams about everyone I cared about being taken from me.

As we sat in her office today, I wasted as much time as I could describing the events of the past week and my nervousness about returning to work.

She finally interrupted me.

"What happens to a child who is bullied once they become an adult?" she asked, repeating the question that had been my homework assignment.

I grimaced.

"It's a simple question, Scott," Dr. Hebron pushed, smiling softly, waiting for me to engage.

But it hadn't seemed a simple question. There are too many unknown variables to predict an outcome like that. I ignored the obvious target of the question—it was specifically about me.

"You didn't work on it, did you?" she asked accusingly.

Dr. Hebron was a woman of about forty. She had thin, angular features and the light cocoa-colored skin of a Pacific Islander. My first guess would be that she was of Filipino descent, but I didn't care to offer that guess. She was quite an attractive woman, but she went to great lengths to appear *all business*, keeping her hair pulled back tightly and donning the most unattractive, heavy-framed, half-rim reading glasses she could find.

"I worked on it," I replied. "The question kept popping up every time I stood still for five seconds. Thanks for that, by the way."

She chuckled mildly and then tipped her head to the side. "What did you come up with?" she asked.

"To be honest, it kept getting wrapped up in the jumble of memories from my childhood," I replied almost apologetically. "Every time I tried to think about it, I kept getting derailed with trying to figure out what happened to my family when I was ten."

"Why do you think my question got mixed up with all that?" she asked with a knowing expression on her face.

"I'm not sure," I replied. "I don't remember enough about it to put it together."

"I thought you had perfect recall," she said with a grin.

"Obviously not that perfect," I replied in frustration. "My dad died, my mom went nuts, and I lost most of my memories—all on the same night. I've never been able to sort it all out."

She opened a folder on her desk and peered into it. "How did your father die again?" she asked.

"Car accident," I replied. "I woke up in the hospital three days later and found out my mom had been institutionalized and my father was dead."

"So you were in the car with him?" she asked.

"No. I was home in bed, according to my aunt…the one who raised me and my sister," I replied as I once again dug into the void of memory. "The police came to the house to notify my mom that Dad had been in an accident, but when they got there, she was wandering around the yard in her nightgown, screaming at the ground. My sister and I were upstairs in bed. According to the police report, they couldn't wake us… They thought Mom had poisoned us."

"But that's not what happened," she recalled, confirming parts of the story from another session.

"No," I replied. "It turned out that there was some sort of well contamination or something. The whole family was affected. That's what they figured caused my dad to have his accident."

Even as I was saying it, the words felt wrong. The whole thing had never made sense to me.

"You don't believe it," she concluded, reading my expression.

"I don't know what to believe," I replied with a sigh. "My aunt raised us on the farm, telling us what great people our parents were and how we owed it to them to be the best we could be."

"That's a pretty heavy burden to place on a child," she observed knowingly.

I shrugged.

"So why do you think my question gets tangled up in all that?" she asked again.

It dawned on me that I hadn't answered it before.

"See what I mean?" I replied, grinning. "I'm not sure. I've got these broken memories...just pieces really...of my father and mother. But one sticks out...no, two." I adjusted myself in my chair, my mental discomfort suddenly becoming a physical discomfort. "I remember on my eighth birthday, my dad caught me getting into his liquor, and—on another occasion—I remember my dad chasing me through the woods...though that might just be part of that recurring dream I told you about."

"Your dad," she highlighted, forming a new line of thought. "Those two memories intrude. So how did his bullying affect you?"

"What makes you think he bullied me?" I asked her, not taking the time to adjust my flow chart to incorporate the new flow of information.

She shrugged. "We've all been bullied, Scott," she pressed. "It's a matter of degrees and how we deal with it. I'm simply asking you how it affected you."

I knew it was a loaded question. There is no single correct answer. As with anyone, much of the answer depends on personal responsibility. Taking it or not.

"He didn't bully me," I protested.

"You said last week your father used to hit you," she reminded me.

"I said I remembered him hitting me...the incident with the liquor," I corrected her. It was a muddled and clouded memory of vague feelings interspersed with flashes of imagery.

"So you maybe got a spank when you broke a window?" she

asked.

"Perhaps," I replied. "But I don't remember anything like that."

"A slap when you were disrespectful?" she continued.

I shrugged.

"A punch when you upset him?" she asked.

I paused, thinking about that last one. "I don't ever remember him punching me," A half-truth.

I clearly remembered being hit on my eighth birthday—but it wasn't closed-handed. I had been snooping around in Dad's study, looking for my birthday presents or something. I came across his "stash"—a small bottle of liquor. It looked kid-sized so I tried it—though to this day I've never tasted liquor anything like that…it was acidic and metallic-tasting. I'd only taken a few swigs of it before he came in and saw me.

He had hit me so hard I flew across the room. I still don't know if it was the hit or the liquor, but I got so sick that I was in bed for weeks. That was one of the few vivid memories I had of my father. The rest were a strange soup of kind patience and the rage of his "episodes."

"How old were you the first time he closed his hand to hit you?" she asked gently, without accusation.

I thought again for a moment. "I'm not sure he ever did," I replied with a little frustration. I felt like we were rehashing the same frustrating dead end over and over. "Mom dealt with Dad when he had an episode. We were usually not around…from what I remember anyway."

"I see. What did your mom say about this?" she asked, again sounding like she was just gathering data, not making any accusations.

Sometimes Mom would wake me and my sister Carol up in the middle of the night and load us into the car. I remembered hearing my dad screaming in their bedroom, smashing furniture and talking—no...arguing—with someone. Those things I remember through a fog.

"She would say that actions have consequences and that even heroes have internal demons to fight," I replied quietly. "She said much the same thing when I got hit."

"So you do remember being hit?" she accused.

"I remember being hit once. I just don't think he ever punched me," I replied.

Dr. Hebron nodded and looked into her folder again. "Was your dad ever in the military?" she asked as she flipped pages in my file. "It almost sounds like he was suffering from PTSD."

I shook my head. "Not that I'm aware of," I replied. "I only ever remember him being a farmer."

"Perhaps the 'poisoning' from the well was a more significant issue than the authorities suspected," she offered.

I shrugged. "I thought about that too," I replied. "It could be, but there isn't even any documentation left on the blood tests from back then...I've looked. It would all be speculation."

This was very hard for me. It had taken me many years to balance my feelings for my parents, and I was being purposely asked to risk upsetting that balance, something I preserved mostly through lack of input.

My mom was in the loony bin, so it was sort of pointless talking to her. She never recognized me on the few occasions I showed up anyway, so I saw her less and less frequently—it did nothing but confuse her and sadden me.

"I've dealt with those things," I continued. "I've moved past them. There are no answers for me there, so I had to let it go."

"Did you let it go?" she asked with an accusation in her voice. "It seems like its present enough to distract you from dealing with a simple question about bullies."

"It's all data," I retorted coldly. "You can't change something that's happened in the past. By its very nature as a past event, it becomes data."

"True," she conceded. "Logically, past events are history, and they contain lessons and information that help us or hurt us moving forward. But when an emotional state is frozen in time, the *feeling* is recorded as data too—in its entirety—threatening to re-emerge and play itself back—in its *entirety*—when that data is accessed."

A few months earlier I would have dismissed that statement as hollow psychobabble, expressed to elicit a response. But after having anxiety after anxiety well up within me over the past eight weeks, I accepted her professional observation for what it was.

"If that's the case, then you never get over it," I said. "You can never move past it."

"I disagree…and so do you,"

"How do you get that?" I asked, raising my eyebrow.

"For example: When you first started climbing, how did your fingers feel?" she asked.

I could see where she was going with this.

"They hurt. Blistered, achy. But I developed calluses over time," I replied.

"Not by the second time you climbed. Not by the third time you climbed," she pointed out correctly. "And when you spent a lot of time in water and your calluses peeled off, or when you went a long time without climbing and they softened—how did they feel the next time you climbed?"

"They hurt again, but not as bad," I replied, rubbing my fingertips with my thumb, feeling the sting from my most recent climb. "I guess I got used to the idea of there being pain and learned to work past it." I suddenly saw her point. "Does that mean I have to keep opening all these closed wounds until I'm used to them?"

She nodded. "That's the hard part…going back and re-experiencing the pain after you've forgotten about it," she offered sympathetically. "On a positive note, though, once you learn to face it all the time, it loses its power over you."

"So you are saying I have to go back and relive all the painful things that have happened to me in my life, over and over again, until feeling the emotions they elicit is so common, they don't bother me anymore?"

"Well..." she said, smiling. "Let's start with being tortured and shot."

"And killing," I added.

"And killing," she agreed, as if in passing, but for some reason I didn't get the impression she was as worried about that.

"What type of person would I be if those things didn't bother me?" I asked incredulously, letting her know I had noted her dismissive response.

"You'd be you. The culmination of your experiences, beliefs, and skills," she replied firmly.

"But would I still be the 'me' that everyone knows—the 'me' that I know?" I asked, suddenly panicking about the reality of her statement.

She paused, seeing my distress, and formulated her words carefully. "You can only be you. *Events that alter us happen every day. It's not a matter of if we change because of our experiences*—they *will* change us...*the better question to ask is: Will we allow those events to be bigger than us?*"

Whoa! That is some seriously deep shit, I thought to myself. *I wonder if I should tell her about my other voice.*

NO! came the resounding, emphatic answer from my hitchhiker.

Big surprise there, I thought sarcastically.

She must have taken my silence as acceptance of her assessment because she abruptly changed subjects on me.

"How's it going with you and Barb?" she asked.

"It's going okay," I deflected flippantly.

Dr. Hebron gave me the "look"—the one that said, "That wasn't small talk. I need details."

"Well, I'm having difficulty dealing with the superficial pandering to my health." I expanded. "Both my physical and mental health."

"Are you still finding yourself suppressing anger with her?" she asked.

I paused for a second, almost embarrassed to admit it, and then nodded.

"Have you talked to her yet?" she asked. "Last week, you said you would work on expressing yourself when that happened, rather than just letting it build."

"Not much luck on that front, I'm afraid," I responded.

"Luck has nothing to do with it," she responded sharply. "It requires a conscious effort."

"I know, Doc," I admitted defensively. "But tomorrow will be the two-month anniversary of the hostages being freed and only the fourth day since I was given permission to work out. How much strength do you think I have to face down my girlfriend over her forcing herself into my life?"

"How much strength does it take to hold down the anger?" she asked with a knowing glare.

Damn! She is being brutal today, I thought.

I sighed in frustration. She smiled at me.

"I know," she offered. "Guilt drove you to Amsterdam to find her. She read your motivations wrong. But you have to understand, that was a pretty mixed message you sent. Not every ex-boyfriend would face mercenaries, torture, and gunfire to help a girl. It really sets you up to be the knight in shining armor."

"More like the frog and the prince," I corrected. "I was a horrible boyfriend before she left. I'm not sure why she thought that would change."

"Because, Scott," she accused, leaning toward me to punch her comment up a notch. "You *died* in the process of saving her. In her mind, *that* is the real you…the rest is just you recovering from the trauma."

I nodded my understanding. I already knew it, but it helped to hear it said out loud.

She watched my face for a few seconds before sitting back in her chair again.

"Monday," she chirped, snapping me out of my internal review of her previous statement.

"Yes," I said with a smile. "Monday. Back to work. I'm excited."

"Good," she replied. "But don't build your expectations too high. Everything changed when you left for Europe. You'll have to accept that."

I nodded.

"And you can call me any time next week if it becomes too overwhelming," she added with a smile. "But I have a feeling you're going to nail it."

That simple expression of confidence changed my mood to the positive.

"Thanks, Doc," I replied. "I'll do my best."

"Of that, I'm certain," she said, rising from her chair and extending her hand. "Next week."

"Yes, ma'am," I replied and then made my way out of her office suite and down to the garage.

On the way, I created an affirmation in my head to help remind me to be honest with Barb.

Stay calm and then speak the truth, I thought.

I felt better already.

four
Saturday, July 17th

9:35 a.m.—Washington, DC

HEINRICH BRAUN was concerned about the new queries into the Combine accounts and the payments to the politicians and agency heads. He had thought for certain that once the Justice Department investigator had been eliminated, the snooping would stop—he had been reassured by individuals high in that agency.

Justice Agents don't disarm mercenaries with their bare hands, Braun thought as he sat in the back seat of his sedan, driving toward the US Capitol. It made him uncomfortable having the unknown wildcard running around—especially a wildcard that could kill trained hit men.

He had been, as yet, unable to determine the identity of the

Department of Justice Agent who had escaped their ambush. Justice had been no help at all. They had no record of Deidre Faulks having a partner on the investigation.

The trace on her phone records had given them a name, but no agency queried had claimed Dominic Tranum as their own—someone was covering for him.

His secure satellite phone chirped to life.

"Braun," he answered.

"God damn it, Braun," came the angry voice of William Spryte. "Please tell me you've found the son of a bitch who's been nosing into our accounts."

"I'm sorry, sir, but I can't—as yet—say that," Braun responded apologetically and then braced himself for the verbal assault.

"Then what the bloody, God-damned hell am I paying you for?!" Spryte exploded.

"Sir, I already have people working on the source of a dead end ID—"

"The agent?" Spryte barked. "Just call Justice and ask who it was! Why are we paying those people if they can't give us a simple name when we want it?!"

Braun shook his head with a bit of frustration. *This is what happens when you micromanage,* he thought.

"Sir," he said calmly, trying to defuse Spryte's anger. "We've done that. The DOJ has no record of another Agent working with Faulks…and the Tranum ID does not appear to be real."

There was silence at the other end of the line as that information was absorbed.

"What are you doing to find him?" Spryte asked more calmly.

"We've discretely distributed an image from the ID to our other assets in various agencies. I'm expecting a facial match shortly."

"How did you get a photo?" Spryte asked incredulously.

Braun smiled. *And this is why you pay others to do this work, you doddering old jackass.*

"For an ID to be believable, it has to be in the various systems representing the IDs...the DMV, the passport office, etc...." Braun replied snidely.

"What sort of—" Spryte began to ask but suddenly stopped cold. "It's a cover ID."

"Yes sir," Braun said mechanically, letting Spryte feel the full weight of what he was up against—a covert government action against his organization.

"Carry on, Heinrich," Spryte said abruptly. "Sorry to have bothered you."

The call ended abruptly. Braun allowed himself a satisfied grin before dialing a new number.

It rang once before being answered. "Homeland Security. Deputy Director Raymond's office. Ned Richards speaking."

"I need to know what progress is being made on the ID search," Braun growled.

There was a pause and the sound of rustling on the other end of the phone. "Are you crazy, calling me here?" the man hissed in an angry whisper.

"Relax, Ned," Braun replied dismissively. "This line is untraceable."

"But that doesn't mean mine isn't being listened to," Ned responded.

"Then switch to secure," Braun said.

There was a click in the connection followed by a tone indicating the call was secure.

"What do you want that's so important you would risk exposing me?" Ned asked, seething anger.

"I need to know the source of the Tranum ID," Braun said

mildly. "Or should I come to your office and ask for the results?"

"This is getting dangerous. I'm not sure it's a good idea for us to be involved with this," Ned whispered. "It took eight hours for us to pull a facial recognition match. Someone is going to notice that much system time being used."

"Why did it take so long for a simple facial match?" Braun asked.

"Because it didn't find a match until it started going through backup files, you bloody, dense Kraut," Ned hissed angrily. "It's a CIA cover."

Braun ignored the weak insult, focusing instead on the cold chill that ran up his spine. "Is it possible he's our mystery DOJ Agent?" Braun asked, tying the pieces together.

"The last cell tower hit on the phone registered to that ID was a quarter mile away from the ambush site," Ned replied. "Ten minutes after it was over."

How long have you been sitting on that tidbit of information? Braun wondered. "Which department at the CIA?" he asked, suddenly drawing up the fire to tackle the new problem.

"It doesn't matter," Ned replied. "The Agent's no longer with the Agency."

"And you know this because…"

"Because once we had a name, we checked pension records," he replied condescendingly. "I'm not a fool. I checked every data warehouse for him."

"Why would an ex-Agent be involved with a DOJ investigation…and why would he have an active cover ID?" Braun muttered.

"I don't know why he'd be working with Justice, but it's an old travel ID." Richards replied with less venom. "It fell apart too easily to be a deep cover ID."

Ex-Agent, Braun thought. *Private security?*

"The name, Ned. Give me the name," Braun said with a

bored tone.

"Mark Gaines," Ned replied. "Is that all?"

"Yes," Braun said. "Thank you." He ended the call and then immediately dialed another number.

"Spryte Industries," came the operator's voice from the other end.

"Heinrich calling for Roman," Braun replied, asking for William Spryte's personal secretary.

"Yes, sir, Mr. Braun," came the reply, followed by the sound of music after being placed on hold.

Roman had been with the Spryte family longer than Braun had; the man had served as the secretary to Spryte's father as well.

"Braun?" Roman's voice came through after a few moments' pause.

"I need everything you can find on a former CIA Agent by the name of Mark Gaines," Braun said.

"Is that our nosy little rat?" Roman asked.

"Indeed," Braun replied.

"I'll have a package for you by noon," Roman replied. "Will you require tactical support?"

"Not this time," Braun responded. "We need to nip this quickly. We'll revert to Mr. Spryte's idea of something more personal. Get me as much background on Gaines's family as you can. Perhaps we can find another pressure point to stop the hemorrhage of information."

"Understood," Roman replied, ending the call.

Braun relaxed into the seat and closed his eyes. *Combine has managed to stay off everyone's radar for decades,* Braun thought. *Then suddenly the CIA gets involved and Mr. Spryte loses his stolen nukes in the Czech Republic, his inside man at State gets pinched after arranging for the nukes, and now another ex-Agent starts sniffing around Combine accounts… Why the sudden interest by the CIA…and how can we stop it before the investigation leads to the Spryte Brothers and Combine?*

"How long until we reach the Capitol, Brian?" Braun asked.

"Almost there, sir," came the driver's reply.

"Call ahead to let Congresswoman Blackman know we are on our way," he ordered. "I don't feel like being kept waiting by that twit…too many other things to get done today."

"Yes, sir," the driver replied, pulling out his cell phone to make the call.

**

When Braun's meeting with the Congresswoman was over and he exited the Capitol, his cell phone rang.

"Braun," he answered.

"Sir, I'm nearly to the entrance," his driver said.

"Hurry it along, Brian," he replied mildly as he looked around for the car.

"Yes, sir," the driver replied. "And sir, your satellite phone rang while you were inside."

"All right," he said as the car pulled up to the curb.

He climbed in and picked up the satellite phone, seeing the missed call was from Roman. He immediately pulled his laptop computer from its case and accessed his email. In a message from Roman was a large, encrypted file that he immediately detached and decrypted.

He scrolled through the digital pages of documents and came to one which piqued his interest.

"Interesting," he muttered as he continued reading. "Perfect!"

"Sir?"

"Brian, make arrangements for me to get to Colorado Springs," he said. "I want to be there by nightfall."

"Yes, sir."

As Brian called to make the flight arrangements, Braun continued reading the documents in the package. There was only one piece of the puzzle missing, and that would be easy enough to access—who to enlist for assistance.

"Hmmph," he grunted as he laid back and closed his eyes. "*Lesbiech.* How fascinating."

**

6:35 p.m.—Fairfax, Virginia

"I'm so excited you are coming back on Monday," Bonbon exclaimed as she downed her second drink since we'd arrived at the restaurant twenty minutes earlier. "But don't you worry; Storc and I are going to be running interference for you in case you get overwhelmed."

Out of the corner of my eye I saw Barb shoot her a warning glance.

"Overwhelmed by what?" I asked gently, hoping to draw more information out of her…information that Barb clearly didn't want me to hear. "It's a contract section. How much different could it be than working for security product development?"

Bonny hesitated. I could tell I wasn't getting the whole story…I just wasn't sure why.

"And how are you and Storc gonna run interference?" I asked. "I'd think Habib would have doubled your workloads with me getting moved to the new section."

"We don't—" Storc started, but an elbow to the ribs from Bonbon stopped him.

"We won't have any problem with Danny," Bonbon inserted. "He got three new developers in exchange for you."

I raised my eyebrows. "I should ask for a raise if it takes three to replace me," I said ironically before taking a sip of my beer.

Bonny grinned...it was her *I've got a secret and I won't tell* grin.

"That's enough about work," Barb warned, inserting herself. "Scott knows things will be different. He'll be able to handle it."

I felt my ears get warm as a little wave of anger washed over me. I suddenly wondered if my new policy of addressing displeasure directly applied when I would have to do it in front of others.

I decided it did not, so I resorted to swallowing my anger...again. So far my desire to do as Dr. Hebron had suggested was not proving a simple task in real life.

So much for honesty and owning my responses, I thought.

Storc was looking rather uncomfortable and a little confused by the lack of candor around him. He reached under the table and pulled out a gift bag, taking the opportunity to fix the awkward silence.

"I got something for you," he said with a grin as he handed me the oversized gift bag. "A welcome back gift."

"Dude! Thanks!" I exclaimed as I opened the top of the bag. Inside was a small camouflaged backpack—just like the ammo packs the SEALs had in Mimon. I pulled it out and saw a biohazard warning placard on its flap. I read the tag:

> The Zombie Emergency Defense kit is our top-of-the-line kit. The pack is not military styled—it contains actual military gear used by troops in the field. So whether you are concerned with the coming zombie apocalypse, nuclear winter, meteor strike, or just a really bad storm, this is the kit for you!
> See more at www.phi-emsolutions.com

"Awesome!" I laughed as I unzipped the pockets to reveal all the various survival goodies contained within. "This is getting hung on the wall in my bedroom, for easy access when the zombies show up."

Storc grinned, pleased with my response to his gift. I noticed

Barb and Bonbon weren't as enthusiastic about it as I was—Barb actually had a bit of a sneer buried beneath her polite smile.

Jesus, Barb, I thought. *Lighten up.*

I continued to go through the pouches, eventually coming to a sturdy metal folding shovel. It had serrated edges on one side so it could be used as an axe in a pinch…or a weapon. I pulled it out and examined it.

"Not at the table," Barb nagged before realizing her comment sounded extremely condescending. She sank back into her seat when I glared at her. "I just meant we could pull it all out and look at it when we get home."

Nice try at a cover, I thought, but I had heard the edge—as had Storc and Bonny. It was all I could do to keep from throwing an insult at her. "Sorry, Mom," I sniped sarcastically. *Oops.*

Storc and Bonny suddenly looked very uncomfortable. Bonny got up from the table. "I have to tinkle," she announced, looking at Barb. "Come with."

Barb got up, embarrassed, and followed Bonny to the ladies' room.

As soon as they were out of earshot, Storc leaned forward. "What was that about?" he asked cautiously. "Should I have cleared it with her before I got you a gift?"

I shrugged. "I'm not sure what the attitude was about, but the gift is awesome," I said, reaching out to bump his fist with mine. "Thank you."

"My pleasure," he replied. "I just hope *I* didn't cause that," he added in a quiet voice, referring to the awkward moment with Barb.

I waved my hand dismissively in the direction of the ladies' room. "She's getting out of control," I complained. "She won't let me do anything without worrying about how it'll affect my wounds or my mood."

"You aren't breaking up again, are you?" he asked.

I sighed. "Honestly, pal, I don't remember getting back together with her," I replied with a grin. "We got back from Germany and suddenly she was living with me."

"Dude." He was incredulous. "You flew to Europe and saved her from terrorists. *That* was when you got back together."

I chuckled and nodded, and then I leaned forward. "Hey. What's up with Bonny and the hush hush about work?"

Storc looked around as if he were passing state secrets. "She's been acting nuts recently too," he said, in almost a whisper. "She gave me a whole list of things I shouldn't talk about around you."

I shook my head. "Those two," I muttered. "They're going to suffocate me."

"That's what I said," Storc volunteered. "I told Bonny it was time for her to butt out."

I grinned.

"She punched me," he continued.

I laughed. "Hit her back!" I joked.

Just then he looked up behind me. I continued staring forward.

"…the way he wants," I heard Bonny say in a whisper as she approached. "It will be okay, I promise."

Barb wrapped her arms around my shoulders from behind and then pressed her lips to my neck and kissed me. "I'm sorry," she whispered into my ear. I immediately felt some of my tension melt away. "I guess I'm just as worried about you going back to work as you are."

And then the tension flooded back. I *wasn't* worried about going back to work… I was stressed about people feeling they needed to shield me from it.

We spent the rest of the visit talking about the people from work: who was dating who, who was not pulling their weight, and how everyone was so excited that I was coming back. By the time we were done, I was exhausted.

Barb and I didn't say a word to each other on the way back home. Out of the corner of my eye, I saw her start to speak a couple of times, but then for some reason, she thought better of it and remained silent.

This tension is going to drive me nuts, I thought.

five
Monday, July 19th

First Day Back to Work—Fairfax, Virginia

I woke with a start. The sun was up, but it took me a moment to realize that meant that I had slept through the night.

Yay for me!

Barb was already out of bed and puttering in the kitchen, judging by the sounds coming from that direction.

I sat up in bed and looked down at my chest and belly.

The presence of the waxy scars on my otherwise smooth and muscular torso created a momentary lapse into self-pity. It quickly evaporated, but the shadow of sadness lingered in the back of my mood.

I climbed out of bed, stretching into the tightness of my man-made deformities as I walked to the bathroom to shower. By the time I was done showering and dressing, I could smell coffee.

I walked into the kitchen to find Barb cutting grapefruit. She looked up and smiled.

"You slept all night!" she exclaimed gleefully.

"Yeah," I replied. "Between the climbing and the sessions with Dr. Hebron, I think my body and brain are just tired enough."

"Are you excited to go back to work?" she asked as she placed the grapefruit and coffee on the kitchen bar.

"I guess," I replied absently, and then thought about my answer more completely. "I'm worried about not being able to get into a routine, though. I can't even seem to get into a routine around here."

"It's okay. It's not like you can't come home if it doesn't feel right. No one is going to push you," she replied supportively.

Stay calm and then speak the truth, I thought, repeating my new mantra.

"That's what I'm worried about," I said, relaxing into possible backlash. "I need to be pushed, and no one seems to be doing any pushing besides me."

An exasperated look washed across her face, quickly hidden behind a smile.

I hated that.

"Hey," I pushed, hoping to create a chink in her armor. "You suffered trauma as well. Why is it that I'm the one who has to be protected from reality?"

"No one is protecting you from 'reality,'" she replied, using air quotes. "And aside from the initial attack on the boat—during which no shots were fired—I spent the entire time in a box, a warehouse, another box, a smelly old barracks, and yet another box," she said, sitting down to breakfast. "I saw no action and no hostility until you showed up to rescue us."

"You exaggerate the lack of action you saw," I said accusingly.

"Exaggerate?" she exclaimed incredulously. "*You* were tortured, abducted, and beaten, fought Bosnian Serb mercenaries, stabbed, jumped out of an airplane, nearly drowned, and were shot twice—and you died three times before we got you back to Germany."

Stay calm and then speak the truth, I repeated in my head, but my willpower had already dissolved.

"Technically, you jumped out of an airplane too," I replied with a grin.

She dropped her spoon and then leaned over and threw her arms around me. "It will all work out. Things will get back to normal," she crooned, squeezing me tightly.

So much for my mantra, I thought.

I was getting tired of the people around me walking on eggshells, treating me like a handicapped person. I didn't need to be humored. I'd rather the physicians tell me I've gone too far and to dial it back than not move forward.

I'd like it if people would expect the old Scott and just be patient if he took a little longer to show up rather than trying to carry me around like an infant and clipping their emotions for fear of not being supportive enough.

I couldn't help but feel I would be testing their limits soon, if for no other reason than to get some honest interaction—or maybe I just wanted to be pissed off at everyone—I honestly couldn't tell.

I ignored her upbeat appraisal and sat at the bar to eat my grapefruit. After a few moments of eating in silence, I spoke up.

"I still haven't heard from Kathrin," I mentioned, hoping to draw out some sort of an honest response.

Barb paused for a split second and then continued to eat. When she had swallowed her spoonful of fruit, she looked up and smiled.

"She's probably out on a new adventure," Barb quipped. "She seems to be sort of a gypsy that way."

Nope...more coddling.

There was something to her tone that I didn't like—something beyond discomfort about me making contact. Not to mention the fact that she had no idea what *sort* Kathrin was. *I had spent days with her and knew next to nothing about the woman.*

Whoa. Am I pissed at Kathrin too?

"I bet she'll pop up when we least expect it," she continued with slightly less bitterness.

I nodded and tucked my observation into the back of my brain. My perceptions were distorted at the moment, and I knew it. I was already paranoid about not getting complete honesty from the people around me. It wouldn't have been a stretch to think I was reading more into the situation than there was.

I finished my grapefruit and my coffee and then got up to brush my teeth.

When I was done and on my way out of the bathroom, Barb was waiting for me. She threw her arms around my neck and kissed me on the lips.

"I want you to have a good day," she ordered, "but if it gets overwhelming, I want you to promise you'll come home."

I nodded and returned her kiss. Her lips stayed stiff.

She's holding something back, I thought. I was tempted to silently recite my mantra again—but then gave up on it.

"I promise," I said and detached myself from her embrace.

Something is going on here, but I am not in the mood to untangle it now, I thought, swallowing my urge to probe her behavior further. In my impatient state, it would more than likely only lead to hurt feelings.

As I walked down the stairs to the front door, I heard her say, almost in a whisper, "I love you."

I paused, turned to her, and smiled.

"What, sweetheart?" I asked.

"Have a good day," she responded with a smile, editing her previous statement.

"You too, baby," I said before turning and walking out, my anger rising.

What the hell is this? I asked myself silently as I got into my car and drove away. *What is going on with me?*

I would have to pay close attention to my responses today. Something was going on, most likely stirred up by Dr. Hebron's sessions, and it didn't bode well for my close relationships.

On the drive into work, Dr. Hebron's question came back to me. *"What happens to a child who is bullied once they become an adult?"*

A keen awareness of injustice, for a start, I said to myself. *Ignoring emotional pain is another trait. I'm aware of that now.*

But was it just pain that was ignored? *Maybe emotional numbness in general?*

"Well, the anger is real enough," I complained aloud as I pulled into the parking garage at TravTech.

As I walked into the lobby, I saw Bonny running towards me, arms wide and smiling. She reached me and threw her arms around my neck, squealing and giggling in delight.

"Don't be angry with me. I may have mentioned what happened to a couple of people here," she confessed cautiously.

I stopped short before walking through the door. "Bonbon. The CIA *debriefed* you. You know you aren't supposed to tell *anyone* about what happened. It was a condition for you and Storc not being indicted."

"I know, I know. But it's just too cool a story not to tell," she whined. "You're a hero!"

I almost turned around and left. I needed things to be normal. This new revelation made it clear that *normal* was not going to be the theme of the day.

We walked into the office together, and I was greeted with a cheer and applause from the vast cube farm as we came around the corner. I could feel my face turning red. Emotion was welling up in me; I wasn't sure if it was pride, anger, embarrassment, or all of the above.

People I had never even spoken to were flooding into the tech area, slapping me on the back, shaking my hand, kissing me on the cheek, and fawning over me—I was *very* uncomfortable.

I leaned over and whispered in Bonny's ear, "I'd hate to be you when John finds out he has to debrief *all* these people."

"He'll get over it," she said dismissively.

I made my way through the ad hoc reception line to my cubicle. I turned the corner into my cube and the first thing I noticed was that all my equipment and personal items were gone.

What the hell?

Bonny linked her arm through mine and continued to pull me down the aisle.

"You're down here now," she informed me.

I followed along to the end of the aisle and into one of the glass-walled offices. Before I left for Europe, the space had been a sales manager's office, and I suddenly wondered if the manager who had been booted had gotten another office. My items were arranged neatly on a desk and on the wall was a huge banner, filled with hundreds of signatures, welcoming me home.

My new office was crowded with balloons and flowers and standing around my new desk were managers and officers from the company, including Bernard Evonitz—founder and president of TravTech.

"Scott," he boomed, silencing the ruckus around us. "We just want to welcome you back and let you know how proud the whole TravTech family is of you. You'll be pleased to know that none of your time off will be deducted from your vacation time."

A burst of laughter erupted in the room as Evonitz leaned over and spoke into my ear.

"…and as gratitude for your service to our country, the board has voted to give you twenty-five thousand shares of TravTech stock options and a raise in your salary."

I smiled and shook his hand. "Thank you, sir, but it really isn't necessary. My actions have already caused enough disruption to business."

"Nonsense. And call me Bernie. I don't think you realize how much you've done for morale," he continued more loudly. "Besides…since your foray into international adventure, security contracts have increased seventy-five percent. That's the biggest one-time jump in sales for the company since I founded it."

"That's great," I said sincerely. "I'm excited to get back to work and into my old routine."

"That's my boy," he said, smiling broadly and patting me on my back. "Okay people, let's clear out of here and let Scott settle into his new office." Then, turning back to me, he confided, "Let logistics know of any resources you need to get you going full swing…now that you've returned, construction will get started. It's good to have you back, son."

"Thanks, Bernie," I said, trying to honor his wishes…but it felt strange calling him by his first name.

After they had all departed, Storc strolled around the room, looking at the bigger space. Bonny plopped down in my chair and put her feet up on my new desk.

"What's first, boss? Are we going after more terrorists? Organized crime?" she asked, smiling.

"Boss?" I asked.

"Yeah," Storc exclaimed. "You're the head of a new

department. Special Projects. Bonny and I now work for you as well as three other people you have to pick...including a personal assistant to manage the office stuff."

"Fuck!" I exclaimed before I could check the emotion.

Bonny rose from my desk quickly, looking at me with worry. "What's wrong? I thought you'd be happy to have autonomy."

I shook my head. It was almost a full minute before I had calmed myself enough to speak.

"What is 'Special Projects' Department?" I asked to neither one specifically.

"It's a special contract branch of tech security," Storc volunteered, "for our new contracts with the government."

I shook my head in disbelief.

"Scott," Bonny offered gently as she came around the desk. "It's a cover contract. The CIA asked Bernie to set it up. The company is getting paid big bucks to provide them access to you. If I had known it was going to upset you this much, I wouldn't have saved it as a surprise."

The blood drained from my face. I had been expecting special contracts from the government, but I hadn't foreseen an entire CIA technical *substation* being built and me being thrown in charge.

It's too much. It's too damned much.

I was looking forward to coming back to my cubicle, jamming my fingers on the keyboard, spinning code, and drinking too much coffee in privacy and quiet—I had autonomy before. Everyone left me alone because I fixed stuff no one else could. This new arrangement was not autonomy. It was the opposite of autonomy—and the opposite of normal.

Dr. Hebron's words came back to me. *"Events that alter us happen every day. It's not a matter of if we change because of our experiences*—they *will* change us...*the better question to ask is: Will we allow those events to be bigger than us?"*

I dropped my tattered shoulder bag on the floor next to my desk and plopped down into the chair. My eyes drifted down to the bag, staring at it listlessly, remembering the morning Kathrin had so eagerly traded it for my backpack in Amsterdam.

It was several seconds before I realized Bonny was speaking to me again.

"Scott. If you need more time, we've got instructions for that. No one is rushing you," she insisted supportively. "You've been through the *shit* and everyone knows it."

"I wish everyone would forget it…I wish I could forget it. I wish—" I was about to say I wish I had never met Barb, but that seemed to go too far, and it wouldn't have been the truth.

"Why don't you go back home? We've got it under control here," Storc offered. "No one expects you to jump right in."

"Nope!" I blurted, suddenly feeling it was time to pull myself together. "I've got to sack up and get to work. I've been on paid vacation long enough."

"That's my boy!" Bonny exclaimed, throwing her arms around me. "Welcome back, Scottmeister!" She kissed me on the cheek and then hopped up onto my desk. "What's first?"

I looked out the window into the tech cube farm, seeing heads popping up occasionally to look in my direction.

"I need to get organized," I murmured absently.

"Well," Bonny said, thinking of a way to get rolling. "You could go ahead and hire the other three people. Start with the office manager. That should help you get organized.

"Office manager?" I asked incredulously.

Bonbon smiled knowingly. "We made sure that *project management* skills were a prerequisite when the job announcement went out. We knew you'd want someone who could keep up with you." She grinned like that had been some sort of insult.

"Okay. Good idea. Who do I have to choose from?" I asked.

"Check your email. You've got hundreds of people clamoring to work for you," Storc suggested. "A bunch of them have been copying me and sending follow-ups every day, asking if I've heard from you."

"Me too," Bonny chirped. "I haven't been this popular since the costume malfunction at the Christmas party two years ago," she added, giggling.

"I didn't see any emails," I replied in confusion.

"Ah," Storc recalled as he got up, fished a piece of paper out of his pack and then sat it on my desk in front of me. "Secure server…new address. This section can't operate on standard servers."

I looked at the new mail server ID and the address I had been assigned—wolfeman. "It would have been nice to know this last week while I was gearing up," I complained without looking up.

"I thought of that too, but Habib wanted you to clear out his project list first…and others," he said, glaring at Bonbon, "wouldn't let me say anything."

I nodded. It made sense that Danny Habib would want as much unfinished work completed before I officially left his department—and Bonbon was Bonbon…probably doing Barb's bidding.

I mentally girded myself for the new role. "Alright. You two pick a systems and networking person you are both comfortable with and another encryption specialist. I'll look for the project manager."

"Personal assistant slash office manager," Bonbon corrected.

"I don't need a personal assistant," I replied a little too sharply, still a little upset she had told the whole office about Europe. "My *person* has all the assistance it needs. I'll need a project manager and a researcher."

I could tell Bonbon was a little put off by my response, so I softened it some. "Besides, once we get going, a researcher slash analyst will do me more good than an assistant."

She smiled and nodded, but I could tell she was a little bruised. Storc intervened through distraction.

"The CIA sent over a list of approved people who'd pass the security checks," Storc said. "I was copied on it. If you can't find it in your box, let me know and I'll forward you another copy."

"Cool. Thanks, man," I responded.

"No problem." He rose to leave but turned before he exited. "Scott," he said seriously. "I'm glad you're back."

"Thanks," I muttered, forcing my face into a smile.

Don't be a douche, Scott, I thought.

Bonny wandered over to the counter on the other side of the office. I hadn't noticed it before due to all the flowers and balloons, but there was an elaborate-looking coffee machine sitting there. It was a rather large office—bigger than Habib's. A large monitor hung on the wall between the two windows and behind me was a work station, though empty of hardware, which could hold several monitors and servers.

"Do you want some coffee?" she asked, snapping me out of my visual inspection. Before I could answer, she continued. "Please say yes. I've been waiting for two weeks to try this thing out."

I laughed. "Yes, Bonbon. I would love some coffee."

"Espresso, cappuccino, latte, or regular?" she asked excitedly.

"Surprise me," I chuckled.

By the time Bonny served me my latte, I had found the email containing the CIA-approved employee list; some candidates had asterisks next to their names, indicating a higher degree of approval—though I wasn't sure what that meant. Perhaps there was a particular personality profile that the Agency considered more desirable.

In any case, I'd make my choice based on my criteria. I wasn't in the mood to play manager, so I just sent a mass email to all the "personal assistant" candidates who also had project management and researcher qualifications, asking them to stop by my office sometime today so we could meet and chat.

I also stumbled across a required facilities alterations list from the CIA, addressed to me, copying Bernie. Bernie had already replied to the message stating that the company and I would happily provide any resources required.

As I waited for the list to print, the first applicant showed up at my door and knocked. I looked up to see a very prim-looking woman in a business suit with her hair pulled back so tightly it probably stretched five years from her face.

"Mr. Wolfe?" she asked as her eyes flashed around my office, pausing briefly at Bonny, tensing—presumably due to her Goth attire or multicolored hair—and then returning her gaze to me. "I received your email. Is now a good time?"

"Yes. And for fuck's sake, don't call me Mr. Wolfe," I ordered with a grin.

She tensed at the language. "Yes, sir," she responded stiffly.

"—or sir," I heaped on as I gestured to the chair in front of the desk. "You have a resume?"

"Yes, s... Yes, I do," she stammered as she sat and then timidly placed it on my desk.

I looked it over, seeing her impressive list of credentials and references. I had already made up my mind, though. If she was uncomfortable with the appearance of Bonny and my intentional F-bomb test, she would not be a good fit for this group.

I saw Bonny wildly gesturing over her shoulder, indicating she did not approve of this one. There was an asterisk next to her name.

It figures.

I wasn't even paying attention to her verbal dissertation of achievements and skills. Once she finished speaking, I thanked her for her interest in the position and told her I would let everyone know of my decision soon.

Two others had arrived while I was interviewing the first. The next was very much like the first, also with an asterisk next to her name—but equally unsuited for this group. And so it was for the next couple of hours; one candidate after another. Each highly qualified for the position but totally unsuited to be part of my team.

Bonny had taken to passing in and out of the office, standing behind the candidates, making faces or rude gestures indicating why they weren't suitable. Most of them failed the Bonny test, all but one failed the F-bomb test. And none of them seemed the slightest bit creative. That was one thing I couldn't abide.

Around twelve o'clock, a delivery person arrived with an assortment of pizza, subs, and wraps, courtesy of upper management. My office filled up with hungry techs from the cube farm outside my door, each eager to have a free meal and chat with me about things I couldn't talk about—such as terrorists and Bosnian Serb mercenaries.

While trying to keep Bonny from lifting my shirt to display my scars to the lunch guests, there was knock on the door. A woman with black hair in dark business attire was standing in my doorway. The collar of her blouse just barely covered the top of a tattoo. She had several piercings in both ears, including a scaffold piercing at the top of her right ear and a tragus piercing on her left.

"Mr. Wolfe?" she asked shyly, looking to see who would respond.

"That's me," I piped and then turned to my lunch companions. "Okay guys. Free lunch is over."

Moans and laughter followed the group as they meandered out the door.

"I can come back a little later if you need me to," she blurted out.

"No. That's fine. Come on in and sit down," I reassured, and then remembered my lines. "And for fuck's sake, don't call me Mr. Wolfe."

She didn't even bat an eye. "Yes, sir," she replied.

Bonny wandered in around my desk and leaned against the wall. The new candidate smiled at her shyly. "Hello," she greeted softly.

Bonny smiled and nodded as I looked at her resume.

Jo Ann Zook. She had a great deal of experience; her skills list was longer than most of the other candidates. It included an elaborate project list, each lasting no more than three months for various managers and executives in this company and several others I recognized in the industry. I quickly checked the CIA's approved list. Her name was there, but no asterisk.

Her resume included glowing recommendations from the managers she had worked with. Conspicuously missing from their statements were the common accolades for being a team player and being well-liked.

"Jo Ann. You have an impressive list of projects here," I remarked.

A look of distaste crossed her face. "Thank you, sir. Please call me Jo."

"Okay. And you could please stop referring to me as 'sir,'" I advised, smiling. "I haven't been knighted."

"Sure," she replied, relaxing her posture a bit.

"Why so many projects with such short duration?" I asked, placing her resume and the CIA list on the desk.

"I have a particular skill set that's geared for organization and problem-solving. More like a troubleshooter than anything else," she said shyly and then reached for, stopped and then reached again across my desk to straighten the two pages I had just laid down, aligning the edges perfectly with the edge of my desk.

"I see," I replied. "Why so many different managers?"

She didn't even pause, but her posture became a little more

rigid. "As I said, I have a particular skill set. Fairly specialized. When projects reach a stage for public or other human interface, I've been told I lack other skills needed to…integrate."

I understood what she meant, but I wanted to test the boundaries of her honesty. "I'm not sure I understand what you mean."

"I think you do understand and are testing me…which is fine," she informed me, and then she gauged my expression before continuing.

I'm impressed so far, Ms. Zook, I thought. *Keep going.*

"My strengths are also my weaknesses. I tend to cut through bullshit to get to the heart of a problem. I'm just as quick to identify team flaws in a new project as I am system or data flaws. I could care less whose sensitive nature I upset. That's fine for getting a project's infrastructure and organization off the ground rapidly. But most managers find my methods abrasive and tend to thank me for my efforts and then shove me out the door before I can embarrass them once things are running smoothly."

"I see," I muttered, getting exactly the answer I had hoped for. "Do you feel you could work in an environment where honesty is essential but rudeness could damage the work environment?"

"Honesty will be no problem," she volunteered without hesitation. "Though I've found the concept of rudeness to be subjective, I can only promise I would try to meet your expectations."

I couldn't have asked for a more perfect answer if I had written it myself. *Finally* someone in my life besides my shrink who will speak her mind—even if I am paying her to do it.

"Jo." I beamed while standing and extending my hand. "Welcome to the island of misfit toys."

She smiled, rose, and shook my hand. Bonny rushed over and gave the girl a hug, clearly making her uncomfortable for a second. She returned the gesture with a gentle, though brief tap on her back. When she pulled away, Jo's face had turned beet red.

"Awww. How cute!" Bonny exclaimed. "You blush."

"Bonbon. Maybe Jo has boundaries you need to recognize," I offered.

"It's fine," Jo replied shyly.

"Yeah. See! It's fine. Everybody likes to hug," Bonny protested, giggling, happy to have another broken doll on the team.

"You can move your personal effects to the cube outside my office as soon as it's convenient," I said. "We'll have some construction at this end of the building soon. But until then, that cube will keep you close to the action."

"Construction?" Bonny asked.

"Yes. The contract we're operating under requires a certain level of physical separation from the rest of the company. A NOC fishbowl has been ordered for this corner of the tech floor," I informed her.

A NOC fishbowl is a glass-enclosed structure for a Network Operations Center. The one that had been contracted for us included biometric entry panels, glass that could be made opaque by remote control, and a separately firewalled mini server room.

"Cool!" Bonny exclaimed. Then she hooked her arm through Jo's and led her outside my office to the cubicle she would be working from.

**

5:30 p.m.—Fairfax, Virginia

"I'm taking you out tonight," Barb chirped excitedly, "to celebrate your first day back at work."

I was tired from the excitement of the day, but a night out sounded like something normal. "I would love that, hon. Great idea," I replied, sounding sincere, playing the adoring boyfriend.

It would have been nice if I felt it as well, but something the shrink said had stuck in my head. *"Sometimes if you start doing normal things, normal feelings come back."*

I was willing to try anything. I was feeling very guilty about not being the person Barb had come to expect after our return from Europe. She wouldn't come out and say it, but I could see the disappointment on her face when I responded counter to her expectations—which left me feeling resentful. It was an ugly cycle.

But my response to her invitation had put a broad smile on her face. She was positively giddy as she readied herself for "date night," singing a tune as she primped and preened. "Hey there, mister. Ain't that sister, sister on the radio," I heard coming from the bedroom as I was drying off from my shower.

Her lyrical confusion usually amused me. But since we had returned from Europe, all I wanted to do was yell out that she had the words backwards.

I resisted the urge, fully aware it would have been a *douchebag* thing to do. The change in my personality was beginning to frighten me. It was like being trapped below deck in a sinking ship, watching out of a portal as the water rose above the window. I was sitting there, warm and dry, not being able to do anything about the ocean swallowing me whole.

When I entered the bedroom, I instead told her how beautiful she looked. She glowed at my compliment. She really did look fantastic. I, however, immediately felt angry at myself for manufacturing a compliment to hide frustration.

You don't want to be here, Scott, I argued with myself. *You don't want to be in the relationship, you don't want to be friends, you don't want to play house. Why aren't you just telling her that?*

Because, my other voice chimed in, startling me, ***you don't trust that you are sane enough to make that decision.***

Shut up or I'll tell Dr. Hebron about you, I thought in reply—a hollow threat.

No response.

While on our way to the restaurant, Barb insisted on hearing every detail of my first day back to work. She giggled and clapped like a little girl when I described the cheering mob when I entered the office. She was very excited about the raise, the stock options, and the promotion.

"You have to let me come by next week and put some stuff up on the walls for you," she insisted.

"Most of the walls will be covered with hardware and monitors," I replied.

"I'll figure something out," she said and then winked.

I told her about the hiring ritual I had practiced. She frowned, but I explained that it was necessary if we were to have a cohesive unit. Bonny swore like a sailor when she was frustrated, and I was known to throw the occasional F-bomb when working on a difficult project as well. Finding someone who didn't take other's habits and foibles personally was critical to a close working group.

She understood my reasoning, but I knew she couldn't picture herself in a work environment like that.

"It's a different culture in tech," I explained. "A subculture, in fact. And often, the more comfortable someone feels with the machines, the less adept they are with people. Tolerance is crucial."

She shrugged it off and began asking about the new office designs as we entered the restaurant. We were seated and then resumed our conversation. I described the fishbowl to her and all the biometric entry requirements, both for the new office cluster and the server room—which would be like a fishbowl inside of a fishbowl.

"Won't you feel isolated, being inside the glass like that?" she asked.

"I don't think so. Even in a cubicle, it's like being in your own little world. And the glass would only be opaque to shoulder level, except when we need more privacy. We'd still have the sense of being surrounded by the rest of the tech floor," I said.

She seemed to accept my take on the subject.

When the waitress arrived with our drinks, we ordered our appetizers and entrees. As we sipped our wine, another couple came into the restaurant and was led past to the table next to us. Perhaps in their mid-thirties, he was a large man with broad shoulders and a round belly and she was a petite woman with long black hair pulled back into a girlish ponytail. They were talking as they went by us.

"Try not to embarrass yourself tonight," I heard the man say as they arrived at their table.

She shot him a shy, hurt look.

"God! I'm just kidding," he snorted. "Don't be so damned sensitive." Then he plopped down heavily in his chair.

Barb and I turned back to each other after shooting him a harsh look and then continued our conversation as the appetizers arrived.

"Aren't you tired of talking about work?" I asked.

"It's your night!" she exclaimed with a smile. "It's supposed to be about you."

It was *always* about me. I hadn't been able get her to talk about what she was doing for weeks. I didn't find out she was signed up for classes at Georgetown until the week before they started…and only then because she was talking to Bonny about it on the phone and I overheard her. It was almost as if she felt that any detail outside of my little protective bubble would crush me.

Maybe there's another approach to get her to show some honesty with me.

"You know," I reasoned with a smile. "I'm the guy who can learn a programming language over the weekend and then plan a

SEAL-assisted assault on a Russian Cargo plane with the time I have left over."

She looked around nervously, checking to see if anyone had overheard me.

"I think I can handle hearing how your day went without requiring medication," I quipped, grinning.

"Sorry," she replied.

"And seriously, please stop apologizing," I added, still smiling but with a little edge of agitation. "You didn't do this to me. And you have gone well above the call of duty to help me since we got back."

"How could I *not*?" she asked quickly, a frantic tone to her voice. She regained her composure before continuing. "You're my hero. I wouldn't be here if it wasn't for you."

And there it was…the reason for it all. The sense of duty and obligation we both felt to each other was keeping us both miserable.

At the table next to us, the man slammed his hand down on the table, interrupting my sudden revelation.

"Don't ask me. Do I look like a fucking chef?" Barb and I, and half the other patrons, heard the big man say coarsely. "Ask the waitress." When he noticed others in the restaurant looking at them, he shook his head and pointed at her, smiling. "I can't take her anywhere." He turned to her, speaking in a threatening whisper. "What did I say about embarrassing me?"

Quiet returned to their table as the woman sulked behind her menu. I let my glance linger long enough to note the matching wedding rings on the couple and a crooked nose on the woman— a bump that flared out at the bridge and set slightly to one side. Sometime in her past, her nose had been broken and never been set properly. It had healed crooked.

As our meals arrived, Barb and I continued to talk about the goings on at the office.

"John told me to expect a lot of work being thrown our way by *the company*," I divulged. "I had no idea the setup would be so elaborate. It's going to be like a business inside of a business."

"Well. I don't think John had much to do with it," she explained with a knowing grin. "I suspect Daddy probably put a bug in someone's ear."

My ire began to rise at the weakly veiled disclosure, but again I was interrupted by the couple next to us.

"Stop making that noise when you eat," the fat man at the table next to us warned—louder than necessary for his wife to hear. She sank down into herself, nearly disappearing below the top of the chair back.

"That's it," he barked. "I'm not taking you out again. You're too much of an embarrassment."

I took a bite of steak, chewed it slowly, and looked at Barb. She was looking at me, clearly upset by the way the woman was being treated. I looked around as I continued to masticate the tasty, bloody flesh and saw that many of the patrons were staring down at the napkins in their laps—a typical response to an assault of any sort; a natural embarrassment for not stepping in and a physical response to a social trigger: "If I don't look, maybe I won't be noticed."

My anger was rising. I could feel it spreading through my cheeks and ears. Barb saw the flush on my face and a worried look crossed hers. Her worry tempered my next action.

I casually turned in my seat toward the couple, swallowed the bite of steak I had been chewing, and then wiped my mouth with my napkin.

"Ma'am?" I interjected politely.

She hesitated to look but social niceties required her to acknowledge me. She turned and looked at me, confused as to why I would be addressing her.

"Do you have children?" I asked.

She looked around nervously and then nodded the affirmative. "Two."

I leaned forward and lowered my voice so she knew the words were for her, though others could hear. "I would recommend you take your children and leave this man before he ruins them the same way he has ruined you," I asserted gently, smiling so she saw kindness in my words.

"Who do you think you are?" the man raged, rising from his chair, bumping the table, and spilling his whiskey.

The patrons in the restaurant were all trying very hard not to look at what was going on…all except Barb, who was wide-eyed, staring at me in shock.

I turned back to my meal and began cutting another piece of steak, ignoring the big man. He stepped toward me on my left. I tensed my left leg and pressed my foot hard into the carpeted floor in anticipation—but continued to eat.

"I'm talking to you, punk," he boomed loudly enough for people on the street to hear. "Who the *fuck* do you think you are!?" His hand came down hard on my left shoulder, his finger digging into the scar from the bullet wound the Serbian mercenary had left, and then he shoved me.

I rolled my left arm up and over his arm as I stood, locking his wrist under my armpit and my forearm under his elbow. Shock and fear washed across his face at the speed and strength of my movement. Before he could formulate a response, physically or verbally, my right fist slammed into his diaphragm, sending the air out his lungs and him to the floor.

He laid there gasping, and as I returned to my meal, I noted a brief flash of satisfaction on the wife's face, followed by a manufactured mask of outrage. A surprised stare from Barb greeted me as I sat. It slowly turned into a smile. She sat up, proud of her knight in shining armor, once again defending the weak. I heard a chorus of chatter, laughs, and a smattering of applause.

I felt anger rising again.

"Don't applaud me!" I reprimanded bitterly, rising from my chair again. The applause stopped abruptly. "He was bullying her all night, and any one of you could have said something. But the napkins in your laps were more interesting,"

The man got up from the floor and left the room hurriedly. His wife hesitated a moment and then followed him out.

I paused, looking around from table to table before sitting and quickly refocusing on finishing my meal. I got a supportive wink from Barb, but the smile was gone from her face. There was silence in the restaurant and mumbling in a corner…and I was suddenly very uncomfortable with my back to the door.

Once we finished eating, I quickly paid for our meal and the other couple's meal. The waiter told me it wasn't necessary for me to pay, but I wasn't interested in a free meal—I just wanted to get home. The tension in my chest had built, and I actually found myself looking over my shoulder, half-expecting to see an assault team burst in.

Barb and I walked to the car in silence. Once in the car, she sat, and a grin slowly started spreading across her face. She looked straight ahead without saying a word for the longest time.

Finally she spoke. "I can't take you anywhere," she joked, and then she broke out in laughter.

It was contagious; I burst out laughing as well. "I really did make a scene, didn't I?" I laughed harder, the manic outburst building on itself. I could feel a tear rolling down my cheek. "At least I didn't kill anyone," I gasped out through a ragged breath.

Barb's laughter stopped abruptly as her head spun to face me, an expression of worry on her face.

Suddenly, all the stress in my life poured out of my chest and my increasingly manic laughter suddenly turned into broken sobs. Tears rolled out; loud, racking shudders assaulted my chest. It was all I could do to pull the car over before I started shaking violently.

She threw her arms around me, and then she began sobbing as well. Not saying a word, she wrapped me warmly in her arms, laying her cheek on my head and pulling me down into her breast. Her soft, warm hands stroked my hair and rubbed my shoulder, trying to absorb the ache into her as she softly shushed in my ear.

"Shhhhh," she whispered. "It's alright. You did a good thing."

I honestly didn't even know why I was collapsing. I had no remorse for my actions. It was almost as if the steam valve just needed to blow…and this was as good a trigger as any.

After a few minutes, I regained my composure and sat up, wiping my eyes.

I took a deep ragged breath. Then, without a word, I put the car in drive and continued home.

six
Tuesday, July 20th

1:15 a.m.—Harvest, Alabama, a suburb of Huntsville

MARK GAINES had been up for hours, reading transaction numbers and account information off to Alisha Gordon, the friend and forensic accountant who had introduced him to Dee. The print on the papers had gotten soggy and smudged with blood and sweat during his escape from the ambush, and he was having difficulty reading a lot of the information.

"Is it a six or an eight, Mark?" Alisha asked him as he paused on another set of numbers. "Because even one number off will prevent me from looking them up."

"Damn it, Alisha," he muttered in exhaustion. "I don't know. I really need you to look at them."

"Then send them to me," she offered softly for the third time.

"The mail isn't monitored here."

"You don't know that for sure," he replied firmly. "If they break through my cover, how hard will it be to find a link from me and Dee to you? As it is, you may already have eyes on you."

"I'm used to eyes being on me," she replied.

Mark chuckled. "Yeah, but not for the same reason."

Just then, his personal phone rang. It was one he had purchased with cash and had kept records of under an assumed company name. Only a handful of people had the number—his family among them.

"I have to call you back, Alisha," he said. "I'm sorry about how hard this is."

"Okay, but if you can't get to a descent document scanner with forensic tools, I'll come and get them from you," she vowed firmly—she wasn't going to let it go.

His phone continued to ring.

"I've gotta go," he insisted again. "I'll call you back later."

He didn't wait for her reply before ending the call and picking up his private phone. He glanced down and saw it was his sister, Marie, in Colorado Springs.

"What's keeping you up so late, sis?" he asked when he answered the phone.

She chuckled before responding. "That's what happens when you have a sick baby," she complained tiredly. "She's been up all night."

Marie and Heather had been together for five years, moving to the quiet suburbs of Colorado Springs last year just before Megan was born. Marie had carried Megan herself after being artificially inseminated, and she'd left her position as a probate attorney when she was within one week of the baby's due date.

"I'm sorry," Mark replied sympathetically. "Nothing serious, I hope."

"She's teething," Marie confided in exasperation. "Nothing we can do except make her feel loved and keep a handful of pacifiers in the freezer."

Mark laughed. "I never thought I'd ever hear words like that come out of *your* mouth," he said, his tone dripping amusement. "My high-powered lawyer of a sister, packing pacifiers in the icebox…it seems impossible."

"Oh, I don't know," she replied. "I think my mediation skills have come in quite handy, haven't they?" Her tone slowly drifted to baby talk, aimed at Megan. "It's Heather who would have a problem being a stay-at-home mom. She likes the conflict…much like you."

"Who me?" Mark asked incredulously. "I'm a teddy bear."

"More like a grizzly bear," she replied, slipping back into baby talk as Megan's crying increased again.

"Aww," Mark crooned. "Let me talk to her."

"You want to talk to Uncle Mark?" he heard her say, followed by the voice of the crying infant on the phone.

"Heeeey, hey, heeeeey," Mark cooed into the phone. "What's all the fuss about?"

The crying began to subside a bit.

"Come on," he continued. "I know it's hard, but you need to grow those teeth to protect you from all those boys who're gonna hound you in school."

He heard Marie chuckle in the background.

"I don't know how you do it," Marie mused. "She's quieting down already."

"She knows Uncle Mark is looking out for her," Mark explained, grateful for the injection of family into his stressful week. "How are you doing aside from the teething crisis?"

There was a short pause before she responded as he listened to her lay Megan back down.

"There was another incident a couple weeks ago," she volunteered in a whispered voice. Her statement was followed by the sound of a door opening and then closing again. "They spray painted the garage door this time."

One morning, three months earlier, as Heather left for work, she'd found someone had left a note written on a paper bag containing what turned out to be dog shit. The note read: *"No Queers in CS. Eat this and die."*

It had been a traumatic and an unpleasant reminder that acceptance of their lifestyle was not universal. Mark had almost come out west then but Marie had talked him out of it.

"Shit," Mark muttered. "What did it say?"

"It's not important," she replied. "Heather had a security system installed, and the police started running more patrols through the neighborhood."

"What did it say?" Mark repeated.

There was a pause. "It was a stick figure of a baby and the word abomination across it."

Mark felt the anger rising in chest and his face began to flush with blood.

"We've got the security system now," she quickly added, "and I've seen three patrols tonight alone."

"When I'm done with this thing I'm working on, I'm coming out to spend some time with my girls," he stated adamantly.

"This 'thing' you're working on?" Marie repeated. "You aren't back with the Agency are you?"

"No," he replied firmly. "Tying up some loose ends on an investigation for a friend."

"You aren't in any danger, are you?" she asked nervously.

"Don't worry about me," he replied, deflecting. "Just stay safe. I don't know what I'd do if something happened to you."

"We'll be fine," she assured. "It's an annoyance, nothing

more."

He didn't respond immediately. He knew very well that the heart of man could harbor intense evil—he had seen it firsthand more times than he cared to remember.

"Stay safe," he repeated. "I'll be out in a few weeks."

"It would be so great to have you around," she admitted. "But please, don't shift your life around because a couple homophobic idiots figured out how to buy a can of spray paint."

"You know I'd come anyway," he replied. "Soon. I promise."

"Okay," she said, "and thanks for helping me put Megan down."

"My pleasure," he offered softly. "Call any time."

"I will. Love you, Mark," she added warmly.

"Love you too, sis. Give Heather and Megan a kiss for me," he replied. "Chat later."

"Bye."

When she had hung up, he went right back to the transaction sheets. He looked at the blood- and sweat-smeared sheets, trying to refocus on the task at hand, but his thoughts kept drifting back to Marie.

Still not a robot, he thought to himself as his chest tightened at the thought of harm befalling Marie, Megan, and Heather.

After another hour of fruitless effort, he stuffed the pages into a folder and lay down to sleep. As he drifted off, the fear of the loss of his sister and niece tainted his rest, leaving him to dream of terror impacting his family.

**

8:40 a.m.—Reston, Virginia

I arrived at TravTech around 8:45 a.m. I would have been earlier, but I had found it very difficult to move my ass out of bed after the prior emotional evening. When I entered the tech area, I could already hear the sounds of construction. An area along the back wall had been covered with clear plastic and there was a construction crew behind it working on taking down a wall.

I walked through my new office door to find Bonbon in my chair sipping a cup of coffee and my new project manager, Jo, sitting on the floor next to my desk. She was reading through printed emails in a binder and aggressively highlighting sections that were important to her.

"Good morning," I muttered as I walked in and moved toward the coffee machine.

"Oh. Let me!" Bonbon sang excitedly as she launched herself out of my chair toward the elaborate coffee station. "What do you want?"

I smiled at her excitement over the new toy. "Quad shot espresso. Please. With a latte chaser."

"Whoo hoo!" she exclaimed as she went to work at the machine.

I sat behind my desk and realized I couldn't see Jo over the top, so I rolled my chair around the side.

"How's it going, Jo?" I asked.

"Well," she stated quietly. Then, as an afterthought, she tossed in, "Thanks for asking."

I chuckled. "Did you understand my notes on the protocol classes and contacts?"

"Yes. Very clear. I'm just setting up the project schedule and procedures," she replied crisply as she continued to flip through pages, highlighting and adding adhesive tabs. "I should have everything mapped out by this afternoon. Most of the briefings and seminars apply to all of us, but there are a few just for you as lead analyst."

"That may change. We may be expanding those roles a bit," I hinted, alluding to my plan for her.

She nodded without looking up.

"Why are you doing it on paper?" I asked with a grin.

She looked up at me, seeing I wasn't going to simply let her work. "I don't have a computer yet," she replied. "I printed these from Story's computer so he could get back to work."

Story...I never heard anyone call him by his proper name anymore.

"Yeah, hopefully we can remedy that soon," I said.

"I'm fine," she responded, quietly returning to her work. After a pause, she spoke again. "But thank you for your concern."

I chuckled again, relieving some of the stress that was building from the construction noise. I turned to my computer, opened the mail interface, and then scanned through all the messages I had received since checking them from home this morning. The only new message of note was one from Mary Browning with Contract Administration at the CIA. Our liaison wrote:

> *"We are anxious to start sending work your way and can't do it until final clearances have been issued. Please forward the completed list of new hires. Again, very excited to be working with you and your team."*

I forwarded the message to Storc, Bonbon, and Jo with a short note:

> *I need your final hire choices. Please forward to Jo for packet completion and copy me.*

The banging of hammers and the buzz of power saws and drills was about to send me over the edge. My head was throbbing already, and I felt a mild welling of anxiety start to creep up my back.

There was a sudden pressure in my chest that was making it difficult for me to breathe as Bonbon appeared beside me with my coffee in her hand. She set it down, staring at me—a worried look spreading across her face.

I smiled. "Thanks, Bon. I just sent you and Storc a note on our other two hires. Can you wrap that up for me?"

"Sure thing. I've got it narrowed down to three people. I'll make a choice this morning and drop it in front of you to review before I notify them," she replied. She leaned close to me and confided in a quieter voice, "This noise is enough to drive anyone nuts. Why don't you head out and keep tabs on things with email today?"

I shook my head. "I'm fine. Just need to get some air," I said, evading her stare before quickly rising and the exiting the office. When I reached the stairwell, I paused and decided to go up instead of down to the street. I climbed the stairs to the roof and propped the door open with a block that sat next to it so the smokers could sneak out without being trapped.

I walked to the edge of the roof and looked out over Reston. It had grown so much in the past few years. It was nearly unrecognizable with all of its tall buildings and new traffic patterns. I sipped at my espresso and breathed in the heavy summer air, taking deep, purposeful breaths through my nose. I started to calm down immediately.

I heard the gravel crunch behind me and turned my head to see Storc approaching. He stopped a few feet behind me.

"Need some privacy?" he asked with a devilish grin on his face.

"Just some air. It was stuffy down there, and the noise was getting to me," I replied.

"I got your email. I'm going to bring Mahesh on if you don't have any objections. He's scary quick and his work rarely needs changes in QA," he related, setting a latte down next to me. "Bonbon said you forgot this when you left."

"Thanks," I replied. "Yeah. Mahesh would be a good choice. But Habib is going to be pissed losing another person to the new section."

"You could fix that by bringing him in as well," Storc

suggested with a grin.

"I don't think he'd deal well working for me," I responded apologetically after considering the option. "Though he'd be a perfect fit otherwise."

He paused and was about to leave, but he changed his mind and leaned on the ledge next to me instead.

"You need to take it easy. You've been out for months, walked into a shitload of new stress, and you still haven't fully recovered from your…uh…adventure," he said, smiling sympathetically.

"I'm fine. I'm just trying to get some balance," I replied insincerely. I felt bad about the deflection since he had taken the effort to confront me with an obvious problem.

I'll have to work on that, I thought to myself. *Tomorrow.*

"You know," he objected cautiously. "The others might stop trying to dance around your stress if you'd stop doing it as well…you can be honest with us."

I smiled. Storc wasn't the social retard he came off as.

"You're right," I replied sincerely. "I'm having trouble trying to fit myself back into my old life. It seems too small."

He nodded his understanding.

"Thanks," I grunted sincerely. "I needed that."

"My pleasure," he retorted. "But I was wrong. You can't say that to Bonbon. She'll have a stroke."

I laughed. "I know! Right?" I replied. "I just wish I didn't have to keep it from Barb as well."

Storc suddenly looked very uncomfortable.

"Sorry you asked now, huh?" I added, grinning. "Come on, let's get back downstairs."

The rest of the day was spent sorting through protocol regulations and a short conference call with Langley and the whole team. As soon as the call concluded, I grabbed my shoulder bag from my office and left the building. By the time I was on the Fairfax County Parkway, I couldn't even remember what I had done all day. As I pulled up to my condo, I realized I had been toying with the strap on my bag most of the way home.

I miss Kathrin, I thought to myself—so clearly, in fact, that for a moment I almost thought I had spoken it out loud.

seven
Thursday, July 22nd

12:30 a.m.—Colorado Springs, Colorado

MARIE GAINES was frantic. Her life partner, Heather, was hours late in coming home. Their daughter, Megan, had finally calmed down and went to sleep in the nursery, but it had been a struggle to tend to her while trying to locate Heather over the phone.

She had called Mark to tell him she was worried.

"I'm going nuts, Mark," she said, doing her best to stay calm. "And unless I wake Megan and pack her into the car, I'm stuck here. I don't want to be one of *those* wives, but it's not like her to not come home and not call."

"No answer on her cell?" Mark asked.

"No," she replied. "Right to voicemail. I must have left a dozen messages already."

"Did you call the office?" he asked calmly. "Is it possible she's just hanging out with people from work and lost track of time?"

"She left the office late, according to her boss, but she was on her own," Marie relayed. "No one at the office heard her say anything about going out. She would have called me anyway."

Just then she heard Heather's key in the door.

"Oh thank God!" she exclaimed into the phone. "I hear her now, Mark. Thanks for listening to me worry."

"No problem, sis. If you need anything else, call," he offered. "That's what big brothers are for."

She hung up the phone and ran for the front door.

"Where the hell have you been?" she asked as the door opened.

Heather fell forward, or rather she was shoved forward into the room. Marie screamed as three men came through the door and moved to restrain her.

She broke free and ran for the phone on the counter, managing to hit only one button on the phone before one of the men grabbed her. He punched her hard in the stomach, sending her to her knees gasping.

The last man through the door closed and bolted it, grabbed Heather by her hair, and dragged her into the living room.

"Good evening ma'am." The other one spoke to Marie smugly. "We will be your instructors this evening."

At which time the three began stripping both of the women of their clothes, punching them brutally when they resisted.

One stood watch by the window while the other two raped and sodomized the women.

"See there?" one of them snidely joked as he rose from

Heather's limp form and the next man prepared for his turn. "All they needed all along was a strong man to break them of their deviant ways."

The other two men laughed.

The two women reached for each other but the older man began punching Heather until she could only curl in on herself, her heaving sobs the only sound aside from the grunts of the men raping them.

After only a few moments—which to Marie seemed like hours—the men straightened themselves, kicking Heather once more for effect.

One of the men drew a handgun from his jacket and leveled it at Marie's head. Just as the man pulled the trigger, Heather screamed and kicked out, sending the shot just wide—the bullet striking Marie across the jaw instead of the forehead.

"Cunt," the man yelled at Heather, kicking her in the head again, knocking her unconscious.

The man at the window yelled something and the three ran through the kitchen toward the back door. Marie could hear, past the ringing in her ears, the sound of appliances moving on the floor.

When she heard the door open and slam shut again, she crawled dizzily toward Heather. She stroked her bruised and blood-soaked face, trying to awaken her.

Her jaw was throbbing and a flash of pain shot down her neck when she tried to move it.

"Baby. They're gone now. You can wake up. Wake up, baby," she pleaded, crying through the pain.

Marie could hear a siren in the distance getting closer as she continued to softly urge Heather to wake up.

"Come on, baby. The ambulance is coming. Wake up for me now. Please, love. Please," she begged as the odor of smoke reached her nostrils.

Heather's eyelids fluttered. She was only able to open one eye. The other was swollen shut.

She looked at Marie. "Love," was all she managed to say.

Just as the sound of sirens stopped outside, the house exploded. The men had broken the gas line on the oven and range, letting the house fill with gas until it reached the burning paper towels they had left on the dining room table.

**

THE LAST THING MARK GAINES heard was his sister pleading with Heather to wake up, and then the signal went dead. As soon as he'd heard the male voices in the house he'd dialed 911 from his secure satellite phone. By the time the dispatcher had figured out he was calling from a phone on behalf of his sister, the rape had begun.

The dispatch went out moments before the gunshot. As soon as the men exited the house, he began calling his sister's name, to no avail. She could not hear him. He heard the siren of the police car and the dispatcher in his ear saying that officers had arrived. In his other ear, he heard his sister pleading with her one true love and partner. Then the line went dead.

Mark didn't cry; he didn't scream. He waited on the cell phone with the dispatcher. When she informed him that the officers just reported that the house had exploded, he calmly ended the call, walked to his bedroom, and began packing a bag.

It was a bag he had packed many times in his old life. Pants, shirts, socks, and underwear rolled tightly and stacked side by side. Then came the belts, two of them, each with integrated scabbards for knives and loops for shoulder-slung holsters. Then came the ammunition, the two matching Desert Eagle .50 caliber automatic handguns, their silencers, and extra mags.

On his way down the hall of his safe house, he opened a closet door, clicked through a layer of drywall, and retrieved a metal box about the size of a large tower computer with wheels and a collapsible handle, like carry-on luggage. He hefted his duffel bag to his shoulder, pulled the box behind him, and exited the house.

It wasn't until he was driving down the street in his stolen black Crown Victoria that he began to cry.

Without thinking about a route, he began driving northwest...toward his sister.

**

8:30 a.m.—Reston, Virginia

When I arrived at work, there were construction workers swarming over the office like ants. Another large plastic sheet had been hung in the back of the building, separating the rest of the tech floor from the new Special Projects department being constructed.

The workers had demolished part of the dividing wall between TravTech and the adjoining suite of offices and had begun constructing the fishbowl enclosure around the area that was still part of the regular tech area.

I had to push past the plastic to get to my office. The door was closed as were the doors of the next three offices between mine and the new hole in the wall. I opened the door to my office and found five people sitting around the room.

Storc was sitting on the counter on the far side of the office, Bonny was sitting in my chair with her feet up on my desk, and a tall, thin Indian man with glasses—who I recognized as Mahesh from the networking department—was sitting in a chair in front of my desk.

A Rubenesque-looking girl with horned-rim glasses, blond braids, a three-quarter sleeve tattoo, and multiple facial piercings was sitting next to him, and then there was Jo, who was sitting on the floor next to my desk, leaning against the wall.

Bonny hopped out of my chair as soon as I came through the door. "Just warming it up for you," she giggled.

"Good morning," I chimed.

A chorus of greetings came back. I looked over my shoulder at the construction and then closed the door.

"It's going to be hard functioning with that going on," I continued.

Everyone lifted their voices in agreement.

"You don't even have a cubicle anymore," I pointed out to Jo.

She nodded her acknowledgment.

"Okay, then. Mahesh! Welcome aboard. I'm glad to have you here," I proclaimed, shaking his hand. "You and Storc can go over to the construction area and make sure the engineer is building to our specs. Storc, I think you were copied on most of that. Right?"

"Yeah. And the specs that came down from the C...from our contract are tight. I'm liking the guy who designed the fishbowl," Storc beamed.

"Yeah. I was impressed too. As for the '*contract*,' I'm pretty sure everyone here knows or has guessed it's with the CIA. That will be common knowledge and discussion among *this* group. No one else in the company is to know any details about the projects we'll be working on, who we are dealing with, or the nature of our work. Not even Bernie, unless we are given clearance by Langley. Is that clear?" I warned, ending my speech while staring directly at Bonny.

"What?!" she exclaimed indignantly. "I can keep a secret."

All the other voices in the office spoke at once. "No, you can't."

"I'm hurt," she whined with a mock pout.

"Bonny," I cautioned, letting my ire color my tone, hoping that singling her out would make an impression. "Your little conversation with Barb revealed your and Storc's involvement in the rescue."

"Bullshit," she blurted defensively. "Barb would never tell anyone anything I told her in confidence."

I raised an eyebrow at her. "Did you tell her in person?"

"No," she reasoned. "She was still in Germany. I told her over the pho—"

Realization struck her and she paused with her mouth open for a second, unable to finish her sentence.

"Yeah," I sniped coolly. "Barb was on a landline at a military installation, and you were on an unsecured cell phone."

She dropped her head as the weight of all that had resulted from her slip suddenly fell on her shoulders.

"It's important we keep our mouths shut for many reasons. Not the least of which is our own safety." I paused and let that sink in. "Bad guys are the kind of people who take revenge when bad stuff happens to them. If we keep our mouths shut, we're just computer people who do some work for the government. If we talk, we make ourselves targets."

I looked around the room. The seriousness had struck a chord with everyone.

"I speak from firsthand experience. You do *not* want the attention of the bad guys."

Though only Bonny and Storc had seen my wounds, the rest had no doubt heard about them. My last statement drove the point home like a hammer.

"There will be classes and assistance for all of us before we start getting Agency projects," I continued. "They will teach us how to keep our mouths shut, how to work with secrecy in mind at all times, and give us instruction on the protocols that we'll come in contact with."

Everyone nodded. I looked at the heavy blonde next to Mahesh. "I'm sorry, I've seen you around, but I don't know your name."

She stood and stuck out her hand. "I'm Anna. I'm excited to

be working with you…for you. In this department."

Bonny laughed.

"Welcome, Anna," I said and then went around to my desk chair. "Okay. Bonny and Anna. Get with purchasing and start picking out our systems. I've already sent you the minimum system requirements and the software expectations. As soon as the work stations are ordered, you can get with Storc and Mahesh on the server and firewall details."

They all nodded and then stared at me.

"Go," I ordered, shooing them away with my hands. As they left, Jo stood and moved in front of my desk. I motioned for her to sit as I took a sip of the coffee Bonny had made and left on the desk.

That was *really* good espresso.

"I'm going to need you to be our expert on Protocol and Security procedures," I mentioned and then waited to see if there was a response. There was none.

"I've sent you all the files and emails I've received from Langley. I need you to organize them into project lists and assign them by category. Do you know what each team member is responsible for?"

"Yes," she assured me. "I just need everyone linked into a team calendar so I can do the scheduling."

"No problem. I'll make sure they all transfer their company calendar entries to the team calendar as soon as it's built," I said.

"It's built," she stated plainly. "It's on a secure drive called TeamWolfe on the fourth floor admin server."

"Great!" I proclaimed, impressed with her head start on things. "I'll do my best to keep my entries up to date. I have to admit I'm not the best at logging my comings and goings."

"Not a problem," she replied. "Until we get into a rhythm, I'll just clear any schedule additions which include you before entering them."

"Excellent," I breathed, relieved by the concession. "I know you don't have a work station today, so if—"

"I checked out a laptop that meets system requirements for the department," she volunteered abruptly. "I hope it's okay that I used your authority to do it. I figured I'd have to start project planning today."

I had made the right choice with this girl.

"Yes. That's fine. Good work. Take my desk and get started then. I'm going to go check the construction schedule and then meet up with Bonbon in purchasing. Do you have any special requests for hardware configuration on your workstation?"

"No. I'm fine with whatever is provided," she stated plainly.

"Okay. Help yourself to whatever you need, and I'll check in with you later," I offered, feeling like my team choice had been so good that I'd be out of a job until we started getting projects from the CIA.

"Is the coffee satisfactory?" she asked rigidly as I began to exit.

"You made that?" I asked, surprised. "I thought Bonny had. Yes. It's great. But please don't feel that it's part of your job description. I can make my own coffee."

"Understood," she stated mechanically and then paused, biting her lip.

"Something else?" I asked.

"It's perfectly alright if you only need me during the build out phase. I'll understand," she said, clearly worried she would be booted to the curb again at the end of the project.

Her mousy tone and sullen carriage seemed at odds with her direct and honest communication traits. I half-expected her to curl up into a ball after each question directed at her, but instead, she leveled her eyes, devoid of emotion, squared her shoulders and spoke clearly and plainly. "I've gotten quite used to being a startup specialist."

"Jo. I've got a feeling you're going to be an important part of this team...well past the build out."

She smiled. It seemed a foreign expression on her sullen face. "Thank you. I'll do my best."

"I know you will," I declared confidently and then left, fighting my way through the plastic sheeting.

As I walked past the broken wall, I saw Storc and Mahesh going over the construction drawings with the engineer. The construction crew must have been working all night; not only was the demolition complete, they had already roughed in the bathroom and kitchen fixtures.

The CIA was insisting on autonomy from the rest of the floor, and though there was an emergency exit planned for the tech office side, the new area carved out of the adjoining office spaces would have its own secure reception area accessible from the floor lobby near the elevators. I hadn't seen budget for reception staff, so I'd have to check on that.

After checking on the progress, I walked through the tech floor on my way to the tech locker but bumped into Bernie Evonitz. That was two times in three days—and two times more than the previous six months combined.

"Scott!" he exclaimed with a smile. "I've been looking for you. Your assistant said you were inspecting the construction."

"I think I've bypassed the 'assistant' position and added a project manager slash researcher instead," I said, warning him that I was altering the org chart a bit.

"Oh! Great! Bonny—Miss Little—suggested the project manager qualifications for your assistant anyway. She was pretty adamant that a run-of-the-mill assistant would commit suicide after a week of trying to keep up with you...her words, not mine."

I laughed. "I think Bonny worries too much," I replied.

A nervous expression flashed across his face for a second, just a second, and then he lowered his voice to a more concerned tone. "If you feel the operation would be better served by a researcher and project manager, that is totally up to you. We were just worried—" He seemed to have trouble finding the right words. "I just didn't want you to get overwhelmed after your...uh—"

"It's okay, sir," I offered, rescuing him from his verbal stumble. "Bonny has been playing mother hen and making sure I don't overwork myself. It's good to be back, though. Not exactly what I expected to find, but it's good nonetheless."

"Good, good," he clucked supportively. "Let's step in here and have a private word."

We went into a small conference room. Two managers were having a meeting about performance reviews or the like. They looked up.

"Can you guys give us the room for a few minutes?" Bernie asked politely.

As they left he smiled and said thank you.

Once the door was closed he sat on the edge of the conference table.

"This new 'Special Projects' department is already bringing us a great deal of revenue. The contracts are written to be very generous to us," he confided.

"That's great! I want to thank you for giving me a shot at running it," I expressed sincerely.

"Well, that's the part I wanted to talk to you about," he said cautiously. For a second I thought he had changed his mind. "I didn't have a choice."

"Come again?" I sputtered.

"The only condition they had for the contract, other than meeting their system and protocol requirements, was that you would be the department head and that you would have full autonomy."

I stared at him blankly.

"So I need to ask you if you are sure you are up to it." He watched me for a moment. When I failed to come up with a response, he continued.

"Scott. I know this is a lot. I can't imagine what you've been through and to come back to this mess, well, I know it's stressful," he said sincerely. "And if you feel this isn't a direction you want to go, just let me know, and the whole thing stops. But I'll be frank. The money is great, the expansion is exciting, and the board is in love with you right now. You could pretty much write your own ticket."

"To be honest, I was caught off balance."

He nodded his head understandingly.

"But I've got this," I continued.

"Good!" he beamed, slapping me on my back, sending a twinge of pain through my shoulder exit wound. "That's all I needed to hear. The construction crews are supposed to work around the clock until the build out is done. Your fishbowl may be ready by the time you come in on Monday."

"That's good news," I said mildly.

"Yep. Now why don't you wrap up here and head on home? No need for you to put in full days before things get off the ground. I want you to be at 100% when the work starts rolling in."

"Thank you, sir. I will," I replied.

"Great. We'll talk again soon," he said and then strode out of the conference room.

The two managers who had been waiting outside came back in, smiling and nodding at me.

"Welcome back," the female manager said, smiling shyly.

"Thanks," I replied sincerely as I turned and left.

I met Bonny and Anna at the IT locker and assisted with the procurement list. When we were done, I texted everyone to meet across the street at the grill for lunch. Bonny, Anna, and I were first there, followed shortly by Storc and Mahesh. Jo came in a few minutes later, carrying her laptop.

I looked at her questioningly as she sat.

"Nothing sensitive on here yet," she proclaimed preemptively, defensively.

"Okay," I conceded, smiling. I was amused by her 'precognitive' powers. People had always accused me of having those traits. It was nice to be in the company of another.

"I wanted to meet down here because it's too loud up there…and I'm hungry," I declared, starting the lunch meeting.

"I just wanted everyone to know the construction crew is supposed to be working round the clock over the weekend. We should see quite a bit of progress on Monday morning." Bonny's attention was drifting to a TV monitor over the bar.

I turned to look as well. On CNN, there was footage from a helicopter flying over a burning house in Colorado Springs. They were night images, so it was not fresh film. A moment later, the scene cut to the ground, with police and fire officials sifting through smoldering remains in the daylight. The caption on the screen read:

> *Lesbian couple and child dead following 911 call. Arson suspected.*

Another banner slid across the bottom of the screen, stating:

> *Couple had reported vandalism and threats in prior weeks.*

"Unbelievable," Bonny muttered.

I could see anger rising in her face—we would not be having a business meeting today.

"Okay," I said, trying to wrap it up. "Let's just order and then head out. I've got a meeting at 2:00 p.m. in McLean, so I'll be leaving after lunch."

Everyone but Bonny picked up a menu. She had drifted over to the TV so she could hear the report. I ordered for her, knowing her usual dish.

When the food arrived, most of us ate and talked about recent goings on—the new construction, the new servers, wondering how jealous the rest of the tech division would be of our new digs. But Bonny and Jo seemed to only pick at their food, looking up occasionally to see if there were any new developments on the arson case.

When we finished eating, I paid the tab and then said my goodbyes. Bonny and Jo were still distracted by the news report. I walked out, crossing the street into the garage to get my car.

On the way to my psychiatrist appointment, Barb called and asked how my day was going.

"It's going well. They are making a lot of progress on the construction," I relayed stiffly.

"How are you doing?" she asked. "That's a lot of activity for your first couple of days back."

"I'm handling it pretty well. Lots to keep me busy," I replied.

"That's good. Don't forget about your appointment," she cautioned, sounding like my mom.

"In the car on my way now," I reassured her, avoiding the temptation to remind her I had always managed my schedule well enough on my own.

"Good," she said in relief. "I'll see you when you get home."

"…'kay," I replied and then took the opportunity to hang up before there was an awkward pause wanting to be filled with "I love you." This was something I was going to have to address soon. The longer Barb stayed at my house, the more she wanted to end every conversation with those words, and the more I wanted her to leave.

I was feeling trapped by a debt she felt she owed to me and the debt I owed her for being there through my recovery. But our relationship would never be as she pictured it. She still wanted the old Scott Wolfe—more precisely, she wanted the *old* Scott

Wolfe to have said he loved her and wanted her to stay in Fairfax instead of going back to Massachusetts—but that Scott Wolfe never existed. More than that, even the flawed and disappointing old Scott Wolfe didn't seem to exist anymore either.

"Damn it!" I said aloud.

**

Afternoon—Dr. Rachel Hebron's Office in Langley, Virginia

"How do you feel about the idea of working for the Agency?" Dr. Hebron asked.

It took me a second to realize she was talking about the contract work at TravTech. For a moment, I thought she was asking me if I wanted to be an Agent. I have to admit, I felt the briefest moment of excitement when she asked it—in addition to a cold chill running down my spine.

"It was a little overwhelming at first," I replied. "But now—"

I tried to form a description around my current feeling on the new section.

"Take your time," she soothed.

"It's pretty exciting," I confessed finally, but my answer didn't quite cover my full feeling. I wasn't sure why.

She looked at me for a moment, waiting to see if I had more detail for her and then shifted in her chair.

"But?" she queried after a moment, sensing the incompleteness of my thought.

"I don't know," I replied finally. "I just thought—"

I hung on the edge of my words for a moment longer, trying to pinpoint what I was feeling.

"Maybe not as satisfying as you hoped it would be?" she asked.

I thought about it for a second as my eyes searched aimlessly across her desk, which was immaculately organized and absent any clutter whatsoever.

Her office was likewise clutter-free. It had been painted a warm, dark beige beneath the chair rail and a lighter beige above, which made one subconsciously feel as if they were rising from darkness each time they sat in her office.

"That may be it," I conceded half-heartedly. "Though I haven't really gotten into any Agency projects yet."

"Are you looking forward to the projects?" she asked. "I mean, they're going to be very different from what you are used to working on. It won't just be servers and code anymore. These projects will have real-world implications."

As I tried to sort through my expectations, my eyes drifted across the rest of the office. The bookshelves and other furniture in the room looked to be made of dark-stained oak, but I immediately saw the telltale edges of veneer, glued and trimmed. Dr. Hebron had gone to a great deal of trouble with a limited budget to make the surroundings look rich and learned while keeping costs down. She had done well.

"That certainly puts an edge on it that I hadn't experienced before," I muttered as I continued to ponder my response. "But it's not like I'm going to have to hone my fighting skills or learn how to speak Mandarin to provide a service. It's definitely well within my comfort zone."

"Your comfort zone," she repeated back to me. "Do you feel like your comfort zone has broadened?"

"Well, yeah!" I replied as if it were self-evident. "In a pinch, I can open the cargo ramp on a heavy aircraft now. If anyone needs that done, I'm the guy to call." I grinned.

She glared at me for a second before her expression softened into a grin. "You learned a lot more than that," she offered gently.

I nodded in acceptance of her truth. The fact is, the week I spent in Europe was probably the most lesson-dense time of my life.

"...and you seemed to learn those lessons quickly," she continued.

I brought my hand up to my shoulder, stroking my thumb across the scar under my shirt.

"Not all of them came fast enough," I replied coolly.

"You're alive, Barb's alive and the other hostages are alive... and everyone who hurt you is dead," she pointed out sharply. "And considering the resources and experience you were up against, I'd say you caught on pretty quickly."

I smiled because it felt like a compliment, but I still wasn't satisfied.

She must have seen that because she suddenly leaned forward and lowered her voice. "Everyone is born into this world with certain traits, good and bad. Most people never figure out how to use those traits as an edge. You're among the rare few who have been given an opportunity to do that. My question to you is simple—do you feel bigger because of it or smaller?"

"Bigger," I blurted out, without even having to think about it.

She smiled at me. "The image you have of yourself is in flux," she observed. "Give it time to readjust."

"How so?" I asked.

"I've heard you call yourself a geek, a computer nerd, a 'skinny kid,' and a whole string of other descriptors that don't actually describe you," she explained coarsely. "I've heard you call yourself a crappy boyfriend and scared. But crappy boyfriends don't fly to halfway around the world to rescue damsels in distress. Skinny kids don't get into fights with mercenaries and win. Computer nerd, though it may describe your talent with automation, certainly isn't the best descriptor of a man who throws himself out of an airplane strapped to a cargo container full of hostages."

I crinkled my face up as I absorbed her words, trying to superimpose her description onto my self-image.

She saw me working on the problem and smiled. "And just so you know, when you walk down the street, people don't see a skinny nerd," she offered with a much softer tone. "Physically, you are quite impressive."

I felt blood flush my ears and cheeks.

She grinned at my physical response.

"Okay. We are about out of time today, but I'd like you to work on something until our next appointment," she stated and paused, waiting for me to be receptive to her words. "Try to cut Barb a little slack."

I raised my eyebrow.

"I don't mean you should let her lead you around by your sense of duty," she quickly added, expanding on her thought. "But remember, she wants what she wants. You're under no obligation to make her happy at your expense, but you have to remember that she has her own wants and desires and many of them may be confused with a new sense of responsibility to you—for saving her life and nearly losing yours in the process."

I nodded. I knew she was right.

"On the other hand," Dr. Hebron continued. "Don't let her push deeper into places you'd prefer not to have her. That is your responsibility—not hers."

I nodded again. "Right. Own my response."

"Also—" she admonished as I began to rise out of my chair. "Let's not have any more provoked physical aggression. You're smarter than the average bully. It's not a fair fight if you can manipulate someone into aggression because you want to teach them a lesson." She stared at me for a moment with a disapproving glare.

"Should I have just sat there and watched it happen?" I asked incredulously, offended by the notion.

"No. But you could have waited until she was alone and given her shelter information. Or had Barb do it so it seemed less threatening. You're smart...very smart. You could have thought of a thousand ways to resolve it without daring the big ape to stand up to you." She paused and examined my face for understanding before she continued. "Admit it Scott... You did what you did because you *wanted* him to challenge you."

I thought about it for a moment. I knew she was right, but there had to be a good defense for what I'd done. It felt right when I did it. I gave up and resigned myself to her argument.

"Okay. I'll keep an eye on my intentions," I finally responded.

On the way out of her office, I recognized that I actually felt better. By the time I was in my car driving toward the highway, I felt as though a huge weight had been lifted from my shoulders.

I was just merging onto the interstate when my phone rang. I didn't recognize the number. I hit the speaker button.

"Hello," I answered.

"Hi, Scott. It's John," came the reply.

"Hey, John. How are you?"

"I'm good. Look. I wanted to apologize for not filling you in more on the contract with TravTech and to ask you a favor," he said.

There was tension in his voice.

"Yeah. I was meaning to call you about that," I complained. "You had two months to tell me before I walked into that bee's nest. What's up with that?"

"Don't judge me too harshly. NoSuch wanted to bring your team in-house. I convinced them it would be a mistake to take them out of their environment and away from you," he explained, referring to the NSA by the Agency nickname *No Such Agency*. "I can't get into more detail than that over the phone, but I want you to know I was running interference for you and your pals."

"Okay. What's the favor?" I asked, swallowing some of my agitation.

"I can't talk about that on the phone either," he replied. "Can we meet?"

"Sure. I'm in my car right now," I responded. "Where are you?"

"Parked outside your place," he informed me with an amused edge. "See you in a bit."

The call abruptly ended.

"Okay," I sniped sarcastically to the dead connection. "I'll meet you in a little while. Thanks for checking in, pal… Bye."

**

4:45 p.m.—Fairfax, Virginia

When I pulled into the court at my condo, John was there leaning against his black Dodge pickup truck, waiting for me.

"Hey man. How are you feeling?" he asked as I got out of my car.

"A little better every day," I reported, reaching my hand out to shake his.

"Good, good," he replied. "You're looking good. How's Barb?"

"She's fine. Taking everything in stride," I chirped, lying.

"Excellent," he said and then lowered his voice. "Do you mind if we go in?"

"Sure," I replied as I unlocked the front door, its loud squeal announcing our entry to the empty condo.

"Nice entry alarm," he teased.

"I need to reset the hinges," I replied sheepishly. "The more humid it gets, the louder it is."

We went upstairs, and I dropped my tattered shoulder bag on the dining alcove table, and then I went right to the fridge.

"Want a beer?" I asked.

"Yeah, sure. That would be great," he responded as he leaned against the pillar that held up the loft above my kitchen and dining room.

I returned with two pop-top "Alts." Several varieties were available from the German grocer in Alexandria, so I was usually fully stocked.

"Wunderbar! Ich kenne dieses Bier. Es ist gut," he exclaimed in perfect German, approving of my beer choice.

"Yeah," I replied. "I've really enjoyed having it around since I got back. Though it's not as good pasteurized."

"Agreed, but it's still better than that horse piss we make here," he quipped, raising his bottle. "Here's to bringing in the bad guys."

We tapped our bottles together and then drank.

"Technically we didn't bring in the bad guys—we killed them," I said with some snark.

"Well, we brought some of them in," he offered with a sly grin before it turned more solemn. "But, about that. How are your sessions going?"

"You don't get reports?" I asked, feigning surprise.

"Doctor patient confidentiality is sacred, even at the Company. We get recommendations from the shrinks, but nothing else," he informed me, but I suspected there were exceptions to that rule.

"They're going okay. Have you gotten a recommendation?" I asked and then took another sip of my beer to hide the amusement in my face.

"Actually…yes," he said, responding quickly to my frank question.

I was surprised. "Well?" I asked.

He stared at me for a few beats, expressionless, trying to decide if he would tell me.

"She thinks you might be a good candidate for recruitment," he relayed cautiously, ready to gauge my response.

I laughed. "I thought I was a loose cannon!" I exclaimed. "*You* named me Monkey Wrench."

"That's not always a bad thing," he replied with a grin. "The Agency likes independent thinkers."

I could tell he was still measuring my response.

I shook my head as I ambled over to my favorite green chair and sat on the edge of the cushion.

"I have a lot of physical healing ahead of me before I can think about something like that," I said, and then quickly added, "Though the thought has crossed my mind a few times."

"Glad to hear it," he said dismissively and then quickly changed the subject, though he was clearly satisfied with my response. "Look. I hate to pile on after everything you've been through, but I need some help—a personal favor."

"Okay. What's up?" I asked, curious as to what I could offer someone with the resources he had at his disposal.

"There's this guy. Someone I know. He's gotten himself into trouble, and I need help locating him," he said, obviously being vague until he had some indication of my willingness to help.

"Really? Why, with the vast arsenal of spying resources you have available, would you need *my* help?" I asked, confused by the request.

"This is unofficial," he confided, pausing.

Something clicked in my mind. "You aren't allowed to use CIA resources to track someone within the United States," I asserted, looking for any changes in his expression. There were none.

"It's a little more than that," he elaborated, clearly dancing around a touchy subject.

I took a deep breath then released it in a sigh. "John. Speak plainly. I've just come back from Dr. Hebron's office and don't feel like playing twenty questions. If you need my help with something, spit it out. I'm certain I'll agree...unless there are Serbs and Russians involved."

He lowered his head and nodded in agreement.

"Sorry. Habit of the trade." He took his beer and sat on the couch opposite me. "There's this guy. He used to be on my team. Good guy. Very skilled. Kind of a Boy Scout...like you," he said, smiling.

"To the Boy Scouts," I toasted mildly, raising my beer. He responded in kind.

"Anyway. A couple of years ago, he was asked to do something that his conscience wouldn't let him do...by someone you've met, in fact—Dwight Miller," he continued.

I raised my eyebrows at the new information.

"So. This guy—Mark—he left the Agency. Started doing some security jobs, a few odd bodyguard assignments for movie stars and such. Nothing to make him rich, but they paid the bills and he wasn't asked to take any—shall we say—morally ambiguous actions," he explained and then took another pull on his beer.

"He was seeing an Agency shrink. Not Hebron, but someone like her, and we were getting updates from time to time. He was on the watch list because of his less-than-flexible sense of right and wrong. Wounded people sometimes magnify those tendencies when they are in pain."

"Okay," I said. "So he disappeared and you are worried he might do something stupid."

"Not exactly," he hinted, hesitating.

"Out with it, John," I urged with a smile on my face, but I was losing patience.

"Have you seen the news today?" he asked.

"Yeah," I responded—and then it clicked and my eyes went wide. "Boy Scouts don't kill families and then burn their houses down."

"No…no, no, no," he responded quickly, holding up his hand. "The family that was murdered—that was his sister, her partner, and their baby."

It made sense then. But the fact that John was already at my house when he called me indicated something else had already happened.

"He found the guys who did it, huh?" I stated more than asked.

"Maybe," he divulged, taking a sip of beer. "But that's not why I'm interested."

"So what do you need from me?" I asked.

"Last week there was an all-agencies search on a cover ID he was using," he revealed, settling back on the couch. "I don't think it's a coincidence that his sister was murdered so soon after there was a query on his cover ID."

"All-agencies," I repeated. "That would mean a government agency was involved. Are you saying someone with the government killed his sister?"

"I hope not," he replied after taking another swig of beer. "It could be he was mixed up in something and it attracted government interest in addition to bad guy interest."

"Why can't you just contact the agency who ordered the search on the ID?" I asked. "Why sneak around using back channels?"

"Because we aren't sure it was a clean search, and we don't want to reveal that it set off a flag," he replied.

I shook my head. "Politics," I sniped, grinning.

"If the cover got blown because of the search, then it's more than politics," he asserted in defense. "It's treason. Any agency with access to cover information is required to coordinate with the owning agency or get a court order to blow it…that never happened."

Whoa! I thought. *That's a pretty heavy load to lay on a new analyst.*

He must have seen the shock on my face. "The Agency can't and won't act on this. They won't clue law enforcement in on it unless they *have to* do it to cover their asses. They won't even take action that might hint they know about it. So I need someone outside of the Agency, with real tracking ability, to help me find him before he does more harm."

"Harm?" I asked, not sure I understood what harm he could do to anyone but himself at this point.

"Yeah. Harm," he replied. "His sister was just about the only person in the world he cared about. She was the reason he was out doing what he did, and the thought of her is what kept him from doing anything he would be ashamed of—*she* was his reality check. Last night, she was brutally raped and then murdered along with the love of her life and their daughter—I know him; he's gone."

"Are you sure you want to be the one to find him? If the Agency won't touch it, what makes you think you should? Won't that show their involvement?" I asked.

"The FBI can't handle this guy. I know. No more than they could handle anyone else on my team," he disclosed with a hint of satisfaction, sitting back and crossing his legs. "I have a feeling if I don't find him, there's going to be a much higher body count before he's done."

"So the FBI was the requesting agency?" I asked.

John shook his head as he took another sip of beer. "Homeland Security," he said.

"And why again are you choosing me over the FBI?" I asked.

"You're an Agency-contracted analyst now," he said with a grin. "I need tech support."

"Oh!" I exclaimed. "So I need to put this into the system at TravTech?"

He tipped his head to the side and shook it. "Not until it's over," he replied. "But yes... It will be a billable job."

"Okay!" I relented. "How can I help?"

"You have an incredible ability to 'link analyze' in your head. I saw it in action in Europe. I don't have access to Agency software or specialists to do that kind of probability analysis, and even then, I'm not sure they would do as well as you could."

I looked up at the living room's vaulted ceiling for a moment, absorbing it all, and then let my gaze wander out the window of the small sun room across from me. John was showing a lot of trust by sharing this. It might have been a test of my willingness, but I believed he was doing it out of a sense of duty.

Barb would have a cow, I thought, but I was suddenly angry for even considering that as a deciding factor. It was all the tipping point I needed to agree.

"Okay. I'll try. What do you know?" I asked, truly wanting to help the man. He had been nothing but supportive of me since the airbase in Mimon.

"I'll brief you on the flight," he said abruptly after downing the rest of his beer and standing.

"The 'flight?'" I asked incredulously.

"Yeah," he replied, setting the empty bottle on my solid maple coffee table. "I don't have many details here, and I can't go digging without raising red flags. We have to be on the ground."

I picked the bottle up and walked it to the recycling container in the kitchen.

"John. I can't just go running off to Colorado without any notice," I said, suddenly regretting my consent to help. "I have new hires that haven't even been officially cleared by Langley yet."

"No choice. We have to head out. Pack a bag for two days, and let's get going. I've got the tab on everything; I just need your brain," he urged, moving his arms as if to shoo me toward my suitcase.

At that moment, I heard Barb come in from downstairs; that annoying door announced her presence. John spun his head in that direction. "Shit," he muttered.

She came upstairs and into the living room, paused upon seeing John, and then smiled thinly. "Hi John," she chirped. "How are you?"

"I'm good, Barb. How are you?" he asked sincerely, but uneasily, as she came over and kissed me 'hello.'

I suddenly realized he was trying to get me out of the house before Barb arrived. His plan had been complicated by her early arrival.

"As well as can be expected," she replied cautiously, sensing that she had entered in the middle of a conversation. "To what do we owe the pleasure of your company?" she asked, always the diplomat but clearly distrustful of his presence.

"Well," he conceded, putting his hand to the back of his head in embarrassment. "I hate to say it, but I'm about to steal Scott from you for a while."

Her face went pale, her smile melting away. "Why? What's going on?" she asked with real concern in her voice.

"I can't really go into it. But rest assured, it's not international in nature," he replied, smiling uneasily.

"Is it Company-related?" she asked, using the CIA vernacular for itself.

"Sort of. More of a personal favor, really, but yes—some housekeeping," he said. "A TravTech contract."

That had been a poor choice of words. "Housekeeping" usually meant taking care of a problem inside the Agency. Barb might not have gotten the reference, but if she talked to her dad, he would.

"Oh," she replied, seeming a little more relaxed. "How long

will you be gone?" she asked, turning to me.

She was asking me to verify what had been said to her already.

"Uh. I'm not sure. We hadn't gotten to that yet," I replied and then turned to John. "How long will we be gone, John?"

I could tell he hated being pinned down to anything like this, but by now it was clear that if he didn't say something that was acceptable to Barb, this probably wouldn't be happening.

"I'll probably have him back to you by Sunday evening," he offered, squirming.

"Promise," Barb said in a tone that indicated that would be the only way she would let him have me.

"Okay. I promise. If we aren't done by Sunday mid-afternoon, I'll put him on a plane back home," he conceded.

She turned to me. "Take it easy and don't let him put you in the way of any terrorists or anything," she murmured patronizingly, kissing me on the cheek.

"You take all the fun out of working for the CIA," I jabbed jokingly, trying to swallow the anger that was building, and then I turned to John. "Okay, looks like you passed inspector number twelve. What do I need to pack?"

"Do you have a black suit?" he asked.

"Yep," I replied.

"Pack it and your shaving kit. If you need any hardware, computer-wise, pack it as well," he added.

In a matter of minutes, I was packed and heading out the door to John's truck. Barb stood in the doorway and watched as we backed out and left, waving before we disappeared around the corner.

"I wish you hadn't said 'housekeeping,'" I confided to him as we pulled out onto Monument Ave.

A confused look crossed his face.

"As soon as we are out of sight, she will be on the phone with her dad to see if he can find out what we're doing," I explained.

Realization spread across his face. "Shit," he swore under his breath. He thought for a moment, and then pulled out his phone and dialed.

"Hey, Nancy!" he chirped into the receiver. "How are you, beautiful?"

I watched him as he schmoozed the woman on the other end of the line.

"I've got a big favor to ask. Feel free to say no if you want."

"Well, I'm supposed to be on call this weekend, but a buddy of mine is in town and we want to go do some fishing."

"Yeah, I know, I'm terrible," he said, smiling as he wove his story. "Anyway. If anyone calls the switchboard asking for me, can you say I had to go and do a debrief out on the coast and won't be back in the office till Monday?"

"I sure do appreciate it darlin'…I owe you a dinner."

"Oh really? Then damn! I owe you two dinners."

"You're the best. Thanks. Bye."

He put his phone in his pocket and then looked at me.

"Nancy is the biggest gossip in communications. She'd never let a whisper of anything go out the door, but in-house, no secret is safe. She either loves me enough to tell the debrief story or is pissed off enough that I haven't taken her to dinner yet to sell me out for fishing," he grinned. "Either way, we're covered."

"Nice," I responded. "Aren't you worried if you let me in on enough of your secrets you won't be able to manipulate me anymore?"

"Son," he smirked. "You're only days away from that anyhow. I might as well teach you what I know."

I could tell by the subtle markers on his expression that he didn't truly believe I could become manipulation resistant, but I sensed sincerity in his desire to teach me.

On the way to the airport, I sent a secure email to my team at TravTech telling them I got called into a three-day orientation workshop, not to try and get hold of me unless it was important, and that I would see them on Monday.

I got a response from Bonbon in a matter of seconds:

> *Tell them I'm sorry about telling the people here and see if you can get me a reduced sentence. :P Don't let them inject you with a homing beacon. The bad guys always use it to find you in the movies. :o))))))*

I smiled.

Hilarious, Bonbon. Just hilarious.

**

6:15 p.m. local time—Colorado Springs, Colorado

MARK GAINES pulled up in front of the convenience store opposite the building and parking lot where Heather Burton had worked. He had driven straight through from Huntsville, the sixteen-hour drive giving him all the time he needed and more to plan.

His grief and anger, however, threatened to undermine his operational objectivity. He knew he needed to use it to keep himself focused on the task at hand, his will sharpened—but reality was proving much harder to deal with.

As he walked into the store, he turned his head as if to look at something behind him, avoiding the store camera. He stepped up to the far end of the counter, keeping himself as far out of camera range as possible, and then cleared his throat to attract the attention of the clerk.

"Special Agent Steel, FBI," he said, pulling out his authentic-looking badge and ID flip. "There was an incident across the street last night, and I need to examine your surveillance footage."

The young man behind the counter looked nervously at the badge and then looked at the hard stare Mark was giving him.

"Don't you need, like, a warrant or something?" the teen asked.

"Absolutely. If you deem procurement of a Federally-issued warrant as necessary in obtaining evidence in a murder investigation, then that, by all means, can be supplied," Gaines offered without altering his stone features. "But usually, only those guilty of a crime force that sort of procedure, which next, requires me to ask you your whereabouts this morning at 2:00 a.m."

The young man turned pale and shifted uncomfortably. "I was at home, asleep," he stuttered.

"And can anyone verify that information?" Gaines asked, leaning forward slightly, accusation suddenly evident in his tone.

"My mom," he whimpered defensively. "Look, I don't want no trouble. I was just askin' is all."

"So you are giving me permission to review your security recordings?" Gaines asked.

"I should call my boss first," he replied.

"That's fine, you can call him from the field office in Denver after you are questioned," Gaines threatened. "Do you need to lock up or anything before I take you?"

"Wait!" the teen exclaimed, fear spreading across his face. "No. It's okay, I'll cooperate. Jeeze!"

"Where are the recordings kept?" Gaines asked.

"Back here," the boy said, leading him to the back office.

Gaines sat in the manager's chair and pulled up the video feed for the previous night. The clerk stood behind him, watching over his shoulder.

"I'm sorry," Gaines sighed in mock regret. "If there's evidence on these recordings, you won't be allowed to see it."

The teen turned to walk out. "Fine," he pouted. "I have to watch the counter anyway."

As soon as the boy was gone, Gaines began scrolling through the video footage. There were two cameras that faced toward the parking lot—one of them had Heather's car in the frame. He watched at high speed until there was movement near her car and then slowed the recording down to get a better look.

"There you are," Gaines whispered as the image of two men appeared in the corner of the screen.

He continued to watch until the men grabbed her from behind and punched her in the face until she fell limp into their arms. Anger swelled up in Gaines, followed by a shadow of grief, realizing these would be the last recorded moments he would see of Heather's life—and there would be none of his sister's or their child.

A pickup truck pulled up beside the scene and stopped. The two men threw Heather's limp body into the back of the truck and sped off. He paused the video as the license plate came into view and zoomed in.

"Gotcha," he muttered in a snarl, memorizing the plate number.

He quickly pulled up the menu on the DVR and deleted the security footage for the time period just before the men attacked Heather to the present time. He then turned off the recording device and rose from the chair.

On his way back out, he stopped at the counter, no longer having to dodge the cameras.

"There wasn't anything useful," he said to the clerk. "There seems to be some sort of flaw in the recording function."

"A flaw?" the clerk exclaimed nervously, possibly worried he would be blamed for that as well.

"It was a long shot anyway," Gaines added as he turned and walked toward the door. "Have a good evening."

"Whatevs," he muttered as Gaines exited the store.

Gaines pulled his phone from his pocket and dialed a number.

"CRIS resource. Operator 14," came a woman's voice from the other end of the call.

"Special Agent Harold Warren, access code Foxtrot 35723 Golf Golf," Gaines replied, using a stolen ID and access code—in fact, stolen from the same FBI Agent who had provided him with the badge. He, of course, had manufactured his own ID card, but the badge and CRIS access were legit—though not his.

"Authorized. Go ahead."

"Colorado Plate, Golf, Alpha, Tango, Tango, Mike, Alpha, November, five," Gaines said. "Pickup truck."

"Searching."

After a short pause her voice returned. "Roy Mullen—Mike, Uniform, Lima, Lima, Echo, November. 38547 C and S Road, Colorado Springs," she replied. "No outstanding warrants."

"Thank you," Gaines said mechanically and then ended the call as he got into his Crown Victoria and started the engine.

"Alright, Roy," he sneered through gritted teeth as he drove out of the parking lot. "Let's see who put you up to this."

eight
Friday, July 23rd

12:15 a.m.—Colorado Springs, Colorado

Once on the ground, John went to procure a rental vehicle while I went and changed into my suit. I did as he instructed, shaved, and cleaned up a bit in the airport restroom. When I emerged, John whistled.

"You look like a proper G-man," he said. It sounded like a compliment.

"Thanks...I guess," I replied.

"Watch my bag. I've got to change too." He disappeared into the men's room with his suit and shaving bag.

When he reemerged, I couldn't help but notice he was walking a little more rigidly...like a soldier.

"Let's go," he commanded before I had time to comment.

Once we were on the road, John reached into the backseat and pulled his carry-on bag up front, setting it on my lap.

"Inside is a shoulder rig with a Glock for you and two bundles wrapped in rubber bands. Pull them out for me," he ordered plainly.

"A gun?" I asked. "Why do I need that?"

"Don't freak out. It's part of your cover," he replied dismissively. "Feds carry *guns*."

"Feds?" I asked, noting his sarcastic repeat of the word *'guns.'*

"You're undercover," he reiterated.

I did as he instructed, handing him the bundles, pulling my suit coat off, and then strapping on the holster.

When I was done, he handed me an envelope.

"You're Agent Scott Rhodes of the ATF," he said as I opened the package.

I opened the wallet to find an ATF badge, complete with an official-looking ATF ID and a small card folio with matching ATF Scott Rhodes business cards.

It was my picture. I looked up at him with a suspicious glare.

"Don't give me the look," he protested defensively. "I figured I'd be using you for projects so I took the liberty of creating a couple of identity packages."

"Kind of presumptuous," I muttered with some snark. "And where the hell did you get my ID photo from?"

He just smiled.

"You know, privacy violations like this are the reason people don't trust their government," I said indignantly. "You *have* heard of the Constitution, right?"

"Relax," he replied. "It's your passport photo."

I nodded. "Still, I don't know why you'd assume I'd need one considering the outcome the last time we worked together."

"Yeah. Well—you aren't the only one who can read people," he said, smiling.

"Fair enough," I muttered. "Who are you?" I asked.

"Special Agent John Stark," he replied.

I laughed.

"What's funny?"

"Who comes up with the covers?"

"I don't know. I put in the requests then the packages get built and sent back," he explained. "Why?"

"Rhodes and Stark?" I asked incredulously. "Ironman?"

"You're such a nerd," he muttered grinning, shaking his head.

"Yeah. I know," I agreed. "Where are we headed?"

"Crime scene," he replied.

"Why? If he's as good as you say, he won't go to the crime scene. We need to find him, not his calling card."

"Okay. Where would you suggest we start?" he asked, seemingly open to my suggestion.

"How about the Colorado Springs Police Department," I replied.

"Huh?" he grunted, questioning my logic.

"Why do leg work that's probably already been done?" I asked. "They have a forensics team. We don't. The evidence has probably already all been gathered and is being analyzed."

"Okay. CSPD it is," he replied.

**

We arrived at the police station, and I followed John through the front doors. He walked in as if he owned the place.

"Who's in charge of the Gaines and Burton murder investigation?" he asked to no one in particular.

"I'm sorry. Who are you?" asked the desk sergeant—a "Sgt. Mills" according to his name tag.

"I'm Special Agent Stark, and this is Agent Rhodes. ATF," John said, producing his badge and ID. I did the same.

Sgt. Mills took them both, examined them, and then handed them back to us. "Stark and Rhodes, huh? Like Ironman," he inserted.

I couldn't help but chuckle.

"Yeah," John muttered with a grimace. "We get that a lot."

"Detective Burns is in charge, but he's gone for the night. Detective Lee is right over there. She'll be able to help you," the sergeant said.

He called her over.

"Hi. I'm Detective Sergeant Lee," she said, reaching her hand out—but not to shake. She wanted to see our IDs as well. After flipping them open, examining them, and closing them again, she handed them back.

"How can I help you?"

"Well, you could point me to your bathroom first. Then I'd like to talk to you about the Gaines Burton murder," John sniffed.

"Bathroom's that way," she pointed. "When you're done, you can find me in that conference room over there."

"Thanks," he replied dismissively as we walked toward the restrooms. When we were out of ear shot, he leaned over toward me.

"They will be expecting us to be dicks," he revealed in a whisper. "Local cops always hate when the feds come in and start marking trees in their territory."

I nodded.

"They'll be expecting it, especially if the FBI has already been here," he continued. "We are going to flank 'em with kindness. The best way to get cops to cooperate is make them think they wronged you by prejudging—thus the shitty first impression."

"I'll remember that next time I get pulled over," I replied.

"Sorry," he said with a grin. "It only works for federal agents."

We stopped at the coffee machine on the way back through the office and poured a couple of cups. John sipped his and then made a face. He shook his head, reached for a salt shaker, and added a dash of salt to the concoction.

He sipped again. "Mmmm. Better," he murmured.

When we entered the conference room, there was a large whiteboard by the wall with photos and labels all over it. I quickly memorized each item as Detective Lee and John started the briefing.

"Not that it matters, but why is the ATF here again?" she asked.

John walked over to her and set his coffee down on the conference table. "To be honest, I think someone is just covering all their bases. I'm not sure we need to be here," he said, feigning more exhaustion than he felt—at least more than he had displayed on the way over.

She was clearly disarmed by John's frankness.

"I'm assuming the FBI has already been in here shuffling through everything," he continued.

"Yeah. They left a little while ago to check in at the Best Western," she sneered.

Judging by her tone and facial expression, I guessed it had not been a pleasant visit for her.

"They left contact info on the board if you want to call them. Agent Barnes and Special Agent Carter."

John wrinkled his face. "I may touch base with them tomorrow," he replied hesitantly, and then lowered his voice a bit. "To be honest, I'd rather not deal with FBI any more than I have to. They can be real pricks sometimes."

Judging by the smile on Detective Lee's face, I'd say John had just won her over. "So what have you got cooking over here?" he asked.

"Photos from the crime scene and an estimated timeline," she offered, her defenses down.

Good work, John!

"How did the scene shake out with CSI?" John asked, again making brownie points asking for her opinion rather than just taking the reports from her.

"It was an all-you-could-eat buffet," she asserted. "I guess the perps figured the fire would cover everything. We got fibers, skin, blood, semen…we could have a CODIS hit any time now. It did take us a while to get in because of the fire, but they were on the first floor. The debris covered them and protected most of the DNA evidence."

My internal flow chart popped up the definition for me:

CODIS: Combined DNA Index System. A centralized system run by the FBI to collect DNA data from Federal, State, and Local jurisdictions that have participating forensic laboratories. CODIS records 13 DNA markers plus Amelogenin (AMEL) to determine gender. The Thirteen markers are CSF1PO, D3S1358, D5S818, D7S820, D8S1179, D13S317, D16S539, D18S51, D21S11, FGA, THO1, TPOX, vWA.

I let the information stream, trying not to let the blank stare be too obvious to John and Detective Lee. When my brain then tried inserting a visual model of a DNA strand, pointing out the marker locations, I breathed a deep sigh.

Enough, I thought, bringing the presentation to an end.

"What about the 911 call?" John asked, though I suspected he already knew the answer to that.

"That was a weird one," she said with some agitation. "We got nothing but garbled digital clutter from that call and the number turned out to be false. One or the other wouldn't have raised too many eyebrows, but untraceable number *and* a corrupt recording... That's peculiar."

"Indeed," John agreed. "What would cause a corrupted recording?"

"You got me," she responded, shrugging. "Bad recording, a corrupt spot on the drive, high tech defeat device, space aliens...it could be anything."

"Hmmm," John muttered, nodding, a perplexed look on his face. "What about video?"

"Yeah. Two. Over here," she said, leading him to a computer.

She pulled up video files from a folder on the desktop and began playing them.

"These are from a convenience store across the street from Heather Burton's place of work," she said. "They show two people coming into the frame as she gets to her car, but the video craps out right before we can make them out."

John scrolled the video out fast and got to the end long before morning. "Why does the video stop there?" he asked.

"Someone—a fed, according to the store clerk—came in and examined the video this afternoon and managed to turn off the security system and wipe the recording in the process. The store didn't find out about it until the state troopers showed up," she said. "The FBI said they didn't know anything about it—though I'm not sure I believe them."

Feds don't wipe surveillance video...even by accident, I thought.

I looked at John with a questioning stare; he discretely shook his head.

Detective Lee noted the awkward silence and looked up at John. "You two didn't go to that store did you?"

John smiled and put his hands up. "Wasn't us. We just got here an hour ago."

She smiled and shook her head. "Okay. Just checking."

"You said there were two videos," I said, jumping in.

She looked at me and smiled. "I forgot you were back there."

"He's the boss. I'm just here to get coffee when he needs it," I deflected, grinning.

"Don't you believe it," John beamed. "That boy has one of the best investigative minds I've ever seen."

The sincerity in his voice made me blush. Detective Lee noticed it and chuckled.

"Cute too," she said, amused by my response.

I diverted my attention back to the computer. "The other video?"

"Yep," she snapped, getting back to the task at hand. "The ATM across the street from the store. Didn't get much because the angle was wrong. The store video was our only real hope of catching them on camera."

"Can I get copies of both?" I asked.

"Sure. Got a memory stick or something? I can dump it from here," she said.

I reached into my pocket and felt around for the right one… I had two in there; a blank one and a *special* one. I handed her the thumb drive and she inserted it to begin the download. When it was complete, she handed it back to me.

"Do you have someplace I can set up my system and plug into the Internet?" I asked.

I got a strange look from John. He wasn't sure what I was doing, and I'm pretty sure he wanted to get out of there.

"Sure, but you could review it right here if you want," she offered, pointing at her computer.

"I've got forensic video software on my system," I explained.

"I just need to plug into a network jack to interface with the ATF server."

"Okay. No problem. You can set up in Burns' office," she offered. "Just don't touch his baseball stuff. He gets bitchy about that."

"That would be perfect. Thanks," I said as I followed her to the office.

I glanced at John as he raised his eyebrow and grinned. He seemed pleased with the level of cooperation—or the swing of her ass—I couldn't tell which. I was happy about a high-speed Internet connection and a whack at the station server.

I set up my laptop and plugged it into the network outlet on the wall. The files from the thumb drive were loaded in a matter of seconds, and I began streaming the ATM video through my player. I spooled it up to just before the time marker that the convenience store video went dark and stopped it on the telltale frame.

There, in front of the store, was a black Crown Victoria. A man in a black suit, similar to mine and John's, was going into the store. A few minutes later, he appeared again—I was able to get a shot of his face. I pushed the still through an enhancement filter and zoomed in.

"John," I called in a low voice.

He came into the office and walked around behind me. He looked at the photo and put his hand on my shoulder.

"That's our boy," he whispered.

I zoomed out and then refocused on the license plate, memorizing it.

"That won't do us any good, I promise you. But now we know what he was driving," he said and then his body language shifted to discomfort. "Damn, I wish they didn't have this."

I looked up at him and smiled. "Really?" I asked.

"Yeah," he mused absently, staring at the photo.

I pulled up a command prompt and tickled the Trojan that Detective Lee had installed on her computer when she inserted my thumb drive—the one I keep handy *just in case*. After a few key strokes and a bracketed hex key push on an erase parameter, the footage containing Mark Gaines was erased—but only those frames. Since the ATM camera only activates with use, no one would ever miss one or two transactions unless they audited the ATM log.

"Done," I announced.

"What?" John asked incredulously.

"I'll explain later," I replied.

"The FBI will have a copy as well," he whispered as I packed up my laptop.

"Not if they use the station network for Internet access tomorrow," I responded with a smile.

"Criminal. I'm working with a criminal," he said, smiling, shaking his head.

"Thanks for your help, Detective Lee," John said warmly as we left the office and walked past the conference room. "We'll be around if anything new pops up."

"Don't you want to hang around a bit?" she responded with disappointment in her voice—apparently John's tactic had worked *very* well on her. "We should have a response from CODIS soon."

The FBI guys would have a hard act to follow tomorrow.

"I'd love to, but it's past the youngster's bed time, and we have a lot of ground to cover in the morning," he explained. "Besides, I wouldn't want to wear out our welcome."

She smiled and nodded, reaching out to shake our hands. "If anything comes up, I'll call," she said.

We thanked her and left the station.

As soon as we were in the SUV, John looked at me.

"What did you do to their system?" he asked as he started the engine.

"The thumb drive Detective Lee put into her computer had a Trojan on it," I explained. "As soon as I logged into their network, I activated it, and it infected the network server."

"What if their virus scanners pick it up?" John asked.

"Pah-lease," I scoffed. "It's a part of their operating system. It removes log entries as it sends data and will self-destruct in two days, deleting all traces of itself unless I send a refresh command."

John laughed. "What about all that self-righteous talk about government intrusions on privacy?"

"This is a police system, not a private citizen. Besides, I'm not *with* the government," I replied.

"—yet," he muttered with a grin as we drove to our hotel.

**

12:45 a.m.—Residence at 38547 C and S Road in Colorado Springs, Colorado

MARK GAINES stood in front of three men who were laying prone in a cluttered garage—his sister's murderers.

He had driven to the remote address only an hour earlier and found the men busily burning clothes and other items in a barrel behind the garage. As soon as he had established that no one was in the house, it had only taken a few seconds to disarm the surprised group and render them unconscious. They were unable to land a single punch on him—despite their best efforts.

The men were securely wired face down on wooden pallets that Gaines had placed on cinderblocks to elevate them. All were still unconscious. He went around the shop, collecting the items he would need, and then pulled a chair in front of the three and waited for them to regain consciousness.

When the first one awoke, his yells and curses brought the

others out of their blackness as well.

"You motherfucker. I'm going to fucking kill you," the oldest man in the group snarled.

You must be Roy, Gaines thought to himself, and then laughed.

"Sorry…do you want me to untie you and let you try again?" he taunted softly, smiling as if these were old pals he was playing a game with.

"Fuck you!" another screamed, and they all began squirming against their bonds to no avail.

"Go ahead," Gaines urged. "Get it out of your system. We've got a long night ahead of us, and it's better if you just work all that nervous energy out now."

He let them fight for a few moments longer until the wire was cutting into their wrists and ankles. Once skin was peeling from the older man's wrists, Gaines walked over and stood in front of him.

The man spat at Gaines. The angle of his head prevented the spittle from even getting close, but Gaines rewarded him with a solid punch to the side of his face anyway.

"Why are you doing this?" the youngest man protested. "We ain't done nothin' to you."

Gaines moved over to stand in front of him. "I'm sure if you think about your activities over the past several hours you can figure out exactly what you did to deserve this," he said, squatting down in front of the boy. He was no more than nineteen or twenty.

"They made me do it," he whined pleadingly. "I said we shouldn't kill 'em. That was Roy!"

"Fuck you, Billy, you just as guilty as we are," the older man yelled.

Gaines moved back to the older man. "Roy, huh? You the father of these two?"

"Fuck you. I wouldn't claim 'em if they was mine. But ain't nobody tried to kill no one," he pleaded, changing the tone of his voice mid-sentence. "We was just tryin' to scare 'em into leaving town. They was pissin' off a bunch of people with their prancin' around with that test tube baby of theirs. All superior and shit like they belonged here with decent folk."

"Decent folk?" Gaines replied in mock amusement. "And do decent folk break into houses, beat, rape, and shoot women, and then burn them down with their children?"

A look of disbelief went across all their faces. It was almost as if this man had been in the house with them last night. They had no idea he had heard every detail of their crime.

Gaines didn't wait for them to answer. "Okay! Let's get this business over with," he said with conviction. "Uncle Sam taught me to first disarm my adversary. Primary weapon first." He moved around behind the men. "And since you clearly can't fight a real opponent, your primary weapon is used against helpless women. So that has to go first."

He took out a knife and sliced the back of the first man's jeans, cutting right through his leather belt, pants, and underwear.

"Wait!" the man screamed. "You're a cop. You can't do this. You have to arrest us."

Gaines laughed. "I've never been a cop," he confided. "I did, however, work for the government. I did their dirty work for many, many years…lots of on-the-job training for *operations* like this. Though I must say…I've gotten more resistance from a house full of crack whores in Thailand than I have from you guys. Almost takes the fun out of it."

The men all started struggling again. The cursing reached a crescendo as Gaines grasped the first man by his fear-shriveled penis and scrotum, pulling it backwards and up so that he could wrap wire around the base at the narrowest point. He didn't want them bleeding out until he was done with them.

He slipped the blade underneath the offending package and

with one swift motion severed it from the man's body. A high-pitched scream emanated from the man followed by silence as he passed back into unconsciousness.

He brought the handful of bloody meat around and set it on the ground in front of the man, letting the other two fully comprehend what was about to happen to them, sending them pulling against their bonds again.

"No. No! Jesus, God, please don't, don't do it," Roy cried out, tears and slobber running down his face. "Please God, don't do it."

He walked around behind the next man, the one who appeared to be nineteen or so, and repeated the same actions on him, slipping the knife under his belt, jeans, and underwear and then wiring his distended scrotum and penis at the base.

"Please man! I didn't rape no one. I just stood watch!" he pleaded.

"'Leave some for me, Roy,'" Gaines mocked, repeating the man's words from the night before. "'Don't I get a turn?'" Then he sliced through the boy's flesh. His scream was shorter than the other man's before he passed out.

Gaines went to Roy, the oldest one of the group. "I've got a family, man. I've got wife and kids," he pleaded. "Don't take my manhood. Please, man. I'll sell everything I own to make up for what we did. Please don't."

Gaines spoke as he worked on the man. "The women you beat, raped, and killed last night had a family," he relayed coolly as he slipped the knife through Roy's belt and pants. "The baby you burned to death had parents who loved her," he continued as he roughly jerked Roy's ball sack and shriveled penis backwards and up. The odor of urine wafted up to Gaines's nostrils from where the man had wet himself.

"All of them had family—mothers, fathers, sisters and *brothers*—who loved them, cared about them, and had no expectation that they would be violated and ripped from their lives." He wrapped the wire tightly around the base of the man's member. "And all of them were better than you," he growled just before he sliced through the flesh.

Roy's scream lingered a long while after the cut, and he didn't fall into unconsciousness. He lingered on the edge of it, whimpering and crying for several minutes. "Just kill me, man," he cried over and over, slobbering on himself.

"I've got questions first," Gaines stated calmly. He picked the pail of water he had prepared and tossed half on each of the two unconscious men. They jerked awake and immediately started wailing.

"Quiet!" Gaines yelled, punching the closest one in the face, sending them all into subdued whimpers.

"The first thing I want to ask…" He paused as he walked slowly in front of sobbing group. "You!" he barked, pointing at the youngest man in the center. "How did you come to know about these women and their family?"

"It was Roy!" the young man squealed, just as he had done earlier. "His wife and these people from some church she belongs to. They have these political meetings at their house. They were always talking about the 'lezzie whores' and that science experiment baby of theirs."

"Really?" Gaines asked, sounding fascinated. "What do they do at these meetings?"

"Nooo," Roy sobbed. "Don't tell him nothin'."

Gaines punched Roy hard in the face, shutting him up, and then refocused his attention on Billy. "As you were saying…"

"They just listen to that Buck guy, and talk about all the things they'd do if they could get away with it," Billy whined.

"Buck?" Gaines asked.

"Yeah. Buck Grimwall. The radio guy," Billy sobbed. "Please let me go. I didn't do nothin' to those girls. Roy made me come along."

"You begged him to let you come," the first guy yelled, sobbing in anger and fear and then strained his neck to look at Gaines. "You ruined us for life. Ain't that enough? Let us go. We won't tell no one."

Gaines ignored the plea, turning his focus back to Billy. "Whose idea was it to go after those girls?"

"It was Roy and his wife," he said, slobbering on himself. "Some German fella was there. Georgia—Roy's old lady—said we had cover. That heavy hitters would have our backs."

Gaines's eyes went wide. "Older gentleman?"

"Yeah," Billy whimpered.

"What was this 'German fella's' name?" Gaines asked.

"I don't know," Billy replied, crying again. "I ain't never met him."

"I see," Gaines muttered, satisfied with his answers. "Billy, you've been very helpful. I want to thank you for your cooperation."

"So you're gonna let me go?" Billy cried hopefully.

"No. I'm sorry, but that's not possible," Gaines said apologetically. "But I will spare you your friends' fate." He pulled his knife out and slipped it under Billy's chin.

"No! You said you'd spare me their fate," he screamed out.

"Believe me, Billy. This is merciful compassion compared to what awaits them." With that, he drew the short, razor-sharp blade across Billy's throat, opening both arteries. Billy struggled for a short while, a gurgling rasp coming from his throat, and then he went limp.

The other two began to struggle again. Gaines calmly picked up the gas can he had located earlier and began pouring it out on the three men. Roy and the other man began tugging at their bonds again, though more weakly than they had earlier. Once the can was empty, he squatted down in front of the men. He looked Roy in the eye.

"What was the German's name?" Gaines asked him.

Roy turned his head to the side. Gaines grabbed the prostrate man by his hair and held his head up.

"Billy got off easy," Gaines said. "Do you want me to show you the hard way?" He brought his knife up to Roy's cheek, the tip pressing at the skin just below his eye.

"Heinrich," Roy whispered through his anger.

"Last name?" Gaines pressed.

"I don't have it," he hissed in reply.

"Two more questions," Gaines said. "How did you meet Heinrich?"

"I don't know. He just showed up after one of those meetings Georgia always has," Roy replied.

"So Georgia was the brains behind this, then?" Gaines asked, accusingly.

Fear raced across Roy's face. He realized he may have just signed his wife's death warrant.

Gaines smiled and rose, not needing an answer.

"Contact information for Heinrich," Gaines said, knowing he probably didn't have it to give.

"I ain't got none," Roy cried out. "He came to us."

"That's a real pity," Gaines claimed in mock regret. "That's the one thing that might have saved you." A lie.

"Wait. I can find him for you," Roy pleaded. "Give me a chance. I know I can find him."

"Tell me how you'd find him, and I might," Mark offered sympathetically.

Roy's eyes darted back and forth rapidly, obviously trying to figure out a suitable answer before it was too late. It was clear he had no more information.

"That's okay. I have another important job for you fellas," he confided, looking them in the eye, one and then the other. Then he pulled a box of matches from his pocket and shook it.

"Anything, man. We'll do anything you want," the younger of the two cried out.

"Oh. You don't have to *do* anything," he chided as he lit a match and held it in front of them. "I need you to be a shining example." He tossed the match onto Billy's back, sending flames spreading across his body and down to the floor, and then onto the other two.

As they twisted, screaming under the flames consuming their skin, Gaines withdrew one of his Desert Eagle automatics and waited. When the flames reached the ceiling of the garage, he fired a round into the top of one man's head and then the other before walking out of the garage.

On the way to his vehicle, he opened the phone belonging to Roy and dialed 911.

When the dispatcher answered he replied "Hello. My name is Roy Mullen. Me and my friends raped and murdered those two women and their baby last night. We are very bad people and are now paying for our crime." Then he tossed the phone on the ground outside the garage without ending the call.

He got in his car and drove away feeling unsatisfied. He had a lot more work to do.

**

1:45 a.m.—Hampton Inn and Suites in Colorado Springs

We checked into the Hampton Inn and Suites near the Air Force Academy. I felt I could breathe again after removing the tie. The dangerous article of clothing sat at the foot of the bed where I could keep an eye on it.

I could hear John in the other room talking on the phone. I laid down on one of the beds and listened in to his side of the conversation.

"Yeah. It's definitely him," John said. "Monkey Wrench

pulled ATM footage and cleaned it up."

"Between 18:00 and 19:00 hours, local time. A convenience store."

"No. He deleted it from the server at CSPD but the FBI might still have a copy."

"Yeah."

"Okay. I'll need a SATINT Package for three hours prior to present."

"Hopefully we can intercept him before he does anything rash."

"How's the recovery op going?"

"Really? Have they been able to get verification yet?"

"Keep me posted. Hopefully we'll have this wrapped up in a day or two and I'll be able to get back there to help."

"Yes, sir. Bye."

John came back into the bedroom area. Stress on his face.

"Try and get a little shuteye," he urged as he grabbed his suit jacket. "I've got to run over to the Air Force Academy and pick up a package."

"I can come," I offered, rising from the bed.

"Nope," he replied, holding out his hand. "You don't have clearance for where I'm going, and it's just a pick up. Get some sleep. I need that brain of yours fresh and alert."

"Okay," I said, plopping back down.

"See you in a couple of hours," he said as he exited the room.

"Hey, John?" I called as he opened the door. "What 'recovery op?'"

He closed the door and moved closer so he could speak in a lower voice.

"I can't really talk about it," he said.

But he wanted to...I could tell. "Sounds important," I probed.

"Just some clean up from a recent incident," he confided.

I saw a trace of a smirk flit, just for a split second, across his face.

It was more than I needed to figure out he felt he was hiding something from me that was right under my nose.

Recent and under my nose? I thought. *Mimon!*

1. Recovery Op

2. Recent Incident

3. Mimon

The nukes! They are hunting the missing nukes and have a strong lead that needs to be verified. John was working on the project and got sidelined by this man hunt. Got it. Thanks, John!

"Okay," I replied. "I understand… National security and all."

"Maybe another time," he said, then turned and left.

I sat there for a few minutes, trying *not* to let my mind start working on nuclear devices—but it was just so damned interesting.

I managed to doze off without even slipping under the covers or turning off the lights.

I had a stressful dream where I was searching my condo for something important. I was pulling items out of my closet, tossing them into the floor, looking under my bed, crawling on my belly—searching for something important that I had misplaced.

When I was done in the bedroom, I moved to the kitchen. There I began pulling things out of the cabinets, pots and pans crashing to the ground with a loud clatter. Next were the closets in the hallway and the foyer. I didn't know exactly what I was looking for, but I'd know it when I saw it, and it was very important that I found it.

I wracked my memory trying to recall what exactly I was looking for. I got the distinct impression it was yellow—

no…wait…Blonde!

**

I awoke as John entered the room.

"Up," he said. "I got a call from Detective Lee while I was out. There's been a development."

I wiped the sleep from my eyes and looked at the clock. It was just after 3:30 a.m.

"Did they get their CODIS matches?" I asked.

"I don't know. There was a 911 call about two hours ago," he said, slinging his bag on the bed and stuffing a package into it. "Someone claimed to be the killer and left an open line for the locals to trace."

I looked at him, dumbfounded. "Why would they do that?"

"They didn't," he said, throwing me my suit jacket. "When CSPD got there, they found three men tied to wooden pallets, burned alive with their manhood cut away. They were tortured."

"Oh, fuck," I muttered as I slipped my shoulder holster and coat on. "He found them."

"Looks that way," he replied, opening the door. "Let's go."

"Where?" I asked.

"The crime scene," he said plainly. "Where else?"

I paused for a second, thinking.

"Is Mark good at what he does?" I asked as the impatience built in his face.

"The best," John replied abruptly.

"How much evidence do you think he would have left at the crime scene?" I asked.

John cocked his head to the side, a confused look on his face, replaced quickly with realization.

"What do you suggest?" he asked, coming back into the room and closing the door.

"He's already got a two-hour head start on us," I replied. "How about I spool up your satellite imagery and see which way he headed?"

He thought about it for all of two seconds, put his bag back up on the bed, unzipped the side pouch, and then retrieved his package.

"That's up to about twenty minutes ago," John said, tossing me a pocket drive.

I plopped down in front of my computer at the table and booted up. I plugged in my password, slipped my finger onto the fingerprint reader, and waited for my desktop to show up while I drank the coffee John had placed in front of me. Bad coffee.

"Why do you salt the coffee?" I asked, making a yuck face.

"It's just like mom used to make," he joked, smiling, and then confessed. "It's a Navy thing."

"How long were you in the Navy?" I asked.

"Seventeen years," he replied.

"Three years from retirement and you just decided you wanted to be a spy?" I asked.

"It's more complicated than that," he admitted. "When I came out of the field, I ended up working for Naval Intelligence. Then I became a liaison under Clinton. Got my rank and thought I'd get a command of my own once I played the DC two-step for a while."

"Huh," I grunted. "Didn't work the way you planned?"

He looked up, realizing I was interrogating him. He gave me a long, measuring stare and then nodded.

"Yeah. The well can get poisoned without warning in Washington," he said. "I spoke my mind a couple of times on some strategic planning. It bit me on the ass."

"Spoke your mind and were wrong?" I asked.

"Worse," he said. "I told them what was going to happen and

they didn't listen. The only thing worse than being wrong in Washington is being right after they screw up—I was blackballed."

"That's when the CIA picked you up?" I asked.

He nodded. "I was no stranger to the Agency, and Burgess likes people who speak their mind," he replied. "He'd never punish a subordinate for an informed opinion…whether he acted on it or not."

"Sounds like a great guy to work for," I commented casually, knowing he would take it as a hint I was interested.

"Indeed he is," he replied. "Tough, but fair."

I nodded and took another sip—not as bad as the first one. "Okay. Let's see where you're going, Mr. Gaines."

"Those are in one-minute increments," he said as I started spooling the index list.

I loaded the data into my map reader and let the auto-labeler mark each layer with the timestamp from the file names. The GPS tags on each image let me synchronize them with a map overlay with longitude and latitude.

"These look tight," I noted, watching my script pull the images into place beneath an opaque road map of the region. "I need the address."

"38547 C and S Road," he replied. "Colorado Springs."

Once the image library finished compiling, I zoomed in to the address around the time John said the 911 call had been made. The garage was a bloom of red on the infrared image, but no sign of the Crown Victoria. I rolled it back more, one minute at a time, until I saw it.

There, parked a short distance from a garage, was the Crown Vic we had seen on the ATM video. The infrared images clearly showed a buildup of heat in the structure.

"Almost three hours," I said as I looked at my watch.

"What?" John asked.

"Yeah. Gaines's car left the scene at 1:17," I elaborated.

"Where's he headed?" John asked.

I ticked the time stamp up in one minute intervals until the car disappeared from the frame. Then I zoomed out and reacquired it as it was leaving the long driveway and merging onto the road. I highlighted the image of the car and tagged it as target one and then zoomed all the way out and ran the time sequence out like a stop frame video.

"South on 25," I replied. "Santa Fe…maybe Albuquerque?"

"Grab your stuff," John said urgently. "We have ground to make up."

"John," I said, wanting him to slow down a bit. "He's flying… Doing at least ninety miles an hour if not more, judging by the distance he's covered already."

"Make your point," John said, losing patience—I'd have to break him of that habit if we were going to work together.

"We need to get ahead of him if we're going to anticipate where he's going," I replied. "Let's fly to Albuquerque, get another image package, and try for an intercept rather than just chasing three or four hours behind him."

He stared at me for a moment, digesting my suggestion.

"Besides putting us ahead of him, it would also let us get more rest than he's getting," I added, trying to sway him. "At some point, he'll have to stop."

"He's a trained Agent," John said, concocting a weak rebuttal. "How much sleep do you think he needs?"

"His sister was killed in the wee hours of the morning yesterday," I replied. "He's probably already driven cross country all day, and now he's driving south on the interstate at a high rate of speed. Eventually, that adrenaline burn is going to wear off and he's going to crash—physically, if not emotionally."

John nodded. "Okay, Albuquerque," he conceded.

I felt a renewed sense of confidence that he valued my opinion enough to change course. That was followed by a renewed sense of pressure to not be wrong.

You are on the right track, I heard my other voice whisper into my ear.

I had almost forgotten about my on-board 'copilot.' Its insertion gave me a momentary respite from the worry.

We packed up our gear and were on our way our way to the airport. If everything worked out right, we'd get there shortly before Gaines did. If not, then at least we will have closed the gap some.

**

4:55 a.m.—Denver International Airport

We arrived at Denver International Airport and got our tickets. As soon as we had them, John nodded his head toward the bathroom, and I followed him in.

"What's up?" I asked after he did a cursory check of all the stalls to make sure we were alone.

"I need your piece," he said in a low voice.

It took me a second to realize he was talking about the gun he had given me. I reached under my coat and withdrew it and then handed it to him. He pulled the slide back a little and looked into the chamber and then opened his bag a bit and shoved it in.

"Spare magazines, too," he added. "TSA won't let you through security with those either."

I handed them over as well. Once they were in his bag and it was zipped up, we proceeded to security.

"How much info can we get from CSPD on the other victims?" I asked as we walked.

"I'm almost certain it raised eyebrows that we didn't show up at the crime scene," he replied.

"Why don't you call Detective Lee and see if you can get the identities of the guys Gaines killed," I suggested. "You can tell her we don't want to get underfoot of CSI and are going to start chasing down leads on connections."

There was a long pause while he considered what I said, or perhaps he was just figuring out what he was going to say to Detective Lee. But in either case, after a moment, he pulled out his phone and dialed.

"Good morning," he said to the person on the other end. "It's Special Agent Stark."

Lee, I thought.

"Oh, no," John explained. "We don't want to step on your CSI. Besides, I figured the FBI would already be up there, getting in your way. I didn't want to add to that."

There was a short pause. "We're still on the case, but my brilliant investigative partner suggested we follow up on connections instead of trying to duplicate your efforts on the forensics," he said. "It's your team, and unless the Bureau brought their own guys, we'd be relying on your findings anyway."

A short pause, and then John laughed. "Don't let them hear you say that," he said with a chuckle. "But yeah, you're right on the money."

"Yeah," he answered soberly. "That'll work."

He paused and then turned and looked at me, smiling. "Yep. He's right here," he teased.

After a second's pause, he laughed. "I'll tell him," he said through his laugh. "Thanks, Detective. I'll let you know what we come up with."

He ended his call and continued to walk toward security with a grin on his face.

"What?" I asked.

"She said she didn't see a wedding ring on your finger and

would like to take you out to dinner after this is all wrapped up," he revealed. "Her treat."

"Right on," I grunted with a grin as we arrived at the TSA portal. "Agent Rhodes got game."

"Oh, it plays," John chuckled as he flashed his ID.

The TSA Agent gestured him around the metal detector and I began to follow.

"Sorry, pal," John said, turning to me. "You have to go through security."

I went through the metal detector and had my bags x-rayed. Once through, we hurried to our gate. I heard the chime on John's phone as we jogged down the corridor.

"That will be the IDs on the vics," he informed me. "Detective Lee said she'd send what she had."

Once on board the plane, he handed me his phone, and I typed in the information on the three victims. When I was done and had started my search, he put a card down on my keyboard. I turned it over and saw a handwritten ID and password.

"What's this?" I asked.

"It's FBI CJIS access info," he said in a low voice.

My mental flowchart filled in the details for me.

> *CJIS: Criminal Justice Information Services. Integration includes, LEO (Law Enforcement Online), National Crime Information Center, IAFIS (Integrated Automated Fingerprint Identification System) and the Uniform Crime Reporting Program.*

Cool! I thought. *Sure beats the heck out of hacking the CSPD system with my virus.*

I nodded and plugged the data into my system quickly before we pulled away from the gate.

"You'll have to put that away, sir," I heard a woman's voice behind me as the data started to spool in.

I turned my head and smiled at the flight attendant.

"Yep," I acknowledged as I closed my laptop, leaving it running in the background. "Sorry."

I slipped it into its case but left the lid up so it wouldn't overheat under the seat in front of me.

As soon as we were airborne, and we were told we could use electronics again, I pulled it back out of its case. The data was extensive.

One of the men Mark had tortured and killed was named Roy Mullen. He and his wife, Georgia, were members of an ultra-conservative splinter of the Tea Party called Limited Access Government, or LAG Party.

I wasn't familiar with the group.

Roy Mullen had been detained a number of times during protests stemming from Tea Party and LAG Party events. His wife also had a few run-ins with law enforcement, along with a few other members of Colorado Springs LAG, for verbal assaults, trespassing, and a couple of instances of shoving counter demonstrators.

Interestingly, Roy and another one of his dead companions had several older assault arrests, including a sexual assault and two assault and battery convictions.

I looked around to make sure the flight attendant wasn't near and then pulled up my web browser to search for "Colorado Springs LAG party."

I got to its member web page and saw a list of events ranging from protest planning meetings to daily, ad-hoc "Radio Parties."

The entries for Radio Parties included several well-known conservative radio shows on the program list, but focused primarily on *System Buckers*, which revolved around the syndicated Buck Grimwall daily radio show.

I browsed the Buck Grimwall website and found a link for the previous day's program. I put my earbuds in and began to listen as I continued to parse the victims' records.

I had heard the man before while flipping through the radio stations in my car in the afternoons. It sounded as though he was talking past a pint of phlegm in his throat. I sat back while I read the arrest information and listened as he started into his daily lineup.

Near the top of his list were the lesbian couple and their baby who were murdered in Colorado Springs. His comments about them were less than complimentary.

"So this *couple—*" he said. "This lesbian *couple* in Colorado Springs was apparently murdered in their home last night—along with *their* baby. *Their* baby."

"How was it *their* baby?" came the producer's voice. "Was it a clone of both their DNA or something?"

"I don't know…I don't know. But let's not be insensitive," Buck said, mockingly taking the high road. "So anyway. This lesbian couple had this baby, blah, blah, blah, and they moved to Colorado Springs to start this new *family* of theirs.

"So last night, apparently someone broke in and set the place on fire, killing the *couple* and *their* baby.

"Anyway…and don't get me wrong. I think it's terrible that these people died. But this morning…oh and the…I guess you'd call her the *daddy* lesbian—she worked for a defense contractor out there in Colorado Springs.

"But this morning, guess who the first group out on the airwaves was to denounce this as a *hate crime*," he asked.

"The Baptist Ministers Association?" his producer responded sarcastically.

A phlegmy laugh rolled out of Buck. "Ha ha. No… The uh… hold on, I have it here. Oh yeah. The LGBT Alliance Against Defamation. The LGBTAAD—Legbitaad," he said, laughing.

"Now…there may very well be some lezzie hater group out there that committed this, uh, this crime. But I haven't heard anything from the police about this being a hate crime…I mean, it might not even be a crime at all. It may just turn out that they forgot and left the stove on."

"You'd think in a house full of women, they'd know how a stove worked," his producer said.

Buck laughed. "No. No," he sputtered between chuckles. "Don't be cruel now, Rob. This is a tragedy."

"Right. Tragedy. No jokes," Rob replied.

"So anyway. Oh, and apparently the mommy lesbian actually gave birth to *their* little baby. A baby girl, I think it was," he said slowly, his judgment dripping from every word. "Looks like they were getting a head start on the next generation.

"Now I'm not condoning violence in any way, shape, or form. Don't read that into my next statement. But…I mean…Colorado Springs is a fairly conservative area, is it not?" he asked, clearly knowing the answer already.

"Yes, it is. Very conservative. We've got a lot of listeners out there," Rob replied.

"That's what I thought," he inserted. "It seems to me that a lesbian *fam-i-ly*…" he said, separating out the syllables for the word. "It just seems to me they wouldn't be happy in a place like Colorado Springs to begin with.

"Not that they don't have a right to be there. But I think they'd be happier someplace else…like…like Gay York or El Gay California."

"I think right now they'd be happier anywhere," Rob added.

"Right. Right. We can't be insensitive. This is a tragedy. A horrible, horrible thing. But I can't help but wonder if their happy little *fam-i-ly* would be alive and well if they had chosen a more suitable place to live—that's all I'm wondering."

He finished his rant and moved on to other news. After a few minutes he took some calls. Several of the callers, who simply wanted to be on the radio, agreed with all Buck had said. One even went so far as to say that maybe this will help other *alternative* families choose their homes more carefully.

"Yes," Buck agreed. "If any good comes from this tragedy, maybe that's it."

I had heard enough. I turned off the feed. I sat back and closed my eyes, inviting my internal flowchart to fill my vision. There were three variables that kept my chart dead ending at question marks.

1. What was Mark doing that required the CIA travel ID?

2. Was the ID blown, and if so, who blew it?

3. Was Mark crazy?

Without answers to those questions, I had no way to formulate a path to him. We'd just have to keep following the satellite imagery. If he were crazy, he might be looking for a new target, unsatisfied by the three men he'd already murdered.

But if he wasn't nuts, and the ID use and his sister's murder were connected, then he might be moving up the food chain.

I leaned over to say something, but I saw John was sleeping so I kept my theory to myself, deciding instead to take a quick nap. I was certain it would be a no-sleep weekend, and this might be my last chance to grab some shut eye.

Jeeze, Buck. What a cockwaffle, I thought as I began to drift off.

**

5:15 a.m.—Colorado Springs, Colorado

HEINRICH BRAUN was awakened by his cell phone. He reached across the bruised prostitute in his bed and picked up the phone without bothering to turn on the light. The prostitute—Violet—flinched and began cowering again as she had only hours before, when she had cried herself to sleep.

"Braun," he answered, ignoring the girl.

"Ned Richards directed me to call this number and to give you any updates concerning activity in Colorado Springs," came the male voice at the other end.

Braun was actually in Colorado Springs—waiting for Gaines to appear. He hadn't expected the morons from the LAG Party group to kill Gaines's sister and her partner, but the assault would do one of two things—either Gaines would get the message and drop his freelance continuation of the Justice Department investigation or he would come to Colorado Springs to seek revenge. Braun had counted on the revenge.

"Well?" Braun asked, rising from the bed.

"The gentleman you had a watch on has been murdered, along with two companions," the man replied.

Revenge, Braun thought as a smile crossed his face. *Now we can track him.*

"And, sir," the man continued. "It appears the men were tortured for some time before they were killed."

That bothered Braun. Tension filled his chest as he realized they had probably revealed his own meeting with them. That would complicate things.

"And you have SATINT on the perpetrator?" Braun asked, uncertain his orders for satellite tracking had been followed.

"Yes, sir," the man replied.

"Where is he now?" Braun asked.

"He's on his way west on Route 40 in New Mexico near the Arizona border," the man replied.

"Arizona?!" Braun exclaimed in anger. "How old is this information?"

"The 911 call was made at 1:17 a.m.," the man replied. "But it wasn't relayed to CSPD until closer to 1:30 a.m."

"Four hours!" Braun yelled. "You waited four hours to tell me?!"

"Sir, I only just received the order to call you ten minutes ago," the man replied nervously.

"You tell Richards—" he started angrily. "Never mind. What is he driving?"

"The perpetrator, sir?" the man asked.

"No! The dead man," he hissed. "Yes, the perpetrator… Gaines. What is he driving?"

"It appears to be a late model Crown Victoria, sir," came the reply. "I can't give you a color until we have daylight imagery."

"Call me back as soon as you have any new information. No more delays," Braun commanded, ending the call before he could hear a reply.

He rose from bed and turned on the light. He stood naked in front of the prostitute, who had pulled the covers up close to her neck. He reached down and tugged on the covers, pulling them from her and exposing his handiwork from the night before. Her body was covered in bruises and bite marks. He smiled before starting to get dressed.

When he was finished dressing, he opened his wallet and pulled a large wad of bills out, tossing them on the bed at her feet.

"Checkout is at noon," he offered with a smirk as he grabbed his bag and was leaving the room. "Feel free to order breakfast and put it on the room tab."

On his way through the lobby, he dropped his room key on the counter.

"I'm not sure," he said with a concerned look on his face, "but I believe I saw a disheveled young woman disappear into my room as I entered the elevator. You might want to have security check."

A surprised expression appeared on the desk clerk's face. "Thank you, sir," she replied. "I'll get them to take a look."

He turned and walked away; a satisfied grin appeared on his

face as soon as he heard the woman at the desk call for security.

I hope they get to see my work, he thought as he handed the valet his ticket.

**

7:30 a.m.—Albuquerque, New Mexico

John slept until the flight attendant woke him to put his seat up. He sat up and rubbed his eyes.

"Shit," he muttered, looking at his watch. "What did you find?"

"Arrest records, Tea Party and LAG party affiliations—the connection between the three men," I replied.

"Anything to connect them to Gaines?" he asked as the plane started its decent.

"Not really," I replied. "But I'm still digging. They just seem to be a bunch of homophobic pricks who get together and listen to other homophobic pricks on the radio."

When the plane had landed and rolled up to the gate, we deplaned and walked up the ramp. John's phone rang as we got to the terminal.

"Temple," he said after looking at his phone. Then, after a short pause, "Where?"

There was another pause. "On our way."

"What?" I asked as he spurred us along the exit tunnel from the plane.

"A new package," he said as we emerged into the terminal. "I called ahead so they'd know the flight."

"They?" I asked.

"Stop it," he replied quietly as we walked out into the open next to the gate. There was a man standing in the gate area with a phone to his ear, staring at John. John closed his phone and walked toward him.

As we approached the man, he put a paper bag on the floor and walked away before we reached him. John picked it up and handed it to me and then pointed toward a corner of the gate seating area.

I sat and then extracted the pocket drive containing the imagery. As soon as my computer was booted up, I began spooling the new images.

"I'm going to go grab us some coffee," he said. "Do you want something to eat?"

"Fruit and meat of some sort," I replied without looking up. Then, as an afterthought as he walked away, I added, "No salt in my coffee, please. I like it bitter."

He chuckled as he trotted off.

When the images had finished spooling, I picked up the overlapping time tags and began tracing Gaines's Crown Victoria along Route 40. The stop frame tracing of his movement stopped west of a small town named Gallup, New Mexico. I zoomed in on the image and watched the heat signature inside the car as it sat in place for what equated to almost an hour.

"What's the scoop?" John asked, arriving with coffee and a breakfast biscuit for me.

"Looks like he stopped outside a place called Gallup to take a nap," I replied.

"How far away from here is that?" he asked.

"A little more than two hours," I replied. "He was really flying to make up that much ground."

"He probably wasn't too worried about troopers in that Crown Vic. It had GS plates on it." John muttered, referring to federal government-issued plates. Police would not be inclined to pull over a car belonging to federal law enforcement.

Just as the feed was about to end, the vehicle pulled out of its parking space on the road and began moving again. The imagery concluded about ten minutes after that, with Gaines still moving west on 40.

"Phoenix or Vegas?" John asked over my shoulder, indicating I was to make the call on the next flight.

Neither sounded quite right, but given the two choices, my internal flowchart pushed me to an answer.

"Vegas," I replied, but it was almost a question it was so laden with doubt.

"I'll be back in a few minutes. Keep digging to see if you can figure out where he's headed."

While he was gone, I went over the crime database information to no avail. Within moments, John had returned with two boarding passes for a flight to Las Vegas.

"Pack it up," he commanded. "We'll have to run to catch our flight."

I closed up my computer, shouldered my bag and jogged behind him toward our new gate. We made it with little time to spare.

On the flight, I thought about our plan and decided it would be much simpler if we could just get tagged coordinate updates.

"If I could get a feed with just coordinate updates, we wouldn't have to anticipate his direction," I suggested as we settled into our seats. "We could jump ahead of him and then close in on the tag instead of following him hours after the fact."

"Can't use Agency resources to track him inside the US," he replied. "All I'm getting is raw Satellite data, no fingerprints on a search."

"Is there a way we can get a feed instead of having to download a whole package then spool it?" I offered.

"We don't have the tech to do that without filtering first, and that would constitute Agency involvement," he replied.

I nodded, and then thought for a second. We had been using an awful lot of CIA manpower and satellite access. "Are we off the books or off the reservation?" I asked him, wondering if we were bending the rules or melting them down completely—and forging a criminal act in the process.

"The books. That's all I can say," he replied, becoming annoyed with my probing.

"But what if—"

"Look, Scott. My boss is already dancing on a thin line with this, and we can't do anything that will turn this into reportable action," he said, lowering his voice but taking a harsh tone. "Before it's over, I may have to retire someone I trained, someone I consider a friend. So how about cutting me some slack with the twenty questions?"

I shut my mouth and leaned back to take another short nap. A few moments later I heard John quietly say, "Sorry."

I didn't open my eyes. "We're cool," I muttered. Without opening my eyes, I smiled and asked, "So why can't you just call Mark and ask him where he is?"

There was no answer, but I heard him shift in his seat. I assumed he was looking at me in agitation, so I opened my eye a slit to confirm…yep.

"I mean, you've gone to all the trouble to come out and help him," I said, turning my head back towards the front of the plane and closing my eyes again. "Is there a reason he wouldn't take your call?"

More silence.

I looked over again to see he was still staring at me, but there was less agitation in his gaze…it looked more like a decision was being made.

"Don't hurt yourself," I said, knowing his nature made it hard to share info. "I'm just curious more than anything. I figured if that was an option, you'd have done it already."

"That might have worked a week or so ago when I found out there'd been a search on his cover ID," John replied quietly. "As soon as the shit with his sister went down, it stopped being an option."

"You don't think he'd trust you?" I asked.

John shook his head. "We didn't end it on the best of terms," he replied. "The mission he was ordered to do that he bailed out of—I had to finish it. And I didn't handle the reprimand well."

"What was it?" I asked, pushing my luck.

He glared at me a second and then softened his expression a bit.

"I can't give you details, but he was ordered to take down a real bad guy before something could happen. The only way to do it was to blow a vehicle. The guy had his wife and son with him and Mark couldn't bring himself to push the button," John replied quietly after leaning toward me to gain some privacy. "I didn't hesitate."

I nodded, absorbing the significance of the disclosure. After a moment, I cautiously asked, "Was it worth it?"

"Totally," he replied without hesitation. "We saved more than three hundred incoming servicemen with that one takedown—but Mark didn't see it that way. He was sure he could've found another opportunity."

"Could he?"

John hesitated that time. "He might have," he replied with a note of regret in his voice. "But we play the odds. We have to."

"You won't get an argument from me," I replied. "Though sometimes someone else might have a better insight into those odds."

He grunted his acknowledgement. I'm certain he would realize I was referring to Mimon and the rescue of the hostages. His odds had told him to take the field with the SEALs to get the nuclear devices, hostages no longer being the primary objective. I had proven both were possible.

I suddenly wondered if *that* made him second guess his actions on the op with Mark and whether that was the source of the regret in his voice.

**

10:15 a.m.

When we arrived in Las Vegas, John went directly to the car rental counter while I stayed with our luggage. I watched as he tapped his foot, impatiently waiting for the clerk to hand over the keys.

He's wound pretty tightly, I thought. *I wonder if I should be more nervous.*

"Okay," he grunted as he grabbed his bags and headed to the door. "We're behind schedule."

Schedule?

On our way to our vehicle, a man approached us from the opposite direction. He was looking up at the tower, shielding his eyes from the sun with his hand. At the last second he looked where he was going, but he bumped into John anyway, knocking his and John's items to the ground along with the man.

"I'm so sorry," the man said.

"No problem," John replied, picking up his belongings and helping the man to his feet. "Watch the road, man."

"Thanks. I will," the man said and then walked on.

John turned to me and handed me a padded envelope from the drop. I took it and tucked it under my arm.

"Real smooth," I muttered sarcastically.

"It does the job," he retorted without looking at me.

We got into the rental vehicle, another SUV like the last. I immediately pulled out my laptop, started it up, and then removed the pocket drive from the envelope.

"Why do you insist on getting industrial-sized vehicles?" I asked while I waited for my computer to boot up again.

"Have you ever tried to do a PIT Maneuver on an American-made sedan with a Mini Cooper?" he replied sarcastically.

"Okay. I get it."

"Tell me something," John chimed as we exited the airport and moved toward the highway. "Why does it take so long for your computer to boot up?"

"Encrypted drive." I replied, watching the startup routines spool across my screen.

"I have an encrypted laptop. It doesn't take that long to boot."

"No. The system is encrypted, yes, but the drive is encrypted at shut down and decrypts at start up—separated by a boot drive," I replied, grinning as the last of the decrypt routine ran. "If the drive is ever separated from the rest of the system, the key gets scrambled and it becomes a random three hundred megabyte crypt key. It would take about two hundred years of random super computer crack gens to unlock it."

He laughed, shaking his head. "And I thought I was paranoid."

I raised my hand. "System security specialist," I responded.

"The NSA doesn't even go to that much effort," he rebuffed, still amused by my encryption overkill.

"That's why their systems are so easy to hack," I replied, plugging in the pocket drive.

His head snapped around and he glared at me. "…from what I've heard," I added with an ironic grin.

As soon as my system was booted up, I started spooling the images. We were just merging onto the highway as I started the review.

Gaines's Crown Vic had driven to a town called Kingman, Arizona, where it had stopped. I ran all the way to the end of the data feed and it hadn't moved, so I backed it up to the frame where it had stopped then zoomed in.

The car had stopped in the parking lot of a small park. I toggled the pictures back and forth for a few seconds and saw no other vehicle movement.

I zoomed out again so I could see more of the park and some of the surrounding streets and then toggled back and forth a few more times. On a side street, one block away from the park, a sedan moved, and then another vehicle on the opposite side of the park—a compact car.

I broadened the view again and expanded the time parameters. To the right of the park was the Mohave County Fairgrounds. I ticked the image stream back and forth and after a ten minute loop, I caught movement on the ground, a long human shadow in the early morning sun.

Okay. Let's look for you on the ground, I thought.

I toggled the time index back to where the Crown Vic had parked and zoomed in again, maximum magnification. There was no movement on the vehicle at all. No people shadows.

Where did you go?

Then I caught a glimpse of a shadow. A couple of pixels in the image that were out of place when compared to the previous frame, in the shadow line of some houses across the street. I followed it a few frames and lost it again.

"This is frustrating as hell," I said aloud.

"What?" John asked.

"The Crown Vic stopped in Kingman, Arizona and stayed there. I'm trying to pick up his ground movement to see where he went, but I get nothing. It's almost as if he knew when the satellite was going to be snapping his picture."

"He does," John said with a smile.

I shot him a smirk. "Yeah. Right."

"Think about it, smart guy. He's used SATINT before. Satellites don't record photos, they record raw digital streams. They are converted to images with software. The photo package we get is in one minute increments because any more than that would be unmanageable in the field."

Understanding hit me. "As long as he keeps to shadow most

of every minute, there is only a one in sixty chance of being caught by the analyst." I replied confidently. "Slick! Okay. I've got this now."

I highlighted a human shadow and copied the image data. Then I opened a script window and programmed a search macro using that shadow data as a general basis for a search. I estimated the distance a man would cover at a leisurely pace and calculated concentric circles out from the Crown Victoria at intervals based on those estimates. I then ran the program, looking for human shadows within those circles in areas that would require more than a minute to cross.

I quickly ran ahead several minutes checking to see if there were any other vehicles or any more "human shadow" walkers within my concentric pacing circles. I tracked and removed all tags that had identifiable origins or that couldn't have walked from the Crown Vic in the time allotted, and then I moved forward roughly thirty minutes. With the eliminated tags belonging to locals just milling about, there was only one possible hit.

"Bingo!" I proclaimed aloud. The only movement within the "human pace" circles were eight frames of a person of the correct height to be Gaines—calculating from the length of the shadow—moving roughly from the parked car toward a series of long, covered buildings at the south end of the fairgrounds. I ticked it forward a few more minutes and saw an older model, white and red short-bodied SUV—probably a Blazer or a Bronco—leaving the covered building he had been headed for. I tagged the SUV as our primary target.

I rolled it forward another hour and saw only a livestock trailer truck and a delivery truck pull up and then leave almost immediately.

When I zoomed out, my guess was confirmed when the new SUV pulled up behind the Crown Vic and stayed stationary for several minutes before continuing toward the highway.

"Okay. It looks like he switched to an older-model, short-body SUV. Red and white," I announced.

"Where is he headed?" John asked.

I moved the time slider all the way out to the image package end.

Uh oh, I thought.

"40 West," I said. "He's not going to Vegas."

"Shit!" John exclaimed and whipped the SUV onto the inside shoulder and through the median. Once we were headed the opposite direction, he floored the gas.

"We're behind him again—fuck, *fuck*, FUCK!" he said, pounding the steering wheel with each utterance.

We took Interstate 15 headed southwest. With the head start he had on us, there was no way we would intercept him. The best we could hope for was to get close to him as he got to Barstow. We'd still be almost an hour behind him, even at this speed.

John pulled out his phone and dialed. "I'm going to need a fresh image package at Barstow in two hours. I'll call again when I'm coming onto the base so they can run it then."

The person on the other end of the phone said something he didn't like. A frustrated look spread across his tired features.

"Yes, sir. I understand," he replied and then hung up.

"This is the last package he can authorize. It's starting to draw attention," John relayed.

"Then it won't do us any good. By the time we get the fresh reel, he'll be past us and be moving in any direction," I pointed out.

He paused, and then, with resignation, said, "It's the best we can do."

**

12:10 p.m.—Kingman, Arizona

HEINRICH BRAUN had just gotten off the phone with his asset at Homeland Security. The Crown Victoria had gone stationary several hours earlier and they had lost track of Gaines.

Braun knew Gaines wasn't stopping in Kingman, so he must have changed vehicles here. The delay was costing him precious time, and his mood was turning sourer as the minutes ticked by. If he didn't locate the man soon, the entire ploy will have been wasted effort, leaving Braun in worse shape than he had been before—and that was something he wasn't willing to accept. William Spryte was not a man to accept failure.

With the murder of the three men in Colorado Springs, he knew he was now fighting the clock, not only in finding Gaines, but with the added urgency of finding him before law enforcement did. It would be bad enough if Gaines evaded capture and continued his covert investigation—but it would be absolute disaster if the Justice Department got their hands on him and sweated information from him. It threatened the entire Combine operation in the US—possibly globally.

He only prayed Gaines's status as a flagged ex-Agent was keeping him from using CIA resources. His murder of the three men would certainly not aid his efforts in getting Agency help.

Braun parked on Main Street and went into the local sheriff's office. He stood at the counter watching a young deputy eat a sandwich and then looked around for any other people—there were none.

"Ehem," Braun grunted, drawing the deputy's attention.

The man placed his sandwich down and walked over to the counter, wiping his hands on a paper napkin and wiping his mouth as he stopped in front of Braun.

"Yes, sir," the deputy said. "How can I help you?"

Braun could smell horseradish from the opposite side of the counter. As unpleasant as it was, it reminded him he hadn't eaten since the previous evening.

"I was wondering if there were any vehicles reported stolen

this morning," Braun said with a thin smile.

Braun wasn't unaware of the distrust some rural populations had for outsiders, especially ones with foreign accents, so he tried to be uncharacteristically diplomatic.

The deputy looked at Braun with suspicion. But thefts would be reported in the local paper anyway, so there was no reason not to disclose the information.

"What's your interest in the theft?" the deputy asked. "I know you don't work for the paper."

"I'm with Great Western Insurance," Braun lied. "There's been a rash of stolen vehicles in the state, and we are trying to create a data model of the pattern. Today the computer predicted they'd show up within a twenty-mile radius of Kingman."

The deputy glared at him, still suspicious.

"It's all right if you aren't able to give me the data," Braun continued. "We'll get the reports from the insurance companies. But if they are in the area, we might be able to put a stop to it before any more vehicles are stolen—if we get the information in a timely fashion."

Appealing to the deputy's sense of preemptive law enforcement was enough to push him over the edge.

"Sometime this morning, a '92 Ford Bronco was stolen from the fairgrounds," he said, looking at his notes from the call earlier in the day. "Two tone, red and white."

"Do you have any idea when it was stolen?" Braun asked.

The deputy looked at Braun through slitted eyes. "Some time this morning," he repeated.

Braun swallowed his annoyance and smiled at the man. "Any other reports of theft or disturbance today?"

"Well…" the deputy sneered, leaning on the counter toward Braun. "A few minutes ago, I got a call from Maple Street. Someone's dog was barking and disturbing the sleep of a second shifter." His tone indicated that his helpfulness was at an end.

"Thank you, Officer," Braun replied. "Have a good day."

"Can I get your name for the log?" the deputy asked as Braun turned to leave.

"Bill Smith," he lied and then walked out the door before any more questions could be asked.

The deputy walked out and stood in the doorway as Braun got into his car and drove away. He looked into the rearview and saw the man writing down the license plate as he cruised down the street.

It was of no concern. The license plate was registered to a rental company in Colorado Springs and rented to one "Bill Smith." There wasn't even a recognizable photo in the file to match him to.

Braun pulled out his map of the western United States and followed with his finger the route he had been traveling. The closest city was Las Vegas, but a cold chill ran down the back of his neck when he saw where Route 40 led.

LA, he thought. *He's going after the media list.*

Braun reached for his satellite phone and then dialed.

"Roman," came the reply.

"We have a problem with Gaines," Braun said coolly.

"Go secure," Roman replied.

Braun hit the encryption setting and put the phone back to his ear.

"What's the problem?" Roman asked.

"I was notified by Homeland far too late to intercept Gaines when he found our patsies," Braun explained, hoping to head off any accusations of dereliction. "He was hours away by the time I got the tracking information."

There was a short pause and then Roman said. "You'll have to tell Mr. Spryte yourself."

"I will, but I'm going to need to arrange tactical support for this op after all," Braun replied quickly before he could be transferred. "I need you to contact Mr. Harbinger and have him make arrangements in LA."

"LA?" Roman exclaimed. "Why there?"

Braun hesitated… Gaines was either going after the media list because Black had betrayed them and given real payment data or because the LAG party people disclosed the connection between Braun and Grimwall. In either case, the news was going to be taken poorly.

"I think Black may have betrayed us and given the DOJ real payment information," he replied, hoping to avoid some wrath from Spryte.

There was silence at the other end while that sank in. "We'll need an alternate plan if you can't locate Gaines," Roman said finally. "I'll contact Mr. Harbinger. You should receive a call from him shortly."

"Very well," Braun said tersely, the tension in his chest ticking up a notch. "Put me through to Mr. Spryte now."

There was no reply, just a click on the line and then a few seconds later, Spryte came on the phone.

"Roman said you have an update for me," Spryte said mildly.

Roman, you snake.

"Yes, sir," Braun replied. "It would appear Gaines is making an attempt to reach some of our media assets. I've ordered a tactical response and am in pursuit. But I thought you should be aware that a clean elimination might not be possible."

There was a very long pause.

"Sir?" Braun said finally.

"I expect this matter to be handled in any way necessary," Spryte hissed. "If a connection is made between us and any of our assets, the damage could be extensive. We've gone to great lengths to hide them…don't let Gaines expose us."

"Yes, sir," Braun replied confidently. "Whatever it takes."

The call ended and Braun sighed deeply—Spryte wouldn't hesitate for a second to hang the payments around Braun's neck and then have Harbinger put a bullet in his head. *I have to clean this up quickly,* he thought.

The phone in his hand chirped while he was lost in thought and it startled him.

"This line isn't secure." A man's voice spoke from the other end.

"I'm headed for LA and would like a private party," Braun replied. "Something small and quiet. Two should be sufficient."

"Understood. What time will you be in town?" the man asked.

"Approximately five hours," Braun responded.

"That's short notice," the man remarked.

"Then perhaps I should call another agency," Braun replied coldly.

"No. We can manage," the man said, seemingly unmoved. "Do you know the location?"

"Not yet. I will need assistance with that as well," Braun replied.

"Understood. So you'll need AV services as well as companionship," the man said. "Any toys for yourself?"

"No," Braun replied. "I have my own supply."

"We'll contact you in five hours for a rendezvous location," he said.

Braun ended the call. He pushed his foot down on the accelerator a bit more without even realizing it. If Gaines successfully reached the radio and TV personalities and was able to extract information from any of them, William Spryte would blame the entire thing on Braun—even though it had been Spryte's plan. It was in his nature to blame others for his own failures.

I can't let Gaines interrogate the media people, he thought, gripping the wheel tighter. *Even one slipping through the cracks could bring the whole house of cards down.*

The man he had just talked to, Harbinger, was a nightmare of a man—a giant of a man. The violence Braun had perpetrated in his lifetime was nothing compared to Harbinger. And he only hired the most capable killers.

Perhaps I should have asked for more men, he thought to himself before quickly dismissing the idea. *No. If two of Harbinger's men and I can't stand against one former CIA Agent with no Agency resources, then I don't deserve to hold my position. Besides—he doesn't even know he's being hunted.*

**

As Mark drove down the highway, he struggled to keep his mind on task. The grief of losing his sister to those animals was more than he could bear. But the thought that she had been violated and murdered because of something he was involved in was helping him focus his anger like a laser.

"Heinrich," Mark muttered.

Mark had been ready to sit and wait for the police to show up after he had killed the shit stains who had killed his family. But when the kid mentioned the "German," the connection had been made.

Grimwall, Mark thought. *We are going to have a chat.*

But first he needed to get some equipment—Mark had been prepared to kill…not for surveillance.

He pulled the map into his lap and looked for a suitable location to obtain what he needed. His finger came to rest on a base and he smiled a grim smile.

"I'll need a uniform," he muttered and then pressed down further on the accelerator.

**

12:40 p.m.—Barstow, California

We drove in silence nearly the rest of the way to the Marine Logistics Base in Barstow. When we arrived, John flashed credentials at the gate and then pulled up in front of a nondescript-looking concrete building with double glass doors.

"Sit tight," he ordered as he exited the vehicle.

While I was waiting for him, I spooled up the reader program in preparation for the fresh data and then checked my phone for any messages. While it was contacting the mail server, I happened to look up and catch a flash of red in the side mirror.

I turned and looked behind me.

"Of all the dumb, fuckin' luck," I muttered.

It was a red and white Bronco. It pulled up to a fence two blocks away and parked. A man in Marine fatigues got out, looked around once, and then walked toward the gate house. He showed an ID and continued across the lot, disappearing as he entered a brick building.

I quickly dialed John's phone number. One second later, I heard the phone ring in the center console next to me.

"Shit!" I exclaimed.

I grabbed a T-shirt out of my bag, jumped out of the SUV, and then walked quickly and with purpose toward the Bronco. As I went, I set my phone to mute and activated location services.

As I approached the old Ford, I wrapped the T-shirt around the phone and then quickly stuffed it under the spare tire wheel cover, jamming it hard under the taut Naugahyde, and then stepped back to make sure I couldn't visually detect its presence. When I was satisfied, I walked casually back to our SUV and immediately logged onto "Find my phone."

The signal correctly placed the flag on our location.

A few moments later, the man reemerged from the building, carrying a cardboard box. He exited through the gate and walked casually to his vehicle. Two Marines passing him saluted and he stiffly returned the gesture, his hand snapping up crisply and then back down again.

An officer's uniform, I thought.

As he approached his vehicle, I got a good look at his face. It was definitely our guy.

He swung the spare tire rack out of the way, opened the back door of the SUV, and placed the box inside next to another, larger box. Once everything was closed back up, he calmly got into the truck and drove away.

I watched my screen as the blip got further and further away from us. It was another ten minutes before John reappeared through the doors. He broke into a run as soon as he exited the building.

He hopped into the SUV and tossed me the pocket drive. "Load it up…quick," he said urgently as he started the engine.

"No need," I replied, smiling.

"Why the fuck not?" he asked in exasperation, tension in his face.

I turned my laptop toward him and showed him the map with the blinking dot moving away from Barstow at a quick pace.

"He pulled up over there a few minutes after you left…dressed in fatigues," I recounted calmly, nodding in the direction our target had just left from. "He went into a building down the street then came back out a few minutes later with a small cardboard box."

"Why the hell didn't you call me?" he asked incredulously.

I pointed at the center console, drawing his attention to the phone he had left sitting there. He dropped his head and shook it in disbelief.

"Where did he go in?" he asked.

"Into that building," I said, pointing.

We drove around to the entrance and parked next to the gate house. John flashed credentials to the guard and we passed through. Once inside the building, we walked up to the cage-covered counter and hit the bell. A sharp-looking corporal approached us.

John pulled out his ID flip and showed it to the corporal as he spoke. "Corporal. About fifteen minutes ago, a soldier—"

"An officer," I interrupted.

"...an officer left here with a cardboard box. Can you tell me what was in that box?"

The corporal lifted a clipboard from behind the counter and opened the metal cover. His finger traced down a short list, stopped on one entry briefly, and then he reached into a file box and extracted a sheet of paper with official markings on it.

"Eight training rounds for a LAW, two smoke grenades, white smoke, and four tactical wireless cameras and receivers," he said. "But he would have gotten the training rounds and the smoke grenades from the ammo bunker. The camera would have been all we had here."

My brain recalled: *The LAW (Light Anti-Tank Weapon) a portable one-shot 66mm unguided anti-tank weapon, United States production of the weapon began in the 60s and ended in the 80s.*

"Thanks, Corporal," John said, and then we turned and walked out.

Once we were back on the road, I pulled our tracking screen back up. Gaines wasn't moving as fast as he had in the Crown Vic—probably more sensitive to notice by state troopers. I quickly calculated his speed at seventy-five miles per hour.

"He's a quarter of the way to LA already," I reported, prompting John to push down further on the gas.

"Why did he get training rounds for the LAW?" I asked.

"He needs a rocket for something, and since the LAW is no

longer in production, the stockpiled training rounds have had their classification lowered. They fall under the same category as small arms ammunition. The Marines always get the castoffs from other branches, so the older munitions are stored with them longer," he explained.

"How big is a LAW training round?" I asked.

"35mm," he replied. "Not big enough to take out a vehicle, even if it had an explosive head, which the training round does not."

The new data flowed into my brain's version of an evidence board. Pieces moved around, lines crossed, and huge question marks opened in areas with insufficient data. I'd know more when we discovered where he was heading.

The two-hour, long-distance pursuit ended in a public garage in Burbank, California.

**

3:35 p.m.—Burbank, California

John drove into the parking garage where the signal was coming from roughly thirty minutes after it had stopped moving. He drove past the vehicle without looking at it and continued up to the next level, parking in a space on the slope just above and behind the Bronco so we could see it without being obvious. Gaines was not in the vehicle.

"The boxes are still in the back," he said as he turned the engine off. "But I couldn't tell if they were empty or not."

"Want me to go over and look in?" I asked.

He thought about it for a second before answering.

"No. He could be using that tactical camera and receiver to monitor," he finally replied. "Let's just sit tight for a while."

We watched it for an hour, seeing no movement. My stomach was making horrific noises, and after about thirty minutes of John listening to it without so much as an acknowledgment, he abruptly turned to me.

"Oh for God's sake. Here," he said, handing me two twenty-dollar bills. "Go and get us some food."

"But what if he comes back?" I asked, feeling as if I'd been asked to scrub the toilet.

"We've got the tracker. I'll wait for you."

I left the truck, happy to be able to stretch my legs. I walked down the stairs of the parking garage and let my mind unspool from the puzzle it was working on. I took a deep breath and looked up into the LA sky as the sun beat down on the top of my head.

"Damn, LA is hot in July," I muttered.

I looked around the corner for a place to get food and spotted a deli about a block away. I walked along, enjoying the beautiful people and their lack of modesty. *So much skin.*

I arrived at the deli and fell in place behind a small line of customers. I finally got to the counter, ordered food and drinks for both of us, and then, while my order was being prepared, I stopped at the bathroom. By the time I came back out, my food was ready, so I picked it up and took a leisurely stroll back toward the garage, snacking on French fries as I went.

I got to the staircase, and as I moved to go up, my other voice chimed in.

Careful, it whispered into my ear.

I looked down at my feet and then up the stairs and saw no obvious hazards.

"I know how to walk up a flight of stairs," I muttered as I began to climb.

Quiet, it whispered as I got to the level we were parked on.

When I came around the corner, a man in Marine fatigues was standing by the passenger-side door. It was open and he was rummaging through my bag and computer case.

I set the food and drinks down quietly and walked along the back edge of the wall, careful to step with the sides of my feet to remain as quiet as possible. When I was within two parking spaces from him, I started to move out so I could get behind him.

I could see John through the open back door, lying in the seat, handcuffed and unconscious—but I could no longer see Gaines.

As I stepped across an empty space, he suddenly appeared out of nowhere, flying down on top of me from above. He knocked me to the ground with a kick to my shoulder, and I rolled backwards, trying to avoid a stomp to my chest.

I rolled down through the narrow gap between levels and managed to get back to my feet before he came through the same way. There was no way I was going to be able to beat this guy. He was too fast and too strong, and I still wasn't 100% because of my wounds.

He made a rapid movement toward me, pulling a knife from behind him.

"Not again," I whined aloud.

That comment caused him to hesitate for a split second, but it didn't stop his advancement toward me.

"Dude! I'm tech support," I protested, throwing my hands up in the universal sign of "Whoa."

Amazingly, this stopped him, but he kept the knife held high.

"How'd you find me here?" he asked.

There was no point in lying to him. We were no longer working undetected.

"My phone. It's in your spare," I revealed, jerking my thumb back towards the Bronco.

A confused look crossed his face. "Your phone?" he asked incredulously.

He walked over to the Bronco and sliced the cover on the spare with his knife. The T-shirt-wrapped phone dropped to the ground. He reached down and picked it up, opening the T-shirt, allowing the phone to drop to the ground. I reached out to try and catch it before it hit, but he stepped forward with the knife.

Crack! went the phone. I rolled my eyes and let my shoulders slump.

"A phone?" he asked.

"It's all I had," I replied honestly. "I'm not Company. I don't have all your cool toys."

"Not Company?" he smirked, verifying he had heard correctly.

I nodded.

He dropped my Melvin's T-shirt after looking at it, and then opened the rear window of his Bronco with his free hand.

"Then why are you here with Temple?" he asked as he reached into the back without looking and withdrew a very mean-looking automatic handgun.

My adventure in Europe had awoken an interest in guns. I recognized it as a Desert Eagle .50 Cal from my research. There were papers wrapped around it; he removed them and tossed them back into the Bronco.

"He's not under orders," I said, raising my hands higher. "He told me he needed help finding a friend who was in trouble."

"Scott! Shut up!" I heard John yell from behind me. He had regained consciousness.

Gaines looked in the direction of our SUV and then back at me.

"Scott?" he asked, narrowing his eyes at me. "Lift your shirt."

The request caught me off guard. I hesitated for a second.

"Now! Lift it," he repeated, the tension in his voice growing.

I did as I was ordered. He saw my scars and a broad grin appeared on his face.

"So you're the one, huh?" he choked, breaking into a laugh. "The Boy Scout who took out Jovanovich and Popovich. Tech support, my ass."

"I don't know what you've heard, but those were accidents," I replied defensively.

"Scott! Shut the hell up!" I heard John yell again from behind me.

Gaines pointed his gun in the direction of our SUV, indicating he wanted me to move that way. Once beside the vehicle, he pressed his gun against John's head and then unlocked one side of the cuffs.

"Cuff yourselves through the wheel," he ordered.

John leaned across the front seat and we complied with the command.

"You didn't have to give me up, Captain," Gaines accused. "It cost me my family."

"I didn't give you up, Mark," John replied sincerely as he closed the cuff around my wrist through the wheel. "I got a flagged call for an all-agencies search on the Tranum ID last week and ordered it zipped up unless there was a warrant attached. If someone gave you up, it wasn't anyone at the Agency."

He paused and looked at John, measuring his statement. "You should have warned me," he muttered finally.

"I know that in hindsight," John replied. "But you have to remember, we didn't leave on the best terms. I didn't know if a call from me would help you or hurt you."

Gaines stared at John for a second longer and then turned and walked away toward his stolen vehicle.

"I'm sorry about your sister and her family, Mark," John called to his back.

"Hey, Boy Scout," Gaines barked as he stopped and turned back toward us. "He's not your friend. You're a throwaway."

I saw the set of John's jaw change as Gaines got back into his Bronco and sped away, tires squealing. John was embarrassed; I could tell—I just wasn't sure if it was because he had been caught by Gaines or because Gaines had told me he wasn't my friend.

John reached under his shirt and down into his waistband with his free hand, extracting a small cloth pouch. He tugged on the opening with his teeth and then dumped its contents on the center console, retrieving a key from the small pile of items. He unlocked the cuffs and then got out without a word, leaving me to unlock my side of the cuffs. He went to the back of the SUV and opened the hatch.

"What now?" I asked across the back seat.

"You're going home," he grunted as he pulled his bag out.

"I've still got two days," I protested.

He reached into a side pocket of his luggage and retrieved the spare key for the Explorer as I got out and started to walk back toward him. He tossed his bag back in and marched to the driver's side.

"In," he commanded.

I stood there, staring at him.

"Scott. Despite what he said, I had no intention of putting you in harm's way. We've lost our tracking on him now anyway. No need for you to be here," he said sincerely. "So get in the car. I'm taking you to LAX."

I grudgingly started to get in, but then remembered my phone. I turned and ran toward the spot where the Bronco had been parked.

"Scott," he yelled. "What are you doing?"

"Getting my phone and T-shirt," I insisted.

My phone was still there. I picked it up and checked it.

Whew! I thought. It still worked.

I bent to retrieve my Melvin's T-shirt as well, and then, as I stood up, a 'recall moment' struck me. I froze and stared at the location the Bronco had been in.

After a moment of virtual playback in my head, John yelled at me.

"Scott. Car. Now," he yelled over the cars.

I forced my legs to move against the 'zone out' I was experiencing and walked back to the SUV slowly, letting the memory roll out.

John's expression indicated he was in no mood for screwing around.

"Get in," he ordered.

I did, mechanically, my mind still spooling the imagery and playing back one frame at a time. As soon as I closed the door, he backed out aggressively and sped toward the exit on the opposite side Gaines had fled through. We were on the street heading toward LAX without a word.

My eyes were closed as I continued to review the images in my head.

I saw something. What was it? I asked myself. *The gun, the newspaper it had been wrapped in, the other papers folded into the crease: a map and a brochure.*

My mind replayed the scene. It slowed down the moment and focused on the papers wrapped around the gun. My mind froze on the brochure, and I mentally zoomed in on the writing.

Bad Hare Studios.

I smiled to myself and then turned to John.

"If you'll let me stay, I'll tell who he's going after," I said with a confident smirk.

"What?" he asked incredulously. "Did he tell you his plan before he locked us up and sped away?"

"Yes, he did," I said, smiling.

John raised an eyebrow as he pulled the truck over. "Okay. Spill it," he commanded.

"Then I can stay?" I asked, verifying his intent.

"Only until Sunday afternoon," he said. "I made a promise…remember?"

"No sense in me staying, then. I'd be surprised if you caught up to him before Monday," I said tauntingly.

"Why Monday? Enough games. What do you know?" He sighed in exasperation.

"He's after Buck Grimwall," I said. "If he hasn't been spooked, he'll probably hit him during his broadcast on Monday. You'll have the weekend to pick him up again."

"What makes you think that?" he asked, not doubting me but wanting my logic.

I looked at my watch. "Buck's show ended two hours ago," I said. "Unless Gaines is here to follow him, my guess is he's going to set up an automated firing system."

You're getting warm, my other voice said. I ignored it, not wanting to break the momentum I had just established with John.

"What makes you think he's going after Grimwall?" John asked doubtfully.

"He left Colorado Springs and came straight to Burbank, home of Bad Hare studios, after making a stop to procure rockets and remote equipment," I said, explaining my theory. "His sister was just killed by three men whose only connection to Burbank is Buck Grimwall. He's on a crusade."

"Flimsy," John muttered.

My voice had said I was getting warm. So far, my voice had been an asset, though annoying. I had to trust I was working in the right direction.

"Yes," I replied firmly. "Very flimsy. Not worth a call to the police even as a passing thought. But since we've tracked him across the whole country and ended up here and since that is the only tie we have at the moment, don't you think it's worth checking out?"

"Okay. It's more than anything I have. Let's work with that," he reasoned, making me smile inwardly. "The range on those projectiles is short, so the first thing we have to do is find out where Grimwall broadcasts from and see if there are any suitable places to fire from."

**

We drove to the Bad Hare studios and parked in the garage across the street.

"We should change," John said.

"Why?" I asked.

"Tourists don't dress like G-Men," he replied.

I squinted one eye at him and then thought of an idea to confirm my theory.

"No…but family visiting from out of town for a Marine award ceremony might," I said with a grin.

He looked at me for a moment, his mouth open, poised to say something. Then, he smiled. "Okay, son," he said through a smirk. "Don't go showing up your old man. It makes for awkward Thanksgivings."

"Yes, Pa," I replied as we started out of the garage toward the studio.

We entered the lobby of the studios and approached the guard desk.

"My son and I are stuck in town over the weekend and thought it would be nice if we could get a tour," John said. "We're both huge fans of Buck's. It would be such a thrill to see where he broadcasts from."

"Sorry. No tours after office hours," the guard replied, barely interested enough to look up from his Tom Clancy novel. "Come back on Monday. When the office is open, they sometimes allow meet and greets. But it's rare."

"That's a shame," John said in disappointment. "Like I said, we'll only be here over the weekend. We were here for an award ceremony for my other son. He's a Marine. He got the Silver Star this afternoon."

"Sorry. Can't help you," the guard said, unimpressed.

"Well can you tell me what floor the studio is on?" John asked. "Maybe we can see it from outside if we know where it is."

"Dad," I said, mocking his cover story. "Leave the man alone. He's just doing his job."

The guard looked at me and then back at John. "Buck broadcasts from the fifth floor. He has his own studio," he conveyed to John. "But your son is correct. I have to do a job, and I can't while chatting with you."

"Right. Right," John mumbled. "Sorry to be any trouble."

The guard rose from his chair, standing to an impressive height of about six foot two.

"I'm going to have to ask you to leave now," he announced, walking toward the door, clearly about to usher us out.

"I think Mark said he was going to tour the studio earlier," I said to John, and then turned to the guard. "My brother might have come in earlier. You couldn't miss him; he would have been in Marine fatigues."

"Yeah," the guard replied impatiently. "He came in during business hours, so he got a tour. Now I'm going to have to ask you to leave so I can get back to work."

"Would it be alright if I used your bathroom?" I asked, pointing at the restroom by the lobby.

The guard looked at me for a second before deciding it would be okay and nodding.

Having been granted permission, I walked behind the security desk and through the bathroom door. On my way, I glanced at the reception cubicle and noticed a stapled bundle of fire evacuation instructions taped to the inside wall of the cubicle.

Once in the bathroom, I urinated and washed my hands and then I removed my right shoe. On the way back out, I stopped at the reception desk and bent over, leaning against the cubicle and knocking the shoe on the floor as if to get a pebble or something out.

John and the security guard looked over to see me leaning against the cubicle, putting my shoe back on. They turned back to each other without noticing my hand had slipped to the inside wall of the low cube.

With my shoe back on, I stuffed the now-rolled packet of pages into the back of my waistband as if I were tucking in my shirt, and then straightened my jacket over them.

"Thanks," I said gratefully as the guard opened the door for us.

I heard the click of the lock as we exited.

As we walked back to the garage, I pulled out the papers I had stolen and began to go through them. He looked over and smiled.

"Okay," he muttered. "I'll give you that one."

"Just one?" I asked.

"Don't get greedy," he replied with a grin as we reached the SUV. "Let's find something close by and set up surveillance."

nine
Saturday, July 24th

Early a.m.—Burbank, California

John got us a hotel room outside of what he considered to be the range of the rockets Gaines had obtained. The room was at a suitable angle to view the windows on the broadcast studio from which Grimwall did his daily radio show, and the buildings were close enough to effectively shoot from.

We had set up wireless cameras, delivered to us in a nondescript-looking cardboard box at the hotel. Within an hour, we had all the equipment up and running, a nearly 180-degree view of the buildings surrounding and facing the studio side of the building.

John was convinced any attack Gaines would launch would be frontal. I wasn't sure. My biggest problem with John's scenario was the fact that it would take a great deal of effort for Gaines to configure a launch array to fire on and kill his target using the rockets. It would be far simpler to sit on a rooftop and shoot the man with a high-powered rifle—something that would be easily attainable.

"Windows on a broadcast studio would be thicker than regular glass," he said to me, "with multiple layers to deaden the sound in the booth. A rifle could be his end game, but he has to blast though the windows first. The rockets, on the other hand, could all be fired at once, or in two volleys, one after another."

I wasn't convinced. "It just seems like a really complex scenario for what would otherwise be a straightforward attack," I said. "Why wouldn't he just wait outside for Buck to show up for work and put one through his head from the roof across the street?"

John shrugged. "He got rockets," he replied. "If he had picked up a rifle in Barstow, I would agree with you, but he picked up eight rockets."

Mini rockets, my other voice suddenly inserted in my ear.

"Mini rockets," I repeated for John's benefit.

He didn't respond as he continued to watch the monitors on the wireless cameras he had set up facing various directions.

Over the next several hours, we saw nothing of interest—in fact, we saw little activity on any of the monitors. By 2:00 a.m., my eyes had started to cross from trying to pull together other clues from the data I had on my computer.

Shortly after 2:30 a.m., boredom and hunger finally got the best of me.

"I need a break," I stated. "Mind if I go down to the street and find some food?"

"Bring back some coffee," John replied without looking away from the monitors. "We already used up everything the hotel gave us for the room."

"Cool," I replied, grabbing a handful of bills off the table. "Back in a bit."

"Scott," he said as I was about to leave. "Be careful."

"Will do, boss," I responded and then closed the door behind me.

Once on the street, I located a greasy-looking pizza shop next to a medical marijuana dispensary. As in other cities where marijuana was legal, entrepreneurs had long ago discovered you could make as much money on food as you could with marijuana if it was located in close proximity to the marijuana. California towns were no different.

One could find all manner of food establishments selling overpriced munchies only feet away from dispensaries. Another benefit of selling food rather than marijuana was that there was no chance of DEA raids. As long as California considered it legal and the federal government did not, the safest way to make money on pot was to sell food *next door* to the pot.

As I entered the restaurant, I wondered what John would want. I had left my phone charging in the room, so there was no way for me to call and find out. I decided he was a roast beef sandwich man.

"Two roast beef subs, please," I said to the cute, but tired-looking, girl behind the counter.

She smiled weakly, punching the order into the computer.

"Everything?" she asked.

"Please," I said. "I'm going to get four waters from your cooler as well."

She nodded and rang them up.

While I waited for her to make my sandwiches, I took one of the waters and strolled leisurely back to the street. There I stood and drank my water as I looked around at the strange night creatures.

Early morning on a Saturday in Burbank was interesting to

observe. A number of people, dressed in their finest club attire, staggered down the sidewalk, most likely looking for breakfast or an after-party to crash.

After a moment of people watching, I turned to go back in, but as I did, the hairs on the back of my neck stood on end and a shiver rolled its way up my spine. I turned quickly to look around, but saw no immediate threat. I shrugged it off and went inside to collect my food.

Just as I exited the pizza and sub shop and was heading toward the small convenience store on the corner, I felt someone approaching me from the right side. I felt the gun in my ribs before it occurred to me to look.

"Hi, Scott," Gaines said in a friendly voice. "Let's take a walk."

Thanks for the warning, I thought crossly to my other voice. I looked at him, noting he had changed into civilian clothing—black jeans, a T-shirt, and a black zip-up hoodie.

"Hi, Mark," I said in a similarly friendly tone. "Want a sandwich? I have enough for two."

"No thanks," he replied, placing his arm across my shoulder. "I've eaten. But keep a firm grip on those bags."

In all the rush to find him and thwart his plans, it had never occurred to me to be on guard—though it should have. He had already detected our presence once and let us go—or maybe I was just a computer geek playing spy and didn't really know what the hell I was doing.

"Down here," he muttered, steering me into an alley.

He walked me down a narrow driveway between buildings and then around a corner so he had some privacy.

"Twice in one day," he observed. He was behind me, the barrel of his gun now pressed against the base of my skull.

Slowly, non-threateningly, I raised my hands as I turned. When I was about halfway into my turn, I lifted my hand, gently, without sudden movement, and began to push his barrel away from my head.

The subtle movement seemed to confuse him for a moment. He shoved me away from him and brought the barrel back in line with my face.

Damn, that's a big gun!

"Don't think you know me, boy," he barked threateningly. "You'll end up a chalk outline."

"I don't claim to know you, but I do understand what you are doing," I claimed, trying to lower my heart rate and appear calm.

"You don't know shit," he sneered.

"I know more than you think I do," I said—maybe a mistake.

"Yeah?" he questioned, suddenly looking at me with curiosity. "No way did John find me twice. It had to be you. Maybe I should just pop you here and change directions again."

"Then you wouldn't be fixing anything. You'd just be another psycho with a gun," I stated coldly, having to flip a coin and guess his motivation—I went with "he's bat shit crazy."

I saw anger flash across his face and his grasp on the pistol grip tighten. I had struck a nerve. He wasn't fully at peace with his actions and was having a hard time reconciling them with his concept of self. *Apparently my psych sessions are paying off,* I thought.

"I did the same thing," I said, adjusting my approach. "Don't get me wrong. I haven't seen nearly what you have, I know that. And my experience is that of rank amateur compared to your training and missions. But I was in a similar place several months ago."

"You know nothing," he hissed through his teeth, but I could see the doubt on his face.

"I don't claim to. Just…I know what it's like to go on autopilot when someone you love gets hurt," I said, slowing my speech and softening the tone.

I could see the pain cross his face. But it was quickly replaced by anger.

"Move," he ordered, pointing down the alley.

We walked for a short distance and then turned down another side alley.

"We're not here to hurt you," I added, trying to keep the dialogue flowing. "If we were, it wouldn't be just me and John."

"Shut up," he replied in a hiss.

We passed a couple of restaurant workers taking a smoke break behind one building, and I saw him put his gun into the folds of the jacket he carried. A brief desire to bolt came over me, but it quickly dissipated as the two nodded at us and then disappeared back through the door into the kitchen.

After a short distance further down the alley, we came to a stairway that descended half a story from street level.

"Down there," he said, giving me a slight shove toward the stairs.

I descended the stairs and went through the door at the bottom. Once in, he took my arm and shoved me roughly down a narrow hallway and through a door at the end.

"Sit," he commanded, pointing at an old metal office chair on wheels.

I did as ordered, and he began tying my hands and feet with a cotton cord. I wasn't afraid. I may have been a little naïve about my situation, but I didn't feel he would do me any harm—or at the least, he wouldn't kill me. This guy, after all, was a Boy Scout like me.

"Nothing you've done so far would be held against you," I said calmly as he tied me to the chair.

"Shut up," he said.

"I don't think a jury in Colorado would convict you for killing the murderers of your sister and her family," I continued. "Especially since it appears you drove straight there without—"

My sentence was cut off with a sharp backhand to my face. So much for not being hurt. I couldn't let myself forget this guy was a trained killer who was suffering great grief and under tremendous stress.

I tasted blood in my mouth, turned my head away from him and spat dark red on the floor. I remained silent for a moment.

When he had finished binding me, he walked over to a box and set his handgun down and grabbed a bottle of water, drinking deeply. He plopped down in a chair identical to mine.

"How did you find me?" he asked calmly. I'd heard the tone before—the calm, emotionless question followed by flame applied to my shoulder, arm, and chest in Amsterdam at the hands of Majmun the "Monkey." I wouldn't give him a reason to be any more of a bad guy. I wanted to be his friend.

"When you pulled the gun on me in the garage. I saw the map and studio brochure," I replied, trying to sound as helpful as possible. I even smiled a little.

"The garage, huh? Do you think this is a game?" he asked.

"Not at all. I'm taking it very seriously. Seriously enough to hop on a plane on a Thursday night and start searching for someone who, *I was told*, was a friend of John's." I let my tone slip into a sort of annoyed lecture as if I were pissed off that I had been somewhat misled by John.

"Pffft. *John* is no friend to anyone but John," he scoffed, placing emphasis on the first name.

I guessed he found it somewhat distasteful that someone like me might be on a first name basis with someone he called *Captain*.

"He's been pretty friendly to me. Among other things, he saved my life and broke the rules to get me access to someone I cared about," I explained. "Once I was back home, he followed up, making sure I got the treatment I needed…annoyingly so," I said, turning my head to spit more blood.

"Oh he's good at breaking the rules when it suits his

purposes. As for saving your life—I know the story. If you had been outside of his op when shit went south, he wouldn't have lifted a finger," he said with a knowing grin. "You'd have been on your own with your dick flapping in the wind."

I loved the colorful phrases I'd heard since being around the military set.

"I didn't get that sense," I replied unemotionally.

"Whatever. What do I know anyway?" he muttered.

A pout? This is a guy who doesn't feel understood, I thought. I could use that.

"You didn't feel finished after you killed Roy Mullen and his pals, did you?" I asked.

He turned and looked at me for a moment, as if he were trying to see behind my skin.

I looked around the cluttered basement, soaking in the scenery. We were apparently downstairs from a closed restaurant, judging by the old canned food and the stacks of cheap plates and bowls.

"It takes longer for the fire to die when you act on anger," I continued.

"Shut up."

I didn't. I could tell he was having a moral crisis over what he had done to his sister's murderers—I was going to use it to my advantage.

"Sometimes it just feeds the fire," I added, as if in passing, as I continued to search my surroundings with my eyes. *Kitchen knives.* If left alone, I would be able to cut myself free. I didn't let my eyes linger on them but rather continued to scan the room.

"It took me a long time to realize that after justice was served, the anger I felt was at myself," I said, manufacturing a fictional parallel to his situation.

He looked at me, tilting his head. I had him interested.

"And for every asshole I put down, it only made me want to handle more."

"Ha! You're more fucked up than I am."

I gave short matter-of-fact nod as I continued to look around, noting the metal storage cage behind us.

"For a long time I became the bully," I continued. "Or the 'bully hunter,' rather."

"If you think your high school vigilante story is going to impress me, you aren't as smart as I thought," he warned.

I shrugged.

"The personalities we form in school follow us the rest of our lives," I said. "I have no doubt I wouldn't have even considered getting on the plane for Amsterdam if it hadn't been for how I was in school."

He sat and listened, turning his head to the side as my words played. It seemed he was trying to overlay what I was saying onto his life. It's possible he knew what he was doing was wrong and desperately wanted to find a way of extricating himself from it—or maybe he thought he was just learning more about me.

"I have to admit though. I felt it popping up in Mimon," I said, turning my gaze to him, reminding him I had seen action as well. A brother in arms.

"Did you get the rush?" he asked.

"The rush?" I asked.

"The big endorphin flood when you kill someone in an adrenaline moment?" he explained.

"No endorphin rush," I replied casually, as if I knew all the psychological ins and outs of killing someone.

"Ah. So you got the time warp," he said knowingly.

He really seems to want to talk, I thought. "Yeah," I said with mild surprise.

He sat back in his chair, showing less tension than he had

earlier. "How many did you kill?"

"I shot four. Though I don't remember the last one." I spoke as if I had already worked through it, but there was a sudden pinch in my chest. It must have showed on my face because he commented on it.

"Still working on it, huh?" he asked, smiling, though not sympathetically.

I nodded. Something was wrong though—a shift in the tone, and it was starting to worry me.

"You said you shot four," he continued, trying to draw more information out. This was turning in a direction I hadn't anticipated.

"Yeah. There were also about a dozen who got pulled out the back of a cargo plane when Nick and I left the plane," I added.

"Nick?!" he exclaimed with raised eyebrows. "How is the old Spartan?"

"Don't know. I haven't seen him since Europe. But he was fine then—Spartan?"

"Yeah. A real live relic of the warrior class. His family name is older than the Battle of Thermopylae. He didn't regale you with stories of Horiatis fighting at the hot gates?"

I shook my head.

"Too bad," he mused. "He's a real hoot when he acts out the Phalanx."

My database brain accessed information on 'Phalanx,' complete with imagery:

A battle configuration consisting of lines of soldiers with large shields, twelve men deep, in which the soldier behind you pushed you forward, in formation, to slowly roll over the opposing army's line, stabbing with spears and short swords as you went. Once the enemy line had collapsed on one side, the Phalanx would split and then flank the remaining enemy, crushing them between an L-

shaped wedge.

I nodded as the visualization played through my head.

"So you're having dreams still?" he asked.

"Sometimes," I replied solemnly, but I couldn't help but feel I was being led into an ambush of some sort. "Less and less."

He nodded and then a sly grin appeared on his face. "They don't ever go away for good."

That was disconcerting. His simple statement shook me, and it must have shown on my face.

"And after you kill and get a rush the first time, it comes back and visits all the time," he continued. "Like an old friend, rating your actions. Comparing each kill to all the others."

His tone had changed. His face grew dark and his smile more sinister. I had made a mistake.

"And before long, the rush is counseling you on what to do. Whipping you into a frenzy as you are about to add another notch on your trophy stick." He was getting calmer, cooler. His mood had taken a dark turn—he *was* crazy and he was here to execute more revenge, and I was dumb enough to think I could work with that.

Don't let your fear make those sorts of judgments, came a whisper from my other voice.

He stood and walked toward me. For a brief, panic-stricken moment, I thought I was about to die. But he grabbed the back to the office chair, spun me around facing the other direction, and then rolled me into the storage cage. He tossed a five-gallon bucket in behind me, the bag of food I had purchased before he captured me, and two liter bottles of water.

"I have no doubt you will make short work of those ropes once I'm gone," he conceded as he padlocked the cage closed. "But I'll bring back a change of clothes for you just in case. See you tomorrow." Then he shouldered his bag and walked out.

As soon as he was gone, I looked around for something to cut myself free. The knives, unfortunately, were on the other side of the cage door. On the floor was a lid from a can. Its ragged metal edge was perfect to slice the ropes.

I tipped the chair over sideways and landed with a crash and then pushed myself around sideways with the toe of my shoe until I could reach the lid with my fingers. As soon as I got my fingers on it, I began slicing the thick cotton cord with the edge.

What the hell is going on in your head, Mark? Are you or aren't you nuts?

As I sliced through the first few strands, I began feeling more optimistic again.

Well, you didn't kill me—that's a promising start.

**

4:02 a.m.

JOHN TEMPLE looked at his watch before looking around the room just to confirm he hadn't missed Scott's return.

He pulled out his phone and dialed Scott's number. A second later, he heard the phone ring on the other side of the room, plugged into the wall and sitting next to Scott's laptop.

"Shit!" he exclaimed as he ended the call.

"God damn it, Scott," he muttered under his breath as he left the room.

He was mentally kicking himself for not being more careful. Scott seemed to be so capable that John sometimes forgot he was not a trained operative.

This op was blown because Scott had been captured. At least, he hoped he had only been captured. He didn't want to think of the other possibility. He didn't honestly believe Mark Gaines would kill Scott unless he felt threatened by him. But then again, two days earlier, he didn't think Gaines was capable of castrating and burning three men alive, either.

As he walked out onto the street, distracted by the thought of losing Scott, he didn't notice the man watching him exit the hotel.

**

THE MAN Harbinger had sent to find Gaines watched as John exited the hotel and turned right down the street.

As soon as John disappeared around the corner, the man pulled out his phone and dialed Heinrich Braun.

"We might have a complication," he said. "I think I just saw the former CIA Deputy Station Chief for Berlin."

"How sure are you that it's him?" Braun asked.

"Pretty sure," the man replied. "I saw him a few years ago in Riyadh at a summit. I was on a security detail for the Syrian delegation."

There was a pause.

"Would he recognize you?" Braun finally asked.

"I can't be sure," he replied as he rounded the corner, catching sight of John again.

"I can't emphasize this enough. *Discreetly* follow him," Braun said. "If he finds Gaines before we do, I want to be able to act immediately."

"Yes, sir," the man replied. "Do you want the surveillance techs on him as well?"

"No sense in putting all our eggs in one basket," Braun argued. "One set of eyes at a time should be enough. Hand off to the others in rotation."

"Understood," he replied. "I'm on him now."

"Call me if anything changes," Braun said, then hung up.

The man, a mercenary hired by Harbinger and detailed to Braun, began following John at a discreet distance. Unlike many of his combat-hardened comrades, this man had worked private security and was quite adept at disappearing in a crowd of people.

He watched from a good distance away, but at one point, his

quarry inexplicably stopped and looked around as if he felt something was off.

The man was much more careful after that and began his handoff earlier than planned.

By the time the mercenary handed the tail off to his partner, he was convinced that John was blindly searching in circles.

He wondered if Temple was acting as a decoy of some sort but then dismissed the thought immediately. There was no APB out on Gaines, the former Station Chief had not made any indication he was communicating with anyone, and there was a certain *desperation* to his movements.

Temple was acting alone, the man concluded.

He said as much to his relief before the hand off. "I don't think he's got any idea where he's going," he said to his partner. "But don't let him lull you into being sloppy. He's been at this longer than we've been alive."

"Got it," his partner said. "Anything else?"

"If he finds something, don't move in on your own," he warned. "He's a stone-cold killer."

His partner rolled his eyes. "If you say so."

"I say so," he reiterated.

**

Time Unknown

I had managed to get myself cut free in a matter of minutes using the ragged edge of the tin can top. I took a few minutes to test the strength of the supply cage I was trapped in before sitting to figure out my next steps.

I absently reached into the food bag and grabbed whatever was closest. I ate one of the two subs I had purchased and drank one of the bottles of water. As I sat and chewed the soggy sandwich, I looked at every inch of the cage, letting my flowchart brain absorb all of the information.

My mind began randomly throwing ideas and calculations about weak points, material strength, and design flaws. I let it flow without trying to control the stream of information.

"Any ideas on how we can get out of here?" I muttered to my other voice.

No response; it was quite a one-sided relationship.

Once I had finished enough of the sandwich to give me a stomachache, I stood and went to the wall of the cage. I moved boxes and cans away from the metal mesh and examined the connection to the bottom rail.

It was welded.

I kicked at the base a few times, testing the strength of the weld, and I was able to break it in a couple of locations, but all it did was bow the mesh out a little… Not even enough to slip my fingers through.

After testing various locations of the cage for weakness for a very long time—though I couldn't be sure since I had left my watch sitting next to my phone in the hotel room—the flow of ideas had shrunk to a trickle. I had bruised the ball of my foot kicking at the metal mesh and bars, my leg was tired and heavy, and my breath was labored from stress and exertion. I plopped down on a pile of flattened cardboard boxes and leaned against a stack of cartons

"Shit, shit, shit," I muttered, knocking the back of my head against the cartons with each utterance.

It didn't work…I still couldn't think of anything.

As I sat in the dim light of the single light bulb on the ceiling of the cage, I let my eyes wander across the room outside my prison. In the corner of the room opposite the cage, I saw a box of the same size Gaines had picked up in Barstow. Next to it was a larger cardboard box and what looked like a metal case of some sort.

I couldn't bring myself to get up and take a closer look as I knew it would only frustrate me more.

"Jooooohn!" I yelled at the ceiling.

I listened to see if there was any response. All I heard were the sounds of rodents chewing on something in the next room.

I dropped my head and rubbed my tired eyes.

"I changed my mind, John," I muttered. "I don't want to be a spy."

I turned my head, rubbing my eye against the palm of my hand, and when I opened it, my sight came to rest on the crossbar of the heavy shelving unit in the cage.

My flow chart mind examined the structure and superimposed even the hidden parts of it, such as the hooks and screws that held it together.

Use it, my other voice whispered into my ear.

Spurred on by the voice, I got up from my resting place and examined it more closely.

There was nothing of use to hammer or cut heavy wire mesh with, but the shelves themselves were made of heavy, square, tubular steel with thick steel hooks for hanging on the posts. I closed my eyes.

Virtual images of the shelf pieces flitted across my eyelids in a jumble and then coalesced into a recognizable form—

A fulcrum and lever! I thought. *Give me a place to stand and with a lever I will move the whole world.*

"Thank you, Archimedes," I muttered.

I unloaded the cans from the bottom shelf and kicked one of the crossbars several times until it unhooked from the frame. Then I went to the other side and did the same at that end.

As soon as it was free, I grabbed a wooden rolling pin from the top shelf and placed it on the floor parallel to the cage wall.

"Okay, Archimedes," I muttered. "Don't let me down."

I wedged the heavy hook into the mesh of the cage and pressed on the other end of the bar with all my weight.

It moved.

I bounced. *ZIP*. The mesh made a sound as the hook sliced through several strands.

"Not exactly what I had in mind, but I'll take it," I muttered, pleased with the accidental discovery of a slicing tool.

I moved the bar over about two feet and repeated the procedure. *ZIP!*

I kicked at the mesh with my foot until the weld broke at the base, and I continued to kick until it rolled up outside the cage. It still wasn't enough to crawl under, but it was a start.

I pulled a short section of square tubing from the shelves and took down another rolling pin. I placed the tubing across the two rolling pins, raising my fulcrum a few extra inches, and then I placed the hook through the mesh and jumped on it.

ZIP. Several more inches of mesh were cut loose. As soon as I had kicked the mesh out so that it curled up, I got down on the floor and tried to squeeze through. It was tight, but I managed to work my head and shoulders through.

It's funny how your priorities change once you've had a windfall. While in the cage, all I could think about was getting out and going back home with an interesting story to tell. But as soon as I pulled myself free, all I wanted was to look in the boxes in the corner.

I lay on the cool concrete floor for a few minutes, breathing heavily from my exertion, and then pushed myself to my feet. Without so much as looking at the exit, I went to the corner and opened the cardboard boxes. The small one was empty, but the larger one had two remote surveillance screens inside, one focused on a parking space somewhere and the other facing down a street.

It only took me a moment longer to realize it was the same street, and sub shop I had just gotten my food from.

"That's how you found me," I muttered in admiration. "But what did you do with the rockets, Mark?" I asked quietly.

Next to the boxes was a pile of torn cardboard covered in metal filings. I also saw cardboard with fresh black spray paint on it. I reached over and touched it with my fingertips. It was still tacky to the touch.

I lifted the cardboard and saw a small device. I didn't know what I was looking at, but it was about the size of a notebook, made of metal, and had an angular frame under it, tilting it up approximately forty-five degrees from the ground. On top was a strip of black plastic taped across the top edge. I lifted the plastic and saw the tips of eight projectiles.

The rockets!

"What are you going to do with these?" I muttered.

On the flat part of the metal device were four large magnets. I picked up a metal can and placed it on one of them. The powerful magnet nearly jerked it out of my hands as it got close and it took a great deal of effort to pull it off again. They were very powerful magnets.

Looking around, I saw nothing else of interest and reached for the wheeled metal case pressed against the wall. I pulled on its hinged lid by the latch, opening it to reveal an interesting array of items. On top were several pages of printout. I reached in and gently lifted one corner to look beneath, and I discovered a phone, some tools, and remote key fobs.

I pulled the sheets of paper all the way out and began thumbing through them as I picked up the phone and then dialed John's number.

"Oh!" I exclaimed as the phone started to ring. "Multi-tool!"

I grabbed the substantial-looking modern equivalent to a Swiss army knife, turning it over once before John answered.

"Temple," came John's voice from the other end as I stuffed the tool into my pocket.

"Hey there," I said casually as I started looking at the numbers on the sheets.

"Where the hell are you?" he asked, the tension in his voice higher than I had ever heard it.

"I'm about three blocks from the hotel," I replied, noting the sheets were split printouts—not all the information was on one line. "Gaines caught me when I went to get food."

There was a short pause. "Where is he now?" John asked.

"I don't know," I replied as I continued to flip through the pages. "He left several hours ago. But he left some of his stuff here, including this phone."

"Jesus," John muttered. "Are you hurt?"

"Not really. But one of those subs I got for us really did a number on my stomach," I replied, grinning. "He locked me in a metal cage, but I got out."

"You got… Where are you?" he asked again.

"Starting from the corner where the pizza shop is, walk north to the next street and turn left," I said, as I discovered the names portion of the data was on the back sheets. "Then—"

"Who the hell are you?" came a voice from behind me.

I turned and saw a woman holding a large revolver in my face—*large* being relative of course. Any gun in your face is going to seem large.

She was gorgeous. If not for the fact that she was holding a gun on me, I might have flirted with her. She had light brown skin with a glow that suggested she spent a lot of time in the sun. Her long hair looked like onyx, poured in liquid form over her shoulders—and her lips…I had seen those lips before… Angelina. Yeah, definitely Angelina lips. She was a real knockout.

"I asked you a question," she reiterated, her features calm, her hand steady. The tone of her voice suggested I was going to have to answer her—she wasn't nervous about holding a gun on someone.

"I have to go," I said to John. "A very attractive woman is

holding a gun on me."

Her cheeks flushed.

I pressed one of the number keys instead of the 'end' button, and then tossed the phone back into the box, followed by the papers, making sure they covered it. If I was lucky, she wouldn't look in and see I still had a live connection.

"Hi," I chirped, smiling and reaching my hand out to shake. "I'm Scott Wolfe."

She raised her gun a few inches, indicating she would not be shaking hands with me.

"That doesn't really answer my question," she said, flicking her gun with her wrist in the universal sign of *hands up or else*. "Why are you here?"

"That's technically a different question than the one you asked before," I said, smiling as I lifted my hands.

"Do you really think this is a good time to be a smart ass?" she threatened.

"Funny. You aren't the first person to ask me that today." I smirked.

She pressed her lips together tightly and tensed her gun hand.

"But I'm here because a big, goofy-looking guy with a hoodie stuck a gun in my back and brought me here. He locked me in there." I pointed at the cage.

"Jesus, Mark," she muttered and then looked at me through slitted eyes. "How'd you get out?"

I shrugged. I didn't want to give up all my secrets. Besides, if I could get her to look for my escape route, she might drop her focus momentarily so I could escape or get her gun away from her.

She looked over at the cage, seeing it was still padlocked, and began to scan the sides. As soon as she saw the bent metal mesh, she returned her attention to me. I had moved a step closer to her.

Oops!

She raised her gun up to my nose threateningly, her brow etched with a deep furrow of anger.

"Back up."

I did as ordered.

"Who are you with?" she asked.

"TravTech," I replied calmly. "We are a travel technology and computer security company."

She must have figured she wouldn't get a straight answer from me because she reached into her shoulder bag and pulled out a pair of black zip cuffs like law enforcement uses. She tossed them on the floor in front of me.

"Put those on," she ordered, her gun and voice never wavering—there was a command quality in her voice that made me suspect she was law enforcement.

I picked up the zip cuffs and did as she ordered.

"Behind your back," she added as I slipped my hand through one side.

I put them on behind me and then turned my back to her when she flicked her gun directing me to do so. She then reached out and cinched them down very tightly.

"Ow," I complained.

"Now, sit," she commanded, pointing at a stack of boxed cans next to the wall.

I again complied, being very careful not to give her the impression I would disobey her at all.

"Who are you?" I asked.

"None of your fuckin' business," she responded mildly, though with no anger.

"I know who Mark is," I said. "How do you know him?"

She squinted her eyes at me and tilted her head to the side. "How do you know who Mark is?" she asked.

"I'm here to help find him," I said. "I work with his old boss."

"You said you're with TravTech," she said, testing my knowledge and truthfulness.

"Contract, tech support," I replied, smiling.

"So who is his old boss?" the woman asked. "Who does he work for?"

It was my turn to narrow my eyes at her. "I'm sorry, but I'm not at liberty to discuss it," I replied. "Besides, how do I even know you're friends with Mark? You could be hunting him."

"Ha!" she exclaimed. "You were the one who was locked up."

I looked over at the cage. "Yeah, well, not everybody sees when you're trying to help them."

She thought about that response for a moment and then reached into her bag and pulled her phone out. She dialed. The phone in the box beeped, and she immediately walked over to it.

"Son of a bitch," she muttered—presumably because she saw that the previous call was still active.

She quickly pulled the phone out of the box and ended the call.

"Who were you talking to?" she asked.

I plastered an innocent look on my face and shrugged.

"This isn't a fucking game!" she yelled, crossing the room quickly.

"I've heard that one today too," I muttered.

She was about to strike me across the face with her revolver when John came into the room behind her, pointing his gun at her.

"Stop," he commanded quietly.

She turned, but he had the drop on her. She immediately resigned herself to her fate and held her hands up, letting the revolver dangle from her finger by the trigger guard.

"Thanks." I turned toward John, relief evident in my voice. "I wasn't looking forward to losing any teeth."

"Why didn't you just get out of here when you got free?" he asked as he took her revolver and tossed it across the room onto a stack of cardboard.

"Then I wouldn't have met this lovely lady," I responded, grinning. "Besides. If he had come back and seen me gone, he might have cleared out."

"What were you going to do if he came back?" John asked as he shoved the woman down to a seated position. "Disarm him with your charm? You left your phone, your weapon, and your wallet in the room."

I shrugged. "You're the spy, I'm just tech support." *Why is everyone so dead set on complaining about me today?*

The look on his face instantly revealed his displeasure at my statement.

"Spy?" the woman asked, looking at me. "So you were telling the truth?"

"I always tell the truth," I replied with a grin.

"Bullshit," John muttered as he walked toward me, presumably to free me—but he never got the chance. Mark Gaines suddenly appeared in the doorway behind John—he was flying through the air before John knew he was there.

"Behind you!" I yelled, but it was too late. Gaines had brought the pistol grip of his giant handgun down on the back of John's skull. He dropped like a sack of potatoes into the floor.

Gaines wasted no time admiring his handiwork. His gun was in my face immediately.

**

THE MAN who had been following John Temple watched from a block away as he turned down an alley with his phone pressed to his ear. Temple had seemed to change directions abruptly and head off in single-minded fashion.

The man pulled his phone out as he approached the corner. The call was answered on the first ring.

"Yes," Heinrich Braun answered.

"I think Temple might have found something," the man said. "I just lost sight of him, but I should—"

The man stopped in his tracks, seeing Gaines maneuver around a dumpster and then disappear down the alley as well.

"I just saw Gaines," he said. "Hold on."

He ran to the corner and carefully looked around the edge of the building. He saw no one.

"They are in an alley on Third about half a block from Olive," he said. "If you'll give me a few minutes, I'll tell you which building they are in."

"No," Braun snapped. "Wait until we can rendezvous. I can be there in fifteen minutes."

"But what if—" the man started to reply.

"Wait," Braun said firmly. "Unless they look to be leaving, do not compromise yourself. Wait for backup."

Braun ended the call before he could respond. The man tucked himself into a window well so he could look down the alley discretely.

I could take 'em, he thought sullenly.

**

"You annoying prick," Gaines growled with a sneer.

"What?" I asked innocently, trying not to show my anger over the assault on John. "I was just sitting here."

"When I came in, he was going through your box," the woman said, rising to join him in front of me. "He got a call out on your phone."

"What did you tell them?" Gaines asked the woman without taking his eyes off me. I guessed he didn't ask me because he knew he wouldn't get a straight answer.

"Nothing," she replied defensively. "He was in the middle of the call when I came in on him. I cuffed him and was questioning him when that other guy came in."

"That's John Fucking Temple," Gaines said. "My old boss."

I looked at the woman and smiled. "See, I always tell the truth."

She shot me a hard look and then turned to Mark. "What do you want me to do?" she asked with a hushed voice, as if it would prevent me from hearing.

"Get the account lists and go," he said—normal voice. "It's a problem anyone knows you were here."

"What does that mean?" she asked and then looked down at John's limp form. "Mark, you can't kill them."

"I wouldn't count on that," he countered with a sneer, but I could tell he had no intention of killing us—he was trying to instill fear in me, most likely to get me to behave.

"Mark—" she protested.

"Get the list and go before you end up like Dee," he snapped with anger bubbling up in his voice.

I wasn't sure who Dee was, but whatever happened to her clearly wasn't pleasant. The woman pulled the papers out of the top of his metal box and stuffed them into her bag.

Gaines looked over at the curled mesh on the cage. "Do you have more cuffs?" he asked her, again without turning his attention from me. For some reason, I got the feeling he didn't trust me.

The woman reached into her bag and pulled out several more sets of zip cuffs and then handed them to him. He took them without looking.

"You won't hear from me again for a while," he said. "Take those pages and find out what the upstream source is. It's going to get sloppy soon."

"Are you going to be okay?" she asked.

"Go," he ordered sharply.

She started to leave and then, at the doorway, she turned. "I'm sorry about your sister," she said with sadness in her voice.

"Go!" he yelled.

She paused for a moment, staring at his back, and then turned and left. There was another moment of him just staring at me with anger on his face, and then he abruptly dropped to his knee and rolled John onto his belly, zip cuffing his hands behind his back.

"Who's Dee?" I asked.

No response, but I saw his jaw set in a hard line. The mention of her caused anger to well up in him.

"I don't understand what it is you are involved with," I said calmly. "I thought you were just after the guys who killed your sister. If there's more, you should ask John for help. I know—"

Gaines rose abruptly and kicked me in the chest, sending me and the stack of cartons tumbling backwards.

"Keep your fucking mouth shut," he yelled. "Don't talk to me. Don't talk about my sister and don't talk about Dee. One more fucking word and I'll put a bullet in your head."

I rolled onto my side and looked at him. He stood there, red-faced, veins bulging in his neck and forehead and, more importantly, that hand canon of his pointing directly at my face. I decided to keep my mouth shut for the time being.

As soon as he had John tightly cuffed, he walked over to his metal box and pulled out his phone, stuffing it in his pocket after checking the call log. He began to move back toward John when he suddenly stopped and looked into his box again, pausing over it briefly.

SNIP.

He abruptly launched himself toward me upon discovering his multi-tool missing, but he was too late—my hands were free.

Just as he arrived over me, I pushed sideways and kicked out, the toe of my boot making solid contact with his wrist as I rolled. His heavy hand cannon went clanking to the ground.

He didn't go for the gun, instead, he let his momentum propel him toward me in my roll. He fell down heavily on my side, his elbow striking my shoulder and chest. He tried to bring his knee up, but I had rolled too far for it to make contact. In desperation, I shoved one of the can-filled cartons between us and used the moment to push myself backwards toward his metal box. I picked it up, accidentally dumping its contents, and used it as a shield as his foot came stomping down toward me.

I pushed him away with the box, sending him several feet backwards. A stunned look appeared on his face; he hadn't expected me to display such strength, I assumed. But he quickly regained his bearings and charged again, feet and fists flying as I struggled to get back to my feet and evade his assault.

He launched into a spinning back punch, connecting solidly with my cheekbone—but while his back was to me, I heard a metallic clacking sound. It dawned on me too late that he had produced a collapsible striking baton and was whipping it around with his other arm as he continued into his spin. My shoulder went up to try and deflect it, and though it glanced painfully off my shoulder, it still connected solidly with my head.

Panic welled up in me as the darkness started to close in like it had another time before.

Where was that? I heard my other voice ask tauntingly.

Then I remembered.

Amsterdam. Majmun. The Bosnian Serb thug who had tortured me in the Russian safe house.

As the darkness closed in, I felt my knees begin to buckle. Pain shot through my skull to the backs of my eyes. Then I suddenly remembered flame against my skin and the smell of my own burning flesh.

Rage exploded through my head and my chest like the torch

fire that had burned me. I would *not* be weak again. I would *not* allow anyone to turn me into a victim. The rage bubbled up through my throat.

I heard my voice as if it had come from another room. "Fuck you."

And the rage continued to rise. It stiffened my legs, tensed the muscles in my neck. The darkness stopped closing in on me.

Then suddenly, as if I were watching from above, I saw my body twist—frighteningly fast. Powerful climber's hands grasped Gaines's wrist before he could react.

The look on his face made me chuckle to myself. No fear—genuine surprise.

I heard myself again. "Fuck you." My fingers pressed into the junction of bones in his wrist as if they were granite and I was holding on for dear life.

I felt and then saw his other hand whipping toward me. I watched as if a spectator as my arm flew up in defense—elbow and forearm—blocking his other blow, my grip still firmly around his wrist.

I saw pain in his face as he tried to twist away. I let him roll to the floor without releasing him, clearly sending more pain up his arm. He tried to bring his leg up for a kick.

"Fuck you!" I heard myself yell as I continued to float above the scene, watching as my knee rose of its own volition—giving me a brief flashback of the fight in the cargo plane above the Czech countryside. My knee caught the entire blow with a kick of its own, and then I was falling forward on top of him.

I watched from the ceiling as my head came crashing forward against the bridge of his nose, making it erupt with blood.

He tried to wrench his left hand free. I crushed down hard on his wrist, feeling the bones begin to separate and crunch beneath my grip.

"Fuck you!" I screamed.

I could feel my face flush with blood. From my ethereal position above the fray, I could see the veins in my neck and face bulging—looking almost as if they were about to burst, yet I also felt my body in a way I never had before—every nerve and muscle a precise mechanism in a complex system.

His other elbow struck down toward my head and shoulder, but my arm was there to deflect it before it reached its target, and then I followed it into the side of his head with a brutal punch. I lifted my head high and then let it fall again, pounding my forehead again into his nose.

I was suddenly more in my body again. Gaines was on the ground, choking on the blood from his nose, his wrists tucked under him in some sort of reflexive protective move.

I stood over him, eyes wide, breathing heavily, my hands still curled and tense, ready for more. He wouldn't look up at me. It pissed me off.

"Get up!" I yelled.

With that, I kicked his back. He curled more tightly, but he flailed with his feet in a weak defensive move.

The rage just kept rolling in on me, crashing, one wave on top of another.

I jumped on him and began pounding his already-bloodied face. The spray of blood into my eyes just made me more angry, and I raised my hands, clasped together, ready to hammer double-fisted blows down on his face—but I heard something that made me stop, my hands still raised high above my head.

"Scott!" I heard the voice as if it were being yelled from a long distance away.

I stood, looking down at the bloodied mess on the floor in front of me. For a moment I tried to get my mind to assess my surroundings, but it wouldn't focus. My body seemed to want to fight some more. I looked down at Gaines; he was wheezing through his broken nose. His mouth and eyes were now broken, bruised, and swelling.

I kicked a stack of boxes to let off the last round of blows I still had coiled up inside me and then stormed out of the storage cellar and into the alley.

It was nearly midday. I breathed in deeply, leaning against the wall, trying to calm myself and then slid to the ground, still breathing heavily. I looked at my hands. They were shaking—skin had peeled from my knuckles, and they were covered in blood—a lot of blood

All sense of time and bearing was absent. I had no idea how long I sat there.

"Scott!" I heard from the side.

I ignored the voice as I continued to examine the bloody hands, wondering who they belonged to. They didn't appear to be mine, even though they were right in front of me. I heard foot falls as someone ran toward me from the cellar below.

I felt a hand on my shoulder, and I lashed out with my bloody claw, grabbing another wrist. My foot went up, looking for something warm to crush. An arm rose up and blocked my kick, but I sent my opponent rolling to the ground. I looked him in the face…it was a familiar face.

The man lay on the ground, a few feet away from me, cradling his wrist with the other hand.

"Scott!" he yelled. "Snap out of it! It's over."

It was John. I was looking down at him. I didn't remember getting to my feet, but there I was, standing over him, the blood back in my face, fists clenched, breathing heavily through my mouth. I immediately plopped back down on the ground and dropped my head between my knees.

I was suddenly aware of everything around me, as if in a super-heightened state of being. It was almost as if I were stuck partially outside myself—unable to 're-seat' fully within my body.

Without even looking up, I knew what was going on around me—how far the walls of the alley were from each other, how many windows looked down, the number of AC units facing the alley, and how many were running.

I was in an intensely heightened state of awareness—more so than I had ever felt before.

John stood, but kept his distance. I heard him as he walked into the cellar. I counted his steps as he disappeared into the half basement. In a few moments, I heard his voice as he approached the door again from inside. He was talking on the phone.

"…an asset. Medical personnel and a cleanup unit," I heard him say as he stepped back into the alley.

He closed his phone and put it back in his pocket. I could sense him standing near, though not too close to me. He squatted down in front of me, and I could feel him staring for long moments before he spoke.

"Are you injured?" he asked calmly.

I couldn't find words yet.

"Scott. Are you injured?" he asked again, more insistently that time.

I still couldn't speak, but I shook my head.

"Okay. Catch your breath. A cleanup team is on its way," he said, staring at me a few moments longer before he returned downstairs to where I had left Gaines.

I felt the man's presence at the end of the alley before I saw him. My first thought was that he was with the cleanup crew John had ordered.

He peeked around the corner twice, a phone to his ear—I knew then he wasn't with John's team. After a few seconds out of sight, he rounded the corner and started walking toward me.

John emerged from the basement. He looked at me, saw my attention was elsewhere, and turned to see what it was. He saw the man and slowly walked up the stairs to where I was. There was a sudden flash of recognition in John's face.

"Down!" he yelled at me as he drew his pistol.

The man walking towards us drew a pair of silenced pistols from under his jacket and began firing at John. I was on my feet and running to the other side of the alley, away from John—toward the other man.

"Scott! Get down!" John screamed as he dropped an empty mag from his pistol and slapped in a fresh one from his shoulder holster.

Masonry and splinters exploded around the doorway John was standing in. The man whipped one of the pistols around at me and began firing.

Running, I kicked off the brick edge of the building in front of me and launched myself sideways, trying to gain as much height as possible.

He raised his arm to match my course, but John began firing again and his attention got drawn away for just a split second. That's all I needed to kick the gun that was pointing at me. I hit the ground hard but tucked into a roll.

John began running toward us. The man began firing at John again, sending him sprawling to the ground, and then he turned his remaining pistol on me. I righted myself and dove for the pistol I had kicked from his hand. He got one shot off, striking the concrete next to me, when the slide locked back on his pistol—out of ammo.

My fingers reached the gun on the ground, but he slid forward, kicking it from my grasp. He popped up immediately and tried to stomp me. I rolled away as his foot came down and then rolled back against his leg. Thinking I had an advantage, I reached around his leg with my arm to trip him, but he produced a knife from behind him and tried to stab down into my chest.

I grabbed his wrist with my hand as it came down and then squeezed—and I could tell I was squeezing hard. It was almost as if I was having a seizure of some sort, clamping down on him without willing it. He grunted in pain as I crushed down on him, dropping the knife on top of me—thankfully, not blade first. I pulled down on his arm and threw my leg up in a kick, catching him in the face. As he fell backwards, I heard the car.

It entered the alleyway and stopped at the entrance briefly before accelerating toward us. The gunman pulled toward the alley wall, trying to extract himself from my grip, but I would not—or could not—let go.

That was my first mistake. I should have let go immediately.

The car swerved toward us, smashing its front fender against the wall and then bouncing out into the center of the alley again. I let go of the man's arm as the car reached us and threw myself backwards onto the hood of the car, smashing my back against the windshield.

That was my second mistake. I should have jumped to the side.

The car stopped as I impacted, throwing me off the hood and to the concrete. I tried to push sideways, but there was too much forward momentum, and I had the wind knocked out of me.

John began firing at the windshield as soon as I was clear. With the barrage of fire, the driver could not pull forward. He instead backed out of the alley, slamming into the walls as he went. The other man was not to be seen. I had to assume he had jumped into the car when it had stopped and I was flat on my back sucking wind.

At least they weren't going to run over me. That was a plus.

John fired his last round into the windshield and the slide on his gun locked back. He dropped the mag and smoothly popped in his last one, flicking the release and letting the slide go forward again. He held his aim on the entrance of the alley until he was certain the vehicle would not return and then he lowered his gun and ran toward me.

"Are you all right?" he asked as I rolled to my side and sat up, my ribs throbbing from the smack against the windshield.

"Where'd the Terminator get to?" I asked.

"He got in the car," John replied. "Are you alright?"

I moved my feet and legs, stretched my arm across my chest, and then nodded.

He pulled out his phone and dialed.

"How far are you?" he asked into the phone. "We just got hit, and we are sitting out in the open. Sooner is better," he snapped, clearly not liking what he had heard.

"Grey sedan, broken windshield. Two men," he said in response to their questions.

"Great. Two minutes," he confirmed and hung up.

He looked up and then down both ends of the alley. I reached for the weapon on the ground—the one that still had bullets, and then got shakily to my feet.

He looked at me then and shook his head.

"What?" I asked, shaking from the adrenaline.

He just continued shaking his head and walked to the alley entrance, tucking his weapon into his holster as he reached the street.

I heard police cars in the area, and they seemed to be getting closer, judging by the sound. Certainly a Saturday shootout in Burbank would draw local law enforcement, but it made me tired just thinking about the questions.

The cleanup team arrived at the alley entrance only moments before the police. I looked up and saw badges being flashed and one of the government vehicles pulling in to block access at the other end of the alley.

A few moments later, John was walking back toward me, a black SUV and two sedans following close behind him.

Men in suits exited the sedans and the SUV discharged three men in coveralls, looking like emergency response crews except for the lack of insignia or any other identifying mark. One of them kneeled next to me, setting a medic's kit on the ground beside me. The other two hurried down into the cellar, pulling a wheeled gurney between them.

"Look at me," the medic urged.

I looked up and he lifted my eyelid and shined a light in eyes. He reached his hand around to the back of my head and felt the knot that was rising there. It stung, but I didn't react. I was still angry. The rage wouldn't bleed off for some reason.

When his hand returned to his medical box, his latex glove had blood on it. He extracted a few items and moved around behind me and busied himself with treating the cut.

Once that was completed, he reached for my hands. I jerked them away and looked up at him, seething. His expression didn't change. "Let me see the abrasions on your hands," he stated plainly.

Out of the corner of my eye I saw John standing next to the lead vehicle, watching me. It made me self-conscious about my actions, so I extended my hands and let the medic examine them. He used a sterile wipe and cleaned most of the blood from them, then treated the four knuckles with the worst of the abuse.

When he had finished, he closed his box and walked over to John. I heard him say something about a concussion, abrasions and "nothing to worry about." I had nearly gotten my breathing under control when the other two medics appeared from the basement carrying the gurney. Gaines was strapped to it, sporting a breathing tube in his nose and an IV attached to his arm.

As they rolled around the vehicles they stopped, and I saw John leaning over Gaines, talking to him. One of Gaines's splinted arms reached up and touched John on the chest. I saw John smile and pat him on his shoulder and say something. I couldn't make out what it was.

Once they loaded him into the back of the SUV, it drove past me and out the other end of the alley. The men in suits began pulling equipment from the cars and disappeared into the cellar.

John came over and sat next to me; he had his phone to his ear again. He looked at me for a moment, and when I didn't turn to meet his gaze, he handed me the phone.

"It's for you," he said.

It took me a few seconds to gather myself together enough to take it from him. While I struggled, he sat patiently, waiting for me. I finally reached over and took it.

"Yep," I snapped curtly into the phone.

"Scott?" I heard a woman's voice speaking softly, sympathy dripping from my name alone. It was Dr. Hebron.

"Yeah," I said, some of my anger melting away.

"Are you alright?" she asked.

"Yeah," I repeated, lying.

"I hear you've been in a fight," she said. More sympathy. No judgment.

"You could say that," I replied stiffly.

"How are you feeling right now?" she asked.

I was still trying to gather my thoughts, but my pause must have taken too long because she started speaking again.

"If you need help coming down, I can be on a flight in a matter of minutes. You don't have to do anything. There's no need to figure anything out," she said.

I paused too long again. I was really having a hard time finding my voice.

"Okay. I'll arrange for transport. I'll see you in a few hours," she said.

"No!" I objected. The glue in my brain had finally allowed my mouth to respond. "I'm coming home. I'll see you when I get there."

"Are you sure?" she asked, probing my response for sincerity. "I can be there in a few hours. You can get some rest. You don't have to carry this all the way home."

"I'm sure," I replied firmly.

"Scott," she warned, to indicate her next words were serious. "I'll wait until you get back on one condition."

I waited to hear the condition. When I didn't say anything she continued.

"You have to see me before you go home to Barb," she said firmly.

"Okay," I replied half-heartedly.

"I mean it, Scott. You land, I'm there, we talk," she insisted sternly but with genuine concern. "No arguments, no evasion, no exceptions."

"I got it. I land, we talk," I replied and then handed the phone back to John.

"Thanks, Doc," he said, then, "No, I'm fine. Just a sore wrist and arm," he relayed dismissively, glaring at me in mock scorn, and then he winked as he turned away from me.

"Okay. See you at Dulles," he said and hung up.

He squatted down in front of me for a minute, looking at the ground. It seemed like he was trying to think of something to say, but decided against it and instead got up and walked over to talk to the men in the suits. A few minutes later the SUV John had rented at the airport rolled into the alley and another suit got out and handed John the keys. Two men climbed out of the back, carrying bags, and walked over to the other group.

There was an active discussion between the new arrivals and the crew that had been there a while. There were passing glances in my direction and whispered words. John walked over and stood between me and the men, prompting them to break their huddle and go back to their duties. John then turned and walked toward me.

"Come on, Scott. Let's go home," he said sympathetically.

That was the last thing he said to me until we were on the plane, about thirty minutes out from Dulles International Airport. I had stared out the window from the time we took off until we started our decent.

He cleared his throat first, so I knew he was about to speak.

"You're a puzzle," he mused aloud.

I continued to stare out the window.

"You sure would make a hell of an Agent, though," he added quietly.

I looked over at him, examining him for a moment, and then returned my gaze to the window. "Can I take a shower first?" I asked.

John laughed.

**

7:50 p.m.—Dulles International Airport

Upon landing at Dulles, the sun was starting to cast long shadows on the ground. We walked toward baggage claim but were intercepted by a man in khakis and a polo shirt.

"Scott Wolfe?" he asked.

I nodded.

"This way, please," he directed.

I looked at John.

"No worries. I've got the bags. I'll meet you out there," he offered reassuringly.

Once in the parking area, I was ushered to a black Ford SUV.

These people and their SUVs, I thought to myself.

The man in the polo shirt opened the back door for me. When I looked in, I saw Dr. Hebron. I climbed in and the door was closed behind me. The man then walked over to a cart return station and lit a cigarette.

"How are you, Scott?" she asked with a subdued tone of concern.

"I'm not sure," I replied looking down at my hands. Silence filled the cabin for a moment, and then she spoke again, a softer voice.

"Having trouble organizing your thoughts?" she asked.

I thought about it for a moment, trying to categorize…categorize what exactly, I wasn't sure. "Yes," I replied absently.

She watched me for a moment, measuring her next words carefully. "Are you still angry?"

"No," I said quietly.

She shifted her questions and came at me from another direction. "You were struck in the head. Was that before or after the fight started?"

"After," I said quickly. Data. Recall. Information. I was a database of memories.

Give her only what she needs, my other voice said.

"What happened?" she asked.

"Gaines had just knocked John out. I was bound," I recalled.

"Wait," she interrupted. "Agent Temple was unconscious?"

I nodded. "Then Mark discovered I had lifted his multi-tool out of his box and came after me," I said.

"How did you get his multi-tool?" she asked.

"He had locked me in a cage earlier, and I got out when he wasn't in the room," I replied.

"So you escaped?" she asked, confused. "How did you get bound again?"

"A woman showed up while I was pilfering his supplies," I said. "She pulled a gun on me."

Dr. Hebron crinkled her brow, trying to digest everything. "What happened to her?" she asked.

I shook my head, letting frustration get the better of me. I decided to start from the beginning and explain more clearly.

"Okay, from the top," I said, taking a deep breath. "John and I had surveillance set up on a building we thought Gaines was trying to access. I left to get some food, and Gaines found me. He locked me in a cage then left. I escaped, then the woman showed up."

"How did John find you?" she asked.

"I called him on Gaines's phone," I replied.

She nodded, but lifted an eyebrow.

"The woman zip cuffed me, and then John found us," I said, trying to explain it as simply as possible. "Gaines came in a bit later and knocked John out, and then sent the woman away with some paperwork."

A confused look crossed Hebron's face. "What kind of paperwork?" she asked.

I shot her a quizzical look, wondering why that was important.

She shook her head. "Never mind," she muttered. "What happened then?"

"Mark discovered I had his multi-tool, but I had just cut my zip cuffs," I replied. "Is this too much information?"

"It's more than I'm used to, but it's fine," she replied.

"When Mark came after me, I started to fight him off," I continued. "I managed to get on my feet and then he hit me in the head with a metal baton. That's when things get fuzzy."

"The fight continued after that?" she asked.

"Yeah. But I wasn't feeling right," I said, trying to find the right words. "Darkness started closing in on me—like when Majmun hit me in Amsterdam—but then the rage came. It felt like 'sick' working its way up from my stomach. Then I felt like I was outside my body watching as I whaled on Mark's head."

"What were you feeling right before he hit you?" she asked quietly, almost in a whisper, as if anything louder would make the memory collapse.

"I was scared and angry." I thought about the moment. "I fought him off twice while I was trapped on the floor."

"How did you do that?" she asked in the same calm, quiet tone.

I shrugged. "I'm not sure. I just did what I had to," I replied.

She nodded.

"But after he hit me, and I started to lose consciousness, it was all rage." I said, touching the back of my head again. "I could actually smell the flesh burning off my chest again. I mean—I could really smell it, like it was happening right then."

"Was there anything else you were feeling before or after he hit you that you can identify?" She asked, almost cautiously, like she was pushing open a door she wasn't sure was completely safe to open.

I thought for a moment. "Like I said. After he hit me I started to black out, then I felt rage and it pulled me out of my collapse… After that I was all fists and feet, like I was watching it from the cheap seats or something."

"When the gunman came after the two of you in the alley, John said you ran toward the gunner," she recounted, somewhat baffled. "Why was that?"

"I didn't have a gun. All I had were my feet" I replied, matter-of-factly. "I had to get them over to him before I could use them."

"And how did you feel then?" she asked.

I thought about it for a second. I honestly didn't remember feeling anything except the hyper-focused need to get his guns away from him.

"Nothing," I replied. "Just focus."

"But you were feeling rage still when you came out of the basement," she pointed out gently. "Weren't you angry when you charged the man with the gun?"

I thought again, trying to replay my thoughts. I shook my head.

"No. I don't think so," I declared finally. "If I was, it

certainly wasn't my central motivator."

She nodded. "That's good, Scott. That's very good. It shows you have the capacity to let reason rule when it needs to."

I nodded my understanding.

She smiled. "I don't think we have anything to worry about," she shared, touching my hand. "It sounds like a combination of stress and flashback got wrapped up in a head trauma. Your memory of Majmun and your torture probably threw you into sort of an 'automatic' response of fear and rage as you started to lose consciousness. The blow to your head would certainly explain the vertigo—that feeling of *floating above yourself.*"

She looked at me for a moment and then continued. "Basically, with your conscious mind drifting into limbo from the blow, your subconscious re-fought the incident in Amsterdam. It seems that in the process you subdued a dangerous opponent."

"Subdued. Ha," I scoffed.

"True. You did do quite a bit of damage. But in your defense, you had been attacked, held prisoner, threatened, and then battered," she countered.

I stared blankly at my hands; they had stopped shaking.

"He created the situation. Not you. You responded as best you could with the resources you had available to you. Your only responsibility now is to ensure you don't let it do more damage—it's over."

I nodded.

She handed me a bottle. "If you have trouble sleeping tonight, take two of these. Otherwise toss them in the trash tomorrow," she said. "I'll call in the morning and check on you. If you need me before then, you have my number. Don't hesitate to call any time."

"Okay. Thanks, Doc," I assured her sincerely. I was suddenly very tired.

I got out of the SUV and saw John talking to the guy in the polo shirt. When he spotted me, he motioned for me to follow him to long-term parking. The guy in the polo shirt passed me and grinned.

"Good job, Monkey Wrench," he said.

I faked a smile and nodded at him, and then headed to long-term parking, catching up with John as he reached the stairs.

"I called Barbara and told her we'd be a little late but that we're at Dulles," he informed me as we climbed the stairs. "I said we'd probably stop and grab a bite to eat on the way home."

"Thanks," I muttered absently.

When we reached his truck, he tossed our bags in the back; we climbed in and headed for the gate, neither of us saying anything until we exited the airport access road.

"So I'm assuming since you aren't in restraints or being loaded up with Thorazine that the doc thinks you're okay," he said smiling; I could hear the edge in his voice.

"Head trauma-induced flashback in a stressful environment," I relayed back as if I were reading it from a medical chart.

"I've had a few of those in my time," he said reassuringly through a chuckle.

"Good to know," I muttered.

I knew John had to have an update on Gaines, but I couldn't bring myself to ask him about it.

We rode in silence into Fairfax and pulled into the parking lot of a local Tex Mex restaurant on Route 50 just east of the exit for Route 28. We went in and ordered.

I asked for a beer. To John's credit, he didn't say anything, though he might have had I ordered tequila.

Once we'd ordered and had our beers in front of us, John leaned toward me, and in a low voice, he said, "Head trauma aside, you did something amazing back there." He took a sip of his beer and then continued. "There aren't many people I've met who could have done what you did. Mark is one of the models of modern hand-to-hand with the Company."

I just grunted in response, unable to see anything positive in what had transpired.

John sat back in his chair, taking another big pull from his beer bottle and then looked at me with a mischievous smile. "Nick always got his ass handed to him by Mark."

That raised my eyebrow. I looked at him for a moment before taking another drink of my own beer.

"If I could get you trained, proper like…" he muttered, letting his sentence trail off as the gears turned in his head.

"I'm a computer nerd," I replied.

"I don't know if you really believe that or if you just like sandbagging," he said, leaning forward with a more serious look on his face. "Computer nerds don't throw down like that on mercenaries and trained Agents."

He had a point. Doc Hebron had said nearly the same thing. Maybe I needed to readjust my self-image.

He leaned back again. "Clearance would be an issue. You've got a shadow," he said, almost as if speaking to himself.

I cocked my head slightly. "A shadow?"

"Yeah. You've got someone with connections running interference on everything involving you," he confided.

It dawned on me who he was talking about. "Barb's dad," I realized quietly.

"I've already said more than I should. But just to let you know…" He paused, looked side to side in some sort of signal that a secret was about to be revealed, and then leaned forward again, lowering his voice. "Gretel has been trying to contact you, and she's being blocked."

I could feel the crease in my forehead deepen. I set my beer down and leaned forward. I could feel the anger start to rise again, but it suddenly dawned on me that this might be an opportunity.

"You have her contact info?" I asked.

A worried look passed across John's face.

"That's not a good idea, Scott," he insisted. "Be patient. She knows it isn't you."

I could feel my face flushing. "It seems everyone knows what's best for me but me," I snapped a little too harshly.

John didn't respond, but I saw something in his expression that indicated he was pleased.

Seriously? You're trying to work me now? I thought.

I smiled and changed tactics. "Do me a favor," I said. "If you can, let her know I'll find a way to catch up with her as soon as I figure out what's going on."

He stared at me for a moment without responding, and then nodded. "Alright. But I'm not playing post office with you two. I'll only do it because chain of command is being abused for personal reasons."

"Thanks," I said, swallowing the bitterness in my voice so it came across as more pleasant than I felt.

"Just so you know, I was specifically ordered *not* to let you know what I just shared with you," he confessed before taking another sip of beer, "but that alone is worth the violation."

That softened me even more. Any anger I had due to his omission of detail suddenly dissolved—though I did get the sense that he was maneuvering me.

John sat back and finished his beer as the waitress appeared and asked if we wanted another. When she returned with two more, John sat back and sighed deeply, looking around the restaurant, and then leaned forward again.

"You haven't asked me how our boy is," he said with a knowing grin, referring to Gaines. "But I know you want to know."

Then he waited, I assumed, for me to confirm I wanted the information. I wasn't sure I wanted to hear what he had to say, but only because I was worried I had done more damage than I wanted to acknowledge.

I nodded hesitantly.

"One arm broken above the wrist, broken nose, fractured brow ridge, both cheek bones fractured, several broken teeth, dislocated jaw, dislocated shoulder, two broken ribs, and a bruised kidney." He stared at me, looking for a reaction.

I was angry again—but at least I had my brain back to manage the emotion. I just stared at my beer and clenched my teeth.

"Is he talking?" I asked.

"Ha!" John exclaimed. "He won't be talking for a while—even if he wanted to."

I cringed and was about to reword my question when our food arrived and the discussion ended. I ate my extra-crispy chimichanga but, though delicious, I found little joy in it.

Once we finished dinner we were on our way again with no more discussion until we reached my condo.

When we arrived, it was after 10:30 p.m. I got out and gathered my belongings from the backseat and as I closed the door, John came around to my side. He stood in my way so there was no mistake he had something to say before I left.

"I just want you to know how much I appreciate your help," he offered sincerely. "I was worried I'd have to kill Mark. Despite the appearances, he's a good guy."

I didn't know what to say, so I stayed silent.

"You saved the life of a good man today." Then he added with a grin, "Probably mine."

"Thanks, John. And thanks for dinner," was all I could muster before shouldering my bag and heading to the door.

As I approached my condo, the door opened, squeaking

loudly. Barb was standing in the threshold, arms crossed with a smirk on her face. John saw this and quickly returned to the driver's side of his truck.

"Fishing huh?" Barb asked as I approached, but as I got closer, her expression began to change—probably noticing the bruises and lacerations on my face.

I smiled and turned back to John as he climbed into the truck.

"Hey John!" I called out before he could drive off. "Nancy's the mole. She spilled the beans about fishing."

John laughed and waved his hand at both of us. "Go ahead and tell her. She'll hear about it soon enough anyway."

I tensed at being exposed while still standing in the parking lot with Barb between me and the door—but I knew he was right. As soon as I turned to face the music, I got a glare from Barb.

"Tell me what? What will I hear about?" she asked, puzzled and agitated.

"I'll tell you inside," I deflected, hauling my gear up the stairs.

I went straight to the bedroom and dropped my bags, got some clean sweats and a T-shirt from the dresser, and then went into the bathroom to shower. My hope was to clean up most of the physical evidence of combat before sitting and explaining what happened; I reasoned that sitting in front of her looking like a used tackling dummy would make things worse. When I finished and came out, Barb had already unpacked my bags and put everything away.

Agitation.

I quickly swallowed it, realizing she wasn't doing it to insert herself, but to be helpful. I'm sure she saw my condition as soon as I was in the light and was trying to be supportive.

"What happened?" she asked nervously as I wandered into the living room and plopped down into my oversized, overstuffed green chair.

I took a deep breath and began to explain. The look on her face as the story unrolled was enough to tell me she didn't like it at all. By the time I was finished, she was staring, shaking her head with tears rolling down her cheeks.

"Scott," she gasped, but she couldn't form her words.

"Barb. I had no idea—" I started.

"No!" she barked, cutting me off sharply. "You're going to let me speak."

I shut my mouth, and she glared at me for a moment until she was certain that I wouldn't interrupt her.

"I can't deal with this. This, this amateur *spy* hobby you've picked up. I'm always on eggshells as it is, and you just keep getting weirder and weirder," she said as she wiped her eyes on her sleeve. "I barely recognize you anymore. It isn't healthy. Not for you and not for me."

My blood had started boiling as soon as she said "amateur spy."

She paused and took a deep shaking breath. "I don't blame you," she started again. "It's mostly John Temple. But I won't have you sneaking around playing junior James Bond with the boys, especially when it affects me. I have to put an end to it. I'm going to ask Daddy to make sure that John stays away from you."

The reference to having my life manipulated at a state level because of my relationship with Barb was more than I could stand—I popped.

"Enough!" I yelled.

Her eyes went wide and her mouth sealed tight.

"You're going to have '*Daddy*' put a stop to it?" I asked incredulously. "Just like he stopped Kathrin from contacting me?"

"What are you talking about?" she asked wide-eyed, seemingly shocked by the accusation.

"Don't give me that shit," I sneered in disbelief. "And you think you've been walking on eggshells? Well let me tell ya darlin'—you don't have the corner on that market."

She stared, uncomprehending.

"You're right about one thing, though. I *am* unrecognizable," I said, careening to a seemingly unavoidable conclusion, "and I will never be the same. So if you were holding out, waiting for the old Scott to show up, you can forget it. He died in the water somewhere outside Mimon."

I don't think I'd ever seen Barb's eyes so wide. I immediately regretted yelling at her. But despite saying it tactlessly, I couldn't bring myself to feel sorry for speaking what I felt.

With that, I got up, went back to the bedroom, grabbed some clothing, stuffed it into my duffel bag, and then stomped back to the front of my apartment—just in time to hear the loud squeaking of my front door followed by the sound of it slamming shut.

I looked out the window to see Barb running to her car.

"Damn!" I muttered to myself. "Smooth. Real smooth."

I turned and went back to my bedroom, unpacked, and got into bed. I was too tired to think about it and too sore to go hunting for her. I wasn't even sure if I wanted her to come back. I was half-hoping that had been the last of the relationship.

With that being my last conscious thought of the day, I slipped into a fitful sleep—and for the first time in weeks, I was visited by Majmun. His hard stare and mechanical actions with the torch haunted me in my sleep. This time, however, I grabbed his throat with my hand and crushed his windpipe until blood and goo oozed between my fingers.

ten
Sunday, July 25th

1:45 a.m.—Somewhere over the Midwest

HEINRICH BRAUN was flying back to the East Coast. His recovery operation had been a complete failure, and William Spryte had made it clear he was quite angry at the loss of Gaines. The fact that the CIA had made the capture gave him only a small window of opportunity to correct the situation; it would require a less-than-covert reliance on procedural measures.

He dialed his contact at Homeland Security.

"Hello," came the groggy voice of Ned Richards.

"Gaines is in CIA custody," Braun said curtly.

"How is that my problem?" Richards responded sneeringly.

Braun didn't reply immediately. This bureaucrat had

forgotten his place and needed to be reminded who was in charge.

"You're right. It's not your problem," Braun replied. "Neither is anything else that affects the organization. I'm sorry to have disturbed you."

"Wait," Richards hissed quickly.

Braun smiled to himself as the silence on the phone lingered a few seconds.

"What do you need from me?" Richards finally asked.

"CIA possession of a US citizen is illegal and wouldn't stand up to a challenge on Constitutional grounds," Braun said. "You need to bring that to the attention of a judge and take possession."

"That's something the Department of Justice would do," Richards replied. "I can't think of a single Judge I could wake in the middle of the night to get the order."

"Gunlock," Braun stated simply.

"Judge Gunlock?" Richards asked in confirmation. "He won't have grounds. Any order he produces would be overturned."

"He will have grounds," Braun said.

There was a long pause as Richards absorbed the statement. "What grounds?" he asked finally.

"On the grounds that Gaines is a threat to National Security and engaged in terrorist activities," Braun replied as if the statement were a known fact.

"But—" Richards replied.

"Put in the request tonight," Braun said. "The evidence is already being transmitted to your office—a list of targets and diagrams of explosive devices."

"What explosives?!" he asked just as Braun severed the connection.

He immediately dialed another number.

"Secure," announced the voice on the other end when the call was answered.

Braun activated the encryption on his satellite phone.

"Progress report," he said.

"Two of the four locations in LA are complete." Harbinger's deep voice spoke on the other end of the call. The timbre of the man's voice was commanding even in casual conversation. "The other two should be done before sunrise. The two locations in Denver and the studio in Albuquerque will have to be done after dark Sunday night. Chicago will be a challenge, but I've been assured our contractor there can complete his work before the broadcast day begins on Monday."

"You required outside assistance?" Braun asked, nervous about the inclusion of an outside entity for such a delicate operation.

"One group has already been dispatched to Europe for your other operation," he replied unapologetically. "That has left a deficit of manpower. The vacuum had to be filled—unless you wish to remove Chicago from the list."

"No," Braun replied quickly. "Chicago is necessary. It places focus on the administration, plus I've already had Gaines's Crown Victoria transmitter log altered to reflect he was there."

"Understood," Harbinger replied. "Then I should continue as planned?"

"Yes," Braun responded. "But I would hope you are confident in the discretion of the outside contractor."

"I've already planned for his discretion," Harbinger replied, a hint of amusement in his voice.

"Excellent," he said.

"What do you want to do about the two Agents who captured Gaines?" Harbinger asked.

Braun grimaced at the thought of the two men. If Gaines had

revealed the investigation results to them, the game was already over. If Homeland Security failed to get custody of Gaines, the game was already over. He had to focus on getting Gaines; everything else would have to be dealt with afterward if they were successful.

"If we don't succeed in getting Gaines, it's a moot point," Braun said finally. "If we do succeed," he said and then paused, "we'll cross that bridge when we get to it."

"Understood," Harbinger replied. "I'll wait for your call on that."

"Thank you," Braun said, aware of Harbinger's distaste for rudeness. "Let me know when all your preparations are in place."

"Of course," he replied and ended the call.

Braun leaned back in his seat and closed his eyes.

"Gaines," he muttered. "Why couldn't you just lie down like a good boy?"

**

7:15 a.m.—Fairfax, Virginia

My phone rang, waking me from a deep sleep. I was face down in my pillow—which probably explains the dream I had been having about being suffocated. I rolled, painfully, over to the other side of the bed to grab my phone.

I noted the time and the caller—Dr. Hebron.

"Hello?" I answered groggily.

"Good morning, Scott," she chirped cheerfully.

"Morning, Doc. How are you?" I replied, almost offended by the cheerfulness in her voice.

"I'm well," she responded. "More importantly, how are you?"

"I'm sore," I said, deflecting. I wasn't looking forward to

telling her Barb and I had a fight.

She chuckled.

"Though I'm sorry you aren't feeling well physically, I was actually inquiring as to your state of mind," she said with amusement in her voice.

"I just woke up, so you'll have to give me a second to take stock," I grunted, sitting up and taking a sip of water from the glass on my night stand.

"You sound groggy," she observed. "Did you end up taking the medication I gave you?"

"No," I replied as the cobwebs started to clear from my head.

"Good. Be sure to toss them today," she ordered firmly.

"Yes, ma'am," I replied.

"Do you want me to let you wake up and call you later?" she asked.

Just then someone knocked on my door.

"Hold on a sec, Doc," I said, rising and grabbing my sweatpants. "Someone's at my door."

"I'll call back," she offered.

"No. No, it's okay," I said quickly, not wanting to put it off. "Just let me get the door."

I pulled my sweats on and walked stiffly downstairs to answer. I peeked out the side window and saw it was John. He smiled and lifted a cup of coffee to the window.

"It's John," I said. "Hold on."

I opened the door; the screech from the hinges felt like an ice pick in my skull.

"Sorry," he said quietly, making a face from the noise as he stepped in. "I hope I didn't wake Barb."

"She's not here," I replied and then quickly realized I had revealed something I had wanted to ease Dr. Hebron into. "Come on in. I've got Dr. Hebron on the phone."

We walked back upstairs and John set the coffees down on the dining room table.

"Make yourself at home," I offered.

"No rush," he replied.

"Sorry, Doc," I said into the phone as I walked back to the bedroom. "I'm back."

"Did I hear you say Barb wasn't there?" she asked immediately.

"Yeah," I replied cautiously. "But there's a story with that."

"I'm listening."

"When I got in last night, she launched into me about working for the Agency and said she was going to get her dad to shut it down from his end," I relayed without emotion. "Said she was tired of my junior spy hobby."

"That sounds harsh," she replied. "Is that the way she said it, or did you just hear it that severely?"

"She wasn't that kind," I replied.

"Wow," she responded. "So I take it that didn't go over well."

"I told her Mimon changed me and that I was dealing with things the only way I knew how—that I would probably never be the person she remembered and that it upset me that she and her dad were making life decisions for me without my knowledge."

"Sounds therapeutic," she replied.

"Except I didn't say it that gently," I confessed.

She laughed. "That's no surprise…especially after the day you had yesterday."

I chuckled as well. "I need to apologize to her," I said, reflecting on my words from the night before. "But I don't think I want her back."

"Did she take it as a break up?" Hebron asked.

"I don't know," I replied, and then suddenly wondered if

telling John to make himself at home would be construed as an invitation to go through my personal belongings to collect intel—like inviting a vampire through your threshold. "Other than that, I'm fine. No anxiety, no anger, no fear, no nervous twitches. I'm actually even feeling better physically now that I'm up and moving."

"Good," she replied. "Give Barb a few days before you talk to her again—even if she wants to talk before then. Let it percolate before you make up your mind."

"Will do, Doc," I said quickly. "Listen. John's waiting for me. I guess I should go see what he wants."

"Okay, Scott," she replied as I reached for a sweatshirt. "Try to take it easy today."

"I will," I promised. "Thanks for checking in."

"Happy to," she replied. "Bye."

I ended the call and pulled my hoodie on over my bruised body. My shoulder was stiff around my bullet wound from Europe, and I grunted while pulling my arm through the sleeve.

I opened the door quietly and looked down the hall to see if John was, indeed, searching my belongings. His head appeared, leaning backwards from the dining table.

"Done?" he asked as I joined him.

"Yeah," I replied. "She was just checking in on me."

"So Barb left, huh?" he asked.

I grinned. "Later," I replied firmly. "What's up?"

"Debrief," John said.

I pulled the chair out next to him and was about to sit down.

"Not here," he added, holding out his hand to stop me. "We have to do this one at Langley."

I raised an eyebrow and then turned and walked back to my bedroom. "I'll be dressed in a minute."

On the drive to Langley, he began to prepare me.

"This isn't going to be like the debrief in Germany," he confided as we drove. "This is going to be close to an Agent debrief."

"Okay...tell me how that's different," I probed.

"You won't just be recounting details, you'll also be expected to offer your opinion on subjective data," he replied. "—and although it is recorded as opinion, you have to keep in mind that it will be heavily weighted when action is taken."

"What sort of action?" I asked.

"It's best if I don't tell you that before the debrief," he cautioned. "It may taint your responses."

I nodded my understanding, though it irked me a bit.

"Who's going to be there?" I asked.

"Analysts and two Agents you haven't met," he replied. "And probably my boss, but I doubt he'll be in the room."

"Do I need to prepare myself for being water boarded?" I asked sarcastically.

"Only if you make cracks like that," he replied with a smirk. "This is the real deal." Then, as an afterthought, "Oh yeah. Do me a favor and don't call me John during the interview. It won't go over well."

I suddenly remembered the hint of disdain Gaines had shown when I had referred to John as "John." I nodded my understanding.

"Also, you might want to skip over the part where you hacked Colorado Springs PD's data server," he suggested with a grin. "We'll keep that between us for now. My boss knows about it, but I'd rather not have it in the official record."

"You're the boss," I quipped, dismissing the obvious conflict of interest.

**

Seated around the table were six people in addition to John

and myself. Two of the interviewers were Agents—Special Agent Raimy and Special Agent Johnson.

Agent Johnson was a clean-cut guy with sandy blond hair that had turned white around the temples and on the sides. He was average height and carried himself as a soldier.

Agent Raimy was a thirty-something African American woman with a rigid posture and a piercing stare as questions were being answered. When her face relaxed into a smile, it was a relief—and led to the desire to disclose additional details. It took three questions for me to realize that was by design. She was an excellent interrogator.

"How did you discover he had changed vehicles in Kingman?" Agent Raimy asked. "If you only had one minute increments and magnification levels that prevented facial recognition, it seems it would have been harder to pick up the switch."

Her stare fixed on me, waiting for my response. I actually had to exert effort not to smile once I realized what she was doing.

"I was able to create a distance of travel model," I responded, wondering how much technical detail they wanted. "I superimposed it on the map and looked for movement within the scope of the prediction. There were only a couple of instances of viable movement in the range, and I was able to eliminate all possibilities but one."

"I see," she responded with a smile.

When I didn't volunteer any additional information, I saw a micro-expression of a frown flit across her face.

"Of course, it was a guess," I added. "I could have just as easily sent us across country in pursuit of a retired couple on vacation. My hunch was confirmed when the new vehicle drove back to the Crown Victoria and parked for a few minutes…probably transferring gear."

She smiled and nodded.

The interview went on like that for quite a long time. Occasionally an analyst would ask me to clarify a statement, but for the most part, I just walked them through everything that happened, leaving out the hack on the CSPD server, as requested.

"And you escaped from the cage using the shelving as a cutting tool?" Johnson asked me when we were further along.

"Yes," I replied. "I was just hoping to bend it up, but it worked out better as a slicing tool."

He raised an eyebrow and nodded his understanding and approval.

"And that's when the woman showed up," he added.

"Yes. I had just used Gaines's satellite phone to call Agent Temple when she walked in on me," I replied. "I only had time to pocket the cutters I found in the box and flip through a couple of pages of some account info."

"Describe the account pages," one of the analysts inserted.

"They were summary pages," I replied. "I counted twenty two. They had roughly ten to twelve entries per page, containing bank transaction IDs and receiving accounts."

"What happened to the pages?" he asked, jotting down notes.

"She left with them," I replied.

"You're jumping ahead," John cautioned the analyst.

"Sorry," he replied. "Go back to when the woman came in."

"She caught me going through Gaines's items then ordered me at gunpoint to put zip cuffs on," I replied.

"She had those with her?" another analyst asked.

I nodded. "Yes…and that's about the time Agent Temple came in and disarmed her," I said. "She gave up without a struggle."

"What did the woman look like?" Johnson asked.

"She had a very light cocoa complexion and long black hair framing an oval face," I replied. "Very full, sensual lips—like

Angelina lips. She was quite attractive. If I had to guess, I'd say she was Middle Eastern or possibly Indian, but she also had some Caucasian features so I can't be certain."

Johnson and Raimy exchanged a brief glance and then Raimy leaned forward. "Did she have an accent of any sort?"

I shook my head. "Not foreign, if that's what you mean," I recalled. "East Coast, perhaps. To be honest, she may have been a New York supermodel…she was that hot."

The analyst took the notes, shifting uncomfortably with my description. I actually saw a flush of color work its way to his face. I noted he was not the only one who had been taken off guard by my frank description. Agent Raimy pursed her lips. Johnson just grinned.

"Agent Temple was about to cut me free when Gaines entered the room and hit him with his gun," I said. "I tried to warn him, but Gaines was too fast."

"Go on," Johnson urged.

"Gaines ordered the woman to take the papers and go." I closed my eyes to recall the exact words. "He said, 'Get the account lists and go. It's a problem anyone knows you were here.' She replied, 'Mark, you can't kill them.' He said, 'Don't count on it.'"

"Are these quotes verbatim?" one of the two female analysts asked.

"I believe so. Yes," I replied and then closed my eyes to continue. "Then he said, 'Get the list and go before you end up like Dee.' He seemed to get angry as he mentioned that name. Then he asked her if she had more cuffs. She gave him a few and then left, saying she was sorry about his sister before he yelled at her to leave again."

"Any idea who this 'Dee' is he was talking about?" Johnson asked.

I shook my head. "I asked him, but he kicked me in the chest," I replied. "That's when I pulled the clippers out and cut my cuffs. He discovered his missing multi-tool just then."

"And that's when the fight occurred?" Raimy asked.

"Yes," I replied. "Do you need me to go over that?"

Raimy was shaking her head when Johnson inserted himself. "I'd like to hear about it," he said. "We have Agent Temple's account, but I'd be interested in it from your point of view."

I looked at John, wondering how he could have seen the fight if he was unconscious. He smiled at me and nodded his head.

You son of a bitch, I thought. *You were awake!*

"As soon as he realized I had his cutters, Gaines rushed me," I said, recounting what I remembered. "I was already on the floor from when he had kicked me over. I got a lucky kick in and knocked his gun out of his hand, and he threw himself down on me, trying to use his elbows and knees to subdue me. I managed to roll away from him, and then used his metal container to block the next assault, giving me time to get on my feet. That's when he produced a telescoping metal baton. It glanced off my shoulder and struck me pretty solidly in the skull.

"I actually started to black out, but a strong memory pulled me out of it," I said trying to recall the event without bringing the emotion back to the surface.

"What memory?" Raimy asked.

I looked at John, and he nodded that it was okay to speak freely.

"When I was in Europe last year, a Bosnian Serb Mercenary by the name of Majmun captured me by knocking me unconscious and then tortured me with a propane torch," I said. "As I started blacking out yesterday, I could smell burning flesh. It sent me into a half-delirious rage, and I attacked."

"And that's when you subdued Gaines?" she asked.

I grimaced at the word. I had actually beaten him to within an inch of his life, but I just nodded confirmation.

"What happened next?"

"I was having a hard time getting rid of the cobwebs after the fight, so I walked out into the alley to try and clear my head," I continued, glazing over my delirious attempt on John's life. "That's when the other guy showed up."

"Did you get the impression he was working with Gaines?" Johnson asked.

I shook my head. "I don't know, but I doubt it," I replied.

"What makes you say that?" one of the male analysts asked.

"Gaines drove straight to Colorado Springs after his sister was murdered. Immediately found, tortured, then killed the men responsible, and then proceeded straight to Burbank on his own, stopping only to change vehicles and pick up supplies in Barstow," I said. "Aside from the woman who showed up for the papers—who by the way didn't seem to know what Gaines was doing—he had been acting on his own, using old Agency cover IDs to make his way across country. The guys that came after us in the alley only seemed interested in killing everyone on the scene."

Johnson and Raimy both nodded.

"If we provided you with a sketch artist, do you think you could recall what the gunman in the alley looked like?" one of the female analysts asked.

I nodded.

Just then, the intercom cracked to life. "I'm going to have to pause the debrief," came the burly male voice across the speaker. I assumed it was John's boss—Director Burgess. AKA Papa. "I've just been handed details that change the disposition of this investigation."

"Yes, sir," Special Agent Johnson said.

"John. Can you come into my office?" the man on the intercom asked. "And have Mr. Wolfe hang around a bit longer."

"Yes, sir," John replied. "Alright, folks. Looks like we are in a holding pattern for the moment. I'll let you know what our next steps will be."

Everyone rose and began to leave. I shook hands with the two Agents before they departed and then the analysts, one at a time, as they filed out of the conference room.

Once they were gone, John walked to one of the connecting doors. He turned to me before leaving the room. "I'll be right back," he said in a quiet voice and smiled reassuringly.

While he was gone, I refilled my coffee cup and looked for the least offensive snacks on the other side of the room. There was a tray with various breads, crackers, dips, and some raw veggies. I grabbed a handful of the veggies and wandered around the room crunching them as I inspected the audio and video equipment.

A few moments later, John came back in.

"Okay," he said. "That's it for today."

"What happened?" I asked.

"I'll explain on the way back to Fairfax," he said in a lowered voice.

"I thought I was supposed to hang around."

"Something came up," John replied. "I'll explain on the way back to Fairfax."

**

On the ride back, John was quiet as we left Langley.

"What's going on?" I asked. "Did I say something wrong?"

"No," he replied. "You did great…excellent recall."

"You could have told me you were conscious during my fight with Gaines," I said accusingly.

A serious look washed across his face. "There are varying levels of consciousness," he replied. "I just got to see the end—when you threw him on the ground and started tenderizing his face."

I stared at him for a second, trying to fit the new information into the fuzzy timeline for the fight, and then nodded my understanding.

"So why did the debriefing end so abruptly?"

John took a deep breath before speaking. "My debrief was last night," he said. "We've been up all night trying to find a mug shot match from my description of her."

"You found her then?" I asked. "Who is she?"

"No," he said. "We still don't know who she is yet."

"Then what happened?" I asked again.

"I was unconscious when Gaines talked to her," he said. "That's the main reason I came to get you this morning—to fill in those holes."

"And?"

"And…you did an awesome job," he smirked, knowing that wasn't what I was asking.

"Don't leave me hanging," I said with a mild whine.

"As soon as you mentioned 'Dee,' the research people were on top of it," he said.

"So your boss wasn't the only one listening in," I confirmed.

He nodded. "The reference to 'Dee' changed the search parameters, and they got a hit immediately," he confessed. "Do you remember a couple of weeks ago there was a story in the news about a gang-related attack in Arlington? A federal employee had been caught in the crossfire."

I closed my eyes and let the recall of the news story from two weeks ago flit across my consciousness. I must have only seen the headline because no other details came to me.

"I remember reading something about it," I said. "That was Dee?"

John nodded again. "An unidentified male was seen leaving the area," John continued. "He fit Gaines's description, but no one tied it together until you mentioned 'Dee.'"

"Who was she?" I asked.

"Deidre Faulks, Department of Justice, and as soon as they tested the connection, they found out what she was working on."

I stared at him, waiting for him to reveal his information.

He smiled tauntingly without looking at me. "She was tracking payoffs to government employees," he revealed finally. "Transactions matched to bank accounts."

"The pages!" I breathed.

John nodded. "Looks that way," he replied. "It looks like Gaines was helping her."

"So the thing with his sister," I said, staring blankly at the dashboard as my flow chart started auto filling before my eyes. "That was probably a warning."

"You're jumping too far ahead of the facts," John cautioned. "We don't know that."

"What?" I asked incredulously. "You think he was on his way to hand off the papers and just decided to stop on the way and kill the men who killed his sister?"

He thought for a moment. "Well, when you put it like that—"

"Gaines on the East Coast, with a federal investigator, gets shot up and disappears," I offered, bolstering my theory. "Gaines on West Coast, pops his head up after sister is killed, then gets shot up with federal investigators in an alley."

John set his jaw firmly. Something I said had upset him.

"That means they found him because of something we did," John inserted quietly.

"Yeah," I replied. "Probably."

"Shit," he muttered.

"So what happens now?" I asked.

"More than likely, we'll hand Mark over to Justice and let them figure out what was on those printouts," he said. "But there's another wrinkle."

I let my mind wander across the connections and then took a leap of logic.

"Another agency wants him?" I guessed with the aid of my flow chart.

He snapped his head around and shot me a hard look. "What makes you say that?" he asked.

"Payments to government employees, CIA cover ID blown, and a man who's an expert at disappearing gets sandwiched between killers on two coasts," I said. "Call me paranoid, but it sounds like spy shit to me."

He continued to look at me for a moment longer.

"Watch the road," I said nervously.

He turned his attention back to the highway before speaking again. "Homeland Security wants him," John replied. "They put in the request for transfer of custody last night."

"Hmmmm," I mumbled. "Smells fishy."

"Agreed," John replied. "But they do have a legal leg to stand on."

"Will they get him?" I asked.

"Unlikely," John responded, shaking his head. "Justice will fight tooth and nail for him if for no other reason than to find the connection to Faulks's murder."

"Would the account numbers help?" I asked.

He turned to look at me again. "You got the pages?" he asked.

I shook my head. "No—watch the road," I repeated and then explained. "I looked at them for a good forty-five seconds or so before the hot chick burst in on me. I can probably give you twenty or so transactions and maybe fifteen account numbers."

"Names?" he asked.

I shook my head again. "No. She came in just as I flipped to the names pages," I replied with regret in my voice. "I just saw that there *were* names. I didn't get enough of a look to lock them in."

"Yes," he replied. "Justice will probably want those account numbers if you can remember any."

"No problem."

He grinned. "I'm going to like working with you," he said. "That's some high-speed shit you've got going between your ears."

"Yeah, well—" I started, about to say I was having second thoughts, but then I changed course. "If Barb comes back, I think she's going to demand my resignation from government service."

"Yeah," he said, a question forming on his face. "What happened with Barb last night?"

"She said she was tired of me playing junior James Bond and that she was going to get 'Daddy' to shut it down."

"Oh, shit," he said, his mouth pulling down into a frown. "How'd that go?"

"I told her I was sick of people making life decisions for me without my input and that she probably wasn't going to be happy with the new me," I replied. "She didn't take that well."

"You didn't let her know I spilled the beans on Gretel, did you?" he asked.

I looked away in embarrassment. "I may have let something slip."

"Oh shit," he said.

"Not by name," I inserted quickly. "But I'm sure she figured it out."

"Damn it all," he muttered after a second.

We rode in silence until we were back at my condo.

"I'm sorry, John," I said sincerely as I got out.

"What? Oh, don't worry about it," he said. "You were in a bad way last night. Besides, there won't be any fallout. He can't submit a complaint without revealing he used his influence for personal reasons."

I suddenly realized he had not been upset by my disclosure due to any order he had disobeyed—he was worried Barb would hate him and force me to stop working for him. Though I was following Dr. Hebron's instructions, letting the situation with Barb "percolate," I still felt very strongly that our relationship was over. I didn't mention this to John out of deference to Dr. Hebron's suggestion—but I didn't think he had anything to worry about.

"Hey," he said, as if just remembering something important. "I've got a project cooking—not related to this. I can't give you a frame of reference, but I've got some movement profiles I'd like you to look at tomorrow."

"Cool," I replied. "Another TravTech project?"

"Yeah," he replied. "I'll send the data over tonight on the secure server. Take a look at it and let me know if you see anything interesting."

"Alright," I replied with satisfaction, excited for my next "assignment."

"Get some rest," he said.

"Call me if you need anything else," I said.

"Will do," he replied as he put his truck into gear. "And Scott. Good job, man."

I shot him a crooked smile and waved goodbye. As he drove off, I realized how late it was and how hungry I was. So I went in and rewarded myself with a Delmonico steak from the freezer.

Shortly before I went to bed, my phone chimed—text message from Bonny:

I hope your conference or whatever went okay. Just wanted to see if Barb's dad was okay. She was vague on details. See you in the morning. Bon

What? I thought.

I wasn't touching that one with a ten-foot pole. I had the sudden desire to call Barb and ask if everything was okay, but decided that if it were something important or if he was in the hospital or something, she would call. After all, if she had even been vague with Bonbon, privacy must have been an issue.

It was the second night since returning from Europe that no one else was in my condo but me. Barb, Bonbon, or Storc had spent the night every night during the first week back, and Barb had spent every night since, inching her way into my bed each night until it felt *normal*.

Last night was the first time I'd slept in an empty house in quite a while. Sadly, my first night alone in months had come after an adrenaline-charged couple of days and my restless sleep had reflected the tension and conflict. But when I lay down to sleep tonight, I was out like a light, dead to the world…until the dream with my dad started again.

**

11:35 p.m.—WCAC Radio Studios in Chicago, Illinois

HARRY SCOGGINS was no more than a shadowy figure moving through the darkened hallways of the small radio studio, having entered the building through a roof access only moments earlier. He had expertly disabled the alarm system before continuing into the production area on the same floor. To him, this was easy money—it didn't matter to him that he didn't know who was on the other end of the contract. He liked it that way.

He arrived at the target broadcast booth and deftly picked the lock. He was inside in a matter of moments.

"Okay," he whispered into his cell phone headset. "I'm in."

"You're sure you know which chair belongs to Harmon?" the deep voice at the other end asked, referring to the conservative talk-show host who used the studio.

"Yes," Scoggins replied. "I watched hours of the show on YouTube. He's always in the same chair."

"Excellent. Lift the seat from the central post."

Scoggins proceeded to lift the heavy chair, placing his foot on one of the five radial rollers at the bottom. The chair didn't move from the post.

"It's not coming loose," Scoggins said. "Hold on."

He got down on his knees and looked under the seat with his flashlight.

"It's bolted," he added. "Give me a minute."

"Take your time. We want it done correctly."

"Uh huh," Scoggins grunted as he began loosening the screws.

After a few moments, the last screw dropped to the ground.

"Okay," he said as he lifted the seat off the post. "It's off."

"Good. Now take the first cylinder and place it gently into the opening of the post," the man on the phone said. "Careful not to drop it. The electronics are delicate."

Scoggins did as ordered and lowered the metallic tube he had been given into the opening. When his fingers reached the top of the rim, he released it. It hit roughly at the bottom with a loud clank.

"Okay," Scoggins said. "It's in."

"Good. Now return the seat and bolt it back together."

Scoggins did as directed and then rose, sitting in the seat to make sure it was solid and its lifting and lowering functions were still intact. Satisfied he had completed his task as directed, he picked up his tools and stowed them in the pouch hanging from his shoulder.

"All set," he said. "Where's the second location?"

"South of the city, there is a drawbridge on East 100th Street, where it crosses the Calumet River," the man said. "Pull off on the shoulder just before crossing the bridge and call me back."

"Is there another radio station there?" Scoggins asked.

"A transmitter," the man said. "Call me when you reach the pull off on 100th Street."

The called ended abruptly.

Scoggins left the building the same way he came in, careful to reconnect the alarms on the way out. He was excited that the job was nearly half-complete. It would be the single largest payday he'd ever had—seventy-five thousand dollars for placing a couple of high-tech listening devices.

He had already received the first ten thousand and with great timing. He was in over his head with a local loan shark and was about to have to face some unpleasant confrontations. It was almost as if he had an angel on his shoulder—the timing had been perfect.

He got in his car and drove to the location described by his benefactor. As described, there was a broad dirt shoulder just before the bridge. He pulled off the road and down to the far edge of the parking area near the river, and then pulled out his phone and dialed.

"Okay," Scoggins said into the phone. "I'm here."

"You'll need to cross under the bridge to get to the transmitter," the voice on the other end said.

"You mean I need to go down to the river?" Scoggins asked.

"Yes," the man replied. "There's video surveillance at the entrance, so you have to skirt the edge of the river and go under the bridge. You'll then come up on the other side and move to the building at the base of the transmitter."

"If you say so," Scoggins replied hesitantly.

He began making his way down to the coarse stone lining the bank of the river. Once there he walked carefully over the granite aggregate toward the base of the drawbridge.

"Are you certain you aren't carrying any identifying documents or objects?" the voice said into his ear as he balanced himself on the coarse stone.

"What? Yes. I'm sure," he replied, distracted by the sudden drop off in front of him. "Are you sure I can get under the bridge here?" he asked.

"Certain," the man replied.

"Well I'm almost at the end of the stone, and all I see is a concrete wall," Scoggins said.

"You'll have to walk out into the water a ways."

"Isn't there an easier way to do this?" he asked as he stepped to the edge of the stone and placed his feet in the water.

"If you'd prefer not to do it, you can forgo the remaining payment and we can hire someone else to do the last part of the task." The booming voice responded in an eerily patronizing tone.

"No. No, I'll do it," he responded quickly as he waded out to his waist. "I just wasn't prepared to get wet."

"Are you in the water now?" the man asked.

"Yes," he replied nervously, still unable to see a way around the bridge. "Are you certain I can cross under here?"

"Where is the device?" the man asked suddenly.

"It's on my back," Scoggins replied.

"Make sure it doesn't get wet," the man said. "Put it on your shoulder."

Scoggins did as ordered and adjusted the cylinder in the pouch so it was resting on his shoulder. "It's fine," Scoggins said.

"Are you sure?" the man asked. "Put it to your ear and see if you can still hear it humming."

Scoggins lifted the device to his ear to listen. He heard nothing, causing him to panic for a moment.

"Do you hear anything?"

"No," he replied, and then suddenly there was a buzzing sound from inside it. "Wait, I hear—"

Scoggins's words were cut off by an explosion that spread the upper part of his body across the water. The lower part of his corpse dropped into the water and began to be tugged along by the slow current of the river.

**

HARBINGER ended the call he had been on, and then closed the phone used to detonate the bomb that Scoggins had so graciously placed next to his head. As soon as the deed was complete, he removed the sim cards from both phones and then pulled his satellite phone from the console next to him. He dialed Heinrich Braun.

"Braun."

"Secure," Harbinger said before switching over to encrypted communication.

"You have an update?" Braun asked as soon as the connection went secure.

"All devices are in place and all loose ends have been tied up," he said.

"No problems?" Braun asked.

"None," Harbinger replied mildly.

"Thank you," Braun said. "You know the schedule. I'll leave execution in your capable hands."

"Yes, sir," Harbinger replied and then ended the call.

He sat back in his seat and closed his eyes. "Back to the house," he said to the driver without looking at him. "We can sleep for a few hours."

eleven
Monday, July 26th

7:25 a.m.—Fairfax, Virginia

I woke with a start around 7:30 a.m. It took me a moment to realize it had been a knock at the door that had roused me. I grabbed my sweats from the night before and pulled them on as I made my way through the house. I pulled my T-shirt on as I walked down the stairs to the front door. The action of pulling my shirt on made me realize I would be sore today. My shoulder was tight and my head ached with every movement.

I opened the annoyingly squeaky door and was shocked to find Barb's dad standing there—Robert Whitney, State Department Attorney and former prisoner of Bosnian Serb mercenaries.

Well you look pretty healthy to me, I thought. *I wonder what*

Barb told Bonbon to make her think something was wrong?

He was the man who, as I discovered two nights earlier, was responsible for preventing Kathrin from contacting me. As soon as I remembered that information, my shock was replaced with anger. I needed to keep it in check.

"Mr. Whitney," I said coolly. "This is unexpected."

"Hi, Scott. May I come in?" he replied. I detected a tone of contrition.

Hmmmm. Strange, I thought.

"Sure. Come on in."

We came upstairs, and he followed me into the kitchen where I began preparing a pot of coffee. He leaned against the counter and crossed his arms over his chest.

Defensive before he even starts talking. This is going to be interesting.

"What can I do for you?" I asked commandingly, hands resting on the surface behind me, chest out, head held level.

He wouldn't be getting any shrinking violet here—and he was clearly uncomfortable with my *lack* of discomfort.

He cleared his throat before speaking. "I just want you to know—" He shifted uncomfortably. "This is awkward. I need to tell you that Barb had no knowledge of my actions to block Ms. Fuchs's contact with you. It was all my doing."

I said nothing. I stared at him unmoved, letting him know I expected some elaboration.

"Granted, I did it on her behalf. Which in itself was wholly inappropriate. But again, she knew nothing about it whatsoever," he continued, and then waited to see if I'd respond—I didn't. "In fact, she had mentioned to me that she was surprised that you hadn't been contacted by her."

"Well…" I said, gathering my thoughts, fighting down the urge to lash into him. "Thanks for the disclosure. I'll be sure to adjust my thinking accordingly next time I see Barb." I reached for the coffee pot. "Coffee?"

"No. Thanks," he replied. "But I would like to explain my actions."

"You don't have to explain anything to me," I replied flippantly. "Your actions and motivations were completely transparent."

He pressed his lips together tightly. He wasn't expecting my response. I suspected he thought I would be so grateful that Barb hadn't been involved in his efforts that I would instantly forgive her and everything would be hunky dory. He must have expected I would be pissed at him, though.

"Okay," he said finally. "Maybe 'explain' is the wrong word. But I'm going to speak my piece."

I stared at him, unmoved.

"I saw how that Kathrin girl reacted when you were in the water outside Mimon," he began and then lowered his head. "I saw her running back toward you before the helicopter landed—with no thought for her own safety. She was firing that rifle and screaming your name, doing everything she could to get the Serbs' attention off of you. She didn't even wait to see if the sniper's shot had killed the last one before she was running into the water, screaming your name and crying."

I was stunned. I had no idea that had happened. To be honest, it just made me more pissed at Bob Whitney for blocking my access to her. He must have seen the anger in my face.

"But I also saw Barb," he continued, looking me firmly in the eye. "The one you came to save. I knew she would never let you go after you went to such extremes to save her. I also knew it had no hope of lasting."

I narrowed my eyes at him, not fully understanding his meaning. He saw I didn't get it, so he continued. "Barb would have been plagued with white knight syndrome for the rest of her life if someone else had taken you away from her after that," he said. "I know it sounds petty and small, but she needed find out on her own what you had become."

I could feel anger in my face again, the blood building in my ears and cheeks.

He shook his head. "You have no need to be angry," he said, reading my mood perfectly. "Your incredible boldness set you up for changes she wasn't going to be able to handle. But Barb is tenacious to say the least—and devoted. It would have destroyed her if the man who flew halfway around the world to save her…"

Damn! I'm starting to feel bad for Barb again.

He shook his head. "Like I said. I saw how Kathrin charged in to pull you out of the water," he said and then relaxed his stance a bit. "I watched Barb stand there, stunned by what had happened—unable to move. And I watched the expression on her face change as another woman put herself in harm's way, overwhelmed by emotion and a need to save you."

He reached out and put his hand on my shoulder as I turned my head away from him, momentarily forgetting that I was angry with him.

"It would have destroyed her," he said.

I took a deep breath and looked back into his face, shrugging his hand off my shoulder. "Kathrin saved Barb as well," I said accusingly. "*And* you, *and* the others. She risked her life to help save you *all* when the government had decided that the 'hostages' were no longer the primary mission—and *that's* how you repaid her?"

A pained look crossed his face, followed by a weak smile.

"Barb is my little girl," he said with sorrow in his voice. He shook his head. "What choice did I have?"

It was pointless to offer any alternative suggestions. The damage was done; the facts revealed. Anything else would have been nothing more than a rehashing of the anger I felt—and I wanted this confrontation to end.

"Thank you for being honest," I replied mildly. "Even if it

was a few months too late."

He was done with his apology. I saw his resolve build and a shift took place in his expression. He was about to impart wisdom on me—I braced myself, fighting against another temper tantrum.

"There is one more thing I'd like to talk to you about," he said. I could see the tension in his shoulders as he girded himself.

"Okay. Shoot," I said.

I saw a twitch in his cheek.

"About your activities this weekend with Agent Temple," he said, broaching another subject that was clearly sensitive. "I'd like to know what happened in California."

I was stunned. *What do you have to do with what went down in Burbank?! —unless your name was on that list.*

Don't jump to conclusions based on emotion, my other voice warned.

"I'm sorry, sir, but I can neither confirm nor deny any information concerning Agency activities nor can I confirm or deny my involvement in any such actions without specific authorization," I replied smugly.

I saw a brief, split-second sneer on his lip. Micro expressions—gotta love 'em.

"I don't know if you are aware of the far-reaching ramifications of your actions," he said, pausing to let his words take some sort of effect on me. They didn't. I didn't react.

"If that's all, Mr. Whitney, I have to get ready for work," I said calmly, without expression.

"That's not all, Scott," he said, his tone elevating. He was agitated.

"I don't know what else I can say, Bob," I said, inserting familiarity with a friendly grin. "I can't talk about the things you seem to want me to talk about."

"Scott," he said, shifting to a friendlier tone. "There are some things about this incident you aren't aware of. I'm only going to be able to help you if you cooperate with me."

Help me? You've helped me enough already.

I moved away from the counter and toward the stairway leading to the front door. "Thank you for clearing Barb in the matter of Kathrin. I appreciate your frankness. Now I really must ask you to leave so I can get ready for work."

His lips went tight and a slight flush appeared on his cheeks. He wasn't happy, but he seemed resigned to the fact he wouldn't be able to squeeze any information out of me. He reluctantly moved downstairs, but he turned when he was halfway down.

"I know this is all a little too much to wrap your head around, especially considering the emotional personal issues," he said. "But I want to offer this warning before you become too deeply embroiled in something complex and dangerous. There is a fight going on. Not everyone you are dealing with is on the right side. Be careful who you trust."

He stared at me, waiting for a response. When he didn't get one, he exited the condo and closed the door a little too loudly.

I went about my business getting ready for work. I actually felt good. There seemed to be some emotional closure going on, and it was certainly welcome change.

**

When I arrived at the office, I was shocked to see the fishbowl enclosure completely finished. I discovered I couldn't enter through the secure door on the TravTech side of the office, so I retreated and went back out to the lobby and approached from the other side of the elevators. The glass doors were frosted, so I couldn't see in. The lettering on the door read, "TravTech—Special Projects Division."

"Fancy," I said aloud. I swiped my badge across the access plate and entered in my code. The lock indicator switched from yellow to green, and I pushed the door open. I was greeted by a reception desk manned by a sharp-looking guy with a military haircut and a black suit.

"Good morning sir," the guard said. "Brown" was the name on his name tag.

"Good morning!" I replied mildly. "Nice setup."

"Can I help you, sir?" he asked, his voice crisp and no-nonsense despite the smile on his face.

"Yep. Scott Wolfe. I'm here to work," I replied.

"Ah. Mr. Wolfe. Yes, sir. Your biometrics are loaded into the system already, as are those of your team," he relayed, standing to hand me a folder containing documents and forms. "I'm to inform you that I am not permitted past this reception area unless you specifically require my assistance. And that under no circumstances are there to be any visitors allowed into the secure area unless you or one of your team members escorts them."

"Okay then," I said as I browsed through the contents of the folder.

"This desk will be manned from 6:00 a.m. until 10:00 p.m. in two shifts until further notice. If anyone requires access outside of those hours, it will require an entry code from you or authorized agency personnel."

"Got it. Thanks…What do I call you?" I asked.

"Officer Brown is fine, sir," he replied curtly.

"Okay. Thanks, Officer Brown."

"My pleasure, sir," he said with a stiff smile.

I placed my hand on the biometric reader. It scanned me and then a chime sounded and the door unlatched. When I entered I felt like I was in an episode of *Space 1999*. Smooth, white plastic panels covered the walls, which were lined with office doors. Gleaming white tiles had been laid on the floor, and the outside wall, which faced the tech floor of TravTech, was translucent frosted glass all the way to the ceiling. I stopped in front of the glass wall and tried to see into the tech area on the other side. I was unable to even see movement through the glass.

Suddenly, the glass went clear from my chest level up. The change startled me.

"Pretty cool, huh?" I turned to see Bonbon at the control panel for the glass wall. I suddenly tensed, expecting to be bombarded with insults or at least questions from Bonbon about the situation with Barb.

"Very cool," I replied pensively. "Good morning."

"Morning," she said, though she was watching as the glass shifted back and forth between opaque and clear.

"Don't break it. I'm sure it'll come out of your paycheck," I said with a smile.

She abruptly stopped with the clouding feature on all the way to the ceiling and then looked at me.

"Jesus, Scott!" she exclaimed. "What happened to your face?"

I had a cover story prepared.

"Bicycle accident on Saturday," I said nonchalantly, "I had to swerve on the W&OD to avoid a runner. Anyone else in yet?" I asked, quickly changing the subject.

I was still bracing for a verbal assault and was surprised it had not begun yet.

"Yep. Jo and Mahesh are here. You have to come see our offices. They're awesome." She spoke as if she would burst if she didn't show me immediately. She took me by my hand and led me past a break room to the first door. She glanced down as we went and I saw her raise an eyebrow at the skinned knuckles on my right hand.

She said nothing and instead dragged me through the door after swiping her badge across it. Inside it looked more like a lab than an office. Mahesh was leaning over a router box, painstakingly labeling cables as he plugged them into the ports in the back.

"Good morning Mahesh," I said.

"Oh! Good morning," he beamed with a broad smile. Then his expression changed. "What happened to your face?"

"Bicycle accident this weekend," I replied. "Are you okay with your server room?"

"Absolutely. It's like a dream come true," he replied, immediately forgetting my injuries.

"Excellent. Staff meeting in thirty minutes in the conference room," I said.

"Cool," he replied, his attention already back on the switch box.

We continued down to the next door and Bonny opened it. This was more of an office. It was carpeted instead of tiled. Wood grain desks and cabinets had been arranged into three separate work stations, each divided by a low, double-sided bookshelf. There was a round meeting table in the far corner next to the window surrounded by four matching chairs.

"Cool!" I exclaimed. "I could get used to working in here."

"Not so fast, buster," she said, grabbing me by the arm. "This is mine and Anna's." She dragged me out of her office and past the conference room, which had the same shoulder-height opaqueness on its floor-to-ceiling glass as the outside wall did. Then she opened the second to last door on the end.

It was the same size as Bonbon's, but it had only two work stations, along with a small seating area with two comfy-looking upholstered chairs, a couch, and a coffee table.

"Cool! I can take a nap," I said as I lay down on the couch. I noticed there were two other doors in the room. One led into the conference room. The other was on the opposite side from the conference room.

Bonbon stared at me, shaking her head.

"What?" I asked.

She pointed at the other door. "That's your office. This is

Jo's."

I got up and walked into the next room. There, standing beside my desk and organizing folders in an upright holder, was Jo.

The room was the same size as the others, with one massive workstation facing the door and a small round table in the corner surrounded by four matching chairs. There were two leather chairs in front of my desk and a long couch against the same wall as the door we just entered through. It was huge.

"Good morning Jo," I said, somewhat dumbfounded.

"Good morning. I have several scheduling items I need to discuss with you. I also need to get your approval on some equipment additions that Story and Mahesh put in on Friday," she said, still calling Storc by his given name, and then she looked up at me.

"What happened to your face?" she asked quietly.

"Bicycle accident," Bonbon replied for me, but her tone indicated she didn't believe it to be true.

Jo nodded. "You received an encrypted file package overnight from a J. Temple at Langley," she continued. "I've already got it flagged on your board."

"Okay. Thanks," I said, still dazed by my new surroundings.

"Your bathroom is over here," Bonny said, pushing open yet another door. "It has its own shower," she said in an amused whisper.

I walked over and peeked in. It was appointed with very expensive-looking tile and chrome.

"Our bathrooms are through the break room at the other end of the hall," she continued. "They're okay, I guess."

I grinned. "Bonny. If you want to use my shower, all you have to do is ask."

"I will. Can I make some coffee?" she asked, nodding her head in the direction of my fancy coffee maker.

"Sure. I'll have a quad shot latte if you don't mind," I replied.

"One quad, whole, with foam, coming up. You want one, Jo?" she asked.

Jo shook her head and then refocused on her folders.

Down the hall I heard Storc. "Holy shit!" he exclaimed. In a few moments he was entering my office. "Did you see our server lab?"

"Yeah. Pretty nice, huh?" I said as his expression changed.

He was about to ask about my injuries, but Bonbon responded before he could get the question out.

"Bicycle accident," Bonny said, again with a mocking tone. "A pesky runner knocked him off the bike trail."

Storc lifted an eyebrow and stared at me for a beat, obviously detecting Bonbon's lack of belief in my story. I shifted the subject again.

"You like the server room?" I asked.

"Friggin' awesome!" he said before turning and walking back out. "I'm gonna go play."

"Staff meeting in twenty in the conference room," I yelled behind him.

"Kay!" he yelled back from down the hall.

I sat down at my desk and saw a card in the center. I ignored it while Jo went over her scheduling concerns. By the time she was done, both Bonbon and I had steaming hot lattes in our hands. Jo disappeared back into the outer office, followed by Bonny.

I opened the card on my desk. It read, *"We hope you enjoy your new surroundings. We've taken the liberty of appointing your office with some upgrades and hope they are to your liking. Your presence at TravTech makes us all proud. Sincerely..."* It was signed by Bernie and several of the TravTech board members.

"Nice," I muttered.

I busied myself reviewing and approving software projects for the team. There were a number of other projects I had yet to categorize, but they were more in line with data detective work than software and security, so I divided them into two stacks. One for me and one for Jo. I was eager to get her started on something other than organization and project management.

At our staff meeting, I went over outstanding infrastructure issues and got updates for everyone.

"Is everyone happy with their new spaces?" I asked.

Everyone enthusiastically nodded their approval. "I want a shower in my office," Bonny said with a playful pout.

"I'll make sure Bernie gets the request for that," I replied grinning.

"There is one thing we might have to get looked at," Mahesh said. "I don't think the power supply for the floor was designed for the load we have on it. I checked the levels in the server room and they are within tolerance, but just barely."

I nodded. "I'll put in a request for someone to come and check the amperage and upgrade us if necessary," I replied. "I suspect the massive electromagnets keeping the doors secure out front are sucking quite a bit off the trunk. It may be a simple matter of adjusting the distribution in the junction box."

Mahesh nodded.

"Okay. As soon as we are done here, I want everyone to finish your signups for the online certifications on the classified materials handling and COMSEC," I said.

"Is there a time limit on the course?" Anna asked, looking a little nervous.

I looked at Jo.

"There isn't a time limit on the course itself," she said firmly. "But there is a time requirement on the certification. We are already processing data for the CIA, and technically, these should have been done before we started getting contracts. For some reason, our status was changed to active retroactively, starting Thursday afternoon. Once our status changed, all the queued projects started coming through."

Oh, shit.

"Why did we go active on Thursday?" Anna asked as if it were an inconvenience that she would have to do her certification more quickly than she had originally anticipated.

Jo shrugged.

"I wonder," Bonbon purred sarcastically, looking right at me. "Now what could have happened on Thursday evening that would have put this section on active status? Hmmmm. Let me think."

"Bonny," I said with a warning tone.

"I seem to remember getting a secure email. Hmmm," she continued and then opened her laptop to check her emails. "Oh yeah! Here it is. 'Gang, got called into a three-day orientation workshop. Please don't message or call unless it's important. See you on Monday. Thanks, Scott."

"Seriously Bonny," I cautioned, my tone rising. "You need to stop."

"How'd you say you got those bruises on your face and those skinned knuckles?" Bonny threw in accusingly.

"Something about a bicycle accident this weekend," Storc replied.

Damn it, Storc. Don't encourage her.

"That's enough speculation," I said firmly, all kinds of anger in my voice. "You know who we work for. Stop digging."

"Fine," Bonny pouted.

"And you know better," I said, pointing at Storc.

He shot me a grin, pleased with his little mini coup.

I shook my head and smiled. "As long as we're active, let's

get to work," I said, trying to salvage the meeting. "TravTech gets paid when we're working on projects, and they've already made a fairly substantial investment in infrastructure. So let's start earning their money back."

Everyone nodded enthusiastically. "I've already parsed out the first projects," I continued. "Bonny and Anna. You'll have to get with Storc and Mahesh to build your environment sandboxes. Some of what you have to build could be contagious, so treat it like you do virus work."

"Are these projects being charged by the hour?" Anna asked.

I was about to answer, but Jo interjected first. "Only analyst time is charged by the hour—on a sliding scale depending on the nature of the work," she said. "There is a project-content-based scale for all other work. The cost ceiling is included in the package and should help you determine the urgency and depth of the work required."

"What if they want something but it takes longer?" Anna asked.

"If what is requested can't be completed within the scope of the allotted budget, then I have to contact contract administration and inform them that an adjustment needs to be made," she replied. "But the cost ceilings seem to err on the side of allowing more than necessary. They seem to really prefer quality over quantity."

"Just out of curiosity, how much does an *'analyst'* hour go for?" Bonny asked.

"As I said, it's sliding scale, depending on the nature of the work," Jo said and then looked at me for permission to continue. I shook my head.

"Oh come on, boss," Bonny protested. "I know it's not going in your pocket. What difference does it make?"

I took a deep breath and then nodded to Jo.

"There are six levels of analyst payment on the scale. Level one bills out at three hundred and fifty dollars per hour and the amounts increase for each level up to eight hundred fifty dollars per hour at level six," she said.

Storc whistled.

"Whoa," Bonny said, in shock. "What's the difference between levels?"

"Level one is data review and comment, then there's a stepped level of involvement up to the highest two levels—which don't have descriptions," she said. "Or rather, I'm not cleared to know what they are."

"And the project that got us activated this weekend," Bonny said. "What level did that get recorded at?"

I didn't catch the significance of that question until Jo was already answering it.

"Level five," Jo said.

The words "stop now" were in my brain, but they had not reached my lips by the time Jo had spilled the beans. *Bonbon, you are too damned smart for your own good.*

"So level five analyst work is bruised faces and skinned knuckles," Bonny snarked with a smug grin. "Good to know. Sort of makes me wonder what level six is."

"Meetings like this," I muttered in disgust. I closed my laptop and looked at Bonny. "Please don't make this hard on me," I pleaded.

Her accusative glare softened a bit. "I'm just trying to look out for you," she grumbled. "God only knows what kind of trouble you'd get into without me."

"I know it's going to be hard to get used to, but most of the time we won't be able to share the things we work on with the others unless the job requires it," I reiterated. "I'm pretty excited about the new section, but there will be sacrifices. Let's please do our best to limit them. Okay?"

I got nods from everyone except Bonny who, in classic Bonny form, had sunk her teeth into something and wouldn't let go.

"Calendar entries," Jo said, starting a new topic, but I was still lingering on the tension created by Bonny's prying. If I couldn't get her to stop, I'd have to either isolate her from my work, or—though the thought pained me—replace her.

Please behave, Bonbon. Please.

When we were done with our meeting, we all went back to work in our respective areas.

By lunch time, I had worked my way through most of the stack and was reviewing a couple of the projects I intended to give to Jo. There was a call on the intercom around noon. It was lunch being delivered, courtesy of Bernie.

I always found the 'gift' of lunch from management to be a little self-serving. Yes, it was a free meal for the employees, but lunchtime was usually much shorter when food was delivered. Some would inevitably grab their food and then go back to their desk to eat, providing the company with more productivity than if the employee had gone out for lunch.

I felt a little ungrateful letting that thought pass through my head, but I couldn't stop thinking about it. So I insisted everyone eat together as a team in the conference room rather than at their desks. I was still thinking like a cube farm inhabitant—I'd have to stop that.

After lunch, I sat down next to Jo's desk and waited for her to finish typing an entry into the team calendar. When she was done, I gently placed three folders on the edge of her desk.

"What are these?" she asked.

"Research projects," I elaborated, smiling.

She took them and started to thumb through the contents.

"These are analyst projects," she stated in confusion as she shuffled through them.

"Yes, they are," I replied with a grin.

She looked up at me questioningly. "You want me to do

them?"

"If you feel up to it," I offered.

"Yes," she said, nodding her head enthusiastically. "I do."

"Good," I said as I rose to leave. "I thought you'd like that."

"Thank you," she called out as I went into my office.

It was 2:30 p.m., and no sooner had I seated myself than the phone on my desk chirped at me.

I hit the speaker button by tossing a pen at it. "Scott Wolfe," I said, seeing the ID was a secure Langley line.

"Have you heard?" John Temple's voice came over my speaker.

"Heard what?" I asked.

"Turn on the news," he ordered.

I grabbed the remote for the screen on my wall, turned it on, and then changed the source from computer to cable. As soon as I flipped to CNN, there were images of rescue vehicles in three split screens. It took me only a second to realize they were three different locations, not three views of the same location.

My heart jumped in my chest when I saw the headline banners at the bottom of the images.

"Radio and TV personalities murdered. Terrorism is suspected."

"Oh shit," I muttered, feeling the blood drain from my face.

"Yeah," John replied. "It looks like Grimwall wasn't the only one he was after."

I suddenly realized I was still on speaker phone and my office door was open. I reached over and picked the handset out of its cradle.

"What happened?" I asked.

"We're still trying to gather details, but it looks like there are at least eight of them," John replied. "Looks like it happened in two waves, ten minutes apart."

"Eight?!" I asked incredulously. "He didn't have time!"

"Either he set up some of them in advance or he had help," John replied. "It's possible the mystery woman was helping."

"Send me the info you have," I demanded.

"No," he replied. "Your role in this is over. Go back to work on the movement profiles that I sent you."

"I'm just supposed to sit here and watch and not be able to do anything about it?" I asked.

"Welcome to the Company," he replied. "If it's too much for you, turn the TV off."

I could tell by the stress in his voice that I shouldn't push it.

"Okay," I replied, though I didn't expect to stay out of it.

"I mean it, Scott," he replied. "I need that other data anyway. Drop this."

"Yes, sir," I replied with mock military crispness.

"I'll let you know if anything changes," he shot and then hung up without saying goodbye.

As soon as I hung up the handset, I noticed movement outside my office door.

"Who's that?" I asked.

Bonbon poked her head around the doorway, and then came into my office, followed closely by Storc.

"What's on TV, Scottmeister?" Bonbon asked with reserved knowing in her tone.

I looked at her for a second before responding. "Apparently some sort of terrorist attack in LA," I replied with a tone of concern.

"Not just in LA," Storc replied. "There's two in Denver, one in Albuquerque, and one in Chicago as well."

Not possible, I thought. *Gaines didn't have that kind of time. He never stopped in Albuquerque or Denver unless he did it before he killed his sister's murderers. This feels wrong.*

I looked at the screen, seeing the new additions to the list of cities. Bonny must have heard John on speaker phone and looked for updates on her own.

I nodded my acknowledgment as I stared at the screen.

"Does this have anything to do with your 'bicycle' accident?" Storc asked.

I looked at him and Bonbon for a moment, not wanting to lie, but resolved not to reveal anything—and slightly annoyed that the subject had come up again after my lecture.

"Do you remember who we work for?" I asked.

"Yeah," Bonbon said snidely. "TravTech."

"Wrong," I replied sharply. "As soon as that wall went up out there, TravTech is who we *used* to work for."

The expression on Bonny's face went from stern resolve to placid reflection to resignation in a matter of about four seconds.

"So no scoop then," she finally said, bitterness still tingeing her tone.

"We work for the CIA," I sighed. "We don't do *'scoops.'*"

She nodded and then turned and left, not happy with my response.

"She'll get it," Storc assured me. "You know how she hates not knowing stuff."

I nodded. "I know," I replied.

"And I hope you gave that *'runner'* who knocked you off the trail a good beat down," Storc said with a smile and a wink.

I chuckled despite myself. "Go back to work," I replied with a grin.

He gave a lingering look at the TV on his way out.

I refocused on what John had ordered me to work on—the movement profile for the missing nukes he didn't know I knew about. I started plugging the data into an assumed matrix when Jo appeared in my doorway.

"Bonbon was at my desk when your call from Langley came through," she said. "If you are going to use the speaker phone, you should close your door."

I nodded my understanding. "Thanks, Jo," I replied.

"You should look at this," she said, holding out one of the folders I had given her after lunch. "I think it requires immediate attention."

"I just handed that to you," I said with an impressed smile.

"It was an easy one," she replied, walking it over to me. "I put an updated data file on the server if you want to look at it. The asset they were tracking didn't have his credit card. A woman had it. That's why the phone tag and the purchases didn't match up."

I looked at her notes on the file. "A drugstore purchase?"

"Yes," she replied as I pulled the data up on my screen. "I hacked the transaction database for the pharmacy. Sleeping pills, wine, tampons, and rat poison."

I raised an eyebrow. "Someone is about to have a bad night," I muttered.

"That's what I thought as well," she responded. "We should get this back to Langley as soon as possible. It looks like their witness is about to be murdered by his wife, if it's not too late already."

I picked up the phone and dialed the contact number on the packet.

"Close the door for me," I said to Jo.

She began to leave and close the door behind her.

"No," I called to her. "I need you in here."

She walked back over after closing the door. The secure phone indicator flashed green as soon as the other end picked up.

"Europe West, Jane," came the reply.

"Jane, Hi. This is Scott Wolfe and Jo Zook over at

TravTech," I said.

"Hello," she replied. "How can I help you?"

"The package you sent over this morning on your asset in London, how old is that data?" I asked.

"Last night," she replied.

"You may want to check on him," I said. "Jo found a pharmacy purchase on the card and researched the items. Sleeping pills, wine, tampons, and rat poison. He was where he said he was. Jo and I think his wife had his card last night."

"Shit," Jane replied. "I knew that bitch was trouble."

"Yeah," I replied. "Jo is going to send the file package back to you now, but you should give him a call."

"Thanks," she replied abruptly. "Gotta go."

The line went dead.

I looked at Jo and smiled. "I need you to find and hire a new office manager," I announced.

"I don't understand," she said with a confused look on her face. "I thought you were happy with my performance."

"Very happy," I inserted quickly, heading off her doubts. "That's why you are now my lead analyst."

Her normally stiff expression slipped into something that could almost be considered a smile.

"I'll go back to the list you hired me from," she beamed, obviously struggling to keep her emotions in check.

"Pick someone neither of us will hate," I said as she opened the door to leave.

"I'll do my best," she replied and then disappeared around the corner.

As soon as she was gone, I pulled the movement matrix back up and ran it in simulation mode. It would take more than an hour for it to calculate origins and probability statistics. I watched my screen as lines were drawn from end points to possible origination locations—set after set appeared and then were overlaid with new ones.

I realized after a short time that I had zoned out and my mind had drifted back to Gaines.

"Why?" I muttered.

Why would you kill those people? In your state of mind I might even understand Buck Grimwall...but why the rest of them?

And why the hell did you have teeny tiny little non-explosive rockets if you already had massive amounts of explosive set in all those offices? It doesn't make sense.

I tried to figure out what the victims had in common—other than the obvious—they were all media personalities. But they weren't all even right wing. One of the TV guys in Denver was a lefty as well as one of the radio hosts in LA. And there was no way in hell he could have done the job in Chicago unless he had planted devices before his sister got killed.

I sat back in my chair and let the names and locations of the attacks flow across the inside of my eyelids. Suddenly a thought occurred to me.

The account lists, I thought. *Maybe they are all on there.*

I pulled up a spreadsheet and began entering the account and transaction numbers I had seen on the sheet before being interrupted by the mystery woman in Burbank. I had almost thirty transactions recorded by the time I was done.

"Why couldn't you have waited a minute longer?" I asked the memory of the hot, mystery woman. One more minute and I would have had all the account numbers and all the associated names.

I saved the spreadsheet file and then dumped it to a thumb drive.

When I was done, I sat and stared at the simulation that was still running. I wondered if John would be upset that I had figured out this was for the nukes the Serbs had stolen.

Only if it doesn't help find them, I thought in answer to my own question.

I decided to add more data to my simulation and run it again. I added transport methods, size limitations, network size, and then shielding and handling considerations for nuclear devices. I then took the movement data John had sent and ran a comparison to map data points.

Dead end routes and loop backs were given less weight. I entered the new matrix and overlaid it on a map to match the routes to actual roads. I let it run for a moment and was surprised when it returned a large map segment in the Middle East and into the edges of Africa and eastern Europe. I forced the search to continue, wondering if it matched any other regions. After several minutes, it reached the end of its map-matching routine and returned no other results.

"Middle East," I muttered and then sat back and wondered what else I could use to refine my travel simulation.

What do they have in the Middle East? I asked myself.

"They have wars in the Middle East," I responded sarcastically, and then realized that was a consideration. There were many factions in the region that would go to great lengths to get their hands on nuclear devices. The Serbs wouldn't be using indigenous personnel for fear of word getting out. Which means they have to be there in person for a reason.

"White faces aren't easy to hide in the Middle East," I muttered. "Arms dealers."

Popovich's group was made up of mercenaries and arms dealers. Even without their leadership, they would probably stick to what they knew.

I entered the new data into the simulator and set it running. It would be hours before the new simulation was complete. I took the time to do more research on the murders Gaines had perpetrated *in absentia.*

Several hours later, when my simulation had finished, I dumped the findings on the encrypted delivery drive and marked the project as requiring review by Langley.

It was after 7:00 p.m., so I stretched, shut down my computer, and left the office. Jo was still sitting in front of her computer.

"Are you about done?" I asked.

"Almost," she replied without looking away from her screen. "I just have to type up the notes on the last project you gave me."

"I'll have to give you something harder next time," I joked.

She grunted her acknowledgment.

"I'll see you tomorrow," I said.

She grunted again.

I love working with talented people.

**

9:25 p.m.—Langley, Virginia

NED RICHARDS walked down the corridor of NCS flanked by eight armed men carrying shackles and pushing a prisoner restraint cart. Several steps behind him were two DHS attorneys and a woman—Carrie Cantor from the Department of Justice—who was trying desperately to get Richards to stop walking.

"You don't have the authority," Cantor said. "Gaines is a DOJ prisoner. You can't just walk in and carry him away."

"Miss Cantor," Richards smirked without breaking stride or turning his head. "You will find that not only can I, but I will, in fact, take Gaines away tonight. I have an order signed by Judge Gunlock making sure that neither the CIA nor you can do anything about it."

Cantor pulled out her phone and dropped back, letting the traveling troupe from Homeland Security walk away from her. Richards turned his head, noticing she had peeled off, and smiled to himself.

When they arrived at John Temple's office, Ned knocked on the door. "We're here to take custody of your prisoner."

John glanced up, a look of confusion on his face. He lifted the blotter on his desk, opened and then closed several drawers, and then turned to Richards, patting first his pants pockets and then his jacket pockets. "Sorry," he said snidely. "I seem to have misplaced him."

"Where is he?" Richards asked.

"I'm sorry," John said, coming around his desk toward Richards. "Who are you?"

"Ned Richards, DHS with Director Raymond's office," he said. "I have an order signed by Judge Gunlock directing the CIA to turn Gaines over to us."

"How is Michael?" asked a voice from behind him.

Richards spun around and saw an older gentleman leaning against the wall of the corridor behind the group.

"Who's asking?" Richards asked.

The man raised an eyebrow, apparently feeling no introduction should be necessary.

"Mathew Burgess, *Director* of the National Clandestine Service…CIA," he replied, holding his hand out to shake. "Did Michael send you over here?"

Richards' eyebrows shot up briefly in shock—he knew the name. They shook hands and then Director Burgess leaned in close to Richards' ear. "You should have your stormtroopers wait in the lobby," he said. "They aren't invited to the meeting."

Ned swallowed and then nodded nervously, suddenly realizing that marching armed men into CIA Headquarters might have been less impressive and more threatening than he had pictured in his head.

"Go back up and wait for me to call you," Richards muttered to the commander of the guard who had accompanied him.

The man nodded and marched his men back out the way they had come.

"How about we meet in the conference room next to my office," Burgess suggested with a friendly smile, gesturing with his hand. The Homeland Security contingent followed Burgess down the hall.

Richards looked over his shoulder to see John Temple walking the opposite direction down the hall toward Miss Cantor, who was still on the phone. He leaned over to one of his lawyers and whispered, "Call Judge Gunlock and inform him his order is about to be challenged."

The lawyer nodded and peeled off down a connecting hallway.

When they arrived at the conference room, Richards saw a lavish arrangement of snacks and drinks on the conference room sideboard.

They were expecting us, he thought.

"Please, have a seat," Burgess said, gesturing to the conference table, and then opened a connecting door to the room. "I'll be right with you. Help yourself to refreshments."

As soon as Burgess disappeared into the office, Ned turned to the other lawyer.

"Whatever he says, we have Gunlock's order," he said in a low voice. "We need to get Gaines out of here as fast as possible and to the transport plane. Whatever you have to do to make that happen, you do it."

The lawyer nodded confidently. Several minutes later, Richards watched as the other DHS lawyer wandered past the door of the conference room.

"In here," he yelled into the hall.

The lawyer reappeared in the doorway and joined his colleague at the conference table. Several more minutes passed. Richards began to get antsy and started fidgeting with his pen, whacking it against the pad of paper in front of him in a rhythmic beat. *Tap, tap, tap, tap.*

As more time passed, he got up from his seat and began pacing back and forth across the room, passing by the sideboard once before returning and grabbing a pastry from the stack. He took one bite and then tossed it back on the table next to the platter.

He paced more as the two lawyers began looking nervous.

"What the fuck is taking him so long?" Richards asked to no one in particular.

He looked at his watch and saw that it had been almost forty-five minutes since Burgess had left the room. He suddenly marched to the connecting door Burgess had disappeared through and knocked.

"Mister Burgess," he called through the door.

No response.

He knocked again, longer and louder than before. " Director Burgess," he called.

Again, no response.

He heard voices coming from down the hall and poked his head through the door. Coming toward him he saw Burgess, Temple, Cantor and two people he didn't recognize—one in a Navy dress uniform.

Richards quickly went back into the conference room and sat back in his seat. As the group approached the door, Burgess stuck his head in.

"Just one more moment," he said apologetically. "Trying to get some details tied up before the briefing."

"What? But—" Richards sputtered, but Burgess had already left.

Richards slammed his hand down roughly on the table, sending a spike of pain up his wrist. "Damn it," he muttered as he began to rub the soreness he had just inflicted upon himself.

Several more minutes passed, and Richards was beginning to get very angry. He looked at his watch and saw that they had now been in the conference room for more than an hour. He pulled out his phone and dialed. Just as the phone began to ring, Burgess and the rest of his entourage entered the room from the hallway with two new additions. Richards closed his phone.

"Sorry to keep you waiting," Burgess sighed tiredly but with sincerity as the group began filing around the table. "I have to admit, you caught us a little off guard, and we had to do some scrambling."

"She shouldn't be here," Richards growled, pointing at Cantor.

Burgess looked at Miss Cantor and furrowed his brow. "Miss Cantor, I believe you have an authorization?"

"Yes," she said, dropping a piece of paper on the table in front of Richards before seating herself as far away from him as possible.

Richards picked it up and began to read it.

"As I said," Burgess continued. "We had to do a bit of detective work, but we think we may have located Gaines."

Richards continued to read the paper when Burgess's comment sank in. "Wait. What?" he asked. "I thought Gaines was already in custody."

"Oh, he's in custody," Burgess said. "But the transport was covert, so we had to wait for authorization to get the departure and destination points."

"Transport?!" Richards exclaimed. "Why would he be transported?"

"Well, Mr. Richards," Burgess said as if taken aback. "This is CIA Headquarters. You didn't actually think we'd be housing a dangerous criminal here, did you?"

"So where is he?" Ned screeched, his face turning red in embarrassment and his voice an octave higher than it had been.

"He's in transit," Burgess replied calmly. "Once you indicated you were to take custody, we had to replace the transport and detention orders. The transport team should get the new instructions in about six hours when they reach the secure facility. Then they'll turn him around and take him to the Navy Brig in Norfolk," he said, looking at his watch. "That should make him available for pickup around noon tomorrow in Norfolk, assuming there are no hang-ups with transport."

"What the fuck?!" Richards exclaimed.

"There's no need for that kind of language," Burgess said, an angry grimace settling on his features. "There are ladies present."

Richards wasn't sure if Burgess was being a gentleman of his generation or just taking the opportunity to scold him like schoolboy in front of the others. "You can play the shell game with Gaines if you like, but there will be repercussions," Richards said, rising out of his seat a bit.

Burgess was about to speak again when John Temple cut in.

"Gaines is a trained CIA operative with high-level escape and evasion training and experience," Temple said in a commanding tone. "In addition, he has secrets in that head of his that require safe guarding—and as if that weren't enough, he's one of the most skilled hand-to-hand combatants this agency has ever produced. We couldn't simply stick him on the bus to county lockup."

Richards calmed down a bit and sat back down.

"Transport, escort, and detention have to be arranged and secured in a manner compliant with National Security directives," John continued. "And changing those plans midstream is time and resource consuming. Neither of which are easy to come by after a day of national lockdown such as today."

Richards nodded his understanding, feeling sufficiently chastised.

"In the meantime, the Department of Justice has indicated they have an interest in Gaines as well," Burgess added.

"I have an order from—" Richards began.

"Yes, yes, Judge Gunlock," Burgess interrupted. "But Judge Chambers has asked that Miss Cantor and her attorneys from DOJ be present for the debrief so he can determine the appropriateness of that order."

Ned began to turn red again. He knew that Chambers could dismiss Gunlock's order if given cause. That would complicate things severely.

"So how do we proceed?" Richards asked.

"Well," John said. "Your boys in black are still waiting in the lobby. You can start by sending them home. They won't be needed tonight."

Embarrassment and anger welled up in Richards again. He flicked his wrist at one of his lawyers without looking at him. The man took out his phone and proceeded to make the call.

"Let's start the debrief," Richards said as the man made his call. "Let's start by getting the identities of the Agents involved in Gaines's capture."

John Temple raised his hand. "That would be me," he said with a pleased look on his face.

"I was under the impression there were more people involved," Richards said.

Burgess gave Temple a strange look and then nodded.

"I was the only Agent involved in the capture," Temple said. "But I had technical support accompanying me."

"Is that person in the room?" Richards asked, looking around the table.

"No," Burgess replied. "He is a civilian contractor. He's since been detached to another project."

"Civilian contractor?" Richards asked hopefully. "Baynebridge?"

"No," Burgess replied. "A computer and surveillance

specialist on an Agency contract."

"But—" Richards started, about to ask about the second fighter in the alley before realizing that would reveal too much about his information. "Never mind. When can I meet with him?"

"We haven't established that will be necessary," Burgess said commandingly. "It may expose other operations we have in the works. We can't compromise national security because of a prisoner handover."

"This isn't just a prisoner handover," Richards said, matching Burgess's tone. "I'm also collecting intel on the attacks. I need to know if anyone had direct contact with Gaines and what information may have been relayed."

Burgess shot Temple another strange look and then shook his head.

"I'm sorry," Temple said. "Until we have a determination from Judge Chambers, the contractor stays anonymous. But I can tell you that no information was revealed by Gaines. We were caught completely off guard by the attacks. There was no indication he had the means or the desire to kill those radio and TV hosts."

"What about any other intel on site at the time of his capture?" Richards asked. "Was anything recovered?"

Temple nodded his head. "There was a device that appeared to be constructed to fire eight non-explosive rockets from the undercarriage of a vehicle," he said. "We were aware of the acquisition of the training rounds and all were accounted for at the time of his capture."

"Well that sounds like 'means and desire' to me!" Richards said, a little victory in his voice.

"The rounds were, as I said, non-explosive, set to fire in tandem, and were all accounted for," Temple reiterated. "There was no sign of any explosives or any hint of a target list."

"Well, it would seem the CIA missed some clues then,"

Richards said smugly. "Because he obviously managed to eliminate a rather extensive and very public list of targets."

"How can you be so sure?" Burgess asked.

I hope your evidence is airtight, Heinrich, Richards thought to himself.

"We have route, access, and target evidence from our own sources," Richards replied. "We've had our eye on Gaines for more than a week now."

Temple turned to Burgess and they exchanged a brief look before Temple continued.

"There was no evidence of such a motivation when we caught up to him," Temple reiterated. "But if you've been tracking him, then certainly you would have been aware of the assistance he had been providing on a DOJ investigation."

Ned shifted uncomfortably in his chair. Braun had warned him that subject might come up.

"We were aware of an investigation, but have no details," he replied. "If you have more information on that, DHS would very much appreciate being brought into the loop on its progress and any findings."

John stared at Richards for several seconds before responding. Miss Cantor was looking very confused, and she was about to speak when Temple responded.

"We have no idea what the investigation had uncovered or any details on the subject of the investigation," John said. "All we know is that Mark was aiding a Deidre Faulks at the DOJ and that the investigation ended abruptly when Ms. Faulks was murdered a little more than two weeks ago."

Surprise appeared on Miss Cantor's face. This was clearly news to her.

"I see," Richards said as he tried to hide his discomfort. "So you have no information on the investigation. Gaines didn't share anything about that with you?"

"No," Temple said, relaxing his expression. "He didn't. We didn't exactly chat."

"And how about this civilian contractor?" Richards asked. "Might he have gotten any information from Gaines?"

"Unlikely," Temple replied.

"Unlikely, but you don't know for sure," Richards said.

"If it makes any difference," the Justice lawyer piped up. "We'd be interested in hearing the testimony of this contractor as well."

"Let me make a call to our legal department and see what our exposure level would be if we brought him in," Burgess interjected.

The man next to him nodded his agreement.

"While I'm doing that, why don't we take a short break," Burgess said and then looked at Temple and nodded toward his office.

Everyone began rising from the table as Temple and Burgess retreated into the office next door.

Richards got the sudden feeling a trap was being laid for him.

**

JOHN TEMPLE closed the door to the office. Burgess was standing in front of his desk staring at him when he turned around.

"I don't know what's going on out there, but we are going to be up to our assholes in congressional hearings if this goes south on us," John said. "This is starting to smell real bad."

Burgess nodded. "At least we bought some time," he said. "Richards would have his security team back down here in a second if he knew Gaines was downstairs when he arrived."

"Nice work pulling together that disappearing act on such short notice," John chuckled.

Burgess grinned. "It helps to know all the players," he said.

"Was Judge Chambers terribly upset about the late call?" John asked.

Burgess shook his head. "He was grateful for the heads' up," he replied. "I don't think anyone at Justice knew this was coming, so they were pretty grateful as well."

"Look," John said, plopping down in the chair in front of Burgess's desk. "I don't mind Scott getting debriefed by Justice, but I'll be damned if I'm going to let him get mixed up in whatever this is with Homeland."

"We might not have a choice," Burgess replied, rubbing his eyes with his fingers. "But let me call legal and see if we have a leg to stand on."

John nodded then got up and headed for the door.

"And John," Burgess said as he picked up the phone on his desk. "Be careful what you say to Richards. Whatever it is he's into, he's in over his head. The last thing we want is to spook him."

"Yes, sir," John replied and then exited Burgess's office.

When he got into the conference room, he looked up and saw that two additional people had joined at his end of the table—bringing the Homeland Security contingent up to five.

"This is going to be a long night," John muttered.

twelve
Tuesday, July 27th

2:05 a.m.—Fairfax, Virginia

I was sound asleep for the first time in days when my phone awakened me. I noted it was about 2:00 a.m. as I answered.

"Hello," I said groggily.

"I'm sorry to wake you." John's voice.

"What's up?" I asked, rubbing my eyes.

"I can't talk long, we are just on a short break," he said in a low voice. "You're going to have to debrief again."

"Why? What's going on?" I asked, getting some clarity as I began to boot up.

"Homeland has latched onto this," he said, "*this*" obviously being the situation with Gaines. He wouldn't mention it over the phone.

"Okay. How does that affect me?" I asked.

"Someone will pick you up in the morning," he replied. "We tried to keep you out of it, but they aren't having it."

"Understood," I replied. "Same rules as before?"

"I'm not sure," he said. "I'll know more tomorrow."

"Okay," I replied. "What time?"

"Not sure," he said. Then his voice got even lower. "Gotta go."

The call ended abruptly.

I lay back down and tried to get back to sleep, but Gaines was fresh in my head again. I tossed and turned for a few hours and then finally just gave up and went into the kitchen to make coffee. After my third cup, I got dressed and headed into work early.

I sent John a text as I got into my car: *"On my way to work."*

A moment later I got a reply as I pulled to a stop at the intersection of the Fairfax County Parkway. It read: *"Still in a holding pattern here."*

**

I was at my desk, working on the nuke movement simulation, when my intercom buzzed. I hit speaker.

"Mr. Wolfe. There is a gentleman here from Langley to escort you to a meeting." It was the voice of our security guard at the front desk.

This is it, I thought.

I punched 'mute' with my finger and then yelled into the other office. "Jo? Do I have a meeting at Langley today?" I asked, not wanting to have to face uncomfortable questions upon my departure.

"No," she said immediately.

I hit the speaker button again. "Okay. I'll be up in a second."

I shut down my system and walked into Jo's work area.

"Apparently I do," I said as I walked by her desk. "There are five new projects in the queue. Two of them are going to require Storc's help."

She nodded as she pulled the list up.

"Are you going to be back today?" she asked as I shouldered my canvas shoulder bag and headed for the door.

"I'm not sure," I said. "If anything important pops up, text me."

"Alright," she replied, already opening the files for her new projects.

When I went through the secure door into reception, I was shocked to see Nick Horiatis—the man, the myth, the legend—who, with my assistance, had pulled a cargo container full of hostages out of the back of an in-flight, Russian-built, cargo plane.

"Nick!" I exclaimed, genuinely happy to see him. "It's good to see you, man!" I said, extending my hand to shake his.

He smiled and returned the gesture. "Good to see you, Scott. You look no worse for the wear," he said, knocking me in the shoulder with the side of his closed hand.

"You look sharp too. Nice suit," I complimented.

"There is a uniform for every duty in the job description," he said. I noticed out of the corner of my eye that the security guard lifted his gaze to take another look at Nick. The 'uniform' comment piqued his interest.

"You feeling okay? I heard about this weekend. No broken bones?" he asked jokingly.

I suddenly felt very uncomfortable talking around the security guard.

"Let's get going," I said, and then turned and looked at the guard. "Have a good one, Officer Brown."

"Thank you, sir," he said curtly as we left.

On the ride to Langley, Nick had been directed to bring me up to speed.

"There are things I'm supposed to tell you about and specific things I've been told not to reveal. But for the life of me I can't remember which are which, so I'll just tell you everything and sort it out later," he said, winking at me.

"Okay. Let's start with the second debrief," I responded.

"Homeland is calling the assassinations an act of terror," he said, his face growing serious.

"They want him," I acknowledged. "Why is that a problem?"

"They are classifying him an enemy combatant," he replied. "That means rendition."

"I thought we didn't do rendition anymore," I said, "as a nation."

"Yeah. There are other words that can be used for the same thing," he replied with a cruel grin. "The government has been disappearing people since before we had a Constitution. It's a tradition unlikely to end any time soon."

"Does it make any difference that Gaines was working with a Justice Department investigator who got killed just before all this happened?" I asked.

"You don't have to convince me," he said as we merged onto the highway. "It makes perfect sense to me. As far as I'm concerned, he was on an op that went bad. Whoever he was after found out who he was and killed his sister as a warning. Not too bright, obviously. There are some people you just don't mess with like that."

"So why am I being hauled in?" I asked.

Nick shrugged. "Homeland wants to do the debrief on you themselves," he replied. "I'm not sure why."

"John gave me rules before for what I should and shouldn't say," I mentioned as we slowed behind some heavy traffic.

Nick looked at me with a serious stare. "We can't tell you to lie," he said and waited for me to respond.

"That's it?" I replied incredulously. "You can't tell me to lie?"

He smiled before refocusing on the road as traffic started moving again. "I don't know what it means, so don't tell me, but John said, 'Same rules as before and don't mention the papers.'" He saw the realization on my face. "Seriously. Don't tell me. I don't want to be involved in this shit."

I nodded my understanding.

"How'd Homeland say he did it?" I asked.

"Automation is a wonderful thing," he said. "He modified desk chairs all over LA on Friday and Saturday. The way they figured it, he had already finished with at least Grimwall's before you caught up with him the first time."

"God damn it," I muttered.

"You couldn't have done anything. They had him doped and questioned all night before the attack and he didn't spill anything. It wouldn't have made any difference," he said, trying to let me off the hook. "You have to learn that, first thing—if you are going to do this kind of work—most of the time, delegation means you do your job and then pass it off to the next group to do their job."

I nodded and grunted my understanding, but it didn't make it any easier to handle.

"What about the explosions in Denver, Chicago, and Albuquerque?" I asked.

"They say they have the transponder log on his stolen government vehicle in Chicago before he disabled it," he replied. "And they have satellite imagery of him in Denver and Albuquerque. But more than that, they have his target list."

"That's bullshit," I said. "I had eyes on him all the way from Colorado Springs. He didn't stop in Albuquerque."

Nick shot me a nervous glance. "Does John know that?"

"Yeah!" I exclaimed. "He was with me the whole time."

Nick shook his head. "Not that I want to be involved… Mark isn't a friend of mine. But I'll remind John there is conflicting data," he said seriously in a quieter voice. "But they still have his target list. They say he stole the information from a Baynebridge VP."

"The target list?" I muttered. *I need to get those account numbers to John.* "I bet the Justice investigation is tied to the murders…and Homeland, if they're pushing this bullshit story."

"Keep that sort of insight to yourself in this meeting," he said. "The last thing you want is for Homeland Security to think you know more than you're telling. You could be next on their list."

"Awesome," I said sarcastically. "Just so I know whose side I'm supposed to be on, who am I taking my lead from?"

"The old man," Nick said. "He'll be there as well."

"John?" I asked.

Nick laughed. "Right. I keep forgetting you aren't 'in' yet," he said. "Director of the National Clandestine Service. This is being sold as a containment operation due to the secrets locked away in Gaines's head. National Security and all that nonsense. Justice will be pissed, but unless they come up with a warrant from a FISA judge, Homeland Security is going to get him. This is damage control for us. One of them is already throwing around accusations of CIA complicity in hiding Mark…it's a short hop to accusing us of being coconspirators."

"What do they want?" I asked.

"His brain," he replied solemnly.

I nodded my understanding. "What else do I need to know?"

"The guy that tried to hit you and John in the alley after you caught Gaines… John thought he looked familiar, but we are still having a hard time placing him," he said. "He's been looking through mug shots all morning."

"So, no way to figure out who he's working for now," I added.

"Right. But we're pretty sure he's not a loner," he said. "Even the State Department tried to jump into the mix over this."

"State," I muttered. I suspected I knew who at State was nosing around. "Robert Whitney?"

Nick shook his head. "He may be involved, but there were some serious ES pay grade types wandering the halls this morning from State—Bob Whitney doesn't pull that kind of weight. If he's involved, it's because the Secretary is pulling the strings."

I knew that ES pay grade referred to "Executive Schedule" personnel—many hundreds of senior-level appointees, deputies, cabinet members, etc. People who seriously outranked Barb's "Daddy."

"Secretary? As in the Secretary of State?" I asked. I could feel my eyebrows disappear beneath my hairline. Maybe I should have heard Barb's dad out before booting him out the door yesterday.

Nick chuckled. "Yeah," he replied. "Whatever you're mixed up in, it's got some big names looking at it."

"Great," I replied sarcastically. "And they're bringing me in to be debriefed? In front of them?"

"Don't worry. Follow the old man's lead. He'll let you know what you can and can't answer and in front of who," he replied.

We didn't speak for a few minutes, and then Nick broke the silence again.

"I gotta know. How did you do it?" he asked. "You surprised him, didn't you."

He wanted to know how I beat Gaines. I shook my head and then shrugged.

"He slipped and fell, right?" he asked, mocking me.

I just chuckled.

"Fine," he said. "Don't tell me."

I could tell he felt he needed to know.

"I'm not sure how or why, but the memory of Majmun putting that torch to me pulled me out of a blackout after he hit me," I said. "I whipped around and got hold of him."

Nick laughed. "Good for you. It's about time someone gave that prick an ass whoopin'." But I could tell he didn't believe me.

"It took me a while to come down," I confided. I'm not sure why I told him, but I felt like he would understand.

He didn't reply immediately. I could see he was thinking about what I had said. When he finally spoke, his tone had changed to that of a confidante.

"John said you almost took *him* out as well," he said.

"I was in some serious rage-induced fog," I said quietly.

"Rage-induced? I heard you got whacked in the head with an extendo," he said, looking over briefly with a knowing grin on his face. "I'm not your fucking shrink, but I can tell you from personal experience that fire or steel applied to human flesh will either cause rage or turn you into drooling mental patient. Sometimes both, but it's never ever *not* one of them."

"I guess," I replied.

"Don't guess. It's a fact. And you don't seem to be drooling, so I'd say you're handling it pretty well," he said smiling. "Now tighten up. You've got a meeting with carrion eaters, and we don't need you getting all fucking weepy on us."

Nick continued to brief me on what to expect, who to speak to and when—and most importantly, when to "keep my fucking mouth shut."

**

Upon arrival at Langley, we passed through a special side of security, went up an elevator to the seventh floor, and walked through winding hallways to a large meeting room. Nick had me wait in the hall and then continued a couple doors further down.

I looked across the hall and saw a very short door—too short to be an office—probably a custodial closet. But on the wall next to the door was an office placard like the ones next to each door in the building. I squinted to make sure I was reading it correctly:

Office of Shire Affairs

I chuckled. *Who said spies don't have a sense of humor?*

Nick was back in a matter of seconds and then nodded me toward the conference room. There were several people already seated around the table when we arrived.

When Nick knocked at the door, all heads turned to us. A man in his late fifties or early sixties approached us, smiling.

"Scott Wolfe," he said, extending his hand to shake mine. "We've never been formally introduced, but we've spoken. I'm Mathew Burgess, Director of NCS. It's a pleasure to finally meet you."

He had a firm handshake, and he seemed to be genuinely pleased to meet me. On the other hand, this was the head of the National Clandestine Service, so you never knew for sure.

"It's nice to meet you, sir," I said, smiling in return—after all, it's not every day you get meet the head spy of the nation.

"Thanks, Nick. Someone will give you a yell when it's time to take him back," Burgess said, dismissing Nick.

"Yes, sir," Nick replied, acknowledging the order, and then he looked at me. "Relax, kid. You've got this." He retreated down the hall.

"Scott. This is Carrie Cantor with the Justice Department. She will be *observing* your debrief today," he said.

I got the impression the emphasis on the word "observing" was code to me that the situation with Gaines transfer had changed. I reached out and shook her hand.

"And this is Ned Richards from Homeland Security. He has

some questions for you as well," he said.

I wanted to ask which Department in Homeland Security, but I followed Nick's advice and "kept my fucking mouth shut."

There were four others in the room who I hadn't been introduced to. I guessed they didn't rate it, but I felt it was a bit rude none-the-less. One of them was a recorder. The other three were suits; two stood against the wall, one sat next to Richards. The two against the wall looked badass—security, I guessed.

"Okay. Let's get started shall we?" Director Burgess said.

"Mr. Wolfe. I'd like for you to describe the events of the past four days. From Thursday around noon until your arrival here today," Richards blurted out.

Director Burgess raised his hand, indicating I should not answer.

"That's not how we are going to do things," he said, looking at Richards with piercing, almost menacing eyes—very different from the friendly man who had shaken my hand a few moments earlier. "We will be dissecting only those areas pertinent to your inquiries and only those that are authorized for disclosure."

"I don't see why we can't just hear the whole story and then decide what's important and what's not," Richards protested.

"Well, then you've been out of the loop on security matters. NCS has broad discretion on certain operational matters, and unless you have a little piece of paper signed by a FISA judge, I get to decide what anyone outside the Agency hears."

Richards smiled a smug smile. He had expected the resistance. He just wanted me to see that there was a power struggle and that I should be careful whose side I chose.

The director turned to me.

"I know you don't know it, but this is highly irregular, Scott," he said. "Normally a civilian debrief would not be exposed to this much high-level scrutiny. Rest assured, your answers will not reflect on you."

"Thank you, sir," I replied courteously, letting him know with my body language that I was his to guide through the meeting.

"Why don't we start with how you were approached for assistance in this op," he continued.

"I got a call from Captain Temple on Thursday afternoon, asking if I was available to do some tech support for a field op," I replied.

"Captain Temple?" Ms. Cantor questioned. "You mean Agent Temple. Right?"

"Yes ma'am. Sorry. My first encounter with 'Agent' Temple was in a different uh...format, and I was introduced to him by his honorary."

"I don't think we are aware of the circumstances under which you met Agent Temple," Richards interrupted, looking through his info packet. "I'd like to know more about that as well."

"That's off the table. He's been debriefed on that situation," the director asserted.

"Fine. Just answer the question, Mr. Wolfe," Richards said curtly.

"Agent Temple asked if I was up to doing some tech support in a field capacity," I said again.

"Didn't you consider it a little unusual for Agency personnel to ask an untrained civilian for support on a field operation?" Richards asked.

I looked at the director for a signal that it was okay to continue and he nodded.

"I didn't know what was unusual and what wasn't. I had just been placed in charge of a technical operation that had been created by contract with the company I work for. We hadn't even gotten our infrastructure built yet, so I had nothing to gauge the request by."

"Still. You had to know that computer support personnel

aren't used for field ops," Richards said incredulously.

"I knew no such thing," I replied straight-faced. "I was given the option to decline. I opted to help."

Richards shifted in his chair. He wasn't happy with my responses, but no one else seemed bothered by them. I dismissed it as a case of him being an asshole.

"How did you locate Gaines?" Richards asked.

Just then my phone went off. *"Don't want to be your Monkey Wrench,"* sang out from my pocket, alerting me to a new email.

The director looked at me with a grin before turning back to Richards. "That question is too broad and in some areas involves operational practices," he interrupted before I could reply to the question. "It needs to be narrowed."

"This is a waste of time," Richards said as if bored by the whole process. "Why don't you just ask him the questions you want us to hear the answers to and be done with this farce?"

"You will watch your tone, sir," the director rumbled, clearly impressing upon Richards the boundaries of this meeting.

"Yes, of course. I apologize," Richards said, backing his attitude down a bit. "I'm here to get a clear picture of what happened and what happens next—it's exceedingly difficult with these inter-agency rules."

The director ignored the apology and turned to me. "Scott. We already know that you and Agent Temple flew to Colorado Springs and that you were given access to the investigation materials by the local police force. We are also aware that you obtained some raw data footage from satellite feeds for the region."

"How did you obtain those feeds?" Ms. Cantor interrupted.

The director nodded, indicating I was to answer.

My phone went off again. *"Don't want to be your Monkey Wrench,"* sang Dave Grohl into my pocket one more time.

"Do you need to get that?" Richards asked with a snarl.

"No," I replied quickly as I extracted my phone from my pocket to place it on silent. My heart jumped when I saw there were two new emails from Kathrin on my personal email account. I set my phone to silent and then stowed it again.

"I was handed a pocket drive containing the first three sets. There was a fourth set, but I didn't need it," I replied, suddenly distracted by my waiting messages. I mentally took a deep breath to refocus on the task at hand.

"Under what conditions did you receive this data?" she asked.

"In all three cases they were handed to me by Agent Temple," I replied. Again, she wasn't satisfied.

"And how did Agent Temple get the data he handed to you?" she asked.

"I'm not sure how he got the first or the last pocket drive. The second drive was left in a lunch bag at the airport in Albuquerque, and the third in a padded envelope he picked up off the ground after bumping into a man in a bad suit," I said, resisting an urge to smile.

"You don't know where the data came from before that?"

"No ma'am. I was given data to parse, so I parsed it," I replied.

"Why didn't you need the fourth set of data?" the director asked, clearly already knowing the answer.

"Because I saw Gaines. He rolled into the lot where we were parked and then entered a building. While he was inside, I wrapped my iPhone in one of my T-shirts and stuffed it into his spare tire."

Richards's eyes narrowed to a slit. "An iPhone? Wrapped in a t-shirt?"

"Yes sir. A Melvin's T-shirt," I said stiffly, doing my best to restrain a smirk.

"A Melvin's T—" he replied curtly. "Why didn't you or

Agent Temple subdue him at that time?"

"Agent Temple was inside another building with no way for me to contact him," I replied crisply. "And as you have pointed out, I am untrained tech support—not an Agent. It didn't even occur to me to try and subdue a trained CIA Agent."

"We know what a crock that is," he said under his breath, loud enough for everyone to hear.

"Ned. If you already know what happened, then we don't require Mr. Wolfe's presence any longer," the director inserted.

"Mr. Wolf's actions in Burbank and his history indicate he's considerably more than 'untrained tech support.' I just want some straight answers," Richards said impatiently.

The director looked at me and smiled in a friendly gesture. "Scott. I have to admit, I've been curious about that myself. Could you elaborate?"

"I assume you are asking about the physical confrontations I've been involved in?" I asked, trying to clarify.

"That, and your ability to find that which does not wish to be found," he replied.

"Finding stuff is what I do. All day long, every day. I look for a missing comma in a hundred thousand lines of code. I look for inconsistencies in video feeds, clicks in audio feeds, digital fingerprints on viruses and Trojans," I replied. "I've always been good at seeing things that others don't see. It's my job."

"Understood," said the director. "And the combat?"

"I took karate when I was in elementary school," I offered, shrugging, knowing full well it wouldn't satisfy the question.

Richards rolled his eyes.

"I'm also a climber," I continued. "I've been climbing at least three times a week since I was ten. It creates very dense muscle and an exceptionally strong grip."

"Strong enough to break bone?" Ms. Cantor asked, unbelieving.

Richards scoffed. "I'd like to see that. Do you mind if we have a little demonstration of this incredible 'grip?'" he asked, mocking my comment.

He turned to one of the guys standing against the wall—a big guy. "Glenn, would mind shaking hands with Mr. Wolfe?"

The big guy puffed up his chest, smiled, and walked over to me, extending his hand. I remained seated but turned in my chair to face him.

Just as I gripped his hand, the director leaned over and whispered in my ear.

"No permanent damage, Scott," he said.

I waited for the big guy to squeeze. I'd learned a long time ago that big man-tits don't necessarily equate to great strength. I'd seen enough jocks peel off of rock, time and time again, because they thought their muscle was a match for a slab of granite.

I gripped, not with my full strength, but enough to send him down to his knee with a grimace of pain. I released when he yowled.

All eyes in the room opened wide except for the director, who I assume was briefed on the strength of my hands.

"I think that clears up the mystery a bit," the director said as the muscle man slunk back to his wall position, rubbing his hand.

"Strong hands don't explain how you subdued a combat-trained CIA Agent," Richards sneered. He looked at his notes. "In fact, Agent Temple called him, and I quote, 'One of the most skilled hand-to-hand combatants this Agency has ever produced.'"

How could I possibly explain what I didn't myself understand?

"He had me confined. When I escaped, he showed up and tried to subdue me. I got hold of his wrist and broke it, and then I head butted him—repeatedly—effectively rendering him *combat incapable*," I explained.

"How did he sustain the rest of his injuries?" Ms. Cantor asked.

"As has been pointed out, I am untrained. When I was attacked, I sustained a blow to the back of my head. It left me dazed and very angry. Once he was on the ground, I didn't immediately stop striking him. It was several minutes before I regained my wits."

"Ms. Cantor. It is not uncommon for head trauma to cause violent episodes in anyone, especially those faced with situational stress," the director chimed in. "There is an Agency psychiatrist's report on the incident in your folder. Scott was evaluated by her after the incident and she concluded he acted in an almost-unconscious, instinctive manner. She said it would be quite expected under the circumstances."

She seemed to accept the explanation.

"Did Gaines reveal any plans to you or tell you why he was in LA?" Richards asked. "Did you witness any details or see any documentation that might explain his actions?"

I thought very carefully about answering that question. I wanted to do it honestly if I could.

"I saw nothing nor heard anything that would have suggested he was about to blow up eight high-profile targets," I replied honestly. "The closest I came was thinking that the LAW training rounds were for Buck Grimwall. But the configuration was wrong for that, and we ended up in possession of all of them."

"And what about in retrospect," Richards asked. "Looking back now, did he say or do anything or did you see or read anything that might, in retrospect, have been an indication of his targets?"

He had me trapped in the detail—but beyond that, I could see ripples of discomfort on his face when he said the words "documentation" and "read anything." I had to trust John and do what he asked.

"No," I lied. "I can't think of a thing."

Judging by the micro-expression that flitted across Richards's face, I could tell he didn't believe me.

He wouldn't believe you no matter what you said, whispered my other voice into my ear. *He wants something from you.*

If that was the case, he didn't show it during the rest of the debriefing. The rest of the meeting was a rehashing of all the details of our other encounters with Gaines, the surveillance we set up, and how I had been captured. All without any more second guessing from Richards.

"There is the matter of the unknown gunman," Ms. Cantor said as the debriefing began to wind down.

"Except for the fact that they were attacked, there is no other useful information regarding that matter," Richards said. "Unless there is new information concerning the identity of the man, I recommend holding off on any discussion. We wouldn't want to introduce any classified speculation in the presence of uncleared personnel." He was obviously referring to me.

That statement struck me as wholly self-serving. I recognized the micro-expressions on Richards face—he was hiding something. I noticed out of the corner of my eye that Director Burgess hadn't reacted. Perhaps he didn't see it, or perhaps he was just better at hiding his responses than Ned Richards was.

"I agree," Burgess said. Then I saw it. It was just a flash, but he didn't want to disclose anything more to Richards either. "We need to hunt down more leads on that incident. We aren't even certain they are related…though a coincidence seems unlikely."

Cantor reluctantly accepted the determination and moved on.

"I want it stated for the record that Justice feels Gaines belongs to us," she said, turning to look directly at Richards. "We have already begun the legal procedure to have him transferred." She slid a piece of paper to him.

Richards looked at the paper and anger flashed across his face.

"A stay?" he asked incredulously. "Just because you have a friendly judge doesn't mean you can subvert the process."

"Look again," she said. "It's Judge Chambers. He wants to review the matter before Gaines disappears into a dark hole somewhere."

"This is unacceptable," Richards replied. "Gaines is ours. We are moving him to a secure location."

"That is unlikely," Cantor said. "And to be certain he doesn't just disappear, there are federal marshals escorting him to his holding location."

Ned looked at the paper again and shook his head. "We'll just have to let the lawyers figure it out," he said with a smug grin, clearly not believing he would lose custody of his prisoner.

When we had concluded, I rose and shook hands with Ms. Cantor, who smiled warmly at me. When I reached for Richards' hand, he withdrew it quickly.

"On the off chance that I've offended you, I hope you don't mind if we don't shake," he said and then exited the room briskly.

"Thank you, Scott," the director said. "If you could, I'd like for you to wait in the office next door. I'll be just a minute longer."

"Yes sir," I said, and then entered the office. There in the corner was Captain John Temple.

"Hey there, Scott," John said as I entered. "You did good."

I closed the door. "You could hear?" I asked.

"Me? Nah," he said, smiling, and then winked.

He motioned me to a chair in front of the desk.

I grinned and accepted his invitation to sit. After a few moments, Director Burgess entered the office.

"Thank you, Scott. You did just fine," he said, shaking my hand again. "And, by the way, I can't express enough gratitude to you for saving the life of one or more of my boys."

"There was more chance involved than anything else. I only wish we could have gotten him before he killed all those people," I said with regret, though I suddenly felt as if I had told another lie—but I wasn't ready to take my other voice at its word. Timing issues aside, Buck Grimwall was dead after Gaines had stalked him.

"Not your concern. You did more than was asked and far more than was expected," he said supportively.

"Still…" I started.

"Yes—still," he repeated solemnly. After a moment's pause, he continued. "In either case, it's out of our hands. People further up the food chain than myself have decided to turn this mess over to Homeland Security unless Justice can get the transfer."

John shook his head. "And Baynebridge."

"Baynebridge?" I asked.

"You might know them better as Black River or Executive Decision, Inc.," the director explained. "They change their name every time they get in trouble with the press. They are basically a private military and intelligence company."

"Why would private military and intelligence have hooks in Gaines?" I asked, not sure I got the connection.

"Much of federal security and intelligence is contracted through them," Burgess continued. "The guard at your office is Baynebridge Security."

"Really?" I asked, having assumed he was a civil servant.

"We should really be doing something to keep Gaines with DOJ," John said.

Burgess shook his head. "It's out of our hands, John," he said. "Though I think Justice isn't going to let him go that easily."

"I've got something that might help," I said, reaching into my pocket and extracting the thumb drive with the account and transaction numbers I had remembered.

"What's this?" John asked.

"Thirty transaction numbers with the matching receiving account numbers from the printout I glanced at," I said with a grin.

"Son of a bitch," John said with a grin as he reached out to take the drive. "How long did you have with the sheets?"

"About a minute," I replied.

John looked at the director. "We need to get him a green card," John said. I didn't understand the reference, but I assumed it meant he wanted to keep me around.

The director turned and looked at me, not smiling as John was.

"I need to ask you a few questions," he said. "Not related to Gaines but to a project you did yesterday."

Oops, I thought.

"You returned a movement prediction model that incorporated some data you weren't provided," he said as he sat behind his desk. "Would you explain to me how you came by that information?"

I hesitated.

"The travel routes only fit one set of road parameters anywhere on the globe," I replied, knowing that's not what he was referring to. "I mapped them to the appropriate region so I had terrain and war zone data to include in the simulation."

"You used data that accounted for shielding on nuclear devices and Serbian arms dealer activities," he said, wrinkling his brow at me.

Sorry, John, I thought before giving my explanation.

"It was an assumption on my part," I began. "When John and

I were in Colorado Springs, I overheard a conversation he had with you, I believe, about tracking something. John mentioned he couldn't tell me anything but that it was just clean up from a recent op."

"That's it?" John asked.

I took a deep breath. "No," I replied hesitantly, about to give up a secret of my own. "When you said it was a recent operation, a micro-expression flashed across your face indicating you were amused—as if your vague description was a secret hiding from me in plain view. I only had personal knowledge of one operation and the only one that would result in that particular response—Mimon."

"Son of a bitch," John said, turning slightly pale. "You read micro-expressions?"

I nodded.

"What else have you gleaned from being around here?" he asked, but I could tell it was rhetorical.

"Ned Richards didn't want us digging into the hit man in the alley," I stated boldly.

"Easy there, chief," Burgess said with a warning tone in his voice.

"He's right," John inserted.

"But it's not something that should be said out loud," Burgess replied. "As it is, Homeland thinks we are covering for Gaines somehow. With an accusation like that out there, this could turn into a war very quickly."

John nodded.

"But," Burgess said with a sly smile sliding over his face. "That account data might make it easier for Justice to keep Gaines tied up."

John nodded. "I'll get it down to the analysts," he said.

"Keep it out of the chain of custody," Burgess said. "No sense tipping our hand if it leads to something."

"Understood," John replied and then turned his attention back to me. "As for you. Since you figured out what we're looking for, I might as well bring you up to speed on the search. A fresh set of eyes on the project might be good."

I nodded, relieved I wasn't going to get booted out for using tradecraft on the spies.

"That's it for now," Burgess said abruptly. "Get out of here and get some rest, John. You look like shit."

"Yes, sir," he replied and then turned me around by my shoulder. "Let's go."

"And Scott," Burgess said as we started to exit. "It's good to finally meet you. I'm looking forward to having you with the section."

I smiled. That made me very happy. "Thank you, sir," I replied.

When John had me out in the hallway, he stopped abruptly and turned to me. The expression on his face was of pure anger.

"Just so you know," he said, leaning close to me, "if you ever do that to me in front of my boss again, you'll—" His face turned red and purple and he appeared to be frustrated beyond words. He turned and stomped away down the hall again—but I saw a shadow of amusement tug at his eyebrow and the corner of his lip for just the briefest instant.

I chuckled as I caught up to him.

"Not even that, huh?" he said with a grin.

"Nope," I said in a quiet voice. "Don't worry. Your secrets are safe with me." I smiled.

"Fuck off," he muttered as his grin broadened even more.

**

3:00 p.m.—New York, New York

HEINRICH BRAUN was in the New York offices of

William Spryte, waiting for an update from Ned Richards. When the call finally came through, he closed the door to his office and activated the soundproofing in the room.

"Go secure," Braun said and then switched on the encryption feature on his phone.

"We have a problem," Richards said as soon as the secure link was established.

"Explain," Braun said, tension building in his chest.

"There's a stay on the transfer for Gaines," Richards said in a low voice. "And if we don't do something fast, he's going to get handed over to DOJ."

Braun let this information sink in before responding. "Where is he being held?" he asked finally.

"The Navy Brig in Norfolk," Richards replied. "As far as I can tell, he hasn't revealed anything, but the CIA is keeping something from us."

"What about the Agents who captured him?" Braun asked.

"There was only one Agent and one tech, though there's something fishy about him," Richards replied. "I don't know if the Agent knows why Gaines was in LA or not, but I think the boy does. He's hiding something—I can tell."

"Is he an Agency tech?" Braun asked.

"No. Civilian contractor," Richards responded. "Some outfit called TravTech."

Braun let this new information sink into the frame of his response. At the moment, there was no hope of extracting Gaines from the Navy Brig, but at least he probably wasn't being interrogated there. The tech would be the best hope of finding out what information, if any, was revealed to the CIA.

"What's the tech boy's name?" Braun asked.

"Scott Wolfe," Richards replied. "What should we do?"

"I'll make arrangements for Gaines in the event he's

transferred to Justice custody," Braun said. "In the meantime, I need you to find out what the tech knows. Do you have personnel you can trust to do a black bag op?"

There was a long pause.

"I don't have to remind you what's at stake here," Braun said in a sly hiss. "Your name was on that list. If the boy knows, then you could be facing the same prison time as everyone else."

The lie was a gamble. Braun didn't know whose names were on the list. Black had run the sheet himself with supposedly false information. But the fact that Gaines had gone straight to Burbank after killing his sister's murders hinted that Black had double-crossed everyone—not just Faulks and Gaines.

"I have a couple people I can trust," Richards finally said. "But if they get caught, there will be little we can do to cover ourselves."

"Baynebridge?" Braun asked.

"Yes," Richards said.

"Then don't worry. If they are discovered, we can cover our tracks," Braun replied.

"How?" Richards replied.

"You let me worry about that," he said firmly. "Just focus on getting that tech and interrogating him."

"And what about after he's interrogated?" Richards asked.

"If you have to ask, then you aren't the man for this job," Braun replied coarsely.

"No, I understand," Richards said indignantly.

"Good," Braun said. "Let me know when you have him. I'd like to be present for the interrogation."

"When do you want it done?" Richards asked.

"Now!" Braun yelled. "The longer he has to reveal his information, the more damage there is to the organization. Get it done tonight."

"Understood," Richards replied nervously.

"Call me when it's done," Braun said and then ended the call.

He set his phone on his desk and then dropped heavily into his chair. He was exhausted, mentally and physically. He had gotten little sleep over the past few days—and until Gaines was either captured or killed, he felt that lack of rest would be the new trend.

**

9:10 p.m.—Fairfax, Virginia

John dropped me at my car in Reston around 9:00 p.m.

We had spent the remainder of the day with the analysts at Langley, trying to squeeze more detail from my brain concerning the transaction numbers and accounts. I wasn't able to recall anything else of value. I had been half-distracted all afternoon, thinking about the emails from Kathrin, but I resolved to wait until I was alone to open them.

I sat in my car for several minutes after John dropped me off, reading and rereading the messages from Kathrin. I was so happy I could barely contain myself.

Her first message was brief—not even really a message to me. It read:

And here we go for a 24th time. How long will this one take to bounce? But fear not, there will be a 25th, and a 26th, and so on, until one of them gets through.

Until then, love always, Gretel.

But the second message had a rather different tone. It read:

Oh my GOD! No BOUNCE! Did it actually go through? Is it possible Scott Wolfe FINALLY got my message? I am crossing my fingers and toes and eyes, hoping this is the case and my Monkey Wrench is reading my words finally.

Don't keep me in suspense, please reply so I can sleep tonight.

I couldn't help but chuckle. Those two messages told me everything I needed to know about why Kathrin hadn't responded to my earlier messages. I suppressed a rising urge to be angry at Robert Whitney and hit reply on my phone, typing in my response:

Dear Gretel,

I am pleased to confirm your messages have been delivered to my mailbox, warm, safe, and sound (though I can't guarantee they were unread by others). In the meantime, I suspect we will be able to communicate freely now...just a hunch. I will assume you did NOT receive my messages and will begin by telling you: I've missed you very much since returning to the States. Thank you for not giving up on me.

Monkey Wrench

###-###-####

I included my phone number in the signature then hit send. I had just slipped my keys into the ignition when Dave Grohl sang my theme music again. I pulled the email up and read it:

Dare should I hope? Is that a phone number? Let's give it a try.

As I read, my phone rang. I smiled involuntarily, though I was confused by the display—unknown number—odd, considering I had caller ID even on foreign numbers.

"Hello?" I answered as I backed out of my parking spot.

"It IS you!" Kathrin exclaimed loudly. "I was worried it was a trick!"

I smiled more deeply and felt a flush of blood in my ears. "It's really me," I replied. "I'm so glad you finally got through."

"Why—" she began but abruptly changed course. "Not important. I'm so happy to hear your voice."

"How have you been?" I asked, turning onto the street.

"Missing my partner in crime!" she exclaimed as if it should have been obvious. "It's been so hard to focus on work since you left. And having all my emails bounce back at me—it felt like—never mind. It's you!"

I chuckled. "I've truly missed you too," I replied. "I was worried you'd come to your senses and decided that the crazy American was more trouble than he was worth."

"Never," she said quickly. "I was worried you were blocking me. But then I thought, any man who would hop on a plane and do what you did would never give me the brush off by blocking my email. I'm so glad I was right."

"Have you been able to slip back into quiet civilian life after our adventure?" I asked.

There was a second of hesitation before she responded. "Eh," she replied. "It hasn't been as much fun, but I've managed to get back into my routine…how about you?"

"Glad to hear it," I said, smiling broadly. "There've been a few changes for me, but for the most part, I'm back to doing what I was doing before." I didn't want to lie to her, but I wasn't going to be able to tell her I was doing analyst work for the CIA over an unsecure line—besides, it wasn't a complete lie. I was still solving puzzles for a TravTech paycheck—I was just doing it for the Agency now.

"How is Barb?" she asked with genuine concern in her voice. I didn't want to get into that business on the phone either.

"We've all had to deal with some unpleasant changes," I replied. "But she's doing as well as can be expected."

There was an uncomfortable pause. "The last time I saw you, you didn't look well. Are you healing?"

"Yes," I replied sincerely. "A few days ago, I actually climbed for the first time since Europe. It wasn't a pretty climb, but I'm definitely on my way to full recovery." I left out the part where I nearly beat Mark Gaines to death and disarmed an assassin in the alleyway in LA.

"*Wunderbar*," she exclaimed. "I will come to you and you can take me climbing on my next holiday—if Barb doesn't mind."

"That would be great," I replied, glossing over the lack of concern for Barb's opinion on the matter. "I'll look forward to it."

"I'm sorry to have to make this call so short, *und* I am almost hesitant to break the connection for fear I won't get it back, but I have to go—work stuff," she explained apologetically.

I quickly calculated the time difference and was struck by the oddity of her having to do *"work stuff"* at 3:30 a.m. on a Tuesday in Germany.

"Why so early?" I asked.

"What?" she replied. "Oh! No. I'm not in Germany. I'm in Asia."

Asia!?

I was about to ask her to elaborate when she spoke again. "I'm sorry. I really do have to go," she reiterated urgently. "But I promise, now that I know I can get through, you will receive more emails from me…starting with the first few I sent that bounced."

"Okay," I replied. "I'll be looking for them…and I hope we can talk again soon."

"We will," she assured me. "It's so good to hear your voice. Be well, Scott Wolfe."

I smiled. That had been the last thing she said to me in Germany as well. "Be well, Kathrin Fuchs."

She chuckled and ended the call. I slipped my phone back into my pocket as I merged onto the Fairfax County Parkway.

It amazed me that I had just spoken with the woman I had been trying to reach for so many weeks unhampered by guilt of any sort. It was, in fact, a huge relief. It immediately occurred to me that I hadn't thought of Barb at all in the past couple of days.

I guess I have Doctor Hebron's answer for her, I thought. *Barb and I are done. Now I have to tell Barb—ouch.*

When I got home, it was hard to focus on anything, so I made a small meal and then sat in the living room to watch TV while I ate.

It took no time to get tired of listening to the same repetitious news reports concerning the deaths of the media personalities. When I had finished eating, I flipped to an old movie, turned the volume down a bit so I could concentrate, and then opened my laptop to do some work.

I was organizing my notes for the coming day, having missed much by getting called to Langley. I was about to open a new email from Storc when my phone rang. I took the opportunity to stand and stretch. I answered.

"Hello?"

"Hi, Scott," came Barb's voice from the other end of the line.

I paused for a second, taken off guard. "Hi."

"Daddy told me what he did," she said with embarrassment, and then she waited for me to respond. I didn't, so she continued. "I am furious with him. I told him he had no right."

"Yeah. He told me that as well," I replied.

"I just want you to know—all other issues aside for a second—I didn't know anything about him blocking Kathrin from communicating with you," she added sincerely.

"I believe you," I replied as gently as I could.

"And it really made me understand why you were so pissed off at me for suggesting I'd have Daddy interfere with your contract," she added.

Like that wouldn't be bad enough in itself?

"I know that doesn't fix everything," she admitted quietly. "But I wanted you to know that, at least."

"I appreciate it," I said uncomfortably, suddenly just wanting the call to end.

"Oh, and I probably should have clued you in before—I hope it's not too late," she said. "I told Bonbon that I was going to stay with my dad for a few days. When she asked if everything was alright with you and me, I knew what would happen if I said no…so I didn't. She assumed that meant something was wrong with Dad."

"That explains a lot," I replied.

"If you don't tell her before Friday, we are supposed to have lunch," she continued. "I'll let her know then."

I suddenly found it amusing that we were both more worried about our friend's reaction to our break up than we were about each other.

"Do you think we could talk?" she asked.

"You mean other than over the phone?" I asked, suddenly nervous about a face-to-face.

"Yes," she replied. "I have some things I'd like to say that are better said in person."

"Barb. I know I haven't been easy. But I think we both know where we stand," I said, trying to avoid a face-to-face. I knew it was the coward's way out, but I needed a few more days wrapped around the idea before I faced her. I knew that otherwise I'd be tempted to try and resolve our differences and give it another shot. That damned guilt thing was going to get me killed one day.

"I know," she said, pausing for a second. "But I want you to know that regardless of how difficult post-abduction is to deal with: you are my hero—and I will never forget that. You're the man who traveled halfway around the world to save me."

I didn't know how to respond to that. I wanted to be gracious, but at that point it was easier to stay angry at her for trying to manipulate me.

"I appreciate that," I replied honestly, letting the awkward silence that followed fill our minds—it said far more than I could.

It became more than I could stand.

"It's still a little raw for me, Barb," I said abruptly—a little too abruptly. "Can we hold off on our farewells for a while?"

"I see," she said tersely.

I could tell it was not what she wanted to hear.

"Well. I just wanted to clear that bit up anyway," she continued. "I didn't want you to continue thinking I was complicit in blocking your friend from contacting you."

My friend. This was getting awkward. Any goodwill she had built by calling had dissolved when she said "your friend." Kathrin had risked her life to help save Barb as well. It felt like a personal insult.

"Thanks, Barb," I blurted. "Look. I hate to cut it short, but—"

"No. No. That's okay," she said, cutting me off. "That's really all I wanted to say. Take care, Scott."

"You too, Barb," I replied and then quickly ended the call.

I stared at the phone a moment after hanging up, and though I felt bad for not being ready to have the *face-to-face* goodbye, I really did feel much better having made it clear we were actually done with the relationship. I breathed in deeply through my nose and then sat down, ready to work some more.

I should have known better. There was no possibility of finishing any work after that. I shut down my system and went back to the bedroom to get ready for bed. As I went through my routine—shower, brushing my teeth, setting up the coffee pot for the next morning—I couldn't help but feel alone after that call. Frustratingly so.

I finished up in the rest of the house, turned off the lights, and retreated to the bedroom. I lay on top of the blanket for a few minutes while I scrolled through new emails. When my eyes were too blurry to focus on the screen, I put my iPad on the nightstand to charge and then turned out the lights.

I had barely started to drift off when I heard my front door squeak.

Odd, I thought as I abruptly sat up in bed. *Who had a key besides Barb? Bonbon? Storc?*

And something was different about the sound—it was just a quick squeal, then silence.

Arm yourself, my other voice whispered.

A chill ran up my spine and my muscles tensed as I slid off the bed. I slunk over to my closet to get my baseball bat. It was not the first time I'd wished I had a gun, but after all that had transpired over the last few months, I felt a little ridiculous grabbing a bat.

I walked down the hallway barefoot, shirtless, and only in my underwear. I was only halfway to the living room when I saw a dark figure in the dim light of the landing. I launched myself forward and over the railing, down on top of the figure. He was in all black and carrying what looked like a silenced handgun.

I was so focused on the man I jumped on that I didn't see the second figure just turning the corner on the stairs.

My feet landed squarely on the shoulders of the first man, smashing him face first into the top stair. I heard a disturbing crack come from the vicinity of his neck. He was motionless. I had no time to celebrate before the butt of a handgun struck me on my shoulder from behind. I'm certain the target had been the base of my skull, but I was in motion and it was dark.

I fell forward but immediately grabbed the shoulders of the man I had just put down and flipped his body around so it was facing the second man. I heard the unmistakable clack of silenced gunfire.

Blood splattered my face.

I pushed up on the dead man's shoulders enough to get my feet under his back, and then launched him forward with my legs, slamming him into the second man. Both men rolled down the stairs, the dead one tumbling over the live one.

I didn't wait to see how it turned out. I was on my feet and grabbing my baseball bat in a second. I sailed down the stairs and through the air, dropping the baseball bat down solidly on the arm holding the gun. The man screamed in pain as the gun flipped backwards and down into the downstairs foyer, clanking into the corner.

I was severely off balance and continued to tumble over his head, able to do little more than spin around before my back landed with a hard thud on the foyer floor. My assailant landed solidly on top of me, knocking the wind from my lungs. He wasted no time in trying to turn himself around, but he was hampered by a severely injured arm—damaged by my Louisville Slugger.

He was halfway through his turn when I brought the bat up and pressed it against his throat, trying to push him off me. But he brought his elbow down hard into my stomach, preventing me from taking a deep enough breath to recover.

He managed to turn himself so he was facing me. He forced his damaged arm between the baseball bat and his throat and was raining blows down on my midsection with his knee. Because of the angle, my one leg was crossed over the other, which prevented him from kneeing my groin, but the pain he was inflicting on my midsection was distracting, to say the least.

The light from the lamppost outside shone through the window. I could see his eyes and the anger contained within. I didn't know if this intrusion was meant to be a capture or a kill, but it was *kill* that was written on the man's face.

He looked to the side, scanning the dimly lit alcove.

He's looking for the gun, my other voice said into my ear.

It was only a split second later that his good hand reached out away from my throat toward the wall. He had spotted it. I released my grip on the fat end of the baseball bat and reached out, not to the gun, but to his arm.

"You are going to die," the man growled.

I grunted under his weight. "Not tonight, though," I replied.

I rocked myself to the side, pulling his reach away from the weapon, and then quickly, rashly, I rolled back toward the gun. With his own strength being used to pull us in that direction, I was able to build enough momentum to flip and roll on top of him.

But his hand had reached the gun. A satisfied grunt emanated from his throat. As far as he was concerned, this fight was over—I had to sap that confidence.

I placed my thumb in the center of his wrist and squeezed as hard as I could, pressing his arm away from us as hard as my climber's strength could muster. My other elbow was now across the man's throat, and his injured hand was trapped uselessly between us. While pressing with all my might into his wrist, I found the top of his boot with my bare feet.

My hand was holding his arm away; my thumb dug deeply into the groove of his wrist. As he struggled to get it free, I scissored my legs apart, forcing the bottom of his feet against the staircase.

"Drop it," I hoarsely whispered into his ear.

"Ha," he laughed weakly—but I could hear doubt.

I dug my heel into the toe of his trapped boot and then pressed up with my elbow, forcing his chin up and back.

"Drop it," I croaked again.

I got no response from him that time. With my heel pressed against his foot on the stairs, he was experiencing a "rack" moment—like an ancient torture device created to stretch a person until their joints popped and broke.

"Last…chance…" I grunted from the effort. His breathing had gotten shallow and quick. I reached down to the core of my being and strained with all my strength, continuing to push his head further away from the rest of his body.

After what seemed like an eternity, his arm went limp, followed by a grotesque arch of his neck with my elbow rolling over top of it. The crunch of bone was disturbing and sent a flash of panic through my chest—but it signaled the end of the battle.

A long, slow exhale rasped through his windpipe and whistled out of his mouth. I felt his chest collapsing beneath me, like lying on an inflatable mattress that was losing its air rapidly.

I lay there on top of him for long minutes, trying to catch my breath, when it suddenly dawned on me that these two might not be alone. I struggled to push myself up. I pried the gun out of his dead fingers and then stumbled up the stairs, stepping over the first man who had been killed. There, on the landing, was his gun. I grabbed it as I headed for my bedroom and my cell phone.

I dialed John's number.

"Hey, Scott. What's up?" he asked groggily.

I was still out of breath. "I have two dead guys in my front foyer," I said. "Dressed in black and carrying silenced pistols."

He was awake then. "Are you hurt?" he asked excitedly.

"I don't think so," I replied.

"I'm leaving now. I'll call internal security on the way. They'll probably be there before me," he said, and then hung up.

I reached into my closet and grabbed a pair of pants and a T-shirt and then pulled on my hiking sandals and returned to the living room. I could smell the mixture of gunpowder and strange sweat emanating from my landing and suddenly had an overwhelming desire to retch.

I made it to the hall bathroom toilet just in time.

After cleaning myself up, I returned to the living room and laid the two guns on the floor in front of me as I squatted down to sit in front of my favorite chair. I leaned back and looked at the ceiling, letting the quiet return to my head.

I stared at the lights that flashed across the ceiling from time to time as a car drove by on the street below. After a few moments, I took my first deep breath since my evening had been interrupted.

"What the fuck are you doing, Scott?" I asked aloud.

Is this what I really wanted with my life? I thought to myself.

Yes, was the simple, gentle reply I heard from my other voice.

I thought about my hitchhiker's answer for a moment, exploring my feelings—and then I smiled.

"God help me. You're right," I whispered. "It *is* what I want."

Two armed men had just broken into my house, trying to do me harm—and I had defeated them with nothing but a Louisville Slugger and my bare hands. I had won.

I am happy.

Epilogue

12:15 a.m. on Wednesday, July 28th—Fairfax, Virginia

The CIA security team had been at my house for about five minutes when John arrived. I heard him talking to the guys downstairs before coming up to the living room where I was still sitting on the floor—the handguns had been taken by the security team's forensics guy.

John stood in front of me for a second without saying anything and then sat on the couch across from me.

"I'm sorry," he said.

I looked up at him. "Why? Did *you* send them after me?" I asked quietly with a grim smile.

He chuckled and shook his head.

"I should have set security up immediately," he replied after a moment of silence.

"That's bullshit," I replied, letting him off the hook. "If you had to put security on everyone who ever crossed a bad guy, ninety percent of your budget would be blown on protection details."

He raised his eyebrow at the observation. "That's a rather enlightened response," he said.

"What can I say? I'm an enlightened fellow," I said with a grin, dropping my head back into my hands and rubbing my tired eyes.

"Are you hurt?" he asked.

I shook my head. "Just tired."

"Okay. I'll get the bodies out of the house and get things wrapped up," he said. "Do you want to stay somewhere else tonight?"

"No. I'm fine," I said. "But if you were to drop one of their guns on the way out and a couple of spare mags, I wouldn't be offended."

He looked at me for a second, measuring my request, and then reached into his belt and pulled out his own 9mm handgun and an extra magazine.

"You can use this until we get you one of your own," he said, setting them down on the coffee table in front of me, and then he smiled. "Not that you need it."

I looked up at him quizzically.

"In the last two days, you've disarmed four, killed two, and disabled an American-made sedan…all without the benefit of being armed," he said. "I'm almost afraid of what you could do with a weapon."

I laughed.

He looked at me a moment longer and then rose from the couch. "I'll put a guy outside overnight," he said as he started to look around the apartment.

"Don't bother," I said. "They won't send men in next time. They'll shoot a rocket through the window."

He grunted his acknowledgment and continued to look around.

"Still," he said. "I'd feel better."

I shrugged and then stood to face him. "I'm more interested in who wants me and why someone tried to kill us both after we captured Gaines."

He looked at me for a long moment before saying anything. I could see conflict on his face.

"Look," I said. "I don't want to break Agency rules or protocol or anything, but it doesn't take a genius to see that the hit in the alley and this are tied to Gaines somehow."

"I'm not cleared to tell you anything," he said.

I shook my head and laughed in frustration. He looked at me a bit longer, and then his stance shifted. I could tell he was going to share something before he said it.

"Come in tomorrow. Let me talk to Burgess and get it cleared…proper-like," he said. "Who knows? You might be able to help."

I nodded my agreement.

When the tech team had finally cleared the condo and everyone had left, I went back to the bedroom and put the gun John had given me in the top drawer of my nightstand. I lay down and tossed for a while before finally sitting up in frustration.

In the dark, I reached into my nightstand and pulled the gun out. I popped the magazine out and pulled the slide back, ejecting the round that had been chambered, and then slapped the magazine back in. I dropped the bullet on my nightstand, tucked the gun under my pillow, and then laid my head down again. I drifted off almost immediately.

Four and a half hours later, my alarm went off. When I woke,

I felt refreshed, as if I had slept a full eight hours. My hand was on the gun John had given me. I pulled it out and looked at it, turning it over to examine the detail in the light.

"Best sleep aid I've ever had," I said, and then I stowed it back in my nightstand.

**

8:45 p.m. on Monday, August 2nd—Navy Brig, Norfolk, Virginia

MARK GAINES sat handcuffed to a cushioned seat in the medical wing of the Navy Brig in Norfolk. It had been his only view, other than his room, for the past four days. He wasn't sure how or why Burgess had arranged the shell game with his incarceration, but when the interrogations began, he suspected he was being shielded—at least for the time being.

Across the table were two FBI Agents—Special Agent James and Special Agent Walsh—who had been questioning him in shifts for the past three days. This evening, they were interrogating him together, taking turns firing questions and accusations.

"We aren't going to be able to help you after the doctors clear you for transport," Walsh said. Gaines thought the man had the bearing of a military officer, concluding after the first day that Walsh had served in action somewhere prior to joining the FBI.

Gaines didn't respond.

"What? You don't want to talk to me because I'm black?" Walsh asked. "If my presence offends you, I can leave the room and you can talk to him." Walsh jerked his thumb toward James.

Gaines just smiled at the new tactic. He had stopped talking two days ago—as soon as the FBI showed up, he knew that Homeland Security might lose their claim on him. He was determined to stay quiet until he knew who would win the custody fight. Giving too much information before that could cost him his life if the wrong agency got him.

Walsh shook his head.

"I think there's brain damage," James said with a sneer. "Otherwise, he'd be showing some emotion about the loss of his dyke sister."

Gaines could tell those words were meant to elicit an emotional response. He didn't bite, but the comment pinched his chest and gut nonetheless.

Still human after all, he thought.

"Or maybe he's just glad she's gone," Walsh added. "Or maybe he had something to do with it. Maybe he hired those rednecks to kill her and her family and he was just cleaning up the connection to him."

Gaines could feel blood rising to his head, but he quickly calmed himself. He knew they would do or say anything to get him talking again. He was certain these two knew he had been through *Response to Interrogation* training, more commonly called RTI, with the CIA. But the fact that they kept using these tactics showed they felt they could break it.

He decided he would frustrate them a little more to drive the point home.

"Who did you have helping you place the explosives?" James asked. "Was it the girl? If you tell us who it was, we might be able to help with reduced charges. But you have to cooperate now."

They still don't have a name; that's good for Alisha.

Gaines leaned forward and opened his mouth as if he were about to speak. He could see the hopeful anticipation on the faces of both men. He paused for a second or two and then closed his mouth and settled back into his chair—a grin spreading across his face.

He saw anger well up in James's face. "You mother fucker," he growled, leaning across the table to jerk Gaines forward by the collar. Walsh grabbed his partner by the arm and restrained him.

Gaines could tell they were just as tired and stressed as he was. And though he was injured, his medication had been upped to aid the interrogation, so the throbbing in his head was manageable.

James pushed the chair over behind him and stood, pointing his meaty finger at Gaines. "I don't think you know what's going on here," James said angrily, showing all the markers of real frustration. "What you say here determines where you go after you're cleared medically."

The angry Agent stood there unmoving for several seconds and then abruptly turned and stormed to the door. He pounded until the guard opened it and let him out. When he was gone, Walsh turned his attention back to Gaines.

"You might think that's funny, but he gets to go back to the hotel and catch a nap," Walsh said, implying a false threat of sleep deprivation for Gaines. "We can keep you up as long as we want. Why don't you just tell us what really happened, and then you can go back to your bed in the clinic."

Mark leaned forward again, but Walsh didn't take the bait this time.

You're a quick study, aren't you? Gaines thought and then he smiled at Walsh. He actually felt bad for the man, who clearly had no idea how much shit was stacking up behind him.

"Nothing I say will see the light of day," Gaines said plainly, eliciting a hopeful expression from Walsh. "And to be honest, anything that I tell you would put you and your partner in danger."

Walsh laughed. "We're big boys," he said through a trailing chuckle. "Why don't you let us decide if what you have to say is dangerous?"

"There's a fight going on above your pay grade," Gaines continued. "And you have to ask yourself…hell, maybe you already have. Why is Homeland Security fighting so hard to get me moved to a black site?"

Walsh sat back in his chair, his smile fading. "It could have something to do with the fact that you assassinated eight high profile media personalities with explosives."

Gaines could tell Walsh didn't believe that despite the confidence in his voice.

"You saw the evidence," Gaines said sympathetically. "I haven't."

"So you didn't kill any of those people?" Walsh asked incredulously. "Then it's just a coincidence that every city you passed through happened to be targets of terrorism."

Gaines shook his head. "Not a coincidence at all," he replied plainly. "But I'm assuming you're having a hard time making the timeline work, which is why you think I had someone helping me."

Walsh reflected on that for a moment. Gaines could see the exhaustion on his face and could tell that Walsh had no idea that Gaines had just turned the interrogation around on him.

"We know you had someone helping you because there was no way you could have done Denver and Chicago," Walsh said.

Chicago!? Thanks for the intel.

"Albuquerque would have been tight, but possible," Walsh continued.

"None of them were possible," Gaines replied. "But I'm sure the documented evidence doesn't line up with the facts, and you already know that. Otherwise you wouldn't be pumping me for details on phantom accomplices."

"The girl wasn't a phantom," Walsh said plainly. "And I guess you didn't kill those three guys in Colorado Springs either."

"Oh, I killed those guys," Gaines replied matter-of-factly. "And I'm ready to do my time for that. But I don't know what girl you're talking about—unless you mean the federal officer who came in and tried to stop the CIA from taking me."

How do you react to that? Mark wondered.

A flash of surprise swept across Walsh's face before placid calm replaced it.

"At least I'm assuming she was a federal officer of some sort. But I didn't catch her name," Mark lied.

He had just successfully sown a seed of doubt about the CIA claims and the purpose for Homeland Security's attempt to gain custody of him.

"But until we know for sure where I'm landing, I'm not sharing anything…and you should thank me," he continued. "If what I have in my head is big enough to cause the deaths of eight media personalities, the manufacture of evidence, and a battle between Justice and Homeland over my custody; how much sleep do you think they'd lose over a dead FBI Agent or two?"

Gaines could see his comments were having an effect. He glanced down and noticed Walsh rubbing his thumb over the wedding ring on his finger. The story was plausible enough for Walsh to consider his family.

Good.

Gaines looked at the recorder in front of him and nodded toward it almost imperceptibly. Walsh regarded him for a moment and then reached out and turned it off. He then stood and stretched, discretely hitting the button on the video recorder.

Gaines moved his head, indicating he wanted Walsh closer. The big Agent hesitated a moment and then moved over toward Gaines, bending to hear what Gaines had to say.

"Every one of those media personalities had something in common with the people who are fighting over me right now," Gaines said in a whisper. Walsh hovered a little longer, waiting for an elaboration. "The same money that was used to kill them also paid them all."

Walsh stood back, blinking at the disclosure. He went back around the table, flipping on the video camera as he went, and then turning the recorder back on. He sat slowly, his face still puzzling over what Gaines had said, and then he picked up his pen. It hovered over his notes for a second before he set it purposefully back on the table, deciding not to write what he had just heard.

Good boy, Gaines thought.

"You can keep up the silent treatment only so long," Walsh said, adopting some sort of fiction for the recording devices. "Eventually you'll have to say something, if for no other reason than to avoid the death penalty."

Gaines smiled and nodded at Walsh. The look on the Agent's face was still one of confusion. It was clear he didn't know how to proceed.

"When DOJ has me and my lawyer shows up, I'll be happy to make my statement," he said tauntingly. "Until then, you've heard the last you'll hear from me. I suggest you and your partner stop wasting your time."

"We get paid the same either way," Walsh said defiantly.

"True, but the survivor benefits are what I'd be worried about," Gaines said, a mild grin spreading across his face.

A flush of red appeared on the dark skin of Walsh's cheeks. He slowly closed his notebook, turned off the recorder and the video camera. Before he knocked on the door to leave, he turned and looked at Gaines.

"I hope you know what you're doing," Walsh said with pity in his voice.

A serious look swept across Gaines's face. "I didn't before they killed my sister," he said in a bitter voice. "But I know exactly what I'm doing now."

**

2:00 a.m. on Wednesday, August 4th—New York, New York

HEINRICH BRAUN was on his way down the stairs at Spryte Industries Headquarters when his phone rang.

"Braun," he answered.

"I'm still holding on your other order," came Harbinger's deep voice.

"Go secure," he said and then hit the encryption function on his phone.

"I understand the abduction of the Wolfe boy didn't go as planned," Harbinger said, his voice now having a muffled, digitized quality to it.

"I'm still trying to sort out what happened," Braun replied. "I don't think Richards is up to the task."

"That's rather obvious," Harbinger grunted. "Are you ready for me to send a team in?"

"Just set up surveillance," Braun replied. "This incident is bound to have put him under closer scrutiny by the Agency. We are still trying to get Gaines transferred to Homeland control and I don't want to do anything to endanger that."

"Aren't you concerned about intel collected at the time of his capture?" Harbinger asked.

Braun thought for a moment. He was nervous about that, but the priority was still Gaines. Wolfe appeared to be the weak link on the capture team. The failed abduction attempt, though, could raise more questions about the connection to Homeland Security.

"Surveillance for now," Braun replied, though the loose end left him feeling uneasy.

"Understood," Harbinger replied.

"These distractions come at a most inopportune moment," Braun said.

"It's not a concern," Harbinger replied, reading Braun's apprehension for the other operation that was going on—the recovery of the misplaced nuclear devices that the Serbs still had. "My team in Europe is ready to move as soon as the Serbs stop playing tag with the CIA. So far, their efforts have only been mildly successful. If they don't get the devices in place soon, I will join them and help pick up the pace. In either case, I have enough resources to take Wolfe as soon as I get the go ahead."

"That's good to know," Braun said, relaxing a bit. "But don't forget, we'll need a team ready when Gaines is moved. Even if it's into DHS custody."

"Understood," Harbinger replied. "I'll send a tech team to Virginia to begin watching Wolfe."

"I know I don't have to tell you this, but if the Agency is watching him, discretion will be very important," Braun said.

"No," Harbinger replied coldly. "You didn't have to mention that."

"On the other hand," Braun said, ignoring the attitude. "If an opportunity presents itself, we wouldn't want to waste it."

There was a short pause on the other end of the line. "I'll do what I can," Harbinger replied.

"Excellent," Braun replied, knowing that usually meant success wasn't far away.

"Anything else?" Harbinger asked.

"No," Braun replied. "Updates as changes occur,"

"Yes, sir," he replied and then ended the call from his end.

Braun tucked his phone into his pocket and continued down the stairs. When he reached the garage level, his driver pulled up and Braun climbed wearily into the backseat.

"Home, Brian," Braun said.

"Yes, sir," his driver replied, sounding equally tired.

"And after you drop me off, go home and rest," Braun said. "I won't need you until noon—unless something comes up."

"Thank you, sir," his driver replied.

Though something always comes up, Braun thought as his exhaustion threatened to pull him into sleep right there in the car.

How did you thwart the abduction, young Mr. Wolfe? Braun continued in his sleep-deprived mind. *It's a pity we can't ask the*

Baynebridge men.

He sighed as his burning eyes closed for a moment.

I'll have to ask you myself once we have you, he thought, and then chuckled aloud at the imagery that flashed behind his eyes.

**

9:35 a.m. on Wednesday, August 4th—CIA Headquarters, Langley Virginia

JOHN TEMPLE took a deep breath before he knocked on Director Burgess's door. He knew why he had been called in.

Burgess looked up while on the phone and waved John in.

"Yes, sir," Burgess said into the phone, letting John know it was someone big on the other end.

"It's our number one priority, sir," Burgess continued and then hung up the phone.

"The nukes," John stated plainly, reading the Director's mood upon hanging up.

"Yeah," Burgess muttered. "If we don't get hold of them soon, State wants to bring Russia and Israel in on the search."

John shook his head. "That would be bad news," he said plainly. "Russia has already hurt us on tracking. If we give them intel on the op, we may just be muddying the water."

Burgess stared blankly at the top of his desk for a moment, his mind obviously working on the problem. "Then we need to find them fast," he said finally.

John nodded. He was already feeling responsible for the delay. He knew the Director wasn't placing blame, but he felt the weight of the missing devices as if he had lost them himself.

"Is that why you called me up?" John asked, already knowing the answer.

"No," Burgess said as he reached into his drawer and pulled out a file folder. "I was looking at your request concerning Scott."

John took a deep breath before speaking his mind. "Before you make a decision, I just want to point out that he has basically solo completed two ops in the past two months with no training," he said cautiously. "That's why I want to bring him on...put him in my section."

Burgess narrowed his eyes and stared at John for a few seconds. He set the folder on his desk and leaned forward to examine the contents, slowly flipping through the pages one at a time before sitting back and rubbing his eyes.

"He's good," Burgess finally said. "But do you think he's ready? I mean, he went through the wringer in Europe... Has he been able to shake that off?"

John nodded his acknowledgment to Burgess's question. "I was worried about that as well," John admitted. "But Hebron is convinced that he's not only worked past it but that he's hungry for more... That lines up with what I've seen as well."

Burgess dropped his head in concentration and then suddenly laughed. "He sure took Gaines down with extreme prejudice."

John laughed in reply. "I know. I don't think I've ever seen anyone move that fast and with that much intensity...blow to the head or not," he observed, sitting back more comfortably in his chair. "And the two guys at his condo—Jesus—I wouldn't want to tangle with him."

Burgess stared at John for a second longer. "What do you have in mind?" he asked with a testing quality to his voice, not having made up his mind.

"I want to put him on a real op," John said confidently. "Something with backup, resources—and tracked through the normal process. He's already up to speed on the Serb devices...I was thinking about using him as a field tech."

Burgess leaned forward and flipped through the file once more before closing it. "You've never steered us wrong on a recruit," Burgess replied.

"Except for Gaines," John inserted quickly.

"I don't think you steered us wrong on him," Burgess replied quietly and then leaned back, staring at the ceiling.

"I'll have Nick shadow him to make sure he doesn't make any obvious mistakes," John added quickly, trying to bolster his case. "If he handles the field tech assignment well, and is interested, I'd like to slip him into the new training cycle that's getting ready to start at the farm."

Burgess nodded for a second before his body language suggested he would commit. "Okay," he replied finally. "If he's interested enough and can handle a legit op, then do it. I'll make sure there's a slot open for him in the next cycle if it works out."

"Roger that, sir." John beamed with a satisfied grin. "Excellent. Thank you."

Burgess nodded and then abruptly looked up at John. "What are we going to do about his outfit at TravTech?" he asked as an afterthought.

"If it works out, I thought we'd keep him in place there," John replied with a sly smile. "It's a great cover and he has the background to be a convincing computer nerd."

"Yep," Burgess said nodding his agreement. "Okay. It's your ball, run with it."

"Thank you, sir," John replied sincerely as he rose to leave.

"And John," Burgess called, stopping John at the door. "Get those damned nukes back. It's got everyone scared shitless that they're still floating around free."

John nodded somberly. "Yes, sir."

On the way down to the analyst floor, John let the question of the nuclear devices fill his thoughts. *Let's see if you're my lucky rabbit's foot on this as well, Scott.*

**

11:35 a.m. on Saturday, August 7th—Crescent Rock, Appalachian Trail

"Do you want to climb first this time?" I asked Arlia as she sat contentedly on the edge of the cliff, having just finished another lovely violin piece.

She looked at me and smiled. "It's nice to see you're in better shape than last time," she said, grinning broadly. "But we've been climbing for more than three hours straight. Aren't you tired yet?"

I laughed as I reclined against my equipment bag in the bright midday sun.

"You're the one who wanted to climb," I shot back at her.

"Yeah," she exclaimed defensively. "I wanted to climb with the old *injured* you who took it slow and was impressed by my climbing."

I laughed. "I'm still impressed by your climbing."

"Uh huh," she grunted accusingly.

"For reals," I exclaimed innocently. "You are *quite* impressive."

She turned her head and stretched to look at her yoga pant-clad behind and then glared at me. "Uh huh," she grunted again.

I chuckled in reply as she put her violin back to her chin and started playing again. After a second, she stopped abruptly.

"Hey," she said accusingly. "Don't you have a girlfriend who's worried about you or something? You wouldn't even let me buy you breakfast last time."

"Lunch," I said.

"Whatever," she sighed. "What happened to her?"

I sat up and began toying with the chocks and other devices hanging from my climbing strap.

"She couldn't handle me after I was healed," I said quietly after a moment's pause.

"Really?" she smirked seductively.

I shook my head, grinning at her innuendo.

"No…not like that. But I think she liked the old injured me more than you did."

She cocked her head to the side and pondered that for a moment. "Well," she offered. "Sometimes you have to let a girl catch up to you if you're interested in her."

"True," I replied. "You just have to be careful what she wants once she catches you."

Arlia raised her eyebrow as a crooked smile rippled across her face. "What exactly *did* she want after you let her catch you?" she asked with intense, mocking intrigue in her voice.

I looked up and stared at her for a second, ignoring the innuendo, and then with a very serious tone, I said. "She wanted to steal the real me and replace him with a boring, complacent drone."

Her smile vanished as she thought about my response. Abruptly, she said, "Let's climb…me first."

"I wouldn't have it any other way," I replied with a sly grin.

<<<<>>>>

2nd Amendment Remedies ∞ 355

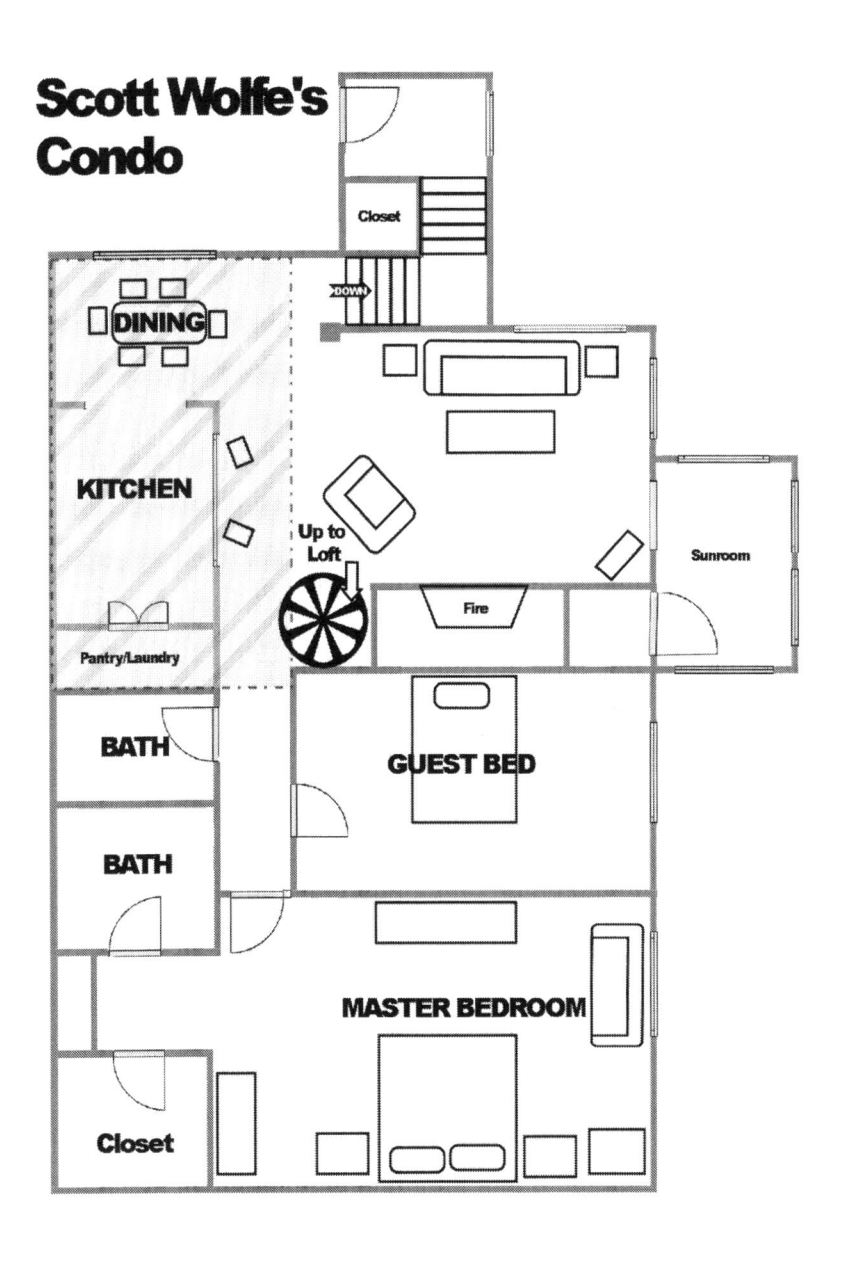

Scott Wolfe's Condo

Closet

DINING

KITCHEN

Up to Loft

Pantry/Laundry

Fire

Sunroom

BATH

GUEST BED

BATH

MASTER BEDROOM

Closet

Acknowledgments

Debts of gratitude to my editor, Brenda Errichiello, for her tireless effort in helping me make the second novel better than the first. Your insights and keen eye have brought out a shining prize.

To my wife, Diane, who has provided me with more support than I ever thought possible and certainly more than I felt I deserved. If not for you, this story would still be knocking around in my head instead of being real.

To my friend, Don Cooper, whose fount of wisdom seems inexhaustible. In matters of law enforcement, military, world events, chemistry, and so much more, I thank you for being my sounding board, encyclopedia, and friend.

I'd also like to thank all of my beta readers and those who have given me feedback on the series. Your opinions and suggestions add to my growing understanding of this dynamic and memorable cast of characters.

For my cheerleaders and enthusiastic friends—particularly Trudy, Wendy, and Ralph…who needs a publicist with friends like you? Thank you for your vocal praise of the project.

And finally, I'd like to thank our children…grown adults, all of you, with your own opinions and interpretations. Your "beta reads" and input are quite valuable throughout the process—thank you Megan, Lauren, and Alex. I love you.

Look for Scott Wolfe's return in
Danger Close

Books by S.L. Shelton:

The Scott Wolfe Series:
A Lamb in Wolfe's Clothing
2nd Amendment Remedies
Back story: Lt. Marsh

Follow S.L. Shelton at:
wolfewriter.tumblr.com
And
facebook.com/SLShelton.Author

Made in the USA
Lexington, KY
23 March 2014